A Banished Land

A Banished Land

Jake Jauch

iUniverse, Inc.
New York Bloomington

iUniverse books may be ordered through booksellers or by contacting:

iUniverse
1663 Liberty Drive
Bloomington, IN 47403
www.iuniverse.com
1-800-Authors (1-800-288-4677)

Because of the dynamic nature of the Internet, any Web addresses or links contained in this book may have changed since publication and may no longer be valid. The views expressed in this work are solely those of the author and do not necessarily reflect the views of the publisher, and the publisher hereby disclaims any responsibility for them.

ISBN: 978-1-4401-7770-5 (sc)
ISBN: 978-1-4401-7768-2 (dj)
ISBN: 978-1-4401-7769-9 (ebook)

Printed in the United States of America

iUniverse rev. date: 09/11/09

This book is dedicated to my family and friends, for their love and undying support. I thank you all.

I

THE EVENING AIR IS warm and humid as I walk along the edge of the forest gathering firewood for the campfire. Sometimes it seems like the nights in Alabama are just as hot as the days. There's not a single cloud in the sky to obstruct the view of the sun as it sinks low in the west. I know that I should be heading back towards the camp before I lose the last rays of the sunlight, but the camp isn't far. I still don't want to have to travel the distance in the dark though. I run my hand through my short brown hair and quicken my pace.

The campsite is set up in a clearing just past the tree line and less than twenty feet from a small stream that trickles through the middle of the clearing. Short soft grass is the only vegetation that seems to grow in this tiny green oasis. Looking back at the sunset through the trees, it reminds me of the end of some romantic movie with the perfect sunset and a happy ever after.

As I get closer I see a lone figure looming near the campfire poking at it, trying to keep the flames going. He turns as he hears me approaching and gives me an annoyed look. He usually gives me that look when I sneak up on him.

"Take your time with the firewood Ivan," he says as he turns back to the fire.

Scott never seems to get mad at people, he just makes jokes. "Sorry," I say setting down the firewood. "Why do we need a fire in the middle of the summer?" "Well, you never know what you might need," Scott says adding a few pieces of wood to the fire. "It should help keep the animals away, but I don't think anything will come around."

I toss a twig in the fire and shrivel before it catches on fire. We sit in silence for a few minutes just listening to the sounds of the fire crackling and the crickets chirping. After about five minutes Scott stands and walks to the tent.

"See you in the morning," he says crawling into the tent and zipping the flap shut.

"Yeah, see you," I say listening to the sounds of the forest as they seem to dominate the camp site. My leg starts to cramp so I stand up and walk to the center of the small clearing. As I listen to the hypnotic sounds of the forest around me, my mind begins to stray to past events. In particular how I managed to be spending my first day of the rest of my life camping in the middle of nowhere.

It was two days before the end of my and Scott's senior year. We had become friends when we were both freshman and over the years we've become good friends. The one thing we shared in common the most was our fascination with swords. We would spend hours at one another's house practicing. Neither one of us ever became exceedingly good, but it was just a pastime that we both enjoyed. On the night of our graduation ceremony, Scott came up to me and wanted to know if I felt like going on a little camping trip. Having nothing else planned so close to the end of school, I readily agreed to the trip.

So this morning I woke up at four o'clock in the morning and drove for twenty-five minutes to Scott's house. Scott lives just outside of a small town called Addison. It's one of those towns where everyone knows everybody, so nothing exciting ever happens, and word spreads like a wildfire on a dry day. Once I got to Scott's house we proceeded to hike to the clearing that we're now at. We decided not to bring anything electronic, except flashlights. This meant no cell phones or portable video games. Two days in the woods with no contact with civilization sounded like fun and there was a slight hint of a challenge in Scott's voice when he asked me to go. This caused me to want to go just to see if it was going to be a challenge.

We started the hiking as soon as I got to his house and parked my car. Scott apparently had been to the area where we were going to be camping. When I asked him what the camp site looked like so I could help search for it, he just said it was a clearing. By the time it was eight o'clock in the morning and after four false clearings we finally reached the right one. After two hours we had the camp set up and the needed provisions set up.

After we had finished setting up the camp we followed the stream to where it emptied into a river. The river was quite a sight to see. There were trees on either side of the river creating a natural canopy over the water. The openings in the canopy sent golden beams of light into the clear water, forming shimmering patterns on the river bottom. Fish darted back and forth in the crystal clear water.

Naturally we thought it would be fun to see who could catch the most fish with their bare hands, since we hadn't packed any fishing poles. It only took a few minutes before we were both soaked through and finding it hard to breathe from trudging waist deep in the water. Eventually we grew tired of the fish evading our every move. It was a good thing we weren't depending on our catch to survive, because we both went back to camp hungry. When we had made it back to camp and had changed into some dry clothes only a few hours of daylight were left. So Scott decided to start a fire while I ventured off to find some firewood.

The sudden sound of the tent flap opening causes me to snap back to reality. I turn to see Scott climb out of the tent and start walking toward me.

"You still up," Scott asks squinting at me through the darkness.

Looking around I notice the sun has set completely and the fire is burning low.

"Yeah," I say. "Why?"

Scott comes up and stands next to me, he stretches and yawns. He rubs sleep from his eyes and yawns again. Scott runs his fingers through his hair to fix it.

"Because it's been about two hours since I left you out here," he says raking his fingers through light brown hair.

"Has it really been that long," I ask trying to hide a yawn.

He stretches again and walks over to the few glow embers left from the fire. He gathers a few twigs and dead foliage from around him.

After a few seconds of blowing on the embers the fire bursts to life once more. I look at Scott in the glowing light of the fire and can see something is troubling him. I yawn and walk over to the fire and immediately feel the heat. I glance at Scott again as he stares into the fire.

"I've seen that look on your face before," I say wanting to help. "What's wrong?"

"When I fell asleep in the tent I had a strange dream," he says adding a few sticks to the fire. "It may have been a premonition."

I can remember Scott having these types of dreams before. He fell asleep in class on e day after a test. When he woke up he said he smelled smoke, but as he became fully awake he couldn't smell it. Near the end of the class the teacher lit a candle, blew the match out and threw it in the trash can. Less than thirty seconds later the trash can burst into flames from the match. I had listened to him tell me about other dreams before, mostly little things like eating something for breakfast. After that dream and the trash can I started listening more intently, because his premonitions could include me as well.

Now that I think something is going to happen every little noise now puts me on edge.

"I packed a machete in my backpack if you want to use it," he says nodding towards the tent.

Knowing that I have some means of protection brings me a little comfort. Now only the louder noises will put me on edge.

"Thanks, that'll make me feel a lot better," I say standing and walking to the tent.

I sit on my knees half inside the tent as I unzip Scott's backpack. Feeling around inside the bag I find the machete and pull it out. I zip the backpack shut and stand to attach the sheath to my belt loop.

"So when is your dream suppose to happen," I ask pacing around the camp.

"I don't know," Scott says as he stares into the fire. "I can't tell when this one is going to happen."

"Well maybe it'll happen on the next camping trip," I say glancing around at the areas of the woods that are left dark without the light of the fire.

"If this trip goes the way my dream did, we won't be having another one," he says staring straight at me in a kind of trance.

"What do you mean," I ask feeling an icy chill run down my spine.

"Exactly what I said, we're not going to be in this world much longer," he says in almost a trance.

"What aren't you telling me Scott," I ask starting to worry. "What do you mean this world?"

"That's the problem," he says as he stands. "I woke up before I could see what's going to happen."

Scott walks over to the small pile of remaining wood. He picks up the last armful and adds it to the fire. In the growing firelight I see him glace at his watch as if he's late for something.

"What are you doing," I ask.

"Getting ready," He says staring blankly into the growing fire.

"Getting ready for what," I ask feeling the heat from the roaring fire. "What's coming?"

Then Scott picks up a long stick from the fire and holds it like a torch. He throws the flaming stick into the open flap of the tent. Sometimes Scott's dreams would trouble him for a day or so, but what he's doing now is all new to me.

"Are you crazy, what are you doing," I yell as panic begins grips me.

"No, I'm perfectly fine," he says picking up and throwing two more flaming sticks at the smoking tent.

A burst of ice cold wind suddenly blasts through the camp. I know that whatever Scott had warned me about is coming. Wintery winds shouldn't be blowing in the middle of summer. All of the other sounds in the forest cease, everything is quiet. Only the sounds of the crackling fire and increasing wind blasting through the trees can be heard.

A sudden static feeling begins to course through my body. The kind of feeling you get when you place your hand too close to a TV screen. Scott walks to the middle of the clearing as the hurricane like winds roar around us. When he reaches the center he turns around and looks straight into my eyes.

"See you later," He says as a bolt of blue lightning flashes out of a cloudless sky.

"Scott," I yell into the deafening wind.

I run towards where he was standing as fast as I can. He's gone and there's not a trace of him anywhere. As I approach the center of the clearing and the static feeling tingles through my body again. I know another bolt is coming, but I only focus is figuring out what has just happened. It feels like a bad dream and no matter what I do I can't wake up. Then the clearing flashes bright blue and I feel my body entire go numb. I fall backwards to the ground, blackness consumes me before I hit.

2

I AWAKE WITH A DULL ache in the back of my head. I slowly move my fingers, then my hands, trying to make sure everything works properly. Once I know every part of my upper body is all right, I struggle into a sitting position sending fresh waves of throbbing pain through my entire body. After the pain subsides I look at my body for physical damage. Nothing was burned, not even a bit of singed hair or clothing. I do notice that my skin is warm to the touch and is steaming as if hot water has just been poured on it, but the inside of my body feels cold. Getting to my feet involves more effort than just sitting upright. Every movement I make causes more pain to course through my body.

When I finally get to my feet I notice for the first time, that my surroundings have changed. Nothing is like it was when I was struck by the strange lightning. The trees are short and gnarled with a grayish colored moss hanging from almost every limb. The ground is almost sand-like, loose, and crunchy underfoot. Even the slight breeze that is moving through the trees has a stale salty smell to it. I tell that this place must be near the ocean, due to the smell and what could possibly be the sound of waves in the distance, not the wind moving through the trees.

I look at the sky and notice the sun is starting to set or it could be rising. With my sense of time lost I decide to travel toward the sound of, what I hope to be crashing waves. What the beach and ocean can do to possibly help me I don't know, but I have to set my mind on something to avoid panicking. With any luck Scott might have landed there. Suddenly I realize something. When people are lost in the wilderness they seek out water. I've got the water, so why not see where it goes. My guess is this stream empties somewhere. That somewhere could be the ocean too. This makes my decision final; I'm going to the beach.

I turn in the direction of the sound of the waves. I tread lightly trying not to send too much pain shooting up my back and to my head. I also know making as little noise as possible in this unknown territory isn't a bad idea either. As I walk quietly through this strange forest I can't shake the feeling that I'm being watched. I stop and look around to see if anything has changed or if something or someone is stalking me. Of course if something is following me, it's probably an inhabitant of this odd place.

I continue walking along the stream listening to its rhythmic gurgle. I stop again to observe the area and notice several things have changed since I started walking. First the sun is sinking lower in the sky, but if the position of this sun is like the one back home, I don't have long before nightfall. Second the sound of what I assume to be waves, have become much louder.

As I turn to continue along the stream my foot slides into a dip in the loose ground. I look down to see several sets of large foot prints. They're larger than my foot and wider too. I kneel down to get a better look at the print. I can make out a pattern, two foot print shaped impressions followed by two almost hand shaped prints. The foot prints in the rear look like large dog paw prints. The front prints look like oversized human hand prints.

A loud snap causes me to jump. Is it the creature that made the huge prints in the sand or something else? Whatever it is I'm not going to stay around long enough to find out. I turn toward the sound of the waves and start running as fast as I can. Pain erupts through my body with every pounding footstep, but I keep pushing myself. I start thinking about the direction of what I hope to be ocean, anything to take my mind off the fact that something could be hunting me.

I try to think of other things as I press painfully on. I decide that if the sun here sets in the west, like it does back home, then the sound of the waves must be coming from the south. Eventually I feel myself begin to tire and my pace begins to slow. I don't want to stop so I change my speed to a steady and painful jog. I glance at my passing surroundings as they slowly creep by. The trees are starting to thin out and the bushes and shrubs are becoming more scarce. The sounds of the waves are becoming louder with each step. Through the remaining trees I can see a blue horizon. I feel the ocean breeze blowing over my aching body as I slow to an agonizing walk. I make my way slowly towards the sea, gazing at the vast dark blue waters stretching on past the horizon. Even with only a few hours of daylight left, it still makes an amazing sight to see. I make my way past the last few trees that separate me from the beach. The sounds of the waves crashing against the white beach are almost hypnotic and I finally realize how exhausted I am. My entire body aches from my long run here. My head is starting to hurt a little less, but every heartbeat sends a small pulse of throbbing pain through my skull. I catch myself before I begin to daydream and start to walk up the beach when a low whistling sound begins to cut through the air above me.

I look up into the evening sky searching for the source of the sound. That's when I see a black sliver traveling straight down toward the sandy beach in front of me. As the object grows closer to the ground I can see it's a spear. I follow the spear's path until it lands in the sand with a soft thud. I walk over to where the spear had landed and pull it out of the sand. Brushing off the sand that still clings to the head of the spear I examine it. The spear is a work of art. The blade consists of two dragons intertwined around the blade and their tales spiral down part of the shaft. The shaft of the spear appears to be a type of hardwood. The wood has been stained so dark that it looks almost black.

A heavy crunching footstep sounds behind me causing me to freeze, my blood feels like ice and each heartbeat sent a chill through me. I grip the spear tight as I turn to face the maker of the sound. I have no idea of what I will be facing, but I know it's not going to be cute and fluffy. As I turn the sight of what I'm seeing causes my heart to beat faster.

This creature is no doubt the creature that made the prints in the sand I had seen earlier. It stands no less than six and a half feet tall with a huge muscle ripped body. Its fur is grayish silver streaked with some black. Claws easily four inches long are ready to tear at flesh, probably mine. The creature's face resembles a wolf with longer and sharper teeth. Saliva drips from its gnashing mouth and its piercing yellow eyes stare at me with the intention of a meal. If this creature is what I think it is, then I am looking into the eyes of a werewolf. But they were only myths, right?

"Whoa," I say, it's all I can manage at the sight of this creature.

The werewolf begins to circle around me snarling and flexing its claws. I position the spear in front of me and the advancing creature. If it wants to eat me it's going to have fight for this meal. I can see the werewolf looking me over, its dart from one part of my body to another. It moves a little closer to me and slashes out with its claws.

"Stay back," I yell hoping to intimidate the beast.

"What will you do if I do not," the werewolf retorts.

It takes me a moment to realize that the werewolf is speaking back to me. Trying not to show my surprise I just stare at the beast.

The werewolf strikes without another word; it lunges at me trying a low sideswipe. I step to my left and jab my attacker in the back of its leg. It lets out a low growl of pain and turns to face me again.

"I'm going to enjoy killing you human," it snarls.

Now it wants to kill me even more, great. Now I move forward to attack him. I step forward and quickly stab at my enemy. The werewolf turns his head sideways and catches the spear in the middle of my attack. I place both hands on the spear shaft and struggle to free it from the werewolf's jaws. Not having the strength to pull it out, I kick the werewolf in the chest with my right leg as hard as I can. My kick lands, but I don't bring my leg back fast enough. The werewolf catches my leg and drives all ten razor sharp claws into my leg. I let out a scream as the pain surges into my leg. I immediately feel the trickle of blood as it begins to pour out my wounds. I hear the werewolf give a satisfied chuckle at the pain it's inflicting on me.

Suddenly a rage overtakes me. The pain in my leg disappears, and the only thing I'm focusing on is killing this enemy before it kills me. I pull on the bottom half of the spear and it breaks off with a loud snap. I continue to hold on to the upper half of the spear with my other hand. Now I use the lower end of the shaft as a club and my right hand to distract my opponent. I pull on the shaft again and this time the werewolf pulls against me. I strike the club across the eyes of my enemy with all the force I can gather. I hear the sound of breaking bone and cartilage as the club makes contact. The werewolf roars with rage and pain as he releases the upper end of the spear, and my leg.

I strike out again and again as fast I can causing the werewolf to block with its arms as it tries to stop the furious onslaught of both halves of the spear. The speed of my attacks increase and my surroundings start to turn black, I'm only focused on my enemy and nothing else. I manage to force him against one of the trees while I keep attacking. As soon as the werewolf's back grazes the tree he glances to see what he's just touched, that's when I strike the final blow. I ram the bladed end of the spear into the werewolf's throat with all the force in my body.

The force is so tremendous that the blade sticks into the tree. I pull the blade out and blood instantly begins to gush from the wound in the werewolf's throat. Its hands reach up to desperately stop the bleeding. As it grips the wound and a strange gurgling sound emits from the werewolf as it falls to the ground. He tries frantically to stop the bleeding, but the damage has already been done. The werewolf falls silent as a puddle of blood leaks from the fatal wound. Still consumed by this odd rage I stab at the back of my fallen foe continuously, as if I can no longer control my own body.

"Enough," I hear a deep voice behind me order.

Thinking it to be another werewolf I swing the lower end of the spear as I turn. A large, rather irritated looking man catches the spear and jerks it from my grasp. As soon as it leaves my hand he redirects the shaft piece and it crashes into the side of my head. I fall to my knees dazed, as the rush of adrenaline slowly leaves my body. He picks me up by my throat roughly, cutting off my air.

"Simon, stop it," I hear a girl order.

Apparently she is in command because the man drops me as soon as the words leave her mouth. All the pain in my body suddenly returns in an instance and I'm unable to move, all I can do is lay in the ground exhausted. I can feel unconsciousness trying to take me into darkness. I fight to keep my eyes open as best I can.

"Let me take a look at him," another girl says as she rushes forward. "Hurry out of my way."

I struggle into a sitting position so I can see who is talking. I see a girl in strange clothing with short black hair and brown eyes rushing towards me. She carries a small bag with her. Kneeling beside me she opens the bag and pulls out a square shaped vial with an orange liquid contained by a cork stopper. She pulls the stopper and hands me the vial.

"Drink this," she orders. "It will ease the pain while I stitch the wounds on your leg."

I sniff the liquid and can make out a slight citrus smell. From the way she is handling the situation she must be some sort of nurse or doctor. Not wanting to feel more pain, I drink the orange liquid without another thought. A few seconds after I drink the contents of the vial I can feel a warm numbness wash over me. My body slumps slightly as I begin to relax a little more. The pain in my leg and everywhere else fades.

She pours a clear liquid on the wounds that she is about to stitch. The wounds bubble for a few seconds then she carefully dabs them off with a white linen cloth. I look down at my leg as she begins to stitch the first wound. I feel a slight pinch each time the needle breaks the skin, even though the pain has been dulled by the medicine. I sit and watch her stitch six more of the ten wounds. She makes it look so effortless. The girl notices that I am watching her and she smiles slightly as she works.

"You are lucky you managed to make him release you," she says as she works. "If he would have pulled his claws down your leg you might not be so fortunate. I am Tori by the way. So tell me a little bit about yourself, where are you from, America?"

"Wait, how do you know that," I ask excitedly as I lean forward. "Are you from the same world as me?"

"No," Tori says, gently pushing me back. "Both of my parents are from your world, they managed to find their way here. They each found out where the other had come from and fell in love. My father used to tell me about his home in America."

"Where was he from," I ask, happy to be talking about my homeland.

"He lived in California," she says. "He was studying to be a doctor."

"You followed in his foot steps, didn't you," I say as I continue to watch her work.

"Yes, I did," Tori says with a sniff. "I have always wanted to help people ever since I was young. I would even go with my father when he would work and hand him the supplies as he needed them. It made me feel so important to help."

"It sounds like you and your father are very close," I say.

"We were until he was killed by werewolves," Tori says in a low voice.

"I'm sorry to hear that," I say quietly. "I didn't know."

"It is all right," she says as she begins to stitch the last wound. "The past cannot be changed."

The girl I assume to be in command of the rescue party walks over after conversing with the large man. She is about a full head shorter than I am, with blue eyes like sapphires. She has blonde hair down to her shoulders; it seems to glimmer in the setting sun. She looks at me and we lock eyes for a moment, then she looks to Tori.

"How is his leg, will we be able to move him before we lose the last of the daylight," she asks glancing around, not looking too thrilled to be here in the fading light.

"I do not know," Tori replies as she finishes the last stitch. "If he places too much pressure on his leg he will reopen the wounds."

"I don't want to stay here any more than you do," I say looking at the girl in command. "Well if you are in command of this group I'll follow your orders. You are in command aren't you?"

"Yes," she snaps. "I am in command and I do not wish to stay here any longer than I have to. You have witnessed first hand the dangers of this place."

Looking at me and then to the body of the fallen werewolf she suddenly has a look of guilt about her.

"I am sorry it must have been difficult to kill the werewolf on your own," she says looking at me. "I am Luna, daughter of Marcus the ruler of Haven. May I ask your name, warrior?"

"My name is Ivan, but I don't think I'm much of a warrior," I say glancing at my injured leg.

"You may not be a warrior now, but I have never seen a newcomer kill a werewolf on the first day of their arrival," Luna says hiding smiling.

"Nor have I," Tori says as she pulls out a bandage and begins to wrap my leg.

She carefully wraps the bandage around my leg. After my leg is properly bandaged she looks around the area for a moment.

"Simon, would you mind cutting down that branch for me?" Tori asks, pointing to a particular tree.

Simon walks to the tree draws a double-edged broadsword and cuts the limb down with a single swipe. He picks up the severed limb and tosses it to Tori. For the first time I notice that Simon has a long scar running across his neck. It runs from the left edge of his jaw and down his neck, and then it disappears under the collar of his shirt. Tori pulls out a small dagger and begins to trim the branch until it looks more and more like a crutch. When she finds the shape satisfying enough she hands me the makeshift crutch. I struggle to my feet as I put all my weight on my left leg. I then place the crutch under my right arm and shift my weight.

"I guess this will work," I say limping around a few times. "So are we going make camp or are we going to travel through the night?"

"We will travel tonight, but not on foot," Luna looks to the sky, places her fingers in her mouth and lets out a shrill whistle.

I look around, not knowing what to expect. Then I hear a distant flapping sound. The sound grows louder and then I see two large shadows move faintly across the ground. I look to the sky, but can not see anything in the rapidly fading light. Just as I think it's my imagination two enormous dragons land on the ground in front of us.

3

AS THE DRAGONS LAND I stand as best I can without the crutch. I draw my machete and place it between me and the two giants. The first dragon is large and muscular, with dark blue scales and lime green eyes. From the looks of this massive creature I assume that it's a male. He stands around twenty feet high and maybe thirty feet long. His wingspan is probably forty feet. The second dragon has a smaller leaner figure. This one could be a female; she has blood red scales with sky blue eyes. Her features are all a few feet shorter than the blue dragon.

"Hello Iris," Luna says patting the red dragon on the neck. "Did anything happen during your flight?"

The dragon looks at me as I hold the machete and she takes a step forward giving a low growl. I hold my ground not moving a single muscle in my body. She stares into my eyes as if she's searching for something. I return her gaze; then she swipes her claws at me without warning. She misses my face by only a few inches, but I don't flinch. I don't know if it's bravery or fear that's keeping me rooted in place.

"I suppose you are braver than you look, newcomer," the dragon says. "I am Iris. May I ask your name?"

Seeing that this dragon is a friend and not an enemy, I relax and sheath the machete.

"I'm Ivan," I say growing somewhat tired of introducing myself so many times in such a short period of time.

"I am honored to meet you," Iris says glancing at the fallen werewolf she adds. "Did they save you from him?"

"Actually he saved himself from that one," Luna says staring at me.

When she says this I have a feeling that Iris thinks I am a warrior, just like Luna does.

"That is very impressive, you will make a formidable warrior," Iris says. "Luna, did not your sister mention something about..."

"We really should be on our way if we wish to make it to Haven by daybreak," Luna interrupts. "There is not much daylight left, let us go."

I pick up my crutch to relieve pressure on my leg. Looking at the blue dragon I notice Simon sitting on him. He is straddling the dragon's shoulders as a small child would sit on his father's shoulders. I see Tori climb onto the dragon as well, sitting behind Simon. I see Luna standing next to Iris whispering something to her. I catch the dragon's eyes as she looks in my direction.

"So how long until we leave," I ask. "Or were you talking about something else?"

Luna turns to me; she almost looks pleased that I'm ready to go.

"No, I was just going over our best course of action with Iris," she says staring at me then mounting Iris. "You will have to ride on Iris as well."

Riding on a dragon with nothing to keep me on its back is not a comforting thought to me. Then there's the couple hundreds feet in between me and the ground, if I fall off. I decide it has to be done if it means finding Scott. Limping forward I slowly climb onto Iris's shoulders; my injured leg is making things much more difficult than I let show. I can feel the stitches pulling as I right myself on Iris's back. I glance at Tori to see if she is watching my progress; as much as it hurts I don't let it show on my face.

"Are we ready," Iris asks looking over her shoulder.

Luna gives a short nod in front of me. I look over at Simon and see him give a stiff nod. Iris spreads her wings to their full extent and beats them a few times. She settles low on her hind legs getting ready to spring off the ground. I know what is coming and adjust myself so the take-off won't cause me too much pain. It only takes one powerful kick of her legs and a single beat of her wings we're in the air. With each beat of her wings we climb higher in the night sky. I'm not able to tighten my legs around Iris's neck due to my leg, so I trust her not to do too much fancy flying. We finally level off and begin to fly in a northeastern direction.

"Where are we going," I ask, not wanting to be the only one not knowing our destination. Luna swings her right leg over Iris's neck and then does the same with her left. Now she's now facing me.

"We are going to the city called Haven," she says over the air that is rushing past us. "It is a city built in the side of a massive mountain range. It was built by the humans and vampires hundreds of years ago."

"Did you say vampires," I ask nervously.

The fact that there were vampires here doesn't surprise me. If there are werewolves and dragons, both of which can talk, why wouldn't there be vampires here too?

"Oh! I forgot to tell you, I am a vampire," Luna says smiling so I can see her teeth in the growing moonlight.

Her canine teeth are longer and sharper than normal, but all the others look perfectly normal, just like a human's would.

"So," I reply hiding the surprise. "Are Simon and Tori vampires too?"

"Tori is a human like you. Simon is a vampire, but he was not born one," Luna glances over at Simon as he flies silently along beside us.

"What do you mean he wasn't born a vampire," I ask trying not to sound totally incompetent.

Luna just smiles. She probably knows that I am trying to learn all I can about this new world.

"Some are born vampire, you know with vampire heritage," She looks at me making sure that I understand. "Then there are humans that are turned by another vampire. Are you getting it so far?"

I nod, soaking up every bit of information she has to offer.

"Normally vampires do not turn a human unless they are going to die and if the human wishes it," Luna explains.

"But wouldn't all humans want to be turned, for a second chance at life," I ask, not being able to stop my constant flow of questions as they flow freely from my mouth.

"Some of the humans here view someone that has been turned as selfish and greedy," Luna says staring down at the back of Iris's neck. "It is sad really, live or not, they treat that person as if they were dead. But not all humans are like this though, only a small group."

I see Simon's dragon fly up along side of Iris. Tori is waving at us trying to get our attention.

"Are we going to make camp later tonight or fly straight to Haven," Tori asks. "Simon's dragon says he can make the flight by mid-morning tomorrow, without having to stop for any rest."

Luna swings her legs around Iris's neck again and begins to converse with her. I look over at Tori again as she digs through a large haversack and pulls out a loaf of bread. She breaks for two pieces and tosses one piece to me as we fly. Looking in the bag again she produces a large chunk of meat. She cuts off two sizable slices and tosses one piece to me, just as she did with the bread. I place the meat on top of the bread and take a bite. The food is good, but I suppose being here for an untold amount of time, almost anything would taste good. I devour the last of the meat and bread in a few more bites. I feel some of the energy in my body return, but not as much as I need. The one thing that I really need is sleep.

"How come you and Simon aren't eating," I ask.

"We don't need to eat very often," Luna says quietly. "When we do need to eat, it is not the kind of food you eat."

"You mean there's nothing that human eat that you do too," I ask.

"We will eat the flesh of some animals," Luna says thinking aloud. "But they are prepared differently for us."

"That's very interesting," I yawn. "I guess I'll learn more about it when we get to the city."

"Yes," Luna says. "You should rest."

"I do need to get some sleep," I say to Luna. "Is it safe to sleep while she is flying?"

"Oh yes. It is perfectly fine," Luna says taking a drink from a flask that Tori tossed to her. "Would you like some water?"

Feeling thirsty from the salted meat I accept the flask and take a long draft of the cool water. Now I feel a level of exhaustion that I hadn't before. I lie down on Iris's back and settle in between her shoulder blades.

"Here is a blanket if you get cold," Luna says handing me a blanket that seems to be made out of some kind of material as thick as wool.

"Thank you," I say taking the blanket and running my hand across it, the blanket feels almost like a type of silk yet it's thick like wool.

I place the blanket on Iris's back and use it as a pillow. In less than a few seconds I fall into a deep sleep. I dream of nothing but blackness and then I have the sensation that I'm falling. Somehow even in my dream I know that I am several hundred feet in the air, but I can't determine if I'm truly falling or if it's just a dream. I feel myself picking up speed and I know that if it's real I'm dead. I look toward the ground that is looming closer in the darkness. Just as I am about to crash to my death, I jolt awake.

I look around to see that I am on the ground and not on Iris's back anymore. I notice that the area I'm at is a sort of prairie with small rolling hills and shrubs dotting the landscape. I think there are some short trees too, but I can't see very far in the darkness. Luna is sitting next to a fire talking with Tori as Simon comes marching into the campsite from the darkness with a small sack bulging with something. I slowly stand feeling the strain on some of my stitches. As I stand Tori turns and rushes over and slowly pushes me back to a sitting position.

"Good you are up, you gave us quite a fright," she says placing her hand gently on my injuries.

I wince as pain blasts through the area she had touched. She looks at her hand and shakes her head.

"You have ripped many of the stitches in your leg," she says showing me her hand.

Her hand is coated with my blood. I can feel the dampness of the blood soaking into the bandages. I look at my leg as more of the white bandages turn red.

"What happened," I ask as I touch the bandages sending pain into my leg and a blood dripping onto the ground.

"You are what happened," Simon says spilling the contents of the sack by the fire. "You yelled something in your sleep and tried to draw your weapon, while we were still in the air. You rolled off Iris's back and fell. She managed to dive and save you."

"The force of the fall when she caught you caused the stitches to rip," Tori says as she opens her medical bag.

She pulls out a small box shaped case and opens it. Inside I recognize a square vial that has an orange liquid in it. I know she will want me drink it.

"He needs to have you stitch him up without the numbing medicine. That will teach him to stop falling off dragons in his sleep," Simon says in the usual irritated voice. He begins to organize the berries from the sack into two piles.

"Simon," Luna exclaims. "You know the pain that he would be in, if not the amount he is in now. Warrior or not it is inhuman."

"I am not human," he says fixing me with a fang-filled smile.

"But at one time you were," Luna almost whispers.

I can hear the sorrow in her voice with every word.

"Give me the vial," I say.

I continue to stare at the smiling vampire I place the bottle back in the case. The look on Simon's face is pure surprise. He isn't smiling at all. He has the most bewildered and shocked expression I've ever seen. I smirk at him, enjoying the moment while it lasts.

"You know that this will hurt a lot more than last time," Tori says with a cautious tone, removing the bloody bandages. "I will still administer the cleansing medicine."

I look over at Luna to see if she is watching, our eyes meet and I can tell she does not approve of this situation at all.

"I know," I say watching the clear liquid begin to bubble on the areas were the stitches have ripped.

From the looks of the damage six entire wounds are open. One other has a few stitches missing. Tori begins to thread the needle. She places her hand on the first wound. Just her touching the wound sends pain pulsating through my leg, but she's going to be pushing a needle through it too. She squeezes the wound together and begins to sew the opening shut again. Pain consumes the wound like a wild fire, but I don't flinch due to Simon watching me. After the first wound has been stitched Simon looks away. Obviously he was hoping for some wincing or me possibly screaming in pain. There may not be screaming, but there is pain, every time the needle punctures the skin.

After what seems like hours of agony, the wounds are stitched shut and the pain is subsiding at an extremely slow rate. I watch Tori wrap fresh bandages around my leg as Luna walks over from the fire and sits next to me. I know she was worried about my decision.

"You did not have to do that you know," she sounds relieved now that the ordeal is over. "But you are much stronger than you look."

"I only did it to shut him up," I whisper leaning in close to Luna. "And it hurt more than I imagined it would."

"I am sure it did," she says with a grin.

"Besides," I say. "What is his problem anyway? Did I do something to make him not like me?"

"Not intentionally, but yes," She says sighing. "I will tell you the whole story of why. It started when he saw the gateway storm, which is what brought you here. Simon and his little sister were assigned the job of protecting the rescue party. We left immediately from Haven with a doctor, a nurse and four warriors. About half way across the open grounds a second gateway storm opened, which was the one that brought you. We figured that the best idea was to split the party in half and investigate each landing site. Simon did not want to do this because it meant leaving his little sister. After a tiresome argument he gave in, so this group is the one that came to find you."

"Okay that explains a lot," I say, content to know why he dislikes me.

"That is not the only reason why," she adds, "There is more and this is the true reason for his dislike of you. When we found you we were going to circle down, pick you up, and fly back to Haven and then meet with the rest of our search party. Unfortunately Simon was rushing things and he managed to lose his spear. That spear has been passed down by his family for generations."

"Oh, it makes sense now," I say finally understanding the full reason. "So he dropped his spear and I picked it up. About the same time the werewolf attacks me and by the end of the battle Simon's spear is in pieces. I had no idea that was the reason."

"Yes, it is very childish," Luna says looking at the pile of bloody bandages sitting at my feet.

"Can't he just have another spear made," I ask thinking out loud.

"Yes, I suppose he will when we return to Haven," she says, still staring at the pile of bandages and shaking her head.

"How long until we reach Haven," I ask moving my leg a little to test the new stitches in my leg.

I keep moving it until I feel a twinge of pain. So I stop to keep the stitches from tearing a second time. I notice that the sun is beginning to rise in the east and know that I've put us behind schedule.

"How long was I out before I woke up," I ask looking at the sun as it continues to rise slowly in the sky.

"I would say, eight or nine hours," Luna says handing me a small pile of the berries Simon had collected.

I look at the berries and notice that they are blackberries. I toss a couple of the berries in my mouth and savor their sweet taste.

"Sorry. I guess I cost us quite a bit of time in getting back to Haven," I say.

"It actually worked to our advantage," Luna says looking down at the berries. "The dragons needed the rest, even if they do not admit it. They were flying all day yesterday across the fields. So I think they are grateful for the rest."

Tori walks over and sits on the other side of Luna. We sit in silence as the minutes creep by slowly, just as the sun does in the sky.

"Simon says we should get moving, he had seen some werewolf prints while he was forging," Tori says eating the last handful of her berries and wiping her hands off on the short green grass. "I think we should go as well, if the werewolves are near they will smell the blood in a short time."

"Is their sense of smell really that good," I ask finishing off my berries and wiping my hands on the grass as well.

"Certainly," Tori replies. "That is why we must burn your clothing after we reach Haven. Your clothes carry a unique scent, unlike our clothing which is masked somewhat better."

"All right," Luna says standing and dusting herself off. "Let us depart. If there are tracks near I agree that our best course of action is to leave."

I reach for my crutch so I will be able to make to my feet. I look up to see Luna with her hand extended to help me. I grip the crutch in my right hand and grasp her hand in my left. I push off and in an instant I'm standing, I place the crutch under my arm and begin limping toward Iris. I very slowly climb onto Iris's back once more and make sure I'm ready for the take off. Luna climbs up onto Iris's back as well and settles down in front of me.

"Are you ready to take off Iris," Luna asks adjusting her position on the dragon's shoulders.

"Of course," Iris says crouching low on her hind legs for take off.

"Sorry if this hurts you Ivan."

"Don't worry," I say with a smile. "I can handle it, trust me." Iris extends her wings as she did during take off last time. She beats them once testing the air, blasting the ashes and embers from the campfire across the open grasslands. I know what's coming this time so I lean forward just as Luna does. Iris kicks off and we become airborne once more. As we climb higher in the morning sunlight I can finally see what my surroundings look like. Iris levels off and I can hardly see the edge of the strange forest that I had landed in. I continue to stare at it noticing something moving across the prairies from the forest. From the height we are at it looks like a sliver speck. Then from the forest comes five more figures, following the one in the lead.

"Hey Luna," I yell over the wind. "Are those werewolves?"

"It would seem so," she says staring down at them. "Did you see were they are coming from?"

"Yeah," I say pointing in their direction. "They came from the forest, and now they're coming this way."

"This is not good," Luna says turning to Simon as he flies alongside us. "Simon there is a pack following us!"

I can tell by the concerned sound in her voice that we are in a troubling situation. Looking back I see the pack slowly gaining on us as we fly at a leisurely pace. I try to think of something that we can do to stop or change their direction. I lean over Iris's shoulders and look for any useful objects on the grasslands. I notice an outcrop of boulders jutting out of the ground.

"Simon," I shout over the constant flap of wings. "Do you see those rocks down at the bottom of that small hill?"

"Yes, what is your point," He says with no interest. "They look just like any other rocks I've seen before."

I don't want to waste time arguing with this stubborn soldier.

"Do they look like any other rock that your dragon can drop on a pack of werewolves," I shoot back.

It's like a light bulb just went off over Simon's head. He leans forward and converses with his dragon for a moment. They immediately start a steep dive toward the small group of rocks. Luna looks from the diving dragon and then over her shoulder at me. I can see the confused look on her face.

"I told him to dive so his dragon can pick up one of those boulders," I explain looking over my shoulder at the werewolves. "Then he can drop it on the werewolves."

Suddenly Luna's face lights up and she leans forward and says something to Iris. I lean forward as well, knowing that we are going to dive and pick up a boulder too. As predicted we dive in an almost vertical line toward the ground. The air roars past us and I can feel the pressure on my chest from the momentum. With less than a hundred feet to impact Iris pulls up and hovers above the stones.

"Pick one that you can fly fast with," Luna instructs to both dragons. She then turns to me. "I am adding to your plan."

Iris picks a boulder about the size of a small sofa. Simon's dragon heaves one the size of a compact car and begins to make his way skyward with Iris trailing right behind him. We turn in the direction of the advancing wolf pack.

"Fly straight at them," Luna orders with a voice an authority I had not heard since I met her. "Right before we pass over them, release the boulders. Fly high enough that they cannot jump and reach you, but no higher."

We begin to fly towards the pack of werewolves that are less than a few hundred yards away. Soaring low over the landscape I look only at our targets as they loom closer and closer. I feel the same odd rage begin to take over my body. The edge of my vision turns black and my heart beat begins to accelerate. We are now less than fifty yards away and closing fast. Just as we are about to pass over the pack the lead werewolf jumps in a futile attempt to reach us. As soon as its feet leave the ground the boulders leave the dragons' claws.

Iris is leading when she releases the boulder; it falls rapidly then crashes into the werewolf in mid-air. The same boulder crushes the werewolf behind the leader. Simon's dragon drops his boulder a second after Iris does. His hits the ground and bounces into the rear of the pack taking out two werewolves in the process.

The two remaining werewolves stop and look around searching for their comrades, who are no longer there. Taking a moment to comprehend the event that has just taken place, they turn and flee before the same fate befalls them. Then the dragons fly back to their original altitude and fly towards Haven once more.

We fly for hours in silence, just listening to the hypnotic flap of the dragons' wings. Then I see something looming in the distance. As we fly closer I can tell it's a mountain range. The minutes continue to pass and with each beat of their wings the dragons bring us closer to the giant mountains. I notice that everyone else is focused on the giant mountains spearing up from the horizon. I clear my throat trying to get Luna's attention without saying anything. She turns and looks at me giving me the opportunity to ask the one question that has been eating at me since I've seen the mountains.

"Is that Haven," I ask.

"Yes," she replies. "That is my home."

4

WE FLY THE LAST of the journey in silence, I watch as the mountain city continues to grow larger the closer we get to our destination. The mountain range is massive against the landscape. Large peaks tower up into the sky. A giant semicircle wall comes out of the western side of the mountains. We begin to fly lower as we near the wall and Luna waves her hand three times in the air to the soldiers on the wall. The soldiers wave back in acknowledgment. As we over the wall I can see soldiers lining the wall on an early morning patrol. They are all equipped with long bows and swords.

Once inside the wall the area is nothing but farmlands and pastures. A small area has soldiers and other people training. I look ahead to see a second wall that is running across the mouth of a gigantic cave. As we approach this wall Luna waves her hand again and the soldiers wave back, just as before. We continue to fly toward the cave, which has plenty of space for the dragons to fly. The distance from the floor of the cave to the ceiling has to be a thousand feet. As we fly inside the cave I see stone buildings covering the entire floor of the cave. Most of the buildings are two or three stories tall with windows on all sides. Some are four stories, but no taller. Torches and lanterns are lit almost everywhere. Torches are spaced along the streets, while lanterns line the windows of many buildings. Flying over the city I see a third wall, extremely smaller than the first two. It cuts a huge white stone palace off from the rest of the city. The palace dwarfs the other dwellings in the city. Easily fifty stories high, it is stands out like a ghost in the darkness of the cave. Large balconies dot the sides of the towering structure. With every balcony is an opening to the room behind it. Some have drapes drawn shut for privacy, while others are open. For the third time Luna waves and the few guards on the wall wave her through. We circle one balcony on the southern side that is twice the size of the other balconies. Flying lower we come to a landing on the polished marble floor.

We all dismount from the dragons; I get off a little slower than the others. Once off Iris's back I observe the large room that we are standing in front of. The room has a long table with ten seats on each side and one on each end. Cloth tapestries line the walls and a golden candle-lit chandelier hangs above the table that lights the room. A large set of polished doors are closed on the opposite side of the room.

As I look around the room, the doors open and a man strides into the room. He stands slightly taller than I do, and has short light brown hair and sapphire eyes that match Luna's. He must be related to her somehow. He walks over to our group and hugs Luna. He then turns to Simon and shakes his hand and he does the same with Tori. The dragons both look at him until he finally nods to them as well. Both of the dragons take flight and fly from the balcony. Their wing beats become faint as they fly away and then there is silence.

"You may return to your duties," he says to Tori and Simon. "I thank you for your services."

Tori and Simon walk to the doors and Simon is actually nice enough to open the door for her. They walk from the room and the doors shut quietly behind them.

He then turns his gaze towards me. He stares at me for a moment as if I'm an old friend and he's trying to place my name.

"So you are the newcomer," he says with a stern yet friendly voice. "I am Marcus ruler of this city. May I ask your name?"

He extends his hand to me.

"I'm Ivan," I say shaking his hand.

"You must be hungry, Ivan," he says. "Would you like something to eat? You can tell me what happened upon your arrival. Please sit down while we wait."

"Thank you," I say making my way slowly to the table and sitting down.

Marcus opens the door and converses with a guard standing at the door. The guard nods and hurries down the hallway. Marcus walks over to the head of the table and sits down. He looks at me and then to Luna.

"So," he says folding his hands on the table and directing his question to Luna. "How did the trip fare?"

Luna tells the story of how they split the search party and were too late to assist with the werewolf attack. She tells of the nightmare that caused my fall and the airborne assault on the werewolf pack. When Luna finishes telling our story the doors open and two servants bearing platters of food walk in. They place the large platters on the table and remove the lids.

A wonderful aroma instantly fills the room, causing my mouth to water. The first platter has an assortment of different meats like steaks, fish, and fowl. Some of the steaks look as if they are rare, due to the small puddle of blood forming at the bottom of the platter. The second platter has a variety of fruits, oranges, grapes, bananas, and variety of other fruits. All are sliced and decoratively placed around a bowl of cream. The servants place plates, forks and knives in front of us and leave the room.

I wait before I reach for any of the food. I don't know if there are any rituals before eating. Marcus looks at me as if waiting for me to do something.

"You are our guest," he says motioning to the food. "Please, after you."

"Oh, thank you," I say spearing a piece of rare steak with my fork. "I didn't know I was to go first."

I cut a piece off and chew it slowly, it's amazing. I've had rare steaks back home on some occasions. Most of the time the people there would say it was disgusting, but they hadn't tried it. It seems that this is the same kind of situation. Luna stares at me with an odd look on her face. I notice that Marcus is also eating a rare steak. I cut off another piece of steak, savoring the favor. Luna also has a rare steak on her plate, so why is she staring at me like that?

"What," I ask cutting off another piece of steak.

"I have never seen a human eat rare meat here," she says cutting off a piece of steak. "Mostly vampires eat them to satisfy their blood lust. Most of the humans eat cooked meat or the fruit."

"I guess I'm just not like most humans," I say eating another piece of steak and letting the juices fill my mouth.

Then something pops into my mind. What is blood lust? So, I decide to ask. There can't be that much harm in learning about their way of life.

"What is blood lust," I ask, noticing Marcus give a stern glance at Luna.

Maybe I touched on a sensitive subject. I guess there could be some harm in learning about them after all.

"The blood lust is the only flaw in being a vampire," Marcus says placing his fork and knife next to his plate. "It happens at different times depending on the individual, causing them to crave blood. So that is why we serve the steaks rare. It satisfies the hunger, but only for a short time."

"Was I not supposed to take one then," I ask, not wanting to offend him.

"Oh, no," he says with a chuckle. "It is perfectly all right."

I finish the steak and eat a few pieces of fruit to try and even things out. After we finish I continue to look around the room and admire the architecture of it. On the ceiling there are four large arcs connecting to each pillar. I look at the table running my hand over the smooth varnished wood. Luna finally finishes her steak and slides her plate forward.

"You must be tired," Marcus says standing and stretching. "Luna, will you show Ivan to his room?"

"Wait a minute," I say quickly. "What do I do about my friend, and how do I get home?"

Marcus sighs and looks down at the table for a moment. When he looks up at me I can tell the news isn't going to be good.

"You cannot go back to where you have come from," Marcus says slowly. "I understand that this must be hard to imagine, but you must. One day you will learn more about this world. Now you must rest. Luna, please take him to a room."

"Yes, father," Luna says getting up and walking over to the door. "This way please."

"It's still morning," I say looking at Marcus. "I'm not tired."

"You need to rest if you are to heal," Marcus says. "Now please, go."

I suppose that there's no need to argue, besides I do feel a little worn down from the fight with the werewolf. I pick up my crutch and make my way through the door. I half walk half hop down the hallways next to Luna. I can't stop my mind from going over our entire conversation during the meal. From what I gathered, vampires periodically want blood and the most stunning thing, Marcus is Luna's father. Now I have more questions nagging at me. One of which is, why can't I go home?

"So," I say hesitantly. "Are you next in line to rule?"

"No," she says turning a corner. "My sister is next to rule, she is two years older than me."

"Do you want to rule," I ask.

It's like I can't stop the questions from flowing out of my mouth. Why do I care this much?

"Never," she says with a smile. "Ruling a city is not one of the things I wish to do. Besides my father says I have too adventurous of a spirit to stay here. He says I got it from my mother."

"I'm the same way," I say, thinking of the camping trip that led me here. "It's that kind of spirit that got me here in this place."

"You know you took the news rather well," Luna says as we walk down the halls.

"What do you mean," I ask.

"Must newcomers here go mad when they find out that they are not returning," Luna says. "Some have even taken their own lives for fear of what is here."

"I'm not going to be that extreme," I say.

"You took the news of vampires rather well too," Luna says with a grin.

"You seem much nicer than the werewolves," I say with a laugh.

I follow Luna down the flight of stairs, which takes longer than I want. We take a few more twists and turns before arriving at another hallway. "Your room is the second door on the left."

I look down the hall and turn to ask Luna how long it would take for the other search party to arrive, but she was gone.

"I have to learn how to do that," I think out loud, and then I turn and hobble down to my room and open the large wooden double doors.

Entering the room I am amazed to see a king sized bed with a canopy. The same large red curtains that blocked my view from some of the rooms earlier are open. I notice a massive cushion on the floor next to the bed. It is about twice the size of the bed. I make my way to the balcony that makes up the area where the fourth wall should be. I place my hands on the rail and look out over the city.

Torches and lanterns dot the entire cave filling it with a dim glow. I continue to stare out over the city and out of the mouth of the massive cave at the morning skies beyond. I wonder where Scott is and if he is going to make it here before the end of the day. As I ponder the thought I hear a knock on the door. I make my way as quickly as I can and open the door. To my surprise I see Tori standing at the doorway.

"Hello," she says in the same cheerful voice as when we met. "I was going to give you a short tour around some of the palace. If you do not have any objections, that is."

"Not at all," I say leaning on my crutch a bit more to relieve the pressure on my stitches. "I would enjoy it."

"It is nothing special," she says glancing at my leg. "I am only going to the infirmary and you need to go to the bathing room anyway."

"Okay," I say not sure how to take the fact that she basically said I stink. "What about my leg, is it okay to get the stitches wet?"

"The bandages need to be changed anyway," she says beginning to walk away. "Water will not affect the stitches at all."

I close the door behind me and hurry to catch up with Tori. We go down a few more flights of stairs before turning down a hallway with three doors. The first door is on the right along with the third. The second door is on the left in between the two on the right.

"There are only three rooms on this floor," Tori says walking to the second door. "This is the floor of palace infirmary."

Tori walks to the middle door on the left and opens it. We walk inside a long rectangular room filled with beds, all covered with white sheets. The wall opposite of the door is completely open, giving a perfect view of the city. There is a balcony attached to this room as well. This balcony was slightly different though. The other balconies were short; this one takes up the entire length of the long opening. The only obstructions of the balcony are the pillars that are placed about every thirty feet. I only notice one patient in the room. A small boy sits holding his wrist close to his body as he just stares at the floor. From the looks of him he might be ten or eleven.

"I see you have a patient," I say nodding in direction of the boy.

"I need to administer to him," she says setting her bag on a bed. "You should go wash up. The men's bathing room is door on the left. I'll wait for you here."

"Okay," I say opening the door and shutting it quietly.

I make my way down the torch lit hallway to the bathing room. I open the door and instantly feel the thick steamy air begin to flow out. I walk into the heat filled room and look around. The room is well lit with lanterns hanging from each pillar. On the left side of the room are niches cut into the wall. Each niche is around two and half feet high and a foot wide. They remind me of a locker at school except without a door. Inside each of the lockers are a small hand towel, a large towel, and a robe. I notice that there is a doorway leading somewhere else. I make my way to the doorway and peer inside.

There is a second room filled with dividers along the walls. Each has a sort of mini waterfall flowing into a small pool. I walk inside the room and kneel at one of the pools. I slosh my hand through the warm water; it's almost to the point of being hot. I look along the inside edge of the pool and notice vertical slits carved out of the sides. I run my hand over the slits and can feel the current of the water lightly tugging at my hand. I slowly stand and walk back to the locker room. I retrieve the contents from one and take them with me to the room with the pools.

I slowly pull off my tattered clothes and place them in a pile at the edge of the pool. I slide into the warm pool and the heat of the water causes me to wince as it touches each wound on my leg. After a moment I allow the warmth to wash away the weariness in my limbs. I take the hand towel and submerse it in the water. It starts to slightly bubble as if it has kind soap on it. I pull it out and rub my hands on it. The substance feels just like soap, so I guess it is. I wash and dry off, reluctant to leave the warm soothing water. I put on the robe, gather up my clothes. I make my way slowly back to the locker room.

I look at the locker that I had taken the towels from. The locker now contains fresh clothes in it. I look around the room for any sign of the person that might have out them there. I take out the clothes and examine them. They feel like a type of silk, the same material that the blanket Luna had given to me during the flight here, only it's not as thick. There is a long sleeved shirt, pants and some kind of slippers that looked like moccasins. They are all a charcoal gray color, with the exception of the shoes. I put on the new clothes and am surprised at how comfortable they are. The shirt and pants are a little baggy, allowing me to move freely. I grab my crutch from next to the lockers, no sense in letting Tori know I was walking around without using the crutch. Well it's more like limping, but she still doesn't need to know.

I place the bundle of old clothes under one arm and half use the crutch with the other. I make my way into the hallway and walk to the infirmary without using the crutch. I open the door and peek inside. Tori is finishing up with the boy, who now has his wrist wrapped in a bandage. I walk into the room being sure to make it look like I am using the crutch. Tori looks up from her conversation with the boy. He gets up and rushes from the room before I even let go of the door.

"Feeling refreshed," Tori asks she rolls up a piece of bandage and places it in her medical bag.

"Yes," I say sitting on a bed across from her. "How do those pool things work anyway?"

"It is a really simple actually," she says taking a fresh roll of bandages from a cabinet by the bed she is sitting on. "This cave has natural hot water springs all over before the city was built here. So we carved and built the city on top of them, making the springs run through openings cut in the stone buildings."

"Okay," I say thinking of the time it must have taking to perfect. "But where does it go after that?"

"Yet again simple," she says rolling up my pant leg to look at the stitches. "There is also an underground waterway that leads to the sea. This allows the waste water to flow to the sea."

"Wouldn't that pollute the water at sea?" I ask watching Tori wrap the bandages around the wounds.

"There are rapids in the waterway," she explains as she works. "They obliterate anything that comes through the waterway."

Tori finishes wrapping the bandages on my leg, she then gets up and walks over to a cabinet that is between the two beds. She places the bandage roll in it then pulls out a small bottle filled with a ruby colored liquid. She hands it to me and sits down on the bed across from me.

"Drink that before you rest," she instructs. "It will help you sleep."

"Thanks," I say staring at the red liquid before placing it in my pocket. "I better get back to my room, I'm exhausted."

I get up and hobble to the door using the crutch as little as possible. I open the door and am surprised to see Marcus standing in the hallway. He looks at me and smiles.

"Greetings Ivan," he says gesturing for me to walk with him.

I walk alongside him as we make our way to the stairs.

"I was hoping I would get to speak with you in private," he says as we reach the stairs. "I wanted to ask you something about your battle with the werewolf."

"Okay," I say, a little bit confused. "What would you like to know?"

"When you started to battle the werewolf," he says. "Did anything strange happen?"

By the tone of his voice I can tell that this is a serious question. I play back the battle in my mind. I can recall the way my vision changed and my agility increased. We turn a corner and begin up one of the staircases.

"Yes," I say hesitantly. "My vision changed, my speed and strength increased. To be perfectly honest that was the first real fight I have ever been in. It was like I could see what I was doing, but I wasn't in control of my own body."

"I see," he says thoughtfully. "I might have an answer to what happened, but it will take some time before I will know for certain."

We climb the stairs until we reach my floor. I walk into the hallway and turn to see if Marcus is following, but he's gone. He did the same as Luna did to me earlier. She is definitely his daughter because they act a lot alike; it must run in the family. I turn to go to my room when I notice a guard heading toward me. He is taller than me and more muscular than me too. He stops in front of me; he looks as if he has run to catch up to me, and then started walking when I noticed him.

"Greetings, sir," he says slightly panting. "I have orders from Tori to have your old clothing burned."

I just remembered that I still had them. I hand them to him and give him a short nod. He does the same before rushing off with them to probably burn them. Then I suddenly realized that he treated me as if I were his commanding officer. I don't understand why he did that. I continue to my room, not wanting anymore surprises for the day.

Hobbling into my room I shut the door and toss the crutch on the bed to the left of the room. I walk over to the balcony and can see that most of the torches and lanterns in the city are now extinguished. The position of the sun is lighting the inside of the cave. Feeling tired and wanting to sleep I draw the large drapes shut. The room is now dim and it takes a moment for my eyes to adjust. I walk over to my bed and set the crutch where I can reach it. I also notice that I hadn't given the machete to the guard. I take the machete out of the sheath. I place the machete behind the crutch to conceal it from view. I slowly crawl into the bed. I instantly relax because of the soft mattress and pillows.

As I roll over on the bed I feel something jab me in the leg. I reach in my pocket and pull out the small bottle. Tori had given my earlier. Popping out the cork I drink the liquid. I instantly feel a slight burn as the liquid flows down my throat, then it turns to a warm feeling. Setting the empty bottle on the nightstand I feel my eyelids begin to droop. I curl up under the warm blanket and mange to ask myself one question before sleep overtakes me. Is Scott even alive?

5

I OPEN MY EYES TO a dark room. As I look around I can't see anything so I wait for a moment and let my eyes adjust to the darkness. The first thing that I notice when I'm able to see is that I am in the same position as when I fell asleep. Whatever the red liquid was, it helped me sleep just like Tori said it would. I slowly slide out of the bed and reach for the crutch. I feel revived and now I'm in the mood to explore this new world that I've landed myself in. My leg is much better then yesterday, but I decide to take it along just in case my leg starts to hurt.

I walk over to the door and open it slowly. Sticking my head out into the hallway I see if anyone is around. Seeing that no one is roaming about, I step into the hall and shut the door behind me. I begin walking down the hallway and a slow pace as I test out my leg. It feels so much better, and I can't fell as much pressure on the stitches. I look around the torch lit halls to see if I can figure out what time of day it is. There are a few stain glass windows, but I can't tell if the light on them is from torches or sunlight. Not knowing my way around I decide to just wander and see where I end up. I know this isn't a good idea, but I need to do something. I find exploring alone helps me clear my mind.

The one question I am trying to answer is where Scott is and most importantly if he's alive. I turn the corner and continue to walk down another hallway. These two questions repeat in my mind over and over as I continue to venture farther from my room. I ascend a few floors of stairs and begin to notice that I have seen no one in the hallways. Before I had gone to sleep I had seen people walking through the halls almost everywhere. Now it is as if the palace is deserted. I suppose it must be nighttime.

Suddenly, I catch a glimpse of movement out of the corner of my eye. For some reason I feel curious, and confident enough to follow the figure. I take short quick steps, holding the crutch at my side to make movement easier. I have used this quick pace when playing evasive type games back home. It allows me to move fast enough to sneak up on or escape my opponent, while the short steps reduce some noise. I turn the corner crouching low and pressing myself into the shadows as best I can. I examine the hallway, thinking I lost the figure and the pursuit is over.

Then I notice a door near the end of the hall slightly open. The light from inside the room sends a line of light to streak across the floor of the dark hallway. I slowly move toward the door, being careful to not make any noise. I peer through the gap of the open door. The room appears to be another bedroom like mine, except much more luxurious. I can make out the sound someone whispering, then a faint reply. Obviously two people are having a late night chat. I strain to hear the conversation, but can only make out pieces. They both sound like females.

"Yes, you were right," one voice says.

"I told you," a second voice says. "I have not had a dream mislead me before."

"But maybe this one is wrong," says the first again. "Besides father thinks he is a berserker."

"I knew you would say that," the second voice says excitedly.

I have no idea what they are talking about, but I don't wish to be standing at the door eavesdropping if this conversation should end soon. I turn and slowly creep away from the door. As soon as turn the corner I hear the door open and close lightly, now I know I'm in trouble. I place the crutch under my arm and look out the window at the dark city below. I can also see the moon full and bright in the cloudless sky outside the cave. As I stare at the moon I can barely hear the footsteps as they round the corner, then they stop. I continue to stare out at the moon lit city. Then I hear the footsteps slowly becoming closer.

"I can hear you," I say continuing to stare out the window.

The footsteps stop and I hear the person sigh.

"Thought I could sneak up on you," says a familiar voice. "I guess you are still proving that you are full of surprises."

Luna walks up and stands at the windowsill with me. She stares out the window for a moment and then looks at me.

"Your friend arrived here a few hours ago," she says.

"What," I exclaim forgetting that it's the middle of the night. "When can I see him?"

"He is resting right now," Luna whispers. "He was not fortunate enough to have only one werewolf follow him, he had a pack chase him. He ran and barely managed to escape before the rescue party found him. But he is here and without a single scratch."

A wave of relief surges through me. He's safe and I'll be able to see him soon.

"What are you doing up here anyway," Luna asks, a hint of concern in her voice.

"I like to walk to clear my mind," I explain. "I guess I walked a little farther than I had expected."

"Or does it take that long to clear your head," she laughs, her concern now replaced with humor.

"Maybe," I shoot back. "Is that why you're up walking around too?"

She just laughs and continues to stare out the window. Suddenly a new set of question come to mind. Was Luna the figure I had seen a moment ago? Was she the one talking to the other person in the room around the corner? The second question made some sense to me. One of them had mentioned her father. Although I'm sure Luna isn't the only person here with a father.

"Well," I say breaking the silence. "I guess I need to head back to my room."

"Do you know the way," Luna asks, looking down the hallway.

"I don't think so," I say with a chuckle. "Can you tell me?"

"Just go down those two flights of stairs, take two lefts, a right, and one more left. Get all of that?"

"I got it all," I say as I try to memorize the lefts and rights. "I guess I'll see you in the morning."

"Yes," Luna says turning and walking away.

I turn and walk in the direction Luna had told me to go. I walk down the stairs with the new set of questions still racing through my mind. After descending the stairs I reach the hallway on my floor. Now comes the part I am not sure about. Was it two lefts then a right or two rights then a left? I decide on two lefts.

As I round the second left my surroundings begin to look more familiar. I manage to make it to my room without having to backtrack. I fall back onto the bed and just stare at the canopy. I know that I should try to get some sleep, but the thought that Scott is here keeps me awake. Since I can't seem to sleep I get up and open the drapes. When I do a slight breeze blows into the room. I walk onto balcony and lean on the railing. I watch the guards patrolling the palace walls. As I watch them walk along the walls I begin to feel like causing a little mischief. I look around the room for something to fuel my growing plan.

I walk over to the bed and sit down, thinking of what I could use. Then my eyes fall on the crutch made from the limb. I decide that will do. I reach over to where I set the machete and notice something. Next to my machete is a new crutch, properly fashioned.

I pick it up and inspect it; this helps my plan a lot. I take the old crutch and the machete and walk out on the balcony. I sit on the cool marble floor of the balcony cutting the old crutch into small pieces, each about the size of golf balls.

After an unknown amount of time the entire crutch is now chunks of wood in a small pile. I pick up a piece and feel the shape as I walk over to the rail of the balcony. I watch and wait for my opportunity. Finally after what seems like hours of waiting I see it. One of the guards has fallen asleep. I figure if I can't sleep why should he be able to, and he's on the job too. I toss the piece of wood towards the sleeping guard. I follow its path, but it falls pitifully short. I pick up another and toss it out a little farther. I watch it hit the shoulder of the sleeping guard. He jumps as he wakes, dropping his spear with a loud metallic clank. I duck down out of sight and peek over the rail.

He literally had no idea what hit him. I continue to do this to any guard that falls asleep. I run out of pieces to throw about the same time that the guards get the idea to start looking up. I look out at the sky and can see it is turning a creamy orange with streaks of light purple. I brush the wood shavings off the side of the balcony and pick up the machete. Walking back to the bed I place the machete back where I can reach it. I lie on the bed and feel sleep slowly working on me. I think of what will happen when I get to meet up with Scott again. As I continue to think of the future I feel my eyes growing heavy. I decide a little nap before starting the day couldn't hurt. I close my eyes and drift off into sleep again.

6

I AWAKE TO THE SOUND of someone knocking on the door. I roll out of bed and grab the new crutch. Looking out at the sky I notice it is now brighter turning from hues of orange to blue. That means that I haven't been asleep for very long, but I feel as if I have gotten more than the needed amount of sleep. I hear the knock on the door again, a little louder this time.

"It's open," I yawn.

I look up to see Luna standing in the doorway with a sword in her hand. I don't really know what is going on, so I causally grab the machete and hold it at my side. She just looks at me and smiles, then I notice the sheath in her other hand. I know that she is not going to attack me, because if she wanted to kill me she could've done it while I was asleep. I pick up the machete and place it in the sheath then attach it to the side of my pants. I turn and walk towards Luna. As I pass by her I gently push the blade out of my way. I look at her and can see that she's puzzled by my reaction.

"How did you know that I was not going to attack you," she asks sheathing the sword.

"If you wanted me dead I would be right now," I say with a smirk.

"You had the chance before I woke up and just now when I walked by."

"I suppose I will not be able to surprise you for some time," she says smiling. "These are all promising traits of a great warrior."

"Please don't start with the warrior stuff again," I sigh. I don't know why everyone here thinks I'm some sort of warrior. I certainly don't feel like a warrior, especially having to carry around a crutch. But for the people here, fighting seems to be a way of life. So maybe they can see things like potential warriors before I can.

"So what do you have planned for us to do today," I say stretching, causing my back to pop a few times.

"I thought I could give you a tour of the Haven," she says as she begins to walk away.

"Wait a second," I say opening the door to my room and throwing the crutch on the bed. "Okay, now I'm ready."

We walk up through the halls and up several flights of stairs to the floor that I had wandered to the night before. Luna tells me which room belongs to whom and what some of the people's roles are in the palace. We reach the room that I had followed the figure to last night.

"This is my older sister's room," Luna says striding past the room to the stair case. "Most of the time she is preparing for the day that she will become ruler of Haven. I am glad she is becoming ruler on day. She has the essence of a true leader."

"You are quite the leader yourself," I say as we continue the little tour. "You seem to be able to take control of a situation, even when under pressure."

Luna only smiles as we continue along the hallway to another flight of stairs. We journey through many halls and passageways, each one bringing us closer to the ground level. As we reach what must be the second or third floor, Luna stops at another wide hallway. This hallway only has two doors with one on each side. Luna walks over to the door on the left and opens it and motions for me to follow her. I follow Luna inside the room and can hardly believe the contents of the room. The room is very long with shelves lining every inch of the walls.

Weapons of every kind and from every place pack the shelves. They also seem to be from different periods of time as well. From ancient arsenals from feudal Japan to Civil War cavalry sabers and so on. There are bows, arrows with various types of heads and even some blow guns. I can also see spears, pikes, lances, throwing stars, and a vast variety of swords.

"This is the armory," Luna says placing the sword she has been carrying with her on a shelf of swords. "You can place your weapon among them and pick a different one if you prefer."

"How did you manage to accumulate this many weapons," I ask taking off the machete and placing it along side Luna's sword.

"Over hundreds of years many people were pulled into this world," Luna explains walking along the rows of swords on the one side of the room. "We simply stored them here and figured out what weapons could be used for which warriors."

"So a warrior can isolate his attributes and pick a weapon that balances him best," I say picking up a double edged long sword and testing the balance.

"You catch on quick," she says leaning against a shelf of spears and pikes. "Pick out one or two that you like. That way you can practice while you continue to recover."

I just remembered that my leg was injured. It hadn't hurt the entire time that I've been up. I can place pressure on it and it feels normal. Looking at a set of hook swords I pick them up and instantly like them. I'd seen them used before and have wanted a pair for a long time.

"I'll take these if you don't mind," I say attaching a kind of double sheath to my lower back. "These have a comfortable feel to them."

"Hook swords are difficult to master," Luna says attaching a set of two short sides to her waist. "You may begin training when we reach the training grounds later today."

"But what about my leg," I say placing a little pressure on my leg.

"Tori gave you a bottle of red medicine did she not," she asks walking back to the door.

"Yes," I say confused. "But that was from sleep, wasn't it."

"That medicine accelerates the healing process," she says opening the door. "Humans call it vampire's touch."

"Why," I ask as I follow her out into the hallway.

"We vampires can heal in seconds," she says drawing one of her short swords.

She presses her hand to the blade and runs it along the blade. I can see crimson blood spill from the cut on the palm of her hand.

She places her hand in front of me and I see the cut instantly begin to fuses itself shut. She then takes out a cloth handkerchief and wipes off the blood on her hand. She then shows me her hand again. There's no trace of the wound is on the palm of her hand.

"You see," Luna says sheathing her sword. "The medicine will not heal you as I was just healed, but that is why you do not need a crutch right now. You are healed enough for Tori to remove the stitches."

"When can I get the stitches taken out," I ask resisting the urge to look at my leg.

"It will be later today," Luna says beginning to walk down the hall toward a massive lobby. "Tori is giving your friend Scott a tour of Haven. We will meet with them at the training grounds."

I follow Luna into a large lobby like room; it seems like a cave itself. A high ceiling with a large golden chandelier with crystals hanging from it lights the room. The crystals send multi- colored patterns all around the room. We are at the top of two sets of decorated stairs. Each curves gently to the down the lower level. Luna descends the stairs and I follow her onto the large lobby floor. Now that I'm standing in the middle of this room, it seems more like a ballroom. I continue to walk slowly across the room towards a set of large polished doors.

I walk ahead of Luna and open the door; she walks by and smiles at me. I step outside with Luna and gaze at the sight of the enormous palace walls. The walls looked so small when I was flying high over them last night. I continue to look around when I notice a small piece of wood on the ground. I push it aside with my foot and continue on my way. As I observe the wall I notice that there are no gates.

"How are we going to get past the wall," I ask still looking for a gate. "There's not a gate."

"We have pulley systems placed along all of the walls," Luna explains. "This way if the outer walls are ever breached there are no gates to be burned. This allows us to keep fighting the enemy."

"But if the outer walls have the same system and they are breached," I pause.

Not wanting to doubt a system that has worked for hundreds of years.

"What do you mean," Luna asks.

"Never mind," I say looking back up at the wall.

"I know what you are thinking," Luna says waving at a guard as we approach the walls. "You think that if all the walls are like this, if one fails they all do."

"Yes, because if your enemies can get past one wall with no gates, can't they get past these," I ask watching one of the wall top guards lower a platform slowly to the ground.

We step onto the platform and Luna waves again; the platform begins to slowly rise from into the air. There are rails along the sides of the platform, but they are only about three feet high. Luna stands on the other side of the platform with her arms crossed. Heights have never bothered me. Flying on the back of Iris had no effect on me either, but this is a little different. When I was on Iris and fell off, she caught me before I hit the ground. This platform can't catch. I adjust my hook swords in their straps. The positions of the swords are in an X shape, with the handles at the top. I don't like this, so I remove the swords from the straps and flip the swords upside down. Now the handles are on the bottom and are easier to draw.

We reach the top of the wall with no problems. I look out over the city and can see the sun shining outside the cave. I can see the second wall that is slightly inside the mouth of the cave. Luna walks over to another platform on the opposite side of the wall. She looks out over the city for a moment and then jumps onto the platform. I walk over and hop onto the platform causing it to sway slightly. The guards wait for the platform to settle before lowering it to the ground. For some reason it seems like it took longer to go up than down. I jump off the platform when it is about five feet off the ground. A small twinge of pain jolts through my leg.

"You know you should still be gentle on your leg," Luna says as the platform touches the ground. "You are not completely healed yet."

"I know," I say rubbing my leg.

Luna steps off of the platform and walks down the main road. I walk alongside her, gazing at the building cut from the stone of the mountain. From the looks of the buildings, each one is made of only a few large pieces of stone. People bustle around with their every day activities. Some of them stop and look at us as we follow the road to the second wall. A few small children even stop and wave at Luna as she passes. We continue to walk along the road as I look at the various lifestyles the people live.

After what was probably a three or four mile walk we reach the middle of the vast city. Streets as wide as the one we followed from the palace now break off into five other directions. This forms a sort of huge six way intersection. A large fountain has been constructed at the center of the roads; unfortunately there is too much noise to hear the flow of water. Vendors everywhere are trying to make sales to people as they pass by. I wonder what they use for currency here.

"Come," Luna says walking toward a small two story building. "Do you like tea?"

"Yes. I do," I say looking at the vendors.

"There is a small tea shop just over there," Luna says pointing at the building she is walking toward.

As we get nearer to the building I can see a wooden sign with a steaming cup on it hanging above the door. I make my way towards the building dodging my way through the crowd. Luna makes it to the door before I do. She stands next the door and waits for me to finish fighting my way to the shop. I approach the tea shop and stand next to Luna for a moment.

"Welcome to Grandma's tea shop," Luna says opening the door.

We walk into a small single room house. Tables for two are spread across the room. Each table has a little lantern in the center. The bar has stools set up in front of it for those that wish to be alone. Luna walks inside and motions for me to follow her. She walks over to an empty table and seats herself. I walk over to the same table and sit down in the chair across the table from her.

I look at the small candle lit lantern and notice a small piece of tattered paper next to it. Picking up the paper I notice it has different types of tea. On the opposite side it has what you can have added to the tea. I look around the shop and see people sipping from cups of steaming tea. A short old woman rushes around the shop refilling cups of tea and picking up coins left on the tables by those who are finished.

The old woman notices us sitting and hurries over to our table. She has snow white hair kept in a bun. Her face was covered with wrinkles which gives her a kind of permanent smile.

"How are you today," she asks placing her teapot on the table. "What will you have today Luna."

"I think I will have white tea with plum juice," she says setting the menu down.

"And what about you sir," she says turning her gaze toward me.
"I'll have green tea," I say flipping the menu to see what to add.
"With honey, please."

"All right," she says turning away.

As she turns her sleeve catches the teapot, pulling it off the table.
As it slides off the table it seems to be in slow motion. I lean over and
catch it before is hits the floor. The old woman turns and sees the
teapot in my grasp just above the floor. I can tell by the look on her
face that she is really smiling this time, sending more wrinkles across
her face.

"Good catch," she says as I hand her the teapot. "In my younger
days I would have caught it myself."

"I'm sure you could have caught it just now," I say with a grin.

"Do not bother trying to flatter me," She says taking the teapot
and walking away laughing to herself.

"That is Grandma," Luna says glancing around the shop.

"Is she really your grandmother," I ask setting down my menu.

"Oh no," she says with a laugh. "Everyone that comes here calls
her Grandma, she owns this tea shop."

"I guess that makes sense," I say watching grandma fixing more tea
behind the bar. "How long has the tea shop been here?"

"I would have to say it has been here for fifty or sixty years," Luna
says looking at the lantern. "It is a sad story really. Her husband ran
the shop after he was wounded in a battle, said it comforted him to
help others relax. Around twelve years ago, her husband passed away
and she now runs the shop with her grandson. She says it was what he
would have wanted."

Grandma comes bustling over to our table with a small tray; on it
are two steaming cups. She sets them on the table in front of us and
rushes off to serve a group that just entered. I pick my cup off tea and
blow on it a few times to cool it down. Luna does the same and then
takes a sip.

"This is the best tea in Haven," she says before taking another sip.
"There are not many other shops like this in Haven to compare it to."

I take a sip from my tea and notice that it isn't burning hot, but
hot enough to cause a relaxing feel to come over me. I take another sip,
letting the warmth wash over me.

"I can see why you say it's the best," I say taking a long draft from my cup.

"It is soothing," Luna says setting her cup down. "She loves tea herself too. One time she told me she married her husband because he was the best tea maker in Haven."

"I think it's great to see people try to make the lives of others better," I say watching Grandma hurrying around the shop.

I finish my tea and wait for Luna to finish her tea. When she finishes Grandma walks over and Luna gives her two copper coins from a small bag at her waist.

"Thank you for the tea," Luna says rising from her chair. "It was wonderful, as always."

"You are welcome, please come back anytime," Grandma says placing our cups on a tray. "Have a nice day Luna."

As Grandma walks away a gruff looking man gets up from the bar. He is tall and thin with an unshaven face. He has the same type of uniform as some of the soldiers I had seen when we entered the city. He also has a katana attached to his belt. He turns and looks at Luna, then at me. We begin to make our way out of the tea shop when the man shouts at us.

"Hey you," he says pointing at Luna. "Your one of the royal vampire family, are you not?"

From the way his word come from his mouth, I can tell he has been putting more than plum juice in his tea. He takes a few staggered steps forward. I step in front of Luna and the intoxicated soldier. He stops and looks at me with bloodshot eyes.

"Step aside I want to talk with her," he says nodding at Luna.

I can smell the alcohol on his breath. From the looks of him he's been drinking for some time. I'm surprised that he can even stand. He seems very irritable about Luna's family. My guess is that I'm only making things worse by intervening.

"I think it would be better if you didn't," I say coolly.

"If you won't move," he says reaching for his sword. "Then I will make you!"

He pulls his sword from its sheath and points it clumsily at me. I place my hands behind my back and tightly grip the handles of my hook swords. I glance over my shoulder at Luna and see she is standing next to the door. The door opens and two young men start to come inside. They stop laughing and joking when they see what's going on. They take a few steps back and rush off, leaving the door open behind them. The man takes the opportunity to make the first move. He performs a stabbing motion with his sword. As he does everything moves in slow motion, just like the teapot. I lean back, dodging the blade as it comes within inches of my face. I grip and twist my hook swords causing them to come out of their straps. I then bring them around to the front of my body, catching the wrist of the man.

I pull hard, making the hooks close tight on his wrist. I then step sideways and pull the swords sharply to the right, releasing the swords on his wrist as I do. The soldier cartwheels out of the open door into the busy streets outside. I turn to see him picking up his sword again, while drawing a second sword. This sword is shorter than his first, but I know it will inflict damage just the same. The people in the streets have stopped there usual routine to stop and watch the fight unfold. They form a semicircle around the shop.

"Just walk away," I say stepping into the streets. "This isn't worth someone getting hurt over."

"It is now," he shouts rushing toward me.

He swings both swords at me, one from each side. I simply raise my swords and catch both of his swords. I then flick my wrist pulling the short sword from his grasp, but the other slips from the hook. Kicking the short sword out of the way I prepare for his next move. He is now holding the sword in both hands as he steadies himself for another attack. He rushes me again trying to get past my defenses, but all his moves seem to be in slow motion. This allows me to easily block each drunken attack.

We continue to battle around making our way closer and closer to the water fountain. I notice his foot movements and can tell the alcohol is affecting him. I take a few swings at him, being sure not hit him. I can see that I'm leading him into a false sense of security. He begins to strike more often and I step back as if he is forcing me back. I side step until the water fountain is at my back. I allow him to push me back again, then the back of my leg hits the edge of the fountain. Then he rushes forward thinking this to be his victory. As he approaches I lean to one side and hook his arm with one sword. I strike him in the stomach with the dull edge of the other sword. The impact causes him to drop his weapon. I quickly pull then release him and he flips into the water.

The soldier doesn't try to get up or retrieve his weapons. He lies in the water taking deep ragged breaths. I guess the cold water sobered him up a little. Seeing the battle is over I put my swords back in the straps. The slow motion effect is slowly wearing off and my vision returns to normal. The crowd that has been watching the fight begins to clap. I look around and walk back to toward the tea shop. I almost make it to the door when the clapping stops. I turn to see the two boys that left the door open; with them is a group of soldiers.

The lead soldier points to my defeated adversary lying in the fountain. Two of the other soldiers walk over to the fountain and pull him out of the water. They bind his hands with thick rope. The lead soldier then points at me.

"Take him too," he says as two more soldiers begin walking toward me.

I grip the handles of my swords, but I don't draw them. The soldiers grab my shoulders and begin to move me. I stiffen and hold my ground causing one to slip and almost fall.

"Stop," Grandma shouts rushing in front of the guards. "He stopped that drunk from hurting someone."

"I am sorry ma'am," says the soldier. "But he was involved in the fight that endangered civilians. I have to take him in well."

"No, you will not," Luna says stepping out of the crowd near the shop. "He is staying here."

The soldier looks at me and then to Luna. He's trying to find the right thing to say.

"Luna," he manages to stammer. "I have orders to apprehend anyone breaking the law."

"And I am overriding that order," Luna says fixing him with a cold stare.

"Your father will not be pleased when he hears about this," he says with some confidence. "He is in direct violation of Haven law."

"He is here in the company of my father," Luna says hardening her glare at him. "It would upset my father even more if he was to find out that his guest of honor has been wrongfully imprisoned."

This seems to make something click in the soldier's mind. He looks at the other soldiers that are holding me and gives them a short nod. They release me and hurry over to the others who are placing the drunken soldier in the back of a horse drawn wagon. I walk over and stand next to Luna, watching the soldiers leave with their prisoner. "Are you okay," I ask Luna. "Thanks for helping me."

"You kept him away from me," Luna says looking at the wagon as it pulls away. "It was the least I could do."

"So why was he so upset with," I ask, rubbing my shoulder were the soldier had gripped it. "Did he have something against you?"

"Yes," Luna sighs. "Sometimes the scouts blame any person in the royal family for their problems. He was a scout, one of the ones that we send on recon missions or patrols outside the walls. Some of them cannot handle it; the werewolves are growing more hostile and savage. They are even feeding on humans and vampires now.

I look up to see Grandma walking toward us; she is smiling widely. Most of the people are still standing around talking about the fight with others that have just arrived.

"Thank you," she says shaking my hand. "I could not have done it without you."

"Well in your younger days you could have taken care of it," I say grinning again.

"Very true," she says smiling even wider. "Let us have a cheer for our friend here!"

The crowd starts cheering and clapping again; I stand and allow the commotion to die down. I hate being the center of attention, but it means a lot to her so I let it go. Many of them shout out about how fantastic the fight was. Others say they had seen better and begin to walk off. After the noise fades the crowd slowly disperses, returning to their activities. I see a few little kids running around with sticks. Acting out the fight they had just witnessed.

"We should make our way to the training grounds," Luna says looking toward the second wall. "We are expected."

"Well come back anytime you want," Grandma says turning walking back inside the shop. "And the next time you come here you both get a free cup of tea."

"Thank you," Luna shouts back as we walk away.

We walk along the road growing closer and closer to the second wall. The sun is shining slightly inside the cave, causing a shadow at the bottom of the wall to eclipse a portion of the city. This wall stands around twice as high as the palace wall. We approach the wall and Luna waves at one of the wall top soldiers. It takes longer for the platform to reach us this time. When the platform finally reaches the ground I wait for Luna to step on before I step onto the platform. Luna waves her hand again and the platform makes it way to the top.

When we reach the top I walk over to the other side of the wall that faces out over the farmlands and the training grounds. The sun shines out from behind a cloud, lighting up certain areas of the ground below us. I stand and stare at the out at the sight before me. Luna comes over and stands next to me. She looks over around at the shade speckled land and points to a section near the north portions of the farmlands.

"That is the training grounds," she says leaning on the edge or the wall. "We can reach it soon. Tori and your friend will arrive there before we do."

"Then let's not keep them waiting," I say eager to see Scott.

We get on the last platform and are lowered to the farmlands below. I jump when it reaches a few feet from the ground. I look back and see Luna jump off as well, she must be somewhat eager to reach the training grounds. Luna leads the way to the training grounds. Everywhere around us people are picking various crops from the fields. I look around and notice that there are no tropical plants. During the dinner with Marcus and Luna when I first arrived there were some tropical fruits. I can see some apple trees and a few vineyards.

"Where did you manage to get other fruits from," I ask continuing to look around at the plants.

"The dragons have a tropical island to the south of here, we call it the Dragon's Den," Luna says slowing her pace to walk beside me. "We trade with them and are very hospitable to their scouts."

"So what do you trade in return," I ask.

"We allow their dragons to stay here as long as they like," Luna says pulling an apple off a tree and polishing it on her sleeve. "They can even live here if they choose. The island is also where you must go if you form a pact with a dragon."

"What is a pact," I ask.

"A pact is a special bond between a human or vampire and a dragon," Luna says setting the apple in a basket near the edge of the path. "You swear to protect each other for the rest of your lives."

"That sounds interesting," I say wondering what it would be like to form a pact with a dragon. We approach the training grounds and I can hear the sound of swords clashing. As we grow closer I can see people fighting with swords, spears, bows, and other weapons. I can make out Simon and a girl battling. Even though Simon has the advantage of size, she has speed. At certain times her attacks are a complete blur. I look around and spot Tori sitting on fallen log. A lone figure stands next to her talking. She glances at me and the person stops talking and looks in our direction. I look at figure and can make no mistake at who it is. He recognizes me and begins to walk towards me. It's Scott.

7

SCOTT WALKS TOWARDS ME at first, and then he breaks into a run. I continue to walk at a steady pace, knowing that Tori is probably watching me approach. Scott slows his pace as he reaches me. He walks up and punches me playfully on the arm.

"Where've you been," I say rubbing my arm. "How are you doing?"

"I'm alive," he says. "Tori told me all about what happened to you."

"Luna told me about what happened to you too," I say noticing the puzzled look on Scott's face.

"Who's Luna," he asks. "I don't think I've met her."

"More introductions," Luna says with a hint of humor in her voice. "I am Luna; it is an honor to meet you at last."

"I'm Scott, it's nice to meet you too," he says. "So Ivan, how long have you been here?"

"I got here about three minutes after you did," I say beginning to walk toward the fallen log Tori is sitting on.

"No," Scott says walking next to me. "How long have you been in this city?"

"Since yesterday morning," I say looking around at the various people training.

We continue to walk through the training grounds around the different warriors. Some of the people are fighting with swords, others fight hand to hand. I walk over to the fallen log and sit down on the opposite end of Tori. Scott sits down in between Tori and me.

"So," Tori says leaning forward so she can see me. "How well did the medicine work? Did it help heal your wounds?"

"Wait a minute," Scott says looking at me. "You were injured?"

"I thought you knew about what happened to me," I say just as puzzled as Scott was a moment ago. "You said Tori told you what happened."

"She mentioned that you fought and killed a werewolf," he says. "She never said anything about you being wounded during the fight."

"We thought it would be best not to put too much stress on you," Tori says to Scott. "I hope you do not think us mistrusting."

"I don't," I say looking at Luna, then to Tori. "Too much bad news at the wrong moment can really wear down on a person."

"I still don't like being left out when it comes to friends," Scott says looking at me. "Where were you injured anyway?"

"My right leg," I say rolling up my pant leg. "The medicine Tori gave me worked pretty well."

This was my first time seeing the wounds on my leg since Tori had placed new bandages on them yesterday. As I remove the bandages I notice there is no pain, but there is a small amount of blood on the bandages touching the wounds. The last of the bandages come off and I can see that all of the wounds are mostly healed. They are still a little bit red and slightly swollen. The medicine also leaves behind no scars, just like when Luna healed.

"Let's take a look," Tori says running her hand over one of the wounds. "It looks like the stitches can come out now."

She takes a small pair of scissors and tweezers from her handbag. She cuts each stitch then pulls it slowly from my leg. When she pulls a stitch out a slight pinch emits from the area it's pulled. After a few minutes all of the stitches are pull out, Tori places all of her equipment back in her bag.

"You can train if you feel up to the challenge," Tori says closing her bag.

"I think I will," I say looking at Scott. "So Scott, do you feel up for a little swordplay?"

"I don't see why not," he says grinning at me. "I won't beat you like I did last time."

"I thought we agreed that was a tie," I say punching him in the arm as pay back for earlier.

"Only so you wouldn't complain," he says dodging my second punch.

"Is that how it happened," I say placing my hand on my hook swords. "Shall we call this a tie breaker then?"

"Okay," Scott says drawing a long double edged sword from behind his back. "Then how does first blood sound?"

We had played by these rules before in the past. The last time we both hit each other at about the same time. His sword nicked my shoulder, while my sword had cut the back of his hand. Neither of our wounds was very serious, but it caused my mother to make us swear to never to play by such rules in the future. But we did anyway, when she wasn't around.

Seeing Scott draw his sword surprises me, I hadn't even noticed that he was carrying it. I draw my hook swords as we begin to circle each other. I know from past duals with Scott that he will attack first. He starts with an upward slash, and then adjusts to a sideways slash after I dodge the first. I'm forced to block with my swords during his second attack. As he moves in again all his movements begin to slow. The strange feeling overcomes me again just as when I battled the werewolf and the drunken soldier. I begin to block less with my swords and start dodging more with leans and sidestep.

I sidestep again and manage to hook Scott's sword with both of mine. We struggle for a moment then he frees his sword and I make an immediate counterattack. I swing both swords sideways, parallel to each other. Scott changes his stance and swings his sword at mine. Then something I've never experienced happens. As our swords connected they shatter into pieces. We both just stand still for a moment looking at the handles of our broken swords.

"Well," I say tossing my broken hook swords on the ground. "I guess we really have to call this one a draw."

"I suppose we do," Scott says taking off the sheath on his back and tossing it on the ground with his sword handle.

I stand still staring at the swords on the ground, allowing my vision to return to normal. I remove my hook sword straps and place them on the pile with our ruined weapons. Scott walks back over to the log and sits down; I make my way over to the log and sit down next to him. Luna strides over and stands in front of me.

"Does that happen often when you train," she asks looking at the bits of shattered metal scattered on the ground.

"No," I say pulling out a fragment of metal in-bedded in the log. "This one's all new to me."

"We can fashion you both new swords," Luna says picking up one of my hook sword handles. "It may take some to though."

"I can find a different sword," I standing up. "I think I'll try a katana this time."

"Follow me then," Luna says gesturing for Scott and me to follow her. "We have supplies of weapons kept near the walls at all times. They are in prime condition for battle as well."

We follow Luna through the training grounds to a building constructed to the side of the wall. There's a trapdoor that makes up half of the roof and a pulley system is suspended above it on the wall top. Luna opens the faded door and walks inside. I walk to the door and look inside the dim lit structure.

The interior is set up about the same as the armory in the palace, with shelves of weapons in rows of type. Swords are on one shelf, spears and pikes on another, and bows and arrows on the last. I turn around to see if Scott is following me. He stands a few feet from the door, not making any effort to come inside.

"Are you coming," I ask standing in the doorway.

"I don't think so," He says rooted in place. "There could be spiders in there and I don't care for them at all, as you well know."

I recall the day that I caught a small spider and set it on Scott's computer desk when I was spending the night at his house. He sat down and began playing a computer game. He became so engrossed in the game he didn't notice the spider that had crawled onto his hand. When I mentioned the spider he knocked spider off his hand and actually killed it with his keyboard. Unfortunately he hit it a little too hard and lost about twenty keys in the process of killing it. After he found out that I was the one behind the spider, he tried to finish off the keyboard on me.

"You've paid me back for that," I say turning to go inside. "Do you want me to find a sword for you then?"

"Yes. See if you can find one like the one before," He says keeping his distance.

"Okay," I say turning to walk inside. "Do you mean a sword like before or spider like before?"

"A sword," he growls.

I turn and walk into the dim lit shack. I rummage through the swords and find a long sword just like what Scott had before our fight. I pull it from the dusty shelf and set it against the wall so I won't forget it. I return to the shelf of swords and look some more for a katana.

"Is this what you are looking for," Luna says holding out a katana with a sheath out to me. "Is it long enough, I think there is a larger one in here if this is not suitable."

"Thank you," I say taking the sword from her and removing it from its sheath. "This is the perfect size for me."

The blade is as long as my arm and with the handle being large enough for two hand making it ideal for when I need a more powerful attack. I blow off the dust to see the color of the handle and sheath. I hold in the light to see it is jet black. The blade is razor sharp with no mirror finish to make it shine. I pick up Scott's sword and start to head out the door.

"Ivan," Luna says walking toward me. "Is Scott truly afraid of spiders?"

"Very," I say quietly. "Watch this."

I place my sword in my belt and hide Scott's sword behind my back. I walk out the door smiling at Scott as mischievously as possible. Scott notices the look on my face and takes a step back, he's not smiling. I continue to keep the sword behind my back.

"I found one," I say walking closer to Scott. "It's just like the last one too."

"Ivan," he says, worry being evident in his voice.

I pull my hand out from behind my back and hold out the sword for Scott. Relief washes over his face as he snatches the sword from my grasp. He attaches the sheath over his back and pulls the sword out. His examines the blade for a moment then places it back in its sheath.

"I hate it when you do that," he says walking over to the log and sitting down again. "So what do we do now?"

"You could go back to the palace and rest or you both could train here for a while," Tori says tossing and catching a small knife. "There are two basic types of training here, direct combat and ranged combat."

"Sounds simple enough," Scott says adjusting the sheath shoulder strap. "I'm going to try out the ranged combat; I haven't had the opportunity to train in it much."

"I'll head over and see what the direct combat training is like," I say as we head in somewhat opposite ways.

"I don't know if you should do the direct training right now," Luna says walking up next to me.

"Why," I ask continuing toward the direct training area.

"For two reasons," she says stopping me so she can make sure I am listening. "First of all your leg is not completely healed and second, the trainer is Simon."

"Really," I say somewhat surprised. "I can't imagine him as a type of person to teach others."

"Yes," she says. "And he just had a new shaft constructed for his spear."

"Will he be willing to train me," I ask starting to doubt if he will after the spear thing.

"He will," Luna says smiling. "I could have him replaced for someone different, which I never would. His training methods have saved many lives over the years."

We approach Simon and the girl he was fighting earlier. They are standing talking to each other and I could have sworn that I saw Simon smile. As we catch their attention the smile disappears from Simon's face.

"Hello Luna," says the girl. "Here to train today?"

I look at the girl and can't help but notice the similarities between her and Simon. Their eyes have almost the same green eyes and the black hair is identical. Simon's eyes are pure emerald, while the girls are less jewel-like, but the similarities are still uncanny. They even mimic the other's hand movements when they were talking.

"Not today Maria," Luna says looking at me. "I am just going to watch him train today. His friend is waiting to train with the bow."

I look over to see Scott testing the string of a longbow. He pulls it back a few times, but loses his grip and the string slaps him in the arm.

I can tell by the look on his face that it hurt, but he just sets the bow down and looks around to see of anyone saw him. He doesn't know that I've seen the accident though.

"Well I suppose I should get back to work," Maria says walking away. "Thanks for the break big brother."

So this was Simon's little sister Luna had mentioned. The one main difference is that she seems much nicer than Simon, although so does everyone else. Simon watches Maria as she walks over to Scott, he then turns to me and glares at me.

"So you think I will train you," he says resting his spear on his shoulder.

"I don't know are you," I shoot back.

"I will train you," he says with a smirk. "But you have to fight me one time. This way I will know what you need to learn and if your victory over the werewolf was luck."

"Okay," I say watching him take a battle stance. "You're the teacher."

I draw my new sword and watch as Simon he begins to circle slowly around me. I hold the sword in both hands loosely at my side, not knowing what he will do. As I watch him circle I can see him change his gaze to where I am holding my sword. I take the opportunity to fake an attack as he looks again. I am satisfied to see him move his spear to protect against the attack that doesn't reach him. I can't help but smile at the fact that I somewhat tricked an experienced soldier, that wasn't drunk.

"Not bad," Simon says continuing to circle. "But it will not happen again."

"We'll see," I say following his movements.

This time I decide to really strike at him, I lunge forward slashing upward in a sort of bladed uppercut. He blocks with the spear and pushes out, forcing me back as he stabs at me with the spear point. I move to one side as the strange slow motion occurs once again. I don't know what this ability is, but I'm not going to make believe that it isn't useful. It saved my life from the werewolf and might help me defeat Simon.

I recover from the push and instantly slash back at his spear trying to find a way around his reach advantage. He repels my attack and begins to circle again, as I try to think of what to do next. I hold my sword in front of me, not relaxed now that the strange ability has infected me again. Suddenly my sword begins to move as if it controls itself. I'm having trouble trying to control my own movements; I don't want to strike yet. My hands start to shake as this internal conflict continues.

This may have stopped me from attacking Simon, but he has no such idea. He rushes me slashing at me with the spear point. I simply slide my feet and dodge each stab, slash, and swing. I seem to be in some control of my body as I continue to evade his every attack. After what feels like hours of his endless assault I decide it's time to strike back. I leap forward and strike down with all the force I can manage to gather. As my sword comes down Simon positions himself to block the attack. The sword crashes into his spear shaft, cleaving it in two pieces. This is the second time in less than two days, that I've destroyed his spear. Simon looks at the two pieces that he is holding in his hands. He throws down the blunt end of the spear and continues to battle with me.

Holding the spear half like a sword he thrusts and slashes at me with untold amounts of strength. We strike back and forth, exchanging blows and blocking each other. If it wasn't for the slow motion I know that he would've made short work of me. I search as best I can for an opening, while trying to block an onslaught of stabs. One of them gazes my cheek and I can feel a stream of hot blood slide down my face. I continue to search for an opening, as I do a notice his foot movements and can make out a pattern. When he strikes he comes forward one step, then retreats two or three steps back. As I watch him I catch a glimpse of the blunt end of the spear he had discarded.

I move to one side until he is directly in front of the spear piece. I then continue as before, blocking and occasionally attacking at make him retreat a little more. Every block and attack causes him to grow closer to the spear piece. Then he attacks and I block, taking a swing at him to ensure his retreat. He takes the first step and his foot lands on the spear piece. As soon as his foot touches the spear piece I strike, he roots himself to brace for the impact. The force of the attack causes Simon to crash to the ground on his back. Before he can recover I place the sword point at his throat, keeping him pinned to ground.

He nods at me and smiles exposing his vampire teeth. I remove the point from his throat and sheath my sword allowing the slow motion to dissipate. Simon remains on the ground breathing heavily, just as I do. I extend my hand and smile back at him. He grabs my hand and I help pull him to his feet.

"Not bad," Simon says dusting himself. "You truly are a warrior. I think your victory over the werewolf might not have been luck."

"Thank you," I say trying to control my ragged breathing. "Sorry about your spear."

"It seems my favored weapon caused my defeat," he sighs sticking the spear into the ground.

"Only half of it," I say nodding at the other half of his spear. "You should've held on to it."

"Very impressive," says someone behind me.

I turn to see Simon's little sister, Maria. Scott is with her, he holds a longbow in his hand. At his waist is a quiver of arrows.

"I would like to test something," she says taking the longbow from Scott. "I promise it will not take up much of your time."

"Of course," I say watching her notch an arrow into the bow. Without a word she then turns and fires the arrow straight at me. The slow motion instantly takes over and I draw my sword. I lean to one side as the arrow flies past my face. Before the arrow completely passes I hit it with the flat of my blade. The arrow flips upwards in the air and then comes straight down towards me. I reach up and pluck the arrow from the air.

"Just as I thought," she says handing the bow back to Scott. "You are a berserker."

"What," I ask walking to Maria and handing her the arrow. "What's a berserker?"

"They are warriors from the moment they are born," she says. "They can move faster and are stronger than normal warriors, in their berserker state. This allows them to obliterate their enemies. Unfortunately there are not many left in this world."

"That is why you where able to kill the werewolf," Luna says appearing out of nowhere. "I thought there was something special about you."

"That's all great," I say not knowing how to handle this information. "But is there anyway to control this ability?"

"Yes," Simon says facing me. "It takes much practice and patience."

"But that is a lesson for another day," Luna says looking at me. "We have a few more things to attend to."

"Okay," I say not knowing what that might be. "See you back at the palace Scott."

"Sounds good," he says notching an arrow and firing at a target in the distance.

I turn around to see Luna facing back toward the city. A girl with long blonde hair down to the middle of her back whispers something to Luna. Then she begins walking towards the walls of the city. Luna looks at me and begins walking in the same direction; I quicken my pace so I can catch up with her. As I walk beside her she seems distance and deep in thought. I don't say anything, not wanting to disturb her. We continue along the path that brought us to the training grounds.

After a few minutes we arrive back at the second wall. I look to see if Luna is going to wave to the guards to let down a platform. Instead she places her fingers in her mouth and lets out a shrill whistle. I stand for a moment, knowing what is going to happen. I look around at the sky, searching for Iris. Continuing to search I feel a heavy gust of wind buffet my body followed by a thunderous crash. I turn to see Iris staring down at me.

"I still don't think I'm used to that," I say looking up at Iris.

"You will," she says lowering herself to my eye level. "The longer you stay in the presence of dragon or form a pact."

"I don't think I'm going to," I say.

I can't imagine having such a powerful bond with a dragon, like Luna and Iris. It would be a wonderful thing, but I only arrived here only a few days ago. Things are moving a little too fast in this place for me.

"There is one place that you have left to see," Luna says breaking my train of thought. "I think you will enjoy it."

"Okay," I say wondering what this last place could be. "How far is it?"

"Not far from here," she says looking up.

I look up, but I'm unable to see over the mouth of the cave. Iris beats her wings sending a gust of wind over me. If she is flexing her wings, which means that we are going to be flying somewhere. Iris lowers herself so Luna and I can climb on her shoulders.

"Here we go," Iris says launching into the air.

We fly up and over the second wall and into the massive cave once more. We fly over the city and I gaze over the edge at the buildings passing below us. As we reach the center of the city I can see the water fountain and the tea shop. I can even make out some small children running under us, trying to keep up. We continue to fly closer to the palace and I expect to see Luna wave to the guards below. Instead she leans forward and whispers something to Iris.

Iris veers to her right then flies straight until we reach the cave wall. She follows the edge of the cave past the wall and behind the palace. Then she stops, hovering for a moment as she searches for something. She flies along the cave wall a few more feet then stops again. This time she spots whatever it is she's looking for. She flies inside an opening in the wall that is almost impossible to see. The entrance is large enough for Iris to move around uninhibited.

Luna gets off and walks silently into the cave with Iris right behind her. I fall in line and follow them around the corner and inside the cave. Once inside the cave I can see it is very spacious and quiet. I look around and see one of the large mats that are like the ones in my room back at the palace. There are also a few cushioned chairs and an extremely fluffy looking sofa. Luna walks over and sits in one of the chairs and lets out a deep sigh. I continue to sit and gaze around the cave and notice that there is also a second mat in the corner.

"You may sit if you wish," Luna says gesturing to a chair near her.

"What is this place," I ask walking over and sitting in the soft chair.

"This is where Iris and I come when we grow tired of usual ways of life," she says resting her head on the back of the chair. "Iris and I found this place after we had formed a pact, then returned to Haven. It is our hideout and no one else in Haven knows about it."

"Except me," I say running my hand over the smooth leather like fabric.

"Yes," she says closing her eyes. "I have wanted to share this place with someone, but someone that I trust."

"You have only known me for about three days," I say. "How do you know I'm trustworthy?"

"My sister told me," she says opening her eyes and looking at me. "She can look into the future by means of dreams. She cannot make herself see a certain thing, but she sees things none the less. It is a rare gift, just as your gift is rare."

"So can you see into the future," I ask. "Does it run in the family?"

"Gifts like those you and my sister posses are not passed on by bloodlines," Luna says closing her eyes once more. "No one really knows how the gifts are acquired."

"Did your sister tell of why you can trust me," I say wanting to figure out what she knows.

"She said you would save my life," Luna looks troubled when the words leave her mouth. "It scares me to think of what kind of danger we are going to face in the future."

"Wait a minute," I say a little confused. "What do you mean, we?"

"You are a great warrior," Luna says looking at me. "And a war is on the way."

"What," I ask. "Who is it between?"

"The werewolves want more territory,' Luna says with a grim sound in her voice. "We have the territory that they want and land here is not taken by diplomacy, when it involves the werewolves."

"If it's to protect this place and its people then I will gladly fight alongside you," I say.

"Thank you. I would understand if you do not want to fight," she says with a distant look in her eyes.

"If I'm going to be here forever then I don't see why not," I say.

"We will need all the help that we can get," Luna sighs. "Let us return to the palace, you need to finish recovering."

"Aren't I healed enough," I ask moving my leg.

"Not if you keep picking fights with vampires," she says walking over to Iris who has fallen asleep on the mat.

"That was only training," I say defensively. "I'm not picking fights."

Luna walks forward and places her hand on the side of my face. She then pulls her hand back and shows it to me. Her hand has blood on it from the cut on my face. I hadn't even noticed the pain because of the berserker ability.

"You see," Luna says walking back to Iris. "You didn't realize a minor injury like that, but you will feel the more damaging ones."

Luna rubs Iris on the shoulder waking her from her slumber. Iris lets out a small growl as she stretches out like a cat that has been basking in the sunlight. She walks over to the mouth of the cave and waits for us to climb on. Luna climbs on Iris's back and I follow without a word. I'm still shocked that I have agreed to fight in a war that has little or nothing to do with me.

Iris takes off and we descend to the palace. As we fly I can't help but wonder who will be willing to fight with us? Here is an entire city protected by walls that are hundreds of feet high, soldiers and virtually unlimited supplies. It looks like these people could handle things themselves. If this war is going to be as big as it sounds we may need help. I just hope they don't look at it like I did.

We reach the balcony of my room and I jump off onto the cool marble floor. I turn to see Iris and Luna about to take flight when a young boy in a soldier uniform blocks the way on a light green dragon. He is wide eyed and is breathing heavily as he jumps off the dragon onto the balcony. Looks at me and then to Luna trying to slow his breathing enough to speak.

"Miss Luna," he finally manages to choke. "I have urgent news!"

"What is it," she says jumping off Iris's back and stands in front of him. "Slow your breathing, what is your name?"

"Isaak," he says gasping a little less for air. "I was patrolling the shores south of here. I found a wounded dragon washed up on the shore. It was alive when I left, but I do not know its condition now."

"How far is it," she asks in a calm, yet urgent voice.

"Half a day's flight," he says hands shaking. "And that was flying fast to get here."

"We will be flying fast to get there then," Luna says climbing onto Iris's back. "Take the message to my father. Ivan try to get some rest, we leave at midnight."

Iris kicks off and puts on an extra burst of speed as she flies away. Isaak's dragon lands and Isaak quickly scrambles onto the dragon's shoulders. The dragon kicks off and they fly away to deliver the news to Marcus. I stand on the balcony and wonder if the dragon is alive at this very moment. If it is, I'm going to try my best to help anyway that is possible. I turn and walk into my room, removing my sword form side and closing the drapes. This place has more drama than my high school back home. Wars, territory hungry werewolves, and midnight flights to wounded dragons. I fall back on the bed too worked up to sleep, yet somehow feeling tired in the middle of the day. I close my eyes and take a deep breath. I lie on the bed for what seems like an eternity until sleep gradually consumes me again.

8

SLEEPING IS NOT AN option tonight. I lie awake on the bed wondering about the wounded dragon laying on the beach somewhere. The few times I managed to sleep my dreams are haunted by the sounds of a dragon roaring in pain. Not being able to sleep, I decide to try and prepare for the journey we are going to take. I look around the room to see a haversack sitting at the foot of the bed. Opening the pack I can see food and everything else I will need for the journey. How is it that someone keeps placing things in here while I'm sleeping and not wake me? I walk to the balcony and look out over the city lit by thousands of torches and lanterns. Beyond I can see that the sky has cleared and the moon is only half full.

A soft knock on the door causes me to turn and see the door slowly open. I dart to the edge of the bed and draw my sword. I watch a familiar face form in the dim room as the figure walks through the doorway. Scott stops a few feet into the room with a haversack slung over his shoulder.

"You ready," he asks adjusting the haversack. "We just about are."

"I didn't know you were going too," I say sheathing my sword. "What's in the pack?"

"Food, bandages, everything we'll need for the trip," he says walking out the door.

I shoulder my pack and follow Scott out onto the palace halls. Torches illuminate the halls in a dull gold as we make our way to the stairs. We walk up several flights of stairs and turn a corner. Luna and Tori walking towards us, both of them are carrying a haversack as well. Tori has a bow slung over the same shoulder as her haversack and a quiver of arrows attached to her waist. Luna carries her double short swords that she had selected from the armory yesterday.

"We were on our way to find you," Tori says adjusting her bow. "Are you ready to depart?"

"Yes," I say looking at Scott. "Are you?"

"Ready as I'll ever be," he says looking out a window at the city below. "When do we leave?"

"After we have a little breakfast," Luna says taking the lead. "Come."

We follow Luna down the twisting halls to the large dining room that we landed at when I first arrived at Haven. Luna quietly opens the door and steps inside, while the rest of us wait outside. She reappears in the doorway and waves at us to come in. I wait for Tori ad Scott to enter before I walk in as well.

The room is dimly lit by four lanterns hanging on the pillars near the corners of the table. Two trays sit on the table, just as before one has different meats and the other has various types of fruits. The only difference in the room is the two figures seated at the table already. One I can tell is Marcus at the head of the table; the other figure is a girl. In the dim light she looks almost just like Luna except her hair is longer and her eyes are light blue, yet the color is intensified. This must be Luna's older sister.

Luna walks over to the table and seats herself next to who I assume to be her sister. Scott sits in front of Luna's sister, while Tori sits next to Luna. I sit next to Scott and in front of Luna. All of us wait in silence for a moment before Marcus stands and clears his throat.

"Lilith has said that you would be going on a journey tonight," he says looking around the table at all of us. "This is a little meal that was prepared for you before you depart, enjoy."

He sits down and selects a steak from the pile of meats on the silver tray. Scott picks a cooked steak as does Tori, the rest of us have rare steaks. I eat the steak, but I don't really taste it. I'm more focused on the journey and getting to the dragon as soon as possible. I'm the first to finish my steak and I sit waiting for the other to finish. The sound of the dragon from my dreams fills my mind every time I try to think of something else.

"Excuse me," I say getting up from the table.

I walk across the room to the balcony and lean against the rail. I stare at the torches that light the city. I can't shake the thought of the dragon. Closing my eyes I take a deep breath and try to clear my mind. After repeating this several more times I feel my body relax a little more. As I stand with me eyes closed I feel someone touch me on the shoulder. I open my eyes and turn to see Luna's sister standing behind me.

"The dragon will live," she says in a comforting tone. "I am Lilith."

"I'm Ivan," I say, wondering how she knows the dragon is alive. "You have the gift of dreams, don't you?"

"Yes," Lilith replies. "That is how I know that you will save my sister's life and that you truly are a great warrior."

"I'm not a great warrior," I sigh.

"You are greater than you believe," she says with a voice calm and gentle. "You killed a werewolf the first day you arrived, did you not?"

"Yes, but that was only because of the berserker thing," I say recalling the strange feeling that overtook me. "I feel that I don't deserve the credit for that, I couldn't control it. I still can't control it."

"Do not let it trouble you," she says her voice soothing. "You will learn to control it in time."

I stand thinking about what she has just said; I will learn to control it. Lilith turns and walks back to the table. I watch her as she begins to converse with Luna. Scott stands up and walks towards me. He stands next to me and looks out at the torch lit city below us. As I think about the dragon, Iris and another dragon land on the balcony.

"We are ready to depart when you are," Iris says looking at us as we gather around. "This one has volunteered his services for this particular journey."

The dragon has scales that are light brown, almost golden.

"Thank you," Luna says bowing in front of the dragon. "May I ask your name?"

"I am Lux," he says bowing to Luna in return. "I am at your service."

"Thank for your help," Luna says. "Your services will be rewarded when we return after the journey."

"I do not wish for anything in return," Lux says glancing around at our group. "I simply want to venture out and see the world outside this place."

"You can fly," I say looking at Lux. "You've the power to leave anytime you wish. Why don't you just leave whenever you want?"

"My father has a pact with a merchant," Lux says looking at the ground. "He wanted me to follow him on his travels. When I refused he said that if I would not travel with him, that I would not travel at all. So he left me here."

"That seems a little harsh," Scott says looking up at Lux.

"So the journey with us is your reward," I say thinking out loud.

"In a way, yes," Lux says. "I did not think of it that way."

"Well we should be going," Luna says placing her pack on Iris's back and climbing on.

Lux lowers himself, allowing Tori to climb onto his back. I stand next to Scott for a moment and see who I'm supposed to ride with. I guess Scott feels the same because he makes no effort to get on either dragon. Luna looks at me and motions me in her direction.

"Who do you wish to ride with," she asks.

"It doesn't matter to me," I say glancing over at Scott. "I guess I'll ride with you, if you don't mind."

"Not at all," Luna says leaning forward on Iris's back.

I get on Iris's shoulders and slide back so I am comfortable. I look back at Scott and see him walking hesitantly toward Lux and Tori. He slowly gets on Lux's back and settles down. I know he has ridden on dragons since he has been here and heights have never bothered him before. So something else must be troubling him.

"Are you ready," Luna asks looking back at Lux.

"Yes," he says rustling his wings.

"Then let the journey begin," Iris says beating her wings and kicking off the ground.

We have no real need to fly higher, being that we launched from the highest balcony on the palace. I look below as we pass over the sleeping city. A few people that are out for a late night stroll look up at us and then returning to what their walk as if they didn't notice us. With every beat of the dragons' wings us near the mouth of the giant cave.

As we reach the mouth of the cave I can see the night sky. The half moon gives some light and clouds are beginning to thin out some since yesterday. We fly outside and a gentle breeze caresses my body as we veer south toward the wounded dragon that awaits us. I know that Lilith said that the dragon would live, but I know that it's in pain.

"How long will it take to reach the beach that the dragon is on," I ask Luna as we fly south.

"We will journey straight through the night," she replies. "That means that we should reach the dragon around sunrise."

"Hey Ivan," Scott says. "Why are you so worried about this dragon anyway?"

"Because you and I both know how hostile this place can be," I say. "And being wounded doesn't improve the situation."

I stare into the night that lies ahead of us and I wish it was morning now. My body feels drained of energy, but I remember what happened the last time I fell asleep while flying. I'm not going to sleep this time, but I need to do something worth while. I think back to what else Lilith said to me before we left. She said I would manage to control the berserker ability. So why not try it out?

"Tori," I shout to her over the breeze. "How many medical supplies did you bring?"

"Triple of the usual," she shouts back.

Not knowing how much the usual is I guess that's a good thing. I decide to focus on controlling the berserker ability. I think back to what triggered the slow motion and enhanced senses. The one thing in common was battle, except the teapot at Grandma's. That time I just really wanted to catch the teapot before it hit the ground.

I don't feel like trying to battle someone hundreds of feet in the air, so I'll work on the teapot type scenario. I open the haversack that is sitting on my lap and see if there is anything I can use. The main compartment is filled with nothing but food and a few medical supplies. As I turn the haversack over on my lap, I feel something hard in the side pocket hit my leg. I open it and find a pouch of small stones and a sling. I open the pouch and retrieve one of the smooth round stones from it. I also find a small dagger, so I take it as well.

I hold the stone in my left hand above my open right hand. I release the stone and watch it fall into the palm of my right hand. I do repeat this several more times, just watching the stone fall. After about five minutes of this I begin to focus on the stone and what I want to happen. I want to drop the stone and catch it with my left hand, when is less than three inches from touching my right hand. This isn't anything special, I can already do this.

Every time that I drop the stone I focus on catching it, but the berserker doesn't come. Two or three hours into the dropping of the stone I start to become frustrated. I take a deep breathe and try to clear my mind of the frustration. As I breathe deep, I calm myself and drop the stone one last time. I follow the stone's descent and then the stone slows down.

The slow motion finally happened at will. I just watch the stone as hits the palm of my right hand. As I close my hand around the stone the slow motion disappears. Now I understand how the slow motion works, but only somewhat. When I lost sight of what I'm focusing on, that's when the slow motion ended.

I take the dagger out of its small leather case and I focus on the stone. This time the slow motion takes effect before the stone leaves my grasp. I move the dagger and flick the stone up into the air. When the stone reaches its climax I flip the dagger around in my hand. Just before the stone falls completely I flick it back up. I do this a few more times before I stop. I look up at Scott, who had apparently been watching my performance. He just sits transfixed on me. I look over to Tori sleeping on Lux's shoulder; she is braver than I am. I then look to Luna, who is now watching. She just looks at me and smiles, not saying a word.

"Did you see that," I ask her, stuffing the stone and the dagger back into the haversack.

"Yes," she replies quietly. "You are learning to master the berserker ability. It only took you about six hours to trigger it."

"Has it been that long," I exclaim. "It only felt like one or two hours to me."

"It will be dawn shortly," Lux says for the first time in hours. "You should eat something now; we don't know when we will find the dragon."

"That is a good idea," Luna says opening a haversack and taking out a small pack of meat. "Everyone has there own food supply."

"Okay," I say opening my haversack again. "Should we wake up Tori?"

"No need to," Tori says sitting and yawning. "Just woke up."

I eat an apple, I don't know if I can handle any heavy foods right now. I look around at the slowly brightening sky. The east is turning hues of orange and yellow as the sun continues to rise. The few clouds that are in the sky are turning a deep purple grayish color. I can finally see the ground below us, shrubs and small bushes mostly. Some trees dot the land here and there. But there's still no sight of the dragon.

As we finish our meals the breeze begins to increase. I drop my apple core and follow its course to the ground. It hits and breaks into several pieces. I start to scan the area looking for any sign of the dragon, or worse werewolves. The wind continues to increase and I think I can hear the sound of waves in the distance. The air has a slight salty smell to it as the dragons bring us ever closer to the beach, and the wounded dragon.

The sky is much brighter now, allowing me to see a line of blue on the horizon. I strain my eyes trying to see any sign of the dragon. As the sky continues to grow brighter I can see more, but no dragon. Then something catches my attention in the distance. A large black figure forms in the growing morning light.

"There," I shout pointing at the figure ahead of us. "That black spot slightly to the left of our current path."

"I see it," Lux shouts back.

The dragons begin to drop slowly as we grow closer to the dragon. As we grow closer to the dragon I can feel my heart begin to beat faster with anticipation. The dragon is far enough up on the shore to avoid the tide when it comes. I can see a lot of blood on the ground around the dragon. I look over at Scott and catch his glance. He nods at the dragon on the shores and gives me a half smile. We're only about a hundred feet from the ground, when the dragons begin to slow to land.

"Don't make any sudden movements," Tori says shouldering her haversack. "He might attack us if he doesn't know that we are allies."

"How do you know it's a he," I ask looking at the dragon then at Tori.

"Larger muscle mass and slightly shorter tail," she says staring at the dragon.

We land a few yards away to ensure that we are at a safe distance. As soon as Iris's feet touch the ground I jump off and stare at the wounded dragon in front of me. It takes all the will in my body to hold myself back and not run to aid the dragon. Even though the dragon is injured I can tell he is a fighter.

His body is large, but lean, not bulky and overly muscular. Jet black scales cover his entire body from his snout to the tip of his tail. Then there are the injuries that cover his body. His right wing is half folded with punctures and a few long gashes. Long cuts and bite marks dot his body. That is only on the side that I can see from were I stand.

The rest of the group is still in the process of dismounting and organizing supplies. I can't stand it any longer, I have to help now. I instantly break into a run toward the dragon.

"Stop," I hear Tori yell. "We don't know..."

I tone her out and continue to run toward the dragon. I slow to a jog as I make my way in front of the dragon. Dropping to my knees I slide the last few feet.

The dragon barely flinches as I stop by its head. It raises its head a few inches off the ground. He lets out a low growl, but I don't back away. I simply stare into his eyes until he breaks the stare. I glance at his left wing which outstretched in an awkward position. One long gash runs across the membrane, allowing me to see the ground under the wing.

"We're here to help you," I say looking back at the dragon. "Do you need any food or water?"

He looks up at me and lets out another low growl and nods the best he can. I stand back up and look back at everyone. They are still standing back, keeping their distance from where I stand. I walk back towards the group. Brushing past them I open my haversack and find a chunk of meat and a full water flask. I turn and walk back past the group, looking back at them as I make my way to the dragon.

"Does anyone care to help me," I ask with a smile.

I kneel in front of the dragon again, offering the meat to him. He accepts the meat and swallows it without even chewing. I then pour the entire flask of water into his mouth. I sit for a moment looking at the wounds on his body again.

"Why are you doing this," the dragon asks in a raspy voice.

I look to see the dragon with his head raised a little higher this time.

"Because you're injured and need help," I say staring at him.

"What is your name," he asks, wincing when he raises his head too far.

"Ivan," I reply. "And yours?"

"I am Arrok," he says returning my stare.

I look over at Luna, who is leading Scott and Tori in a slow advance towards me. Arrok looks over at Luna and the others. They freeze where they are not moving; Luna even has her hands on her swords.

"He isn't going to attack you," I say with a reassuring tone.

"He may not," she says drawing her swords. "But they will."

I follow Luna's gaze over to my left, I let out a deep sigh when I see what it is. Standing and drawing my sword I turn to face the pack of four werewolves. The lead werewolf steps forward, but doesn't attack.

"What do you want," I ask taking a step in front of the werewolf and Arrok.

"We only want the dragon," he says in a casual manner. "Give him to us and you may leave alive."

I risk a glance at Arrok and can see him flex his claws, even though he is in no condition to fight, he will if he wants to. I turn back to face the werewolf, as he continues to watch me. His eyes shift to behind me, then he focuses on my again. Luna and the others form a line beside me. I'm on the left end with Luna beside me, followed by Tori and Scott.

"Give him to us and you may leave alive," the lead werewolf repeats.

"Sorry," I say coldly. "But I think I'm going to leave alive no matter how this ends."

9

"SO BE IT THEN," the werewolf says looking back at his companions. "It does not matter to us how we acquire the dragon."

As soon as the words leave his mouth the other three werewolves spring forward. Luna moves forward with lightning speed and begins to attack the werewolf that is closest to us. Scott and Tori draw their weapons and begin to battle the other werewolves that have moved around Luna. I try to keep my breathing at a steady pace, but I can feel the rage of the berserker rising inside me.

I turn to see one of the werewolves dodge Scott's attack. I run over to the werewolf and deliver a slash into the back of its right shoulder. It roars in pain and spins around to retaliate against me. It flexes its claws and prepares to strike. Just as it takes one step forward a blade pierces through its chest. The berserker inside of me suddenly takes over and I bring my sword down across the werewolf's neck. As the werewolf falls I can see Scott standing behind our fallen adversary. I then turn to view the battle in the slow motion.

Scott is rushing towards Tori to help her with a large werewolf bearing down on her. He jumps in the air and plunges his sword into the werewolf's back. Even Iris and Lux are joining in on the battle as two more werewolves arrive. I look around to see if I can find the leader. I notice him creeping slowly towards Arrok, who is in no condition to fight. Arrok is too busy watching the battle with the remaining werewolves to notice. I run quickly towards the werewolf as he lunges at Arrok.

Arrok can only twist his head and try to deflect the attacks as best he can. I continue to towards the unfair assault. As I approach the werewolf he doesn't even know I'm near him. I swing the sword as hard as I can at the werewolf's arm, just before the blade hits he notices me. He turns to face me causing the blade to graze him. The only reason that I know the blade made some connection is because of the blood flowing from the deep gash in his arm. He jumps back a few feet with his left arm hanging useless at his side.

"I told you," I say preparing for another strike. "Leave now and you can live."

"Hah, it will not matter," he says holding his arm. "We are not the only werewolves out here. There are thousands of us; each ready to fight for what rightfully belong to us."

"What do you mean, what rightfully belongs to you," I ask, trying to distract him.

"You humans and the vampires stole this land from us when you arrived here," he says taking a step back. "We are only taking back what belonged to us in the first place."

Without another word he lunges forward and slashes at me with his one good arm. I sidestep and hold out my sword to the side he is charging. The blade rakes his chest as he turns to counterattack. I continue to face away from my opponent as he rushes toward me from behind. His breathing is ragged and his footsteps heavy. Just as he is almost on top of me I flip the sword around so the blade is facing the werewolf, then I kneel. I feel the blade dig into the werewolf and I let go of the sword as the werewolf crashes into the ground next to me. As I stand I can see my sword protruding from my enemy's motionless chest.

I walk over to the fallen werewolf and pull the blade out of his chest. I clean my sword off on the werewolf's fur and sheath my sword. I look around at the remains of the battle. All of the werewolves have been taken care of, but we sustained some injuries. Scott walks over to me as I continue to look at the red soaked shores.

"How's the dragon," he asks wiping blood from his face.

"I don't know," I say noticing a sizable cut on Scott's forehead. "Looks like one of the werewolves left you with a nice souvenir."

"I suppose so," he says wiping the blood from his face again.

"Did anyone else get injured," I say looking over at Luna and Tori.

"I have no idea," he says as he walks over to the werewolf I had killed moments ago.

I walk over to Luna. She has her sleeve rolled up and removes a blood stained cloth from her arm. As she turns her forearm over I can see four long gashes that run from her elbow diagonally to her wrist. She focuses on her arm and the gashes slowly start close. After a few seconds the wounds are healed and she rolls her sleeve back down, even though it is shredded. When she sees that I am watching she simply smiles and looks to Iris.

"Do you want me to take care of the bodies," Iris asks glancing at the werewolves lying on the beach.

"Yes take them out over the sea," Luna orders. "Make sure they are out far enough out that they will not wash back ashore."

"I will assist you," Lux says walking up to us.

"What are we going to do about Arrok," I ask Luna and the others.

"Who," Luna asks with a puzzled look on her face.

"The black dragon," I reply. "He told me his name just before the werewolves attacked."

I stop for a moment to see Iris pickup a fallen werewolf in her claws and fly off in the direction over the sea. Lux does the same and flies off after Iris. As the dragons fly off to drop the bodies, I notice Tori inspecting Arrok's wounds.

"How is he," I ask watching Tori.

She begins pulling out various items from her bag. She removes some vials and a small bowl.

"He will live," she says setting some herbs in the bowl. "But we need to get him back to Haven as soon as we can."

"Can we move him in that condition," Luna asks.

"We'll have to find a way," Tori says.

She then removes two large needles from the bag as well. She threads one needle and hands it to me.

"Why are you giving this to me," I ask.

"You watch me stitch your leg," Tori says. "Do you think that you can do it too?"

"Okay," I say holding out my hand to Tori for the vials. "Let me give him the medicine, just in case he doesn't know you're here to help him."

"Good idea," she says handing me the vials and taking a step back from Arrok.

I walk around to the front of Arrok and kneel down. Just from the way he is breathing I can tell the sooner we get him to Haven the better.

"This will ease your pain while we administer to your wounds," I say pulling the cork stopper out with my teeth.

He raises his head only a few inches from the ground. I pour the first vial into his mouth and pull the stopper in the second vial and give him I as well. After both of the vials are empty I stand and return to the group.

"Here are your vials," I say handing them to Tori.

"Did he take them," Tori asks looking at Arrok.

"Yes," I say watching the look of pain on Arrok's face grow less with each breath.

After a few minutes of watching Arrok in silence Tori slowly begins to walk towards him. I follow right behind her ready to help stitch where needed. She kneels by his wing that is turned in an awkward position. She looks at the positions of the wing, then stands and dusts the sand off her clothes.

"Lift his wing," she instructs. "And tell him this may hurt."

"Hold on," I say to Arrok. "This might hurt, even with the numbing medicine."

Tori runs her hand over his wing near his body. Tori then grasps his wing and pushes it towards his body. A loud pop sounds followed by an agonizing roar of pain that echoes across the beach. Arrok makes an attempt to turn, but is still too weak. Even though he could not reach Tori it still causes her to jump away from him.

"Not to sound impatient," I say to Tori as I retrieve my needle again. "But when are we going to move him?"

"As soon as we stitch the wounds that are one his wings and seal the wounds on his body" she says as she wipes off the wounds so she can begin stitching. "We also need to find a way to move him."

"How much rope do we have," Scott asks squinting at the now, midmorning sun.

"Not nearly enough to effectively carry him," Luna says cleaning off one of her swords.

I walk around to the right side of Arrok so I can stitch some of the wounds. As I kneel I can see a long gash that penetrates completely through the membrane of his wing. Taking a deep breath I begin to slowly stitch the wound shut. Time seems to drag on just as slowly as my stitching. After the gash is stitched I stitch the other gashes on the wing. As the minutes continue to drag on, I can't keep my mind from trying to figure out a way to move him back to Haven.

"I've got the answer to how we can move Arrok to Haven," Scott says. "Is it possible to make a net out of the seaweed that is scattered on this beach?"

"I suppose it could be done," Luna says looking around the beach. "Let us start then."

"Do you need my help for anything else," I ask Tori as I hand the needle back to her.

"Not right now," she says as she begins to crush up the ingredients in the bowl. "But in a moment I may."

"Okay," I say turning to walk down the beach to gather seaweed.

I walk in the direction away from Scott and the others. I continue until I reach a dune that slopes gently down to a section of the shore that is eroded inward forming a small cove. As I slide down the dune a shadow flashes across the ground, causing me to lose my balance. I roll down to the bottom of the dune before I finally stop.

Once I stand and shake the sand off my clothing, I look to the sky for the source of the shadow. Glaring against the sun I can see Iris and Lux returning for the other werewolves. Knowing what the shadow was caused by puts my mind at some ease. I walk around the cove and begin to gather seaweed. As I place the seaweed in a small pile, I begin to think of home for the first time since I've been in this new world.

I know that my mother is probably heartbroken and spearheading a search for me. My father is more than likely doing the same, while trying to comfort her best he can. I'm sure Scott's family is equally concerned with his disappearance as well. I also know that both of our families will be upset with the charred campsite left on the forest. Do they think Scott and I are dead?

I can recall the image of the lightning striking Scott. That blue bolt out of a cloudless sky. It almost makes me wonder if this is all just a dream. But how could I possibly have a dream this vivid. I can feel the heat of the sun on my body, the cool ocean breeze gently tugging at my clothes, and the sound of the waves crashing softly on the beach, and a loud splash.

The sound snaps me out of my daydreaming. I look out to the sea in the relative direction of the splash. I gaze out at the dark blue water as the sun refracts on the surface causing it to sparkle. After a minute or two of staring at the water I assume it is my imagination. Then a fin breaks the surface of the water. It rolls under only to be followed by another and another. It's not different fins in different locations. They are all attached to one serpent like body. After the fifth fin goes under a tail breaks the surface then the water is calm again.

I continue to gaze at the sparkling waters, even when the crunching sound of footsteps on the sand grows louder. I wait until the footsteps are only a few feet from me, then I draw my sword and swing as I turn. A metallic ring splits through the quiet air.

"You shouldn't sneak up on people," I say to Scott as I lower sword.

"I'm starting to think the same thing," he says as he sheaths his sword behind his shoulders. "What are you doing anyway; it's been about an hour since we started gathering seaweed for the net."

"Has it been that long," I ask sheathing my sword. "I just got thinking about home."

"You too, huh," Scott asks sitting down on the edge of the dune. "I think about home everyday since we landed here."

"This may sound strange," I say sitting next to him. "But today is the first time I have thought about it. I've been so caught up with werewolves and wounded dragons that I almost forgot all about home."

"Everyone 's different," he says drawing circle in the sand with his finger. "I know that I'm not going to stay here, I'm going home one way or another."

"But we don't even know that much about how we got here," I say gazing out at the sea for any sign of the finned creature. "It may only be one way."

"I hope not," he says getting up and dusting himself off. "I'm not giving up that easily."

Then he slowly makes his way up the side of the dune, and out of sight. I walk around the cove and gather up the last of the seaweed. Now that I have a sufficient sized pile I decide it would be best to go around the dune. I notice that the dune ends close to the water's edge. With my arms full of seaweed I begin to trek around the dune.

As I walk along the bottom of the dune I glance out at the sky above the sea, to see if Iris and Lux are returning yet. I can make out two specks in the distance slower moving closer to the shore. Slowly I make my way back to the group so I can begin helping with the construction of the net. With any luck it will work and we will be able to transport Arrok to Haven. Continuing along the shore I once again see the form of Arrok lying still on the sand.

When I finally reach the group, I can see Scott and Luna weaving the seaweed together to make the net. Tori is applying some sort of green paste to the wounds that are on Arrok's body. I walk over to Scott and Luna and drop of seaweed by the side of the net.

"Do you need any help," I ask Luna.

"No," she says continuing to weave the net together. "But I think Tori might need some help applying the medicines."

I turn and walk over to Tori as she smears the paste on a long gash running down Arrok's neck.

"What are you putting on his wounds,' I ask as she smears more of the paste on the wound.

"It keeps the wounds from becoming infected," Tori says wiping her hands off on a piece of seaweed. "You can help on the other side; I have not started on it at the moment."

Tori puts more ingredients in another bowl and begins to mix them together. She then hands the bowl to me and I walk around to the other side of Arrok. I immediately begin to apply the substance to the first wound that I see. Many of the wounds seem to be punctures marks in groups of five, just like a hand. The wounds are too far apart to be the claws of a werewolf; they appear to be from a dragon.

After over half of the wounds are covered with the anti infection medicine, I feel a presence behind me. I look behind me to see Tori watching my progress.

"You are doing a good job," she says. "You really put your mind into what you're doing."

"I suppose," I reply. "Guess that's why I can control the berserker ability a little bit now."

"That is good," she says dipping her hand in the bowl and smearing the paste on a wound. "I will finish this, if you want to see how the net is progressing."

"Thank you," I say picking up a strand of seaweed and wiping off my hands with it.

I stand and stretch, working out the soreness in my legs from crouching by Arrok's side. As I do, I notice Iris and Lux fly overhead and begin to slowly spiral down for a landing. Lux lands with a soft thud as he lands with just a little too much speed. Iris lands without a single sound to betray her presence.

After watching the two dragons land I begin to walk over to Scott and Luna. When I'm only a few feet away from them the pattern of the puncture wounds on Arrok flashes in my mind. I stop walking towards them and turn towards Iris and Lux, who are talking quietly together. As I walk closer they stop talking to each other and watch me approach.

"Greetings Ivan," Iris says as I reach them. "What is on your mind?"

I think that this dragon has the ability to read expressions or something. Just like when I first arrived here and she stared at me while talking with Luna.

"Well, I need your help," I say.

"And what might you need my help for," she say stretching her wings out and folding them back.

"Actually it's more of your opinion," I say hesitantly. "I need to know how you would attack another dragon."

"Most of us dragons live in peace with one another," she says calmly. "So there is little need for fighting amongst ourselves."

"If you had no choice but to defend yourself or be killed," I say trying to intensify the scenario. "What would you do and how would you carry it out?"

"I suppose I would slash at the neck or try to puncture my enemy's side," she replies thoughtfully. "At least make the death quick and as painless as possible."

"When you say puncture what do you mean," I ask, finally getting somewhere with my questions.

"Like this," Iris says stabbing her claws into the sand and pulling them out. "See?"

I lean over and examine the five holes stamped in the sand. The marks look almost identical to the wounds on Arrok. This confirms my theory that he was attacked by a dragon.

"Are there any dragons that do fight each other," I ask, still staring at the sand. "Any group set apart from the rest?"

"None that I can recall," Iris says thoughtfully. "There has been no strife between dragon clans that I know as of late. You could search in the archives, once we return to Haven. There is bound to be information on what you seek…"

"And even by some chance that you are unsuccessful," Luna says walking up behind me without a sound. "You will gain knowledge on many other things while there."

"Hey," I say, sweeping my foot across the marks in the sand as I turn.

"Are you surprised," Luna asks with a hint of a smile on her face.

"Somewhat," I say. "You manage to walk so silently."

"One of the many advantages of being a vampire," she says, this time smiling. "The net is not far from being finished."

"I'll help finish it," I say turning towards the area of the net.

"Actually we could use some firewood," Luna says. "Is that all right with you?"

"Yeah," I say.

I look around for any wood near me, then I notice Scott isn't around the area. I scan the area for any signs of where he might be or been. Then I catch a glimpse of a figure disappear around the bottom of a dune. Not wanting to draw attention I casually walk in the direction of what I hope is Scott. Following the foot prints in the sand I make my way around the edge of the dune. As the beach on the other side of the dune becomes visible, so does Scott.

"I thought no one saw me," Scott says sitting on a large piece of driftwood.

"Think again," I say sitting down next to him on the driftwood. "What's bothering you?"

"I had another dream last night," he says taking a drink from a water flask.

"So that's what's putting you on edge today," I say looking up at the sun to guess the time. "What was the dream?"

"It was a short and simple dream really," he says placing the cap back on the flask. "I'm going to return home, somehow, and you're not."

"That's kind of harsh," I say with a laugh.

"I hope it's one of those that I think is going to come true and doesn't," he say with a sigh. "I really do."

"Me too," I say, more serious. "There are a lot of loose ends on this dream, like why I don't return with you."

"That was the first thing that came to my mind too," he says, worry evident in his voice. "I hope it's because you choose to stay here, not because you have to."

"What is that suppose to mean," I ask, curious to know why I wouldn't want to go home.

"Well you and Luna," he says slowly.

I know his intentions are good, but he used the wrong choice of words, and he knows that he did.

"What do you mean by that," I say, knowing that I can play him.

"I… ah… you," he stutters. "Oh come on."

"Come on what," I shoot back. "What do you mean?"

"You two spend a lot of time together," he says nervously. "She smiles at you from time to time. You don't think there is something there?"

"Scott," I say. "Don't look too much into it. Just because we spend time doesn't mean we're interested in each other. You and Tori have spent some time together since you've been here. Does that mean you two are going to become a package deal?"

"I understand," he says, a little more relaxed. "I'm just saying what I see."

"It's a mutual respect I guess," I say trying to change the subject. "So, any ideas on how we're getting home?"

"But I told you," Scott says. "You aren't going home."

"I know," I say with a smile. "But if I act like I'm going to be returning home, it will make things easier on you and me."

"I guess you're right," he says thoughtfully. "Good mind trick."

"Remember when we had that computer class together," I ask, thinking back to the past once again. "We used that card trick on the teacher."

"Yeah, I remember," he laughs. "We bet him if we could guess his card every time, we wouldn't do any work. He became so fascinated with the trick, that we used the trick the entire class so he could try to figure it out."

"That was fun," I say. "So how much work do we lack on the net?"

"Not much now," Scott says standing up and looking out at the sea. "You want to head back and try to finish it before sundown?"

"Sure," I say standing up next to him. "Wish I knew what time it was. Ever since I arrived here I've been trying to guess by the angle of the sun."

"It's about two o'clock," Scott says looking at the sky.

"How can you tell," I ask curious to know for myself.

"Because," he says pushing his sleeve up. "I managed to keep my watch."

"I don't know whether to be glad you have it," I say, then without warning I punch him in the arm. "Or mad because you could get us killed with it!"

"Ouch, what do you mean," he asks rubbing arm.

"The werewolves can smell the scent of things not of these surroundings," I explain. "Why do you think they took our clothing and had them burned after we arrived here?"

"Sorry," he says pulling his sleeve back down over the watch. "I have an idea."

"What," I ask, picking up a piece of dry driftwood.

"Every hour I'll look at the position of the sun," Scott says. "Then when I can tell by the sun, I'll throw the watch away."

"Sounds good to me," I say picking up more wood.

I gather up firewood and look at Scott who is now doing the same. We gather wood until both of us have a large load.

"Ready to head back," he says taking the lead.

"Sure," I reply. "I need to see how Arrok is doing."

I follow Scott towards the edge of dune near the rest of the group. As we walk around the dune I can see Luna and Tori standing together looking around the area. They spot us and seem relived to see that we're returning in one piece.

"We were starting to wonder where you two had gone," Luna says as she walks over to the net. "I see you found plenty of firewood."

"So how much work do we lack from finishing the net," I say walking over to the large net stretched out on the sand.

"Maybe a few hours of weaving and then we need to attach the ropes," Luna replies as she begins weaving more seaweed together.

"We will be able to move the wounded dragon onto the net," Tori says then pauses and looks at me. 'What was his name again?"

"His name is Arrok," I say setting my bundle of wood down next to Luna. "How do you plan on us moving him?"

"Iris and Lux should be able to lift him onto the net," Tori explains. "Then we will run the two ropes that we have along two sides of the net. Iris will get on one side with a rope and Lux on the other. They should then be able to fly, and together carry Arrok back to Haven, where he can recover."

"Sounds like a pretty good plan to me," I say sitting down next to the net to examine the weave.

I run my hand over the makeshift net. There are gaps in the weave just like a normal net yet the strands are thicker. It's not just one strand thick, but five or six. I guess that a several hundred pound dragon would break it pretty easily if it wasn't.

"If we start now we can finish the net and move Arrok onto it to night," Luna says continuing to weave on the net.

"Okay," Scott says sitting down next to me. "Let's get started."

We all sit around the net weaving seaweed in silence. The time seems to flow into the pattern of the over then under weaving. As the amount of extra seaweed becomes less, so does the amount light. Once all of the seaweed has been used and the ropes attached to the sides of the net, the sun is sinking low in the west.

"Well we are finally finished," Tori says standing and walking over to Iris and Lux. After a moment she returns with Iris and Lux following close behind. "We should get a fire going before we lose all of the sunlight."

"Good idea," Scott says looking at me. "We should have brought back enough."

"Yeah," I say turning and walking with Scott towards the dune. "Let's get a little more, just in case."

We walk around the side of the dune and walk straight towards the large piece of drift wood that we were sitting on earlier. I lift one end of the driftwood to test its weight; the wood is light enough for me to carry alone. As I pick up the piece of wood Scott picks up a few other small pieces of wood that have landed up on shore.

Once he has gathered enough wood for a suitable sized fire to burn through most of the night we begin walking back towards the others. Just as we are about to round the edge of the dune a roar sounds through the darkening night. Scott and I both stop in our tracks and look at each other. We both know what the reason for the roar was; it was a roar of pain. We quicken our pace to see if Arrok has been moved very far.

As I walk around the edge of the dune, I can see that Arrok has been successfully moved onto the net. Iris and Lux are both a few yards away from where Arrok lay. I drop the driftwood on the ground with the rest of the wood and walk over next to Luna. Scott drops his firewood next to mine and stand next to me.

"Tomorrow we begin our journey back to Haven," Luna says staring at Arrok as he breathes slowly. "We had best start a fire and post sentries, I will go first."

"I'll start the fire," Scott says, and walks back the fire wood pile.

"I can take the first shift if you want me too," I say to Luna as she stares into the darkness.

"That will not be necessary," she says walking away from me to stand guard. "I can see better in the dark than you can."

"More vampire abilities," I say with a smile.

"Yes, she says turning away. "I suppose."

I walk around to the front of Arrok and kneel by his head. As I do, he seems to recognize me.

"Are you going to be all right," I ask him. "Do you need anything?"

"Only rest," he replies weakly.

Now that I know he is okay I stand and walk over to where Scott has constructed a fire. He adds a few pieces of driftwood to the fire, then he opens a haversack and pulls out two blankets.

"Here," he says tossing me a blanket. "Tori says it can get cold on these shores at night."

I unroll the blanket on the sand and fold it over to stay warm against the breeze coming off the sea. I look across the fire and see Scott close his eyes, I also see Tori preparing her blanket. Looking around a little more I spot Luna standing with a blanket around her shoulders. She sees me and smiles, I return the smile and drift off to sleep helped by the hypnotic sounds of the waves crashing on the shores.

10

I AWAKE, BUT KEEP MY eyes closed. I can feel that the atmosphere around me has become much cooler than it was before. Everything smells different, there is no salt smell lingering in the air. I listen for any signs of Luna or anyone else up and moving around. Nothing is like it should be; I can't even make out the sounds of the waves crashing on the shore. Then I hear voices whispering. They are not the voices of Scott, Luna, or Tori, yet they're familiar.

I decide it's time to see for myself what's going on. I open my eyes and my eyes adjust to the abnormally bright light. I can't believe what I am seeing. I am in a hospital room, and my mother and father are sitting across the room staring at me. When they see that I am looking at them a shocked expression flashes across their faces. I can tell from the redness around my mother's eyes, she has been crying. My father just has a blank look on his face.

"What's going on," I ask, sitting up. "Where am I?"

Before I can even sit up a nurse, which seems to have appeared from nowhere, pushes gently back down on the bed.

"You need to relax," she says gently.

I push against her push, but she pushes a little harder. I decide it is better to figure out what is happening first, before I make trouble.

"I will when I know what's going on," I say looking at the nurse, who looks almost identical to Luna.

She has the same long blonde hair and blue eyes. Only her eyes are not sapphire colored like Luna's.

"You were struck by lightning," the nurse explains. "You've been unconscious for four days."

"Well," I say looking around the room. "Now I know."

"Hit by lightning and in a coma for days and you still have your sense of humor," my father says smiling at me.

"Not that it was ever that good," a very familiar voice says.

I look over to the door to see Scott walk into the room.

"How are you doing," Scott says closing the door and leaning against the wall.

"Looks like I'm alive," I say grinning at him. "So I can't complain."

"Well, you owe me one," he says, shifting his lean on the wall.

"What do you mean," I ask.

"I carried you back to my house in the dark," he says.

"No," I say feeling my heartbeat starting to increase. "This isn't right. You said I wasn't going to make it back with you."

"What are you talking about," Scott asks, standing up straight. "I never said anything like that."

"Did you get back here before me," I ask, starting to get frustrated. "Where are the others at?"

"Who are you talking about," my father asks concerned.

"Scott," I yell. "Luna, Tori, the others, where are they!"

"There is no one here by those names," Scott says. "The nurse's name is Luan. Maybe you somehow heard her name in your sleep."

"How can you say that," I say growing more impatient. "You were there just like I was."

"I've seen this before," the nurse says. "Patients will dream something and think it is real when they come out of a coma."

"No one asked you," I snap at the nurse. "And it wasn't a dream!"

I can tell by the look on her face that she has never dealt with angered patients, or at least one like me. She just stands with her back against the wall.

"Ivan, listen to me," Scott says slowly as walks towards me. "You have been in this world the entire time. I have been in this world the entire time too. There is no one here by the name of Tori or Luna. It was all a dream."

I know that I can't get out of this hospital unless I play along. I have to get back to the campsite. It doesn't matter what I have to do or how I do it.

"Okay," I say calmly. "I guess I overreacted."

"Yes you did," the nurse says taking a step forward.

I shoot her an icy glare causing her to freeze where she stands.

"I'm just glad your okay," my mother says for the first time since I have been awake.

"I've got to get up," I say glaring at the nurse before she comes closer.

"I'll be back in a few minutes," she says walking out the door. "I have other patients to check on."

I drop the side bar down on the bed so I can get out. I slide out of the bed and my feet touch the cold tile floor. I notice that there are no heart monitoring devices attached to me, but there is an IV in my right hand. I also notice that I only have on a hospital gown.

"Do I have any regular clothes," I ask standing slowly.

"You have some in the bathroom," my mother says staring at the wall. "I had Scott bring them yesterday."

"Thanks," I say. "Good thing I have to head in that direction."

I walk to the bathroom door, which is right next to the door leading to the hallway. I open the bathroom door and step inside the small bathroom. It has a toilet, a sink, and a shower, nothing more. I glance around for my clothes. I see them sitting neatly folded on the sink.

I pull the IV out of my wrist causing a small spasm of pain to course through my right arm. I open the toilet lid and set the IV next to it. I then bite the tube open so it flows into the toilet in a steady stream. While it sounds like I'm using the bathroom, I change into a pair of blue jeans and a white T-shirt. I glance at the IV as the bag empties its contents, now's my chance.

I open the door and rush to the door that leads to the hallway. I jerk it open and don't look back. I look around the hallway to see which way is the best to get out of here. To my left is a small waiting room and reception desk. To the right are the elevators, stairs and more hallways. Then the door to my room begins to open.

I think anywhere is better than being caught. I turn to the right and run as fast as I can. The first set of elevator doors blur by, as I'm about to pass the second set they open. Suddenly I crash into someone coming out of a patient's room.

"Hey," the nurse yells as she makes her way back to her feet. "Wait a minute."

I look up to see the nurse from my room standing above me. She must have stepped out when I was in the bathroom. I scramble to my feet and glance into the open elevator. Two police officers step out and look at me and then to the nurse. One is short and rather large around the middle with thinning hair. The second is taller than the first with a mustache and I can see muscles bulging against his shirt.

"Are you all right," the taller one asks stepping forward.

"Yes," I say, hoping the nurse will be quiet, but I know it's doubtful.

I don't take time for her to speak. I turn and start to run towards the waiting room area. I make it to the reception desk before I here the nurse yell. Looking back I can see the tall police officer running after me, with the shorter one about ten feet behind him. I glance frantically around the dead end waiting room. The taller officer is almost upon me now and the only way out of this hospital is through them.

Suddenly everything begins to move slowly. The berserker ability wasn't a dream! I turn and smirk at the officer as he reaches out to grab me; I lean to one side but leave my left foot in place. He hits my foot and flies forward. As he does, I slide his nightstick from his belt. While he crashes to the floor I turn to confront the second officer.

He reaches for his nightstick as I run towards him. Before he can pull the nightstick around to his front I stab forward with the nightstick. It jabs straight into his stomach, I then bring it up and it connects with his nose with a crunching sound. I start running toward the other end of the hall, passing by Scott and my family as they watch from the doorway. As I reach the nurse she just stands awestruck. I run past the elevators and towards the stairs as the berserker fades.

I reach the staircase and stop to look back at my pursuers. The short officer is kneeling with both hands on his nose. I can see blood streaming from the spaces in between his fingers. Well at least he's already in a hospital. The taller officer has recovered and is now checking on his partner. He looks up and our eyes connect and then he breaks into a run towards me. I'm not very surprised to see the short one point in my direction with a bloody finger. The other officer is covering ground faster than I would like him to. I can see Scott beginning to run behind the officer. Chances are he's not on my side this time.

I open the door and rush down the stairs. I only make it down half of the first flight when the door bursts open and the tall officer begins chasing me again. I continue to run as fast as I can; now I start skipping steps to help put move distance between us.

"Stop," he yells.

I ignore his threat and continue down the staircase. The second floor door passes by and I know I'm running out of time. I make it to the ground floor door and tear it open. A large lobby opens in front of me with people walking casually to their appointments. Instantly I spot the automated sliding doors at the opposite end of the lobby. I run towards the doors, pushing myself even though my body begs for rest. As I weave between the bewildered people I hear the staircase door crash open.

"Stop," the officer yells again. "Stop or I'll shoot!"

For some strange reason I stop, right in front of the opening doors. Five more steps and I can be out of here. Turning I can see the officer walking slowly towards me with his gun fixed on me. Now everything seems to register in the minds of the people in the lobby. Some stand silent watching the scene before them. Others run screaming out of the lobby.

"Drop your weapon and put your hands on your head," he orders. "I said drop it!"

I only smile as I stand rooted in place.

"Ivan," Scott yells as he comes up next to the officer. "What are you doing?"

He stands staring at me as I look at the gun pointed at me. Then he suddenly notices the police officer standing next to him has his gun drawn.

"Don't shoot him," he yells.

"Stay out of this kid," the officer says without looking away from me. "I won't shoot him, if he cooperates."

He takes a step forward and I instinctively take a step back. I can tell this is a move he doesn't want me to take, because I can hear the safety click on his pistol.

"Don't take another step," he orders stepping forward.

This time I stand still. I can feel my heart pounding against my chest. Sweat beads slide down my face as the officer step even closer. I can feel the heat radiating from my body after my run from my room.

Suddenly a breeze of cool air rushes over my body. I turn to see a young man staring at what he has just walked in on. Then a gun shot echoes through the lobby and my right shoulder erupts into pain. I look down at my shoulder to see a red spot blossom on my white shirt. It quickly grows until my entire right side is covered in red, just as the fiery pain continues to spread. I look up at the officer that is now rushing towards me. I throw the nightstick at him and it catches him in the chest but he keeps coming. He tackles me sending us both to the ground and more pain rips through my shoulder as I hit the hard carpeted floor.

I lay on my back as he sits on my midsection, pinning me down.

"Ivan," Scott yells.

"Stay back," the officer yells.

Scott stops only a few feet from me. The pain is too unbearable for me to handle. My vision begins to blur and turn black.

"This can't be," I mumble.

The last thing that I see is the image of Scott standing near my shaking his head.

11

I JOLT AWAKE TO AN immense pressure on my body. My right shoulder burns with pain as I make an attempt to get up. I look at my body to see a werewolf lying on top of me. Panic grips me for a second, but then I notice that the werewolf isn't alive. Even though the werewolf is dead its claw is lodged in my shoulder. There is blood all over the blanket and sand around me. I can't tell how much of the blood belongs to me or if it's the werewolf.

"Are you all right," Luna says standing over me with two blood covered swords.

"Other than the dead werewolf on me and the claw on my shoulder I'm fine," I say pushing at the werewolf. "What happened anyway?"

"I was standing guard when I turned around and there was a werewolf," she says sheathing her swords. "It seemed to be sniffing the air for something, so I took the opportunity to slay it before it noticed me."

"Did it attack me before you could kill it," I ask touching the claw in my shoulder.

"No, that is my fault," Luna says looking at the ground. "When I attacked, it was alive long enough to try and brace itself for the fall. That is how you became injured. I am sorry.

"It's okay," I say looking at the claw in my shoulder. "I would rather be injured than dead."

I grasp the hand of the werewolf and pull it sharply out. I'm unable to contain a shout of pain as it slides out. Apparently the claw punctured into an artery, because blood instantly begins to gush from the wound.

"What's going on," Scott yells groggily as he wakes up.

I look over at him as he sits up and notices the dead werewolf. He scrambles to his feet and rushes over next me.

"Help me push this thing off," I say pushing with my left arm.

Scott and I roll the werewolf off and I sit up, I feel blood begin to run down my chest and side. Scott looks over in the direction were Tori lay sleeping.

"I'll wake up Tori so she can help," Scott says standing and jogging over to her.

As I watch him kneel by Tori and wake her, I feel a hand on my shoulder. I glance over my shoulder to see Luna sitting slightly behind me. She's watching Tori and doesn't seem to notice me watching her. I clear my throat and she notices me, she instantly puts force on her hand. I wince at the pain of the pressure on my wound.

"Again, I am sorry about this," she says.

"It's all right," I say placing my left hand over hers to stop help stop the bleeding. "You did what was best for all of us."

"Except for you," she says.

"It could've been worse," I say smiling. "He could've gotten to me before you did."

"Hey," she says pushing a little harder on my shoulder. "What is that suppose to mean."

"It was just a joke," I say wincing. "Let me see what the wound looks like."

Luna slowly removes her hand and blood instantly starts to flow. I tear my shirt a little and touch the wound. Just placing my hand near the wound sends pain blasting through my shoulder. It looks like I could hide a roll of pennies inside it.

Tori rubs sleep from her eyes as she walk over to us. She kneels beside me and opens her bag and removes a pair of scissors. She moves my hand and cuts the area of my shirt were the wound is. Then she retrieves a vial of clear liquid and pours it on my shoulder. I watch it bubble for a moment then the bubbles begin to turn red from mixing with the blood. After the bubbles settle she dabs the wound and places bandages around the wound. It only takes few minutes before she is finished.

"Are the bandages too tight," she asks with a yawn.

"No it's fine," I say standing up. "What caused the wounds to be so large?"

"I think that when the werewolf landed is twisted the claw in your shoulder," Tori yawns again.

"Okay, well I think this shirt may be ruined though," I say.

"There are fresh clothes in the packs on the ground over there," Tori says pointing to the haversacks that were carried by the dragons.

As I walk over to the haversacks I look around for the dragons that don't seem to be around. The only reason the werewolf must have made it into the camp is because they weren't here. I open a haversack and rummage through until I find a pair of pants and a shirt. I glance around looking for a place to change. I spot a large bush and walk behind it. I take off my blood covered clothes and put on the fresh ones. It takes some struggling to get my shirt on. The strange moccasin-like shoes still seem to be holding up and they only have a little blood on them.

Once I'm in some new clothes I walk back to the camp. Scott sits by the fire, just staring at the flames. Luna and Tori are talking over by Arrok as he sleeps. I see Luna point to portions of the net and Tori nods. I sit down next to Scott and watch the flames slowly consume the pieces of wood.

"Did you get rid of the watch yet," I say.

"Not yet," he says staring into the fire.

"You need to get rid of it," I say looking at him. "Here and now."

"What," he says confused. "Why?"

"Because that's how the werewolf wondered into our camp." I say coldly. "That's why I had a claw in my shoulder, and Luna thinks it's her fault. It smelled your watch and followed the scent. If she hadn't been standing guard we might all be dead."

"I had no idea," he says reaching inside his sleeve. "I'll get rid of it then."

"I'll take care of it," I say holding out my hand.

Scott takes off the watch and drops it in my hand. I set it on the sand and pick up a large conch shell. I slam the shell down on the face of the watch shattering the insides. I pick up the ruined watch and toss it into the fire, along with my bloody clothes.

"I'm sorry I caused you to get hurt," Scott says staring at the fire.

"You did more harm to Luna than to me," I say standing up and turning towards Luna and Tori. "So since we're all up, when are we going to start back to Haven?"

"When the dragons return from their hunt," Luna says walking past me. "But while we wait we should have something to eat."

She opens a haversack and pulls out a water flask and throws it to me. As I see it flying through the air I start to lift both arms to catch it. My left arm goes up like it's supposed to, my right arm stays at my side, while my shoulder burns with pain. I catch with just my left hand. I look at Luna for a moment and she looks towards Arrok.

"Tend to your dragon," she says, then begins rummaging through the haversack for provisions.

I walk over to Arrok and kneel in front of him. I can tell by his deep breathing that he is asleep, so I stand up and turn to leave. As I do my feet crunch on the sand and instantly he awakes and lets out a low growl. I stand unmoving as he raises his head until he is eye level with me.

"I've got some water for you, if you want any," I say kneeling down again. "Are you doing any better?"

"Why do you seem different to me than the others of your group," he asks, lowering his head. "You do not fear me and you befriend me as if you know me."

"I know what it feels like to be out here alone," I say sitting down. "When I arrived here I encountered a werewolf, and had no choice but to fight. I managed to win, but was wounded during fight. I wasn't alone long after I was injured, that's when they found me and helped me."

"So you are a newcomer," he asks, somewhat surprised. "You fight like a seasoned warrior."

"I guess I'm just lucky," I say pulling out the stopper on the flask. "Do you want some water?"

"Yes," he says. "Thank you."

I pour the entire contents of the flask into his mouth and sit for a moment. I look at Arrok's body that is covered with specks of green.

I stand up to leave and Arrok begins to rise. He raises his upper body about two feet when he stops and lowers himself back on his stomach. He lets what sounds like a mix between a sigh and a growl.

"I am still too weak," he says in disappointment. "I cannot stand relying on others for assistance."

"It's nothing to be ashamed of," I say looking at down at him. "Even though you think I'm a great warrior, I need help more than you think."

"I suppose," he says settling back down on the net.

I walk back over to the fire and sit down next to Scott. Luna has an apple on a stick over the fire roasting it. I see Scott and Tori both eating roasted apples as well. Luna turns the apple then plucks it from the stick and tosses it to me. I catch it with my left hand and set it down on the sand next to me before it burns my hand.

"Here," Scott says.

He hands me a handkerchief with a piece salted meat with a slice of bread. I gladly accept the food and set it on my lap. I eat the meat and bread in a few minutes. After I know the apple has cooled down enough, I pick it and brush off the sand. I take a bite and savor its warm sweet taste. I finish the apple and stand up; looking up at the sky I can see Iris and Lux returning from their hunt.

As they fly closer I can made out something clutched in Lux's claws. I continue to look trying to see what it may be. Iris circles a few times then lands a few yards away from Arrok. She looks up at Lux and he drops whatever he was carrying. The object falls towards Iris and I can make out the form a deer. Iris rises on her hind legs and catches the deer carcass. She walks over to Arrok and sets it in front of him.

"What are you doing," Arrok says raising his head.

"You need nourishment," Iris says pushing the deer closer to him. "You have to get your strength back."

"You must share quite a pact with that human," he says tearing off a piece of meat and swallowing it. "He tried to care for me only moments ago."

"I am sorry," Iris says looking back at me. "But I have no pact with him; I have a pact with the vampire standing next to him. He has no pact with any dragon."

I look to my right and see Luna standing next to me. She just smiles at me and looks back to Arrok as he devours the remains of the deer. As he finishes the deer Luna steps forward and looks at us.

"Well let us begin the journey back home," she says.

Iris and Lux stand on either side of Arrok and grip long thick ropes in their claws. They both lower themselves so we can climb onto their backs. Scott hands me a haversack and one to Luna and Tori. Scott and Tori climb onto Lux's back just as when we began our journey here. Luna takes a step and nimbly jumps onto Iris's back. I step and struggle up as best I can with one arm. I finally make it onto Iris's shoulders, then I notice Luna had her hand extended to help me.

"Again, I am sorry," she says, I can see the sorrow on her face and hear it in her voice. "I did not intend for…"

"It wasn't your fault," I say cutting off her apology. "Besides didn't Lilith say I'm supposed to save your life, not you saving mine?"

I smile at her, trying to lighten the mood. She seems to catch some of the humor and sits down in front of me. She looks down at Arrok.

"This may hurt a little," she says.

"You do not seem to know what I have gone through before you arrived here," he replies.

Was that a hint of humor in his voice? Iris beats her wings a few times and Lux does the same. Both of them crouch low and kick off at almost the same time. The jarring of the take off causes my shoulder to throb with pain. I look down at Arrok on the large seaweed net and I can tell the take off caused him pain as well.

"It looks like the net is going to work," Tori yells across to us as we climb into the air.

The dragons level off about a hundred feet lower than they usually do. Even with two dragons sharing the burden of the weight, it's clear it will take some time for them to adjust.

"Do dragons heal as fast as your kind," I ask Luna.

"No," she says swinging her right leg over Iris's and then doing the same with her left. "They do heal faster than humans at a natural rate, but compared to the natural healing of a vampire. You both fall short. The wound on your shoulder, without the vampire's touch, will take a week or more. Arrok's injuries will take a few days at the most."

"Seems like humans have to be the most careful in this world," I say setting my hand gently on my shoulder.

"Yet there are so many humans in our army," Luna says puzzled.

"Your kind is the most vulnerable, yet you fight with determination possessed by no others."

"Back in our world there are people that find what triggers their anger," I explain. "This gives them more determination and power to fight."

"The ways that people survive here are different," Luna says looking up at me. "But the goal is the same."

"Oh. Speaking of goals," I say glancing down at Arrok. "Who do you think attacked him?"

"It is hard to say," Luna says looking down at him too. "I do not believe it was werewolves. He could have simply flown away."

"I think it was another dragon that attacked him," I say looking up at Luna. "What do you think?"

She looks up at me with a shocked look on her face. I can tell she sees what I see or I have somehow offended her.

"You can not be serious," she exclaims. "Dragons rarely fight for a mate. Why would another dragon be behind this?"

"I don't know why," I say holding my gaze on her. "But look at the marks on him. They're too large and spread apart to be werewolves. Do you mind if I check the archives when we return to Haven?"

"Maybe we should ask him," Luna says looking back at Arrok.

"I think that is a good idea," I say. "But let's wait until he recovers first."

"All right," Luna says looking back at me. "We will wait."

"Will it take longer for us to reach Haven since we are carrying Arrok," I ask Iris as we fly.

"He will not hinder us greatly," she says glancing back at me. "We will arrive home before nightfall."

Home, the word sends a wave of guilt and pain through my heart. I know that my family is worried about me and they are looking for me.

"If you do not have any objections I would like to place Arrok in your room," Tori says over a slight gust of wind that has picked up. "You seem to be less afraid of him than any of us."

"That's all right with me," I say remembering the large mats my room. "What does he think of it?"

"Arrok," Tori says. "Do you wish to stay with Ivan in his room, or would you prefer the infirmary?"

Arrok raises his head and looks at Tori, then to me. He seems to ponder it for a moment then looks at Tori again.

"I believe I will stay with him," he says lowering his head back onto the net. "Not that I have the strength to complain at this point."

"I'm honored that you choose to stay with me," I say locking eyes with the pitch black dragon.

"Do not bother," he says staring into my eyes. "It is only temporary."

"So what are we going to do to pass the time," Scott says looking around at all of us.

"I don't know," I say looking at Luna and then to Tori. "Luna what do you usually do to pass the time."

"Well," she says thoughtfully. "Train or study in the archives."

"I don't think we can do any of that on the backs of dragons," I say with a laugh. "Iris do you have any suggestions?"

"Let me see," she says. "I have always been very fond of riddles."

"That sounds like a good idea," Tori says excitedly. "So who will begin?"

"I will," Scott says. "What do you lie out at night, but roll up in the morning?"

I have already heard this riddle before so I think I'll let the others try to guess it. I can see the look on Iris's face; she's unraveling the clues in her mind.

"Is it a blanket," Iris asks over her shoulder.

"Yes," Scott says, a little disappointed that she got the answer on the first try.

"All right I have one," Luna says.

The time seems to go by somewhat faster as we all exchange riddles and puzzles. We laugh when one of us is close to solving a riddle, but not that close. Even Arrok has a few riddles and trick questions to share with us. As time goes on the riddles become more difficult. By the time any of us realize it the sun is already past its peak and is making is way back down in the West.

"Well that was fun," Scott says stretching.

"It certainly helped pass the time," Tori says stretching too. "I can make out the mountain range now."

"How long has it been," I ask looking back over my shoulder.

"Five or six hours," Luna says glancing at the position of the sun.

"From the looks of the mountains, it will be another four or five hours before we reach home."

I know this comment pains Scott more than it does me. He wants to and probably will return home somehow. I will end up stuck here, due to still unknown circumstances. Right now I don't know if that's good or bad. I do enjoy it here, but the upcoming war isn't exactly a reason to want to stay. Neither is ever being able to see my family again. Yet there is something that draws me here, for some reason I feel more comfortable here than back at my home.

"Hey Ivan what's wrong," Tori shouts at me. "You are awful quiet all of the sudden."

"No," I reply. "I'm all right."

"How is your shoulder," Tori asks. "Is it causing you much pain?"

"Not yet," I say moving my right arm until it does. "It only hurts if I move it too much."

"You are probably wondering why I did not give you the vampires touch," she says looking at my shoulder. "If you take too much of the vampires touch within a short period of time, it will kill you."

"How does that happen," I ask, wondering how something that can heal me hurt me.

"Because one of the ingredients of the medicine is the blood of a vampire," she explains. "And since human blood and vampire blood is different, your body tries to fight it off. The body overcompensates and somehow the blood becomes as thin as water."

"That sounds pretty rough," I say wondering if it's painful. "How many people died before you found out the problem?"

"Sixty-three," Tori says quietly. "Fortunately this did not happen recently. This occurred One hundred and twenty-two years ago. Everyone started calling it the vampire's curse."

"It makes me mad when people jump to what they believe as true without knowing the whole story," I say through gritted teeth. "They think they are right and there are no other alternatives."

"It was a sad day in our history," Luna says grimly.

"Hey," I say in a more cheerful voice. "We can't change the mistakes of the past, but we can learn from them."

"That is strange," Luna says swing her legs over Iris's neck so she is facing again. "My father said that during his rule when the incident broke out."

"That is a strange coincident," Tori says considering Luna has just said. "And the words are almost the same too."

"Wait a minute," I say connecting with Luna's gaze. "If that happened was one hundred and twenty-two years ago, how could your father have said that?"

"Just another advantage of being a vampire," Luna says smiling. "On average we can live for six hundred to one thousand years, sometimes longer."

"That's amazing," Scott says staring at Luna. "So how old are you? Two hundred years old?"

"Not quite," Luna says as she stops smiling. "I am only nineteen. Father is one hundred and forty-three years old."

We sit in an awkward silence, no one says anything. I watch the mountains as they creep closer as we fly. Small clouds dot the sky, causing shadows to skirt across the rolling hills below. As the wind blows gently the clouds continue south. Then something catches my attention. Two shadows move to the west then disappear within the shadow of a cloud.

I keep my eyes locked on the shadow of the cloud they traveled into. After a few minutes of staring at one cloud, I look up in the sky to see if there is anything. The only things that I manage to see are clusters of fluffy white clouds and the blue skies beyond.

"Don't worry," Lux says looking straight ahead. "I saw them too."

"What were they," I ask.

"They are dragons," he says still looking ahead. "We are being followed. Do not look up any of you."

"Why would they be following us," Tori asks. "Do you think they know Arrok?"

"It looks like you might be able to prove your theory Ivan," Iris says looking ahead as well.

"This is not good," Luna says crossing her arms.

I can see that she has crossed her arms so both hands are on her swords. I glance over at Tori as she sets a haversack on her lap. She pulls an arrow from the quiver at her side and hides it next to the haversack. Then she notches the arrow while keeping it hidden.

We sit in silence again. Except this time we are all aware of the other dragons that are stalking us. I keep my head still and constantly shift my eyes towards the sky. Luna leans back slightly and she appears to be sleeping with her arms crossed, while still facing me. Scott is lying on his back with both hands behind his head. I know he has one hand one his sword.

"Can you hear that," I whisper.

No one moves or says a word or makes any attempt to move. Over the wind I can make out a faint flapping noise. As time drags on, the noise increases slightly. Luna leans back a little farther, she may actually be asleep. The sun is beginning to hang lower in the sky that is now turning orange.

Then the noise suddenly stops. I shift my eyes skyward searching to see if the dragons are flying above us. It wouldn't be difficult for them to fly higher than us. We're flying at least a hundred feet lower than we usually do. As I bring my eyes lower, I can see how much closer we are to Haven. We might be one hour or less from the mountain stronghold.

Suddenly a whistling sound cuts through the air, followed by a second. The dragons tense their bodies, they know what's coming. Tori pulls back on her bowstring. Scott shifts slightly as he lays on Lux's back. I look forward to Luna and see her hands grip her swords tightly. I set my arm on my right thigh. The whistling noise is right above us now.

Without a shout from the others or a warning a grey dragon, smaller than Arrok, rockets in between Iris and Lux. It pulls up and looks as if it's preparing for another dive. Tori points her bow at the dragon and lets the arrow fly. The arrow falls short and she notches another. As I look over at Tori while she aims again, a second dragon comes down at us. This dragon flies lower than the first.

As it soars past, it rakes its claws deep into Arrok's unprotected back. Arrok let's out a roar of pain and surprise. The dragon pulls up and instantly dives for a second attack. It approaches fast and I can see the blood on his claws. Anger consumes me and then the berserker takes over. The dragon dips low again. I stand on Iris's back and draw my sword, trying to keep my balance on her lean body.

The dragon is a few feet from Iris and Lux now. Luna stands and draws her swords as well. The dragon reaches out to attack and I jump. I fly out over Arrok and into the path of the dragon. My move seems to distract the dragon from its attack on Arrok. It pulls up to avoid colliding with me. It doesn't move fast enough though. I slash as hard as I can with my left arm. The blade glides smoothly through the side of its neck, but not deep enough.

The dragon brings its arm up to protect its neck and roars out at me. As it does its arm crashes into me, sending me straight down. Even with the slow motion the fall is fast. For some reason I sheath my sword and brace myself for the impact with the net. I place my left arm over my face, but my body turns and my right shoulder is the first thing to crash into the taut net.

I scream out in agony as blinding pain burns through my shoulder. I instinctively place pressure on my shoulder. Blood oozes through the bandages and from between my fingers. I look over at Arrok and can see five long gashes on his back. The dragon's claws managed to miss his wings, but they still inflicted damage. As more blood seeps through the bandages I can tell that the wound was ripped open wider by the impact of the fall.

"Ivan," Tori yells down at me.

"Throw me a blanket now," I yell back.

She throws me a blanket of a haversack and I place it on the deep gashes on Arrok's back. I have to stop the bleeding, even though I can feel my own blood slowly leaving me.

"Iris," I shout. "Can you and Lux fly any faster, Arrok is bleeding badly!"

"You're bleeding too Ivan," Scott says hanging over the side of Lux.

I look down the entire right side of my shirt is crimson. My vision blurs a little and I blink it away. I continue to press to on the blanket; it's soaked with blood as much as my shirt.

"We will be at Haven shortly," Luna says looking down at me.

I can hear her gasp when she sees me. I grit my teeth and try to think about something besides blood loss and the burning pain that is searing through my shoulder.

"Iris can you fly faster," Luna asks urgently. "Ivan is looking worse than Arrok."

"We are almost to the wall top," Iris says rather annoyed.

My vision blurs again, more than the first this time. I blink it away again, but it takes a little longer. I look up as we fly into the mouth of the giant cave. I focus on the ceiling of the cave to keep my mind off the pain.

"We are at the infirmary balcony," Tori yells to me. "Hold on."

The bleeding of my shoulder has slowed some, but I still feel the result of the blood loss. The net goes slack and I look up to see the palace towering up before me. I stagger over to the edge of one of the columns and lean against it. Tori rushes over to me and places a hand on me.

"Help Arrok first," I say shaking off her hand.

I look into her eyes and she can see I really want this. She nods at me and rushes to a cabinet and begins grabbing bottles and other supplies. I take a few labored steps towards Arrok and I lose my balance. I fall to the floor and roll onto my back. I can't tell if the cool feeling is the stone floor under me or the blood. My vision blurs for a third time, worse than before. I can see Luna kneeling over me saying something. I see her mouth move, but I can't hear any of the words. Her lips move again, and then everything goes black.

12

I SLOWLY OPEN MY EYES and glance around; I'm in my room again. The drapes are closed keeping most of the light out of the room. I move my right arm slightly and can feel that my shoulder is heavily bandaged. I sit up and look around the rest of the dark room. I can see a figure sitting in a chair a few feet from my bed. Straining my eyes for a moment and I can make out Luna reading a small book. She turns the page and looks up at me.

"So you are finally up," she says as she continues to read. "We were worried when you passed out."

"Arrok," I shout, remembering his wounds. "Is he okay?"

"Tori and Scott stopped his bleeding," she says gently.

"What were you doing," I ask as she flips another page.

"I was busy stopping your bleeding," she says looking up from her book and smiling at me.

"Oh," I say smiling back. "I must have been asleep at the time."

"It was a brave thing you did for him," Luna says closing her book. "Foolish, but brave none the less. I do find it strange that you treat him as if you have a pact with him."

Luna stands and sets her book on the chair and walks towards the drapes. I pull back the cover and slide out of the bed. As my feet hit the cool floor and the room brightens. I put a hand over my eyes until they adjust to the light. I look up as Luna walks back to her chair and sits. She sets her book on her lap and looks at me.

"Were you reading in the dark," I ask glancing at the small red book in her hand.

"Yes," she says opening it. "We vampires have the ability to see in the dark, just as you humans can see in a dim lit room. I found a book about the first pact between dragons and humans. It is very interesting."

"So how is Arrok," I ask stand slowly.

"You can see him right now," she says looking up from her book and past the bed.

I follow her gaze and I walk hesitantly around the bed. I look around the edge of the canopy and gasp at what I see. Arrok is lying on one of the large mats asleep. His breathing isn't deep and long as when something usually sleeps. Instead his are coming in shorter shallow breathes. Both of his wings are stretched out due to the five long gashes running along his back. They have been sealed shut, but I can tell they are causing him pain even in his sleep.

"How long has he been unconscious," I ask.

"Almost as long as you have," she says not looking up from her book.

"And how long has that been," I ask not able to tear my gaze from Arrok.

"He lost consciousness about half way through his operation," she says flipping another page. "So you both have been asleep for almost two days."

"What," I exclaim. "I've been asleep for over a whole day."

"You needed the rest," she says, continuing to read. "Your blood still needs to regenerate. Any activity you engage in will cause you to become fatigued much faster."

I lean against one of the bed posts holding up the canopy. I can't just sit here doing nothing. Even back home when I would get sick and the doctor would tell me to rest I'd do something. This is no different but, I can't bear the sight of Arrok right now. I have to get out of here for a while.

"Where's Scott and Tori," I ask standing up straight.

"Scott is in the archives researching medicines and herbs," she says closing her book and standing. "Tori is probably cleaning up the mess you and Arrok created."

"I can help her clean it up," I say starting for the door.

"No," Luna orders. "You are going to rest."

"I'm sorry," I say opening the door and grabbing my sword that is next to it. "But I have to do something. I have to figure out why those dragons want Arrok dead."

Luna moves the chair next to the wall and looks at me. She lets out a sigh and walks out the door as I hold it open. I watch her begin down the hallway then she stops and looks at me again.

"Well are you coming," she asks. "If you want answers you will need to talk with my father. He may be able to help you."

"Thank you," I say closing the door and following her down the hallway. "You have no idea how much this will help me."

"It is all right, but the first signs of exhaustion and you need to return to your room," she says over her shoulder. "You do not need to be passing out again."

"I understand," I say walking up alongside her. "I don't want to be passing out any more than you do."

We walk along the rest of the hallway and make our way up the stairs to the floor we had dinner on the night we left to rescue Arrok. I follow Luna down the hallway to a set of large wooden double doors. Luna steps forward and opens one of the doors and motions for me to go ahead of her.

I walk into a bed room much like mine, but highly decorative. A large fireplace burns to the right of the door, filling the room with a warm orange glow. A king sized bed with a canopy sits across the room from the fireplace. Straight ahead of the door are the same large drapes that close off the balcony area.

Luna walks past me to another smaller set of double doors. She opens them and steps halfway inside. I can hear her saying something to someone, but I'm unable to make out what. Luna steps back and opens the doors the rest of the way.

"My father will speak with you," she says stepping into the room.

I walk into a room lit by a small hanging candle lit chandelier. Bookcases cover all four walls of the room. Every inch of shelves are full of books, and there are still several piles of books around the room. Marcus sits at a large polished desk near the center of the room. He leans over a large scroll map that takes up more room than the desk has to offer.

"Come in," he says, not looking up from the map. "Luna says you have some questions."

"Yes," I say looking at the many books surrounding me. "One of them being, is this the archives?"

"No," he chuckles. "This is the family library. With every generation that goes by it grows. Hard to imagine all of this started with a single book. Now what are the questions you came here to ask?"

"I need to know about the different groups of dragons in this land," I say. "Mostly I want to know why a dragon would attack one of its own."

"I do not know if I have the answers to the question you seek," he says continuing to look at the map.

"Can you help me at all," I ask walking to his desk and placing my hands on the edge. "Do you know much about dragons?"

"I do not have a great knowledge about dragons," he says with a sigh.

"So you don't have a pact with a dragon," I ask somewhat surprised. "I assumed that since Luna has a pact with a dragon, that you do as well."

"Father believes in diplomacy before fighting," Luna says sitting down in a chair to the side of the desk. "That's what we are trying to accomplish with the werewolves."

"But we've both seen what they are like out there," I say looking at Luna. "Do you really think that they will stop their advance to listen to peaceful propositions?"

"That is with I am trying to convince the counsel," Marcus shouts, slamming his hands down on the desk and standing up. "I do not want bloodshed over something that can be avoided!"

"Father, please calm down," Luna says placing a hand on Marcus's shoulder. "I know that you are frustrated."

"Sorry to keep bothering you," I say hesitantly. "How can there be bloodshed when the people here are protected."

I point at the area of the map where Haven is located.

"The people here have walls to protect them and plenty of supplies," I continue. "Why would the werewolves even try to attack?"

"That is one of the questions I am trying to answer," Marcus says slowly. "The werewolves have never cooperated like this. They usually stay together in packs consisting of their families. But recently they have joined together and are slowly taking more territory."

"Do any of your people need anything outside these walls," I ask. "They have farm land, water, and homes."

"Exactly," Marcus says looking at me. "If the werewolves think they can easily seize the land that does not belong to them, how long until they think they can take this stronghold too?"

"I understand," I say trying to avoid Marcus's piercing gaze. "Okay. You want to avoid fight right?"

"Of course," Marcus says. "That is why I have arranged for a meeting with the werewolves."

"What," Luna shouts. "What are you talking about?"

"Do not worry Luna," Marcus says soothing. "The meeting is being held on the wall top. I will be safe from harm."

"Marcus," I say cautiously. "Have you held a counsel of war yet?"

"No," he says sternly. "And I pray I will not have to."

"Will you consider it," I say. "If the were negotiations fail."

"If they fail, then yes," he says with sorrow in his voice. "I will, and I wish for you and Luna to accommodate me. I hope war is not the answer."

"We all do father," Luna says quietly.

"Now I must leave for the meeting," Marcus says walking quickly out of the room.

"I came here for answers and now I only have more questions," I say rather annoyed.

"Then let us go to the archives," Luna says walking past me. "There may be some answers for you there."

I follow Luna to the bedroom and out into the hallways again. She walks faster than when we came here. I can tell by the look on her face she's worried about her father. I continue to walk at a steady pace behind Luna. She glances over her shoulder and stops when she sees she's about twenty feet ahead of me.

"Are you all right," I ask as I catch up with her. "What's wrong?"

"The negotiations will fail," she whispers. "We are going to go to war, I just know it. You are going to fight with the rest of our army."

"How do you know the negotiations are going to fail," I ask, somewhat concerned. "And why would I fight with your army. Unless, no."

"What," Luna says looking at me. "What is it?"

"Scott has dreams like Lilith," I explain as I begin to walk. "He says that I am not going to return home with him, if he finds a way out of this world."

"He has the gift of dreams too," Luna asks walking next to me. "How do you know?"

"Because his dreams are the reason why we are here now," I say staring down the hallway.

"You seem to say this with regret," Luna says turning down a staircase. "Do you dislike here?"

"No," I say quickly. "I feel that I have more purpose here than back at my home. I'm not sure what this purpose is, but I would like to find out. I just hope the reason I stay here is by choice."

"What did you do in your world," Luna asks as she begins to walk down the stairs. "Were you a fighter like you are here?"

"Back where I come from I just finished school," I say following Luna down the stairs. "People in my world go to school for thirteen years and then they decide on what they want to do with the rest of their lives."

"That is many years of education," Luna says continuing down the stairs. "Here that would make one a scholar. What were you going to do with the rest of your life after, school?"

"I was going to be a teacher," I say.

"What does that allow you to do," Luna asks eagerly.

It's nice to be the one answering questions for once.

"I would teach others just like how I was taught," I say as we walk even farther down the stairs. "I would help them learn and chose what they would want to do with their futures."

"It sounds very important," Luna says stepping into another hallway.

"Well it doesn't let me make new friends like I have here," I say. "Or kill werewolves and jump from the backs of flying dragons."

"Or fall off them in your sleep," Luna says smiling at me over her shoulder.

"Yeah, that too," I laugh.

I look down the hallway and can see only two doors. One is on the left side of the hall and the other on the right. It looks just like the hall that the armory is on.

"Is this the floor that the armory is on," I ask.

"Yes it is," Luna says walking to the door on the right. "The archives make up the rest of this floor, and one more."

Luna turns the tarnished door handle and pushes the door open. She walks inside and holds the door open for me. As I step past Luna I stop dead in my tracks, the rest of this floor as massive. The ceiling is two stories high, with bookcases that reach the ceiling. The shelves are packed with books just as Luna's family library. All of the walls are covered with bookcases. Near the middle of the room are more bookcases, almost as high as the ones lining the walls. There are also circular tables placed around the room, each with four chairs. At one of the tables near the corner of the room, Scott sits with a small stack of books.

"How long did it take to gather this many books," I ask gazing around the thousands of books.

"We have been collecting these since Haven was constructed," Luna says shutting the door and walking towards the table that Scott is sitting at.

I walk behind Luna to where Scott is sitting. Luna sits down in the chair that is across from Scott. She pulls the small book she had been reading earlier and begins leafing through the pages until she finds the one she wants. Scott suddenly seems to realize that he's not the only one sitting at the table. He looks up at Luna, but doesn't notice me standing slightly behind him.

"How long have you been here," he asks as closing his book.

"Not long," I say. "We just walked in."

Scott turns and looks rather surprised that I'm here. His eyes instantly lock on my heavily bandaged shoulder.

"You seem surprised that I'm here," I say walking around to an empty chair. "Did you think I would be out longer than this?"

"Kind of, yeah," Scott says setting the book down on the table. "You were in really rough shape."

"Well you know I don't stay down as long as I'm supposed to," I say sitting down and picking up the book Scott was reading. "So what are you doing studying medicines anyway?"

"I figured if you keep up fighting like this, Tori will need some help taking care of you," Scott says taking the book from me and setting it on top of the stack. "Sorry, don't want to lose my page. So why are you here?"

"I'm going to look into the dragon clans," I say looking at the thousands of books surrounding us. "Surely there are a few books that can help me with what I'm looking for."

"Then I may be of some assistance," a raspy voice says.

I look up to a tall thin man, with short light brown hair and cloudy green eyes. He wears a golden colored robe that flows to the floor on his thin bony frame. His skin is a pale white, almost translucent. He doesn't appear to be much older than Lilith, but his breathing and voice sound aged beyond his appearance.

"I am one of the caretakers of the archives," he says gesturing to the many books around us. "What is it that you seek?"

"I'm looking for anything about the dragon clans of past," I say standing and sliding the chair back under the table.

"Any particular clan or are you just wanting to learn about them all in general," he asks turning towards the rows of bookcases in the middle of the room.

"About them all," I say following the strange man.

"Right this way," he says as begins towards the rows of books.

This man almost seems to glide as he leads me through the archives. He walks down the center of the vast library. He turns down one of the rows and looks around one area of the bookcase. After a few minutes of searching he pulls out a small green dust covered book. As he blows the dust off the book he sounds like an old man wheezing for breath.

"This may be able to answer some of your questions," he rasps.

"Thank you," I say taking the book and looking at it.

I look up only to see him gliding away. I turn and walk out of the row and back down the between the rows. After I feel like I've walk for hours I reach the front of the archives. I sit down at the table with Scott and Luna. I set the book on the table and examine it. It's slightly larger than the book Luna is reading. I brush off the dust that clings to the cover and the form of two dragons fighting etched in gold lines become visible.

I open the book and the pages crackle. The pages are yellow and stiff from the ages of being on the shelf. I look inside the first few pages to see if there is a title. Instead I find dates and a few lines under them. It's not a book it's really a journal.

"What's wrong," Scott says looking up from his book.

"It's a journal," I say flipping through the pages. "I wonder how old it is."

I look at one of the dates on the first page, but it only has question marks on the day and month. The year says 1587.

"How many years old is it," Scott asks setting his book down on the table.

"It's from 1587," I say calculating the numbers in my head. "This would make it four hundred and twenty-two years old."

"That's pretty old," he says staring at the ancient journal.

"That is around the same time as," Luna starts to say. "I will be back in a moment."

She stands up and then rushes off down one of the rows of books and out of sight.

"I wonder what that was about," I say looking down at the story of someone's life.

??/??/1587

I have lost track of the days since I have arrived in this strange land. After many days alone in the wilderness I have found other people that arrived here over the years. They have taken me in and given me food, clothing, a place to sleep, as well as the materials to write this journal.

The people here are very friendly, but there is a darker side to them. They seem to have a fear of the skies. Their homes are constructed only under large trees and thick shrubbery. I will continue to live among them and observe them. I only pray that while I am here I will not have to fear what they fear.

??/??/1587

Today I was allowed to go with a forging party to gather food and supplies. While we were in the forest some of my companions and I noticed a large shadow move across the ground. Before I could ask what it was I was shoved into an area of thick undergrowth and told to make no noise. The shadow passed, but we remained hidden. After minutes of silence a scream rose from near us. The shadow moved near us again and I watched until it disappeared. Once the others deemed it safe, we continued our forging.

We returned to the village just before nightfall. The others seemed relieved that we had made it back. But one of the villagers came forward and asked if I had seen the shadow. After I told him and the others what I had seen we were rushed into an underground home. It seemed that one of the villagers from another forging party was taken by a dragon. How this is possible I do not know. What would the dragons want with us? I still do not know if I should fear the sky as they do. There is something about this that does not feel right. I will try to observe the dragons whenever I am able to.

"So is that guy's writing any good," Scott asks as he continues to read his book.

I glance up him and then to Luna's empty chair. I look around and spot Luna conversing with one of the caretakers.

"Yeah, it's pretty interesting," I say flipping a few pages skipping farther into this man's future.

??/??/1587

I have done it! After days of fruitless effort I was able to actually watch two dragons. Amazingly they are capable of speech and problem solving. Not only that, but they are different colors. One was a brilliant green, while the other was a red darker than blood. These two did not appear to be savage in any form. I watched them until they flew away. I also noticed they did not fly in the direction the one that took one of the villagers. I will continue to watch the dragons that land in this area. With a little luck I may be able to converse with one myself.

??/??/1587

Today I was able to eavesdrop on the same two dragons from yesterday. They do not seem to be interested in capturing or devouring the people of this village. From the information I gathered from their conversation there are many groups of dragons called clans. One of these clans seems to be becoming larger than the others. This one clan now threatens the others and these two believe a war is on the way.

I wanted to burst from my hiding place, just as the questions inside of me yearned to get out. I will return to the same location tomorrow. It seems that my comings and going in and out of the village have many concerned I will, one day not return. If they become too suspicious of me getting nearer to the dragon I may fear what is on the ground more than in the sky.

??/??/1587

It has been weeks since my last entry. The people of the village are beginning to ask too many questions about where I have been going. I also do not wish to risk their lives if I am discovered. So I have decided to leave the village and live on my own. I have still been observing the dragons while I was constructing my own hidden dwelling. I have chosen a large dead oak, but still remains standing. There was a small hole at the base of the tree made by some animal. I bored the hole out some so I could fit inside. After ten days of constant work I now have a home of my own.

I have discovered the clan of dragons that has become exceedingly large. Most of them are a grayish color, while some are different colors like the two I have been observing. Only their color is somehow dulled and seems to be turning gray as well. These dragons are most irritable and hostile more than the others. I can tell when they are coming because they smell of brimstone. Perhaps these are the dragons that are abducting the villagers.

??/??/1587

Today I was awakened by the sound of roars and screams filling the air. I believe today I will stay inside of my dwelling. It seems the gray dragons have discovered the hidden villages in the forest. No matter how hard I try I can not stop from hearing the screams of my former villagers. Tomorrow I will journey back to the village and search for survivors. All I can do today is stay hidden and keep silent.

??/??/1587

I journeyed to the remains of the village today. I will not write about what I have witnessed. It seems that my decision to leave the village was wise. But was it because of me that they were discovered? On my journey back to my dwelling I noticed the skies in the direction of the gray dragons are darker than usual. Perhaps a storm is on the way. I will gather extra supplies today while there is still light.

??/??/1587

A storm is on the horizon. It is not a storm of wind and rain, but wings and claws. The darkness to the northeast is a vast horde of gray dragons and they are flying this way. I look to the south and all other directions for any sign of the other dragons. But I see none.

??/??/1587

Today has been an amazing day indeed. My dwelling was discovered by one of the dragons that I heard about the war from. It seems the red one is a male and the green is a female. I am hiding on the back of the female as I write this very entry. They are very kind to me and are taking me to their den.

It seems that there is a mountain range with a large cave. This cave is where the other dragon clans are mounting a resistance against the larger clan. I will write of what I find when I arrive.

??/??/1587

Extraordinary! This den is a giant cave in the side of the mountains. I am writing this as I fly through it. There are dragons everywhere, all of different sizes, colors and personalities. It also seems that these dragons have been gathering others that have arrived in this world just as I have. We are landing now I will write more in a moment.

It seems that some of these people are vampires too! This world never ceases to amaze me. I have met one of them and he appears to be in charge of the people and vampires here, they call him Xander. He claims that we should fight against the dragons that threaten our land. We should fight for peace. I for one agree with his logic. Being a blacksmith from England I have forged many swords for soldiers and sailors alike. I will use my skills to assist however I can.

??/??/1587

It has been four days since my last entry. Have lost count of the many weapons I have forged, arrowheads, spearheads, swords, daggers, and armor. My arms and hands ache from shaping and folding of metal. I am barely able to writ in this journal. I will rest now and continue making more weapons. We only have a few more days before the storm arrives.

"Ivan," Scott says. "Are you okay? Your shoulder is starting to bleed again."

"I'm fine," I say looking at my shoulder and then back to the journal. "Let me finish these last few entries. Then I'll go to the infirmary."

I flip past a few more pages were there are only two entries left.

??/??/1587

Today may be the last day I write in this journal. The horde of dragons is almost upon us. I will be going into one of the side dens in the cave to hide with those not able to fight. But before I go I will present Xander his sword. I have worked for two days forging a grand blade for a grand warrior. If this is my last entry I only hope is that someday someone will know my story.

??/??/1587

This will be my last entry in this journal. Not because of injury or capture by the enemy. For today we are victorious! After a battle that lasted two weeks it is over. There are still thousands of gray dragons left, but we have dispatched thousands of our own to follow and hopefully end this conflict. The dragons of this den have agreed to let us live here in harmony with them as well.

I will stay here with the others. Xander has plans to extend the cave and build a city for the dragons and people to live together. Somehow I am happy that I arrived in this turbulent world, because it is no more.

"Ivan, you are bleeding," Luna exclaims as I close the journal.

"I know I must have moved wrong," I say standing. "I'm going to the infirmary right now."

"We'll come with you," Scott says setting his book down and standing up.

"Thanks, but you don't have to," I say walking towards the door. "I know the way."

"Yes we do," Luna says walking past me and opening the door.

I walk out the door and hold it open with my right arm. Just extending my arm sends a small twinge of pain through my shoulder. Luna and Scott walk out and I walk alongside them.

"So what was written in the journal," Luna says walking slightly ahead of me.

"Just the story of a blacksmith that was brought here," I say following Luna around a corner. "He forged weapons for the resistance when the dragons attack this cave. He also mentioned gray dragons that were ruthless and took humans and vampires."

"Why would they take people," Scott asks as we turn into a staircase. "Wait a minute; the dragons that attacked us were gray."

"I know," I say as we walk up the stairs. "Their clan grew too large and they threatened the other clans. They then mounted an attack against the other dragons that held up here. Luna, were they completely wiped out during the war?"

"We thought they were," she says continuing up the stairs. "But as Scott has pointed out, it seems we were wrong."

"Now there are more than just the werewolves to worry about," I say.

"It would seem that way," Luna replies.

We walk out of the staircase and turn down a hallway. There are two doors on the left and one on the right. We must have come up a different set of stairs. Scott and I both walk a little faster and we get to the door just as Luna does. I open the door for Luna and Scott. After they pass I walk inside and shut the door.

"So what did he do this time," Tori asks from a table at the far end of the infirmary.

"Very funny," I say, walking towards her. "I moved my arm wrong and ripped the wound open."

"Give me a moment," she says mixing a dark red liquid in a beaker. "All right, take off your shirt so I can see the wound."

"Okay," I say pulling off my shirt and looking down at the red spot on the bandages.

"Let me see," Tori mumbles as she removes the thick bandages from my shoulder. "Oh. This is nothing serious. You only opened the wound slightly. When did you notice the blood?"

"About five or ten minutes ago," I say.

"Well this probably happened when you woke up," Tori says retrieving a bandage from a cabinet. "It just took a while for the blood to seep through the bandages. Speaking of blood, Luna do you feel like contributing some so I can make more medicine. I used the last few drops just now."

"Certainly," Luna says rolling up her sleeve.

Tori applies new bandages to my shoulder and walks to the other end of the infirmary. She selects a large vial and two smaller vials. She picks up a strange looking knife. It has a small triangular tip, like a straw with a handle molded around it. I pull my shirt back on and watch Luna give blood. Tori examines Luna's arm for a moment then selects about the same area a nurse would when a patient gives blood.

"This is going to hurt a little bit," Tori says placing the tip of the knife on Luna's arm.

"I know," Luna says.

Tori presses the knife into Luna's arm and the tip punctures into Luna's arm. Tori then holds the vial under the handle and a small stream of blood leaks from the end. When the vial is about three quarters full

Tori removes the knife and the blood finishes pouring from the knife. Luna wipes off the blood on her arm were the small hole was. Tori repeats the process again and then they are finished.

"Thank you," Tori says putting stoppers in the vials.

She walks back to the table and kneels down at the edge of the table. She pulls on a handle on the floor and a tall rack with openings for other vials rises. She places the two vials in it and pushes it back into the floor.

"What was that," Scott asks walking over and examining the handle.

"I had part of the cold spring that has redirected here," Tori says dropping the blood drawing knife into a small pot of boiling water. "That way I am able to keep blood and other medicines from spoiling."

"That's a good idea," Scott says.

I look over at Luna as she rolls her sleeve back down. As I do I spot a red dragon flying through the cave rather fast. I stand up and walk to the long balcony. I squint against the light coming in from the mouth of the cave to make out the dragon. As the dragon flies closer I can see that it's Iris.

"What is it," Luna says walking up next to me.

She holds up her hand to shield her eyes from the sun. Suddenly her expression changes from curious to concern.

"It's Iris," I say. "Do you think something is wrong?"

"I do not know," she replies. "We will see."

We both watch as Iris flies closer and veers up to stop from crashing into the balcony.

"Luna, Ivan," she says in short breathes. "Something has gone wrong with the negotiations."

13

"LET US GO, NOW," Luna says. "We have to see what has gone wrong."

"What's going on," Scott asks as Iris lands on the balcony. "What's happening?"

"The negotiations with the werewolves have gone wrong," I say as Luna climbs onto Iris's back. "We're going to the wall to see."

Scott looks around the balcony as if expecting a second dragon.

"Well, I'll just stay here," he says. "You go ahead."

"We'll be back as soon as possible," I say climbing onto Iris's back. "Let's go."

Iris kicks off hard and fast causing me to almost fall off. She beats her wings faster than normal so we can reach the wall top. We reach the mouth of the cave in half the time as usual. As we fly over the farm land I can see a group on the wall top. They are focused on whatever is on the other side of the wall. Iris drops until she is flying straight at the edge of the wall. Just before I think she is going to hit she pulls up and lands softly on the walkway of the walls.

Luna and I both jump off at almost the same time. We both land and before I can straighten my body Luna is already running towards the group of soldiers.

"What is going on," Luna orders. "Where is my father?"

"I am perfectly capable of taking care of myself," Marcus says beside me. "I was on the other side of Iris when she landed."

"What's happened with the negotiations," I ask as I walk to the edge of the wall top.

"The werewolves have a hostage," one of the soldiers blurts out. "They are demanding that we give them all of the land to these walls."

"And we will not," Marcus shouts. "We will think of some alternative."

"Who do they have hostage," Luna says walking towards Marcus.

"They have one of our long range scouts," Marcus says looking at me. "If I am not mistaken, it was the same scout that told you of the black dragon you rescued."

"You still have not given us your answer vampire," a werewolf says with his claws at the scout's throat. "Your time will be up some, as will this one's life."

I look at the werewolves below us, there are four of them. There are two on the left, one in front with the hostage and one on the right.

"We can not risk shooting them with arrows, because they will see us," another soldier says in a hopeless tone.

"There's no way to fly around them and surprise them from behind either," Luna says looking at Iris. "What are we going to do?"

I look behind the group of werewolves and can see two more sneaking up behind them. One is large with a haversack on its back. The other is smaller and much leaner.

"It looks like we have more trouble," I say quietly to Marcus and Luna. "Look."

"This is not good," Luna says.

"Perhaps we can use their arrival to our advantage, a distraction," Marcus says.

I look back down at the two werewolves that are almost to the group. Just before they reach the group they slow down and begin to creep towards the group.

"What are they doing," Luna says as we watch the scene below us unfold.

The two werewolves reach the group and the larger one tackles the werewolf holding the hostage. The smaller werewolf jumps over the two on the left and rakes its claws along their backs then turns to face them. I'm somewhat surprised by what I'm seeing, as is everyone else. The remaining werewolf jumps onto the back of the larger werewolf, which has made quick work of the leader. They begin to roll around on the ground. The smaller werewolf switches its attacks from one opponent to the other.

After several well placed jabs of its claws, the smaller werewolf kills one enemy and shortly after the second werewolf falls. The larger werewolf is still wrestling with the remaining werewolf. It picks up the other and throws it against the wall. Even from high on the wall top I can still hear the crunch of bone as it hits.

"What just happened," one of the soldiers asks confused.

"It looks like not all of the werewolves are power hungry," I say looking over the edge at the fallen werewolves. "Where is the hostage?"

"We are bringing him up on the pulley system right now," one soldier says as he turns a hand crank.

"Thank you for your assistance," Marcus yells to the werewolves. "Is there something you require from us?"

"Only to try and negotiate with you," says the werewolf with the haversack.

"I am sorry, but that is what the others were doing," Marcus replies calmly.

"Yes, you were doing a grand job of negotiating with them," he shoots back. "We are here to negotiate, so we may join you. We do not share the same out look as my father."

"Did he just say his father," Luna asks, rather confused.

"Yes," I say. "Marcus, let them up."

"What," Marcus shouts turning towards them. "They could easily be lying."

"Trust me," I say coolly. "Let them up, but we only let them up half way. We question them; if they lie let go, if they tell the truth let them up."

"That is actually a go idea," one of the soldiers says looking over the edge.

"All right," Marcus shouts to the werewolves. "We will let you up, but be warned we are all armed."

"As you wish," the werewolf says.

A few soldiers move out of the way and allow the hostage to step onto the wall. He wobbles a little, but catches his balance.

"I hate going up those things," he says placing a hand on his head.

The soldiers lower the platform down to the ground again. I watch the two werewolves climb onto the platform and crouch low. The soldiers strain against the extra weight and two more soldiers rush over to help.

"Hold the platform," Marcus says. "It is time to question them."

I look over at the soldiers who are struggling to hold onto the crank. Suddenly they slip as if the weight has been lessened. I look over the edge to see if the ropes have broken or they jumped.

"What has happened," Marcus asks looking over the edge. "Half breeds!"

There are no longer two werewolves crouching on the platform, but two people standing in tattered clothes. One is a young man with long hair and a haversack slung over one shoulder. The other is a woman with long hair half way down her back; she appears to be a few years younger than the man. Their hair is pure silver. No color at all shows, even their eyebrows are silver.

"We are not going to harm you," the man says.

"Let them up," Marcus orders. "Now!"

The soldiers bring the platform to the edge of the wall and the two jump off. They walk over to where Luna and I stand. We all stand and just look at each other for a moment. The man doesn't appear to be much older than me. The woman looks to be slightly older than Luna, but younger than the man. She stares at the ground as if she does not want to make eye contact with anyone.

"Greetings," Luna says. "Welcome to Haven."

"Thank you," the man says. "I am Kain and this is my mate Violet."

"It's nice to meet both of you," I say. "I'm Ivan."

As soon as the words leave my mouth Violet looks up. Now I understand why her name is Violet. Her eyes are a light purple color.

"I know who you are," Violet says blankly. "I watched you fight a member of my pack when you first arrived here."

"You were one of the werewolves following me," I ask.

"No," she says. "Kain and I were running away from our pack, you killed the werewolf that was trying to kill us."

"My brother was a stubborn one," Kain says almost cheerfully. "I told him that Violet and I would have no part in the war they plan on starting."

"What," Marcus shouts pushing between Luna and I. "They intend on starting a war?"

"Yes," Kain says. "About four months ago two gray dragons came to our land with promises of more land and hunting grounds. They also said the great city would belong to us. Of course my father will seize any opportunity to gain more power."

"So their clan wasn't destroyed," I say looking at Luna. "Those two dragons may be the same ones that attacked us."

"If that is the case we must hold a council of war at once," Marcus says looking at me then to Luna. "I would like for both of you to attend. Ivan you have a good head on your shoulders, Luna has told me of your strategies while rescuing the dragon."

"I'm honored," I say bowing slightly. "I will try my best."

"I would also like for our two new allies to join us as well," he says, shifting his gaze to Kain and Violet. "Both of you have valuable information, and if you truly want to stop this war."

"I will, but Violet is rather weary from our journey," Kain says as he placing an arm around her.

"That is perfectly fine," Marcus says, and then his face turns hard. "But if either one of you are lying, you will have a harder time surviving inside these walls than from running away from your pack."

"Understood," Kain says with a nod.

Luna walks over to Iris and climbs on her back. I stand for a moment, somewhat stunned by Marcus's sudden transformation.

"Are you coming," Luna says.

"What? Oh, sorry. Yes I'm coming," I say as I climb onto Iris's back. "Your father must really hate war. I've never seen him act like that before."

"He does not believe in unnecessary bloodshed," Luna says as Iris takes off. "And that is all that this war is going to be."

I look back at the wall top as two dragons land to carry Marcus and the two, half breeds as he called them, to the palace.

"What exactly are half breeds," I ask as I turn back around.

"No one really knows where they came from," Luna says over her shoulder. "They are somehow half werewolf and half human. That is how they can take on both forms, but the werewolf in them causes all hair on their body to be pure silver."

"What about Violet's eyes," I ask. "How did that happen?"

"That I do not know," Luna says looking over her shoulder at me.

"Have you ever been to a council of war," I ask as we fly over the second wall.

"No, I have never been asked to go," she says looking to the left. "To be honest we have never really needed to hold a council of war."

Two other dragons land on the wall and Marcus climbs onto one. It seems Kain and Violet are not to happy about flying on a dragon, I'm sure they would have rather walked to the palace. They climb hesitantly onto the back of the other dragon. Luna and I climb onto Iris and all three dragons launch themselves off the wall. It only takes a few minutes for the dragons to cover the area that make up the farm lands. We fly over the vast city in silence. I look over at Marcus as he rides alone; he has a distant and troubled look on his face.

We circle the large balcony that is connected to the dining room. Iris continues to circle while the two dragons land and let their passengers get off. Once the other dragons have taken off, Iris lands on the balcony. I jump off Iris's back and look at Kain and Violet. They seem happy to be on solid ground again. I hear Luna jump off Iris's back and land almost silently behind me. She walks across the balcony to Violet and begins talking quietly to her. Kain walks over to me and smiles.

"I do not think I will ever become accustomed to flying," he says looking at the dragons as they fly away.

"I kind of like it," I say walking towards Marcus. "My first time flying on a dragon I fell off. So you did better than me."

"That is precisely the reason I do not wish to fly very often," Kain says, no longer smiling.

"I will go to the council chamber," Marcus says walking to the door. "Luna, would you show our new friends to their room?"

"Yes," she says. "I will."

Marcus opens the door and hurries from the room. Luna then walks with Violet to the door and opens it. I walk to the door and hold it open for them, I wait until I'm the only one left in the room before shutting the door behind me. I walk next to Kain as Luna leads us down the halls.

"This is truly a beautiful place," Kain says as he gazes around the torch lit halls. "It is more peaceful than living in a pack."

"I suppose," I say looking Kain straight in the face. "I'm sorry about your brother; I couldn't control my ability at the time. To be honest I still can't completely control it."

"Do not be troubled by the past," Kain says looking ahead at Luna and Violet. "You actually helped me."

"How did me killing your brother help you," I ask, very confused.

"My brother was going to ask Violet to be his mate, but I asked before him," Kain explains. "I did not know of his intentions. So when she said yes, he became obsessed with wanting revenge. He followed us after we left the pack and began hunting us. I knew I would have to face him, but I did not know how to approach the situation. Luckily you took care of him for me."

"Well that makes much more sense," I say as we enter a staircase. "But if that happened at the time you say it did, why didn't you arrived at Haven sooner?"

"Because we returned to our pack so I could try to convince my father one last time not to start a war," he says sadly.

"I take it he didn't listen," I say mumble.

"No he did not," Kain says quietly. "If Violet and I would have come straight here this war might have had a chance to start. You see, my father knew my brother followed me. So when we returned and he did not, he wanted to know what happened. I told my father what we had witnessed. Now there is going to be a war."

"From what you've just told me your father is going to listen to those two dragons," I say, trying to pick my words carefully. "It's not your fault."

"It sure feels that way," he says with a laugh.

"Here we are," Luna says stopping at a door. "This will be your room, while you are here."

"Is this the same floor that my room's on," I ask Luna as I look at the door across the hall.

"Yes it is," she says opening the door for Kain and Violet.

"I'm going to check on Arrok while you show them their room," I say walking to the door to my room.

"That sounds good," Luna says as she follows Kain and Violet into their room. "I will come and get you if you are not out."

"Okay," I say opening the door and quietly stepping inside.

I shut the door and walk over to where Arrok is lying. His wounds are still hard for me to look at. His breathing is slower and not as shallow. I can't tell if he is awake or still asleep.

"I know that someone is there," he grumbles. "I can smell you."

"Sorry," I say as walk around so he can see me. "I just wanted to make sure you're all right. Do you need anything?"

"I need real food, the leaves and liquids that girl brings me taste horrid," he says moving his head so he can better see me.

"I'll see what I can do," I say sitting down on the floor. "Is it all right if I ask you about how you became injured on that beach?"

"I suppose," he says looking up at me. "Where else am I going to go?"

"Were you attacked by dragons," I ask slowly.

"Yes, I was," he sighs. "I lived on the island to the south of here."

"Is it the same island one goes to when making a pact," I ask, recalling what Luna had said.

"Yes. But how do you know of the pacts if you have no pact with a dragon," he asks in a puzzled tone.

"I know someone who has a pact," I say thinking of the special bond Luna and Iris share. "So why do you have to travel to the island if you form a pact?"

"There are tests both must take to prove they trust each other," he explains. "If they both pass the tests then there is a ceremony. After that the two have a pact for the rest of their lives."

"What are the tests that have to be taken," I ask, wanting to know more about these tests.

"I cannot reveal what the tests are," he says resting his head on the back of his forearm. "I am sorry."

"I understand," I say as I stand up. "I'll be back later."

"All right," he mumbles.

I walk across the room and stop at the door. I turn and look back at Arrok as he lies resting. I reach for the door knob and feel it slip from my grasp. I turn back around and am staring at Luna.

"Looks like I was just in time," she says. "How is Arrok doing?"

"He needs more rest," I say as I walk past Luna and out into the hallway. "He says he's tired of Tori giving him leaves and medicines, he wants real food."

"Well let us see if we can do that," Luna says with a smile. "Come, we must go to the council chamber now."

"Where's Kain," I ask looking around the hall.

"I am here," he says walking out of his room. "Violet is resting now; she has had a long day. Well so have I, so can we make this quick?"

"It all depends on if we can convince the other members of the council to go to war," Luna says. "I hope we can avoid a fight, if necessary."

Luna turns and walks down the hall. I follow almost next to her and Kain walks alongside me. We walk around several corners and up another staircase.

"So what is the council," I ask as we walk.

"It is a group of people put together in times of hardship," Luna explains. "If the current ruler of Haven is having difficulties due to a crisis, usually war, they can take the minor problems of the ruler's hands."

"So how long has this council been here," I ask.

"Long enough to be an annoyance," Luna sighs. "They are trying to become involved with matters that are not theirs."

"Okay," I say. "I was just wondering."

After a few minutes we arrive at a large set of red wooden doors. I can hear the murmurs of people inside. I reach down and turn the brass doorknob.

As we walk into the room all the talking and movements stop. The room is built like a mini coliseum. The seats are built in near complete circle; straight ahead of the doorway is a flat circular area. Steps go up either side of the walls to the seating above. There are probably twenty people spread out on the semicircle above us.

"We may now begin, please be seated," Marcus says as he stands. "We are gathered here to discuss the ever growing threat that is the werewolf expansion. They are becoming braver in their attempts to conquer this land. Unfortunately they are succeeding in their quest, and their sights have fallen on our city."

"We are not giving them any land," one old man shouts.

"We should in order to prevent war," shout another.

"No," shouts another.

The room breaks into shouts and bickering. People stand and yell in each others faces. We all make it to our seats as Marcus raises a hand for silence, but the arguing continues.

"They are only interested in their personal opinions," Luna whispers to me as she sits down.

"Silence," Marcus shouts. "We need to worry about the werewolves starting a war, not starting a war with ourselves. Now we have valuable information from an outsider about the werewolves."

Marcus looks at Kain and nods. Kain stands and clears his throat. Apparently some of the others have seen half breeds before. Some just shake their heads as if insulted by his presence.

"I can tell by your expressions that you do not care for me to be here," Kain says to the hushed audience before him. "But I do not share the lust for power and land like many others of my kind. About four months ago two gray dragons came to our land from the north. They filled our minds with promises of more land, new hunting grounds, and the great city of Haven."

"Impossible," one man with a long red beard shouts. "No one has ever been able to penetrate our walls, and to think dragons would want to start the war. This is absurd!"

"I know this sounds rather bizarre," Kain continues. "The negotiations failed today and if the werewolves think they can over throw this city, they will try. Why they believe they need this place I do not know. You should be making yourselves ready for an attack, soon."

"Attack or not," says a woman with a bow and quiver on her back. "We have enough supplies here to wait them out for years."

I just sit and listen to their futile claims and false hopes. They believe whatever they want to believe. They see what they want and hear what they want to. They hear only themselves and see a great fortress city.

"Ivan what is your opinion on this matter," Marcus says as the room quiets.

"Who is this, another outsider," someone shouts.

"He is a new arrival that killed a werewolf his first day here," Marcus says to the others. "He is also a berserker. Go ahead."

I slowly stand and look around at the others members of the council. All eyes in the room are on me now.

"I agree with Kain," I say, pausing for shouts and objections.

But none come. This surprises me, so I think of what to say next. I don't want to upset these people any more than they already are.

"I have seen the gray dragons he has spoken of," I continue. "They are a threat to us more than the werewolves, but together they are an even larger threat. The werewolves may not be able to scale these walls, but those dragons can fly over them. Therefore we're in danger."

"That is it," an old man says. "There are evil dragons that are going to fly over the walls and attack us?"

"Four hundred and twenty-two years ago," I say over the old man. "A horde of dragons came from the north and attacked this place, before the city was ever built. They were supposedly wiped out after the conflict. But what if some of them survived? Four hundred years gives them plenty of time to plot revenge."

"So let us say that the werewolves and these dragons are going to attack us," says the woman with the bow. "What should we do in order to prevent this?"

"I do not think there is any preventing this now," Luna says as she stands next to me. "Our enemies have allies, so that is what we need. The dragons to the south would surely join our cause."

"What makes you so sure," another elderly man asks.

"Do you think that the northern dragons were the only ones to have casualties in the last conflict," Luna snaps at the man. "If they choose they could overtake that island to our south and we will be fighting a two front war. If your home is in danger you would protect it, well so would anyone else whose home is in danger."

"Then what do you suggest," says a pale woman.

"I propose that a small party travels south," Luna says looking at me. "One that is small enough to avoid too much attention. Once the group reaches the Dragon's Den they can try and convince as many of the dragons there as possible to join us."

"Who do you intend on sending," says the man with the red beard.

There is a long pause of silence. Everyone just looks at one another.

"I'll go," I say looking around the room until a see Marcus staring at me. "What?"

"So shall I," Luna says. "There are others we will ask to join us."

"It is settled then," Marcus says over the murmuring that has arisen. "You will depart for the island in three days. Everyone is dismissed."

Marcus just stands and stares at me just as he did a moment before. I have to figure out what is going on. I walk over to him and stand for a moment, thinking of what to say.

"Why do you keep looking at me," I finally say.

"You hardly know anything about this place yet you are willing to do so much to protect it," he says. "Why is that?"

"Because I have a hunch I'm going to be here for a while," I say. "That and I feel more at home here then at my home."

"I understand," he says. "Stop by my library later there is something that I want to ask you. I would ask you here but it is a private matter."

"Okay," I say turning and walking back to where Luna and Kain are standing.

"So what made you want to go," Luna asks.

"I don't really know, I guess I just like to travel," I say looking at the people slowly filing through the doors. "What made you want to?"

"I have a few friends on the island," Luna says walking towards the steps. "We have to find a few others to accompany us."

"I think I know who you're talking about," I say thinking back to our last trip. "Are they Scott and Tori?"

"Yes," Luna says making her way down the steps. "Who else would we take with us?"

We walk out the door and down the halls. Kain walks with until we reach the hall that our bedrooms are on.

"I am going to rest," he says opening the door. "See you tomorrow."

"See you later," I say. "Hey Luna, are we going to the infirmary to see if they will come with us?"

"Sounds good enough to me," Luna says.

We start towards one of the staircase the takes us to the floor that the infirmary is on. Just as we are about to enter the staircase a guard walks out. We must have startled him because he points his spear at us before realizing who I'm with.

"Oh, my apologies," he says as he stands at attention.

"That is fine." Luna says. "Do you know which room the injured dragon is in?"

"Yes ma'am," he says. "It is across from the room I am supposed to guard tonight."

"What do you mean," Luna says taking a step forward.

"I have orders from your father to make sure no one leaves that room," he stammers.

"Well before you go on guard I have a task for you," Luna says with a smile. "Bring a whole side of beef to the wounded dragon in that room, and make sure to be polite. He is in a rather ill mood."

"Yes ma'am," he stammers again. "Is there anything else ma'am?"

"No," Luna says. "That is all."

He hurries off down the staircase and I can hear his rapid foot steps echoing through the halls. Luna and I walk down the staircase and onto the floor of the infirmary in silence. I open the infirmary door and walk inside after Luna. Tori has Scott wearing an apron mixing something in a copper pot boiling above a small fire.

"About time you two got back," Scott says. "You have no idea what Tori has had me doing."

"You wanted to learn about medicines," Tori says smiling. "You are learning the same way I did, so stop complaining."

"So what took you two so long," Scott says as he takes the pot off of the fire.

"Just planning a little trip," I say looking from Scott to Tori. "Feel like coming along?"

14

"WHAT," Scott exclaims. "WHERE are we going now? We just got back a few days ago, why do we have to go so soon?"

"Not right now," I say looking at Scott's stained apron. "We're leaving in three days. For the island called the Dragon's Den."

"Okay that explains where we're going," Scott says taking off his apron. "But why are we going to this island? What are we going to do, take Arrok back to his home?"

"Maybe," I say slowly. "But our main job is to gather allies for the war."

"Oh," Scott says gloomily. "You know there might be the chance that this war could be avoided, peacefully."

"Doubtful," Luna says coldly. "The werewolves had a hostage, but two renegade half breeds killed them and are giving us vital information."

"Wow," Tori says sitting down on a bed. "Do we have them locked up in the lower levels?"

"No," Luna says. "They are across the hall from Ivan."

"Well we should all be careful," Tori says, staring at the floor. "In case they are lying about being on our side."

"I don't know," I reply. "Their story is pretty convincing, but I'll keep an open mind when I'm around them."

"You would be wise to do so," Luna says looking at me.

"So what if they are spies," Scott asks. "What is going to happen to them?"

"Well, they have already given us a lot of valuable information," Luna says as she sits down on a bed across from Tori. "If they are we can give them two options, death or leave Haven forever."

"I hope they aren't lying," I say.

"As do I," Luna replies.

A knock on the door causes me to turn. The door opens and a guard with a short beard walks into the room. He bows to Luna and then looks at me.

"Marcus has requested your presence," he says with a gruff voice. "He is in his chambers."

Before I can even respond he walks out of the room. I look at Luna and can tell by the expression on her face that she knows why Marcus is summoning me.

"Well I guess I should go and see what he wants," I say as I walk to the door and open it. "I'll check on Arrok on my way there."

"We will begin to plan for the journey," Luna says as she stands and looks at the others.

I nod and walk out into the hallway. I make my way through the twists and turns until I reach my room. As I reach for the door knob it turns and opens. I instantly place my hand on my sword hilt. The young guard that Luna had ordered to take the meat to Arrok rushes out. He stops in front of me and looks at me carefully.

"So now you want to kill me to," he huffs.

"Catch your breath," I say calmly. "Is the dragon in there all right?"

"Ha! He nearly took my hand off," he says as he breathes slower. "I tried to clean up some of the bones that were left over. Then, snap, he almost got me!"

I can't help but smile as I play the image of the Arrok snapping at the guard. I can imagine the guard pulling his hand back at the last moment.

"I'll talk to him," I say as I brush past him.

"Well I had better get back to my duties," he says rubbing his hand.

Then he walks across the hall and stands next to the door that leads to Kain and Violet's room. I push the door open and step inside my room. Arrok is gnawing on a piece of bone as he lies on his large sleeping mat. He looks up at me as he cracks a bone open with his powerful jaws.

"How's the food," I ask as I walk across the room and sit down on the bed. "Is there anything else that you need?"

"No," he says swallowing the bone. "Is there something that you need? That is why you are here, is it not?"

"Yes and no," I say. "I came to check on you, but since you asked I do have a few more questions. I want to know why those two dragons attacked you on the beach. I also want to know why they tried to finish you off during the flight here."

"I am not in the mood to tell you now," he says picking up one of the last bones and cracking it with his teeth.

I stand up and walk over to Arrok. I stand right in front of the last bone that lay on the floor.

"Why are you so interested in my past," he says reaching for the last bone.

"Because," I say picking up the last bone and taking a few steps back. "I'm going to be traveling to the island you spoke of, and you seem like you've had an interesting past."

"I suppose that you are right," he says. "But I still do not feel like telling you."

"Like you said earlier you have nowhere to go right now," I say looking at him.

"Fine," he says glancing at the bone in my hand. "The two dragons are from the north. They seem to be of the same dragons that caused the war hundreds of years ago. They came to the island with offers of restoring the honor that we lost in the war."

"But only the dragons from the north fought against the humans and vampires," I say. "The other dragons didn't lose any honor."

"That is what we told them," Arrok says gazing out the window. "Our leader refused their offer, but allowed them to stay for a few days as a sign of his hospitality. They took the time to ask the individuals of the island. I was one of the dragons that was, somewhat rebellious to my elders."

I can picture Arrok as one of the loners in such a dull place. Doing what he pleased when he pleased without causing trouble.

"This seemed to make me a likely candidate for their group," he says looking up at me. "But I refused the offer and threatened them after they continued to follow me around the island. Eventually they left and that was the end of them, until I left the island and they happened to find me."

"Why did they attack you then," I ask taking a step forward. "Or did you attack them first?"

"No they appeared at separate times," he says as he shifts uneasily. "Just like when they attacked us in the air. The first appeared, claiming that he had seen me somewhere before. I had the same feeling as we eyed each other carefully. Then he recalled the day on the island when he made his offer. He asked me again, and I refused just as before."

"Then the other one attacked you," I interrupt.

"Yes," he says quietly. "They left me for dead, I know that they are the ones that sent the werewolves."

"We can't let them go unpunished," I say stepping even closer and dropping the bone in front of him. "They have recruited the werewolves to fight with them. So if we defeat the werewolves in this war, we can get to those dragons too."

"You seem very confident that the werewolves will fall," Arrok says as he picks up the bone with a claw. "If only all wars were won as they were planned."

"But they can still be won," I say shortly.

Arrok sits for a moment, gnawing at the bone. The bone breaks with a sharp crack that causes me to wince.

"You are going to the Dragon's Den in order to recruit allies for the war," Arrok says. "Are you not?"

"How do you know that," I ask, wanting to know how he can read people just as Iris.

"Because I think that you have an interesting future ahead of you," he says as he rests his head on his bed. "You said that you are going to travel to the island, and a war is approaching."

"Okay," I say walking to my bed and sitting down. "But there is one thing that I do want know."

"And that is," Arrok asking looking at me.

"Will you be coming with us," I ask. "We leave in three days."

"I will have to consider you offer," Arrok says thoughtfully. "I have enjoyed our conversations, I truly mean that."

"So have I," I say as I stand. "Now I've a few other errands to attend to. I will see you later."

"Farwell, Ivan," he says as he closes his eyes.

I walk to the door and open it to the maze-like halls. Closing the door quietly behind me I head in the direction of the staircase. I walk slowly by Kain and Violet's room and strain to hear anything hint of conversation. There is only silence so I quicken my pace to meet with Marcus. I reach the staircase and begin trekking up them.

As I walk up the stairs I can't help but wonder about our upcoming journey. Will Arrok choose to come with us? Will he be healed enough to come with us if does choose to come? I almost miss the floor I'm supposed to get off at, due to the questions swirling through my mind. I step out of the staircase door and into the halls that lead to Marcus's room and his library.

Walking closer to my destination, more question flood my mind. Why does Marcus want to see me? Does it have something to with me wanting to help his city against the werewolves? I walk around a corner and can see some sunlight streaming through the windows from outside the cave. It must be close to midday or early afternoon.

I reach Marcus's chamber and knock gently on the door. I wait and listen for any signs of movement, but hear nothing. I knock again and continue to stand, waiting. Just as I turn to leave the door opens and Marcus is standing before me.

"Ah, you are here," he says as he steps to the side and motions me inside. "I have some important matters to discuss with you. I also have a few questions to ask you."

"What do you want to know," I say stepping inside. "I only hope I have the answers."

Marcus chuckles as he closes the door and walks ahead of me to his family's library.

"I do not intend on asking anything that you cannot answer," he says as he strides into the library and behind his desk. "Do you know of Arrok's intentions?"

"What do you mean by intentions," I ask, somewhat confused.

"Do you mean about the two dragons that attacked him, or after he has healed?"

"After he has healed," he replies simply as he sits in his chair. "I talked with Arrok just before the guard brought him his meal. He told me of you."

"Really," I say somewhat surprised. "When I spoke to him, he seemed to act somewhat different."

"But that is not why I have called you here," Marcus says changing the subject. "I want to know if you understand the importance of this journey. You are going to the Dragon's Den to try and recruit allies. My daughter is going as well. I want you to accompany her as her Guardian."

"What exactly is a Guardian," I ask.

"They are bodyguards, to a certain extent," Marcus says. "They are chosen to protect those of great importance, and in many cases guardians are berserkers."

"So you want me to protect Luna on this trip," I say.

"Precisely," Marcus says.

"I understand," I say.

"Do you accept this offer," Marcus asks leaning forward in his chair.

"Yes I will," I say with a grin. "I swear nothing will happen to her."

"Good because my other daughter Lilith has told me of a dream," he says then pauses. "It is most troubling to me.

"About me saving Luna's life," I say quietly. "That's why you have chosen me to be her guardian, isn't it?"

"Yes," Marcus says. "Now I have only one more question for you. Were you a fighter in your homeland?"

"No," I say looking at the floor. "I was just an ordinary person that no one ever paid any attention to. Like one of the farmers or merchants here in your world."

"Well, I am glad that you have found your way here," Marcus says leaning back in his chair. "These are difficult times now."

"Thank you," I say taking a step back. "I'm going to get ready for our trip."

"Yes, that would be wise," Marcus says opening a small red book on his desk.

I walk out of the library and into Marcus's bed chamber. I continue across the smooth marble floor and open the door. I step out into the hallway and close the door quietly behind me. Then a strange question sudden finds its way into my mind. What are Arrok's intentions? Then the same questions as before begin to burden me once more. I begin down the halls to the infirmary, where Scott and the others are.

I walk by a window that gives another view of the city. I stop and stand at the window sill and gaze out at all the people carrying on with their lives. Most of them are oblivious to the dangers mounting outside the walls of the city. I turn to continue to the infirmary and come face to face with Lilith.

"Hello Ivan," she says with a smile.

"Hi, Lilith," I say a little surprised.

"May I speak with you for a moment," she asks. "I have something I want to tell you, if you have time."

"Sure," I reply. "What do you need?"

"It is about the war," she says quietly. "The werewolves will attack here."

"Are you sure," I ask. "That's some very important information, you should tell the council."

"They will not believe me," she says as a tear slides down her cheek. "They think we are safe, but our walls will fall. None of us can imagine the numbers that the werewolves will come in."

"All we can do is fight as best we can," I say placing a hand on Lilith's shoulder.

"I pray that more will be revealed in my dreams," she says wiping a hand across her face.

"I'm sorry, but I'm not very useful at comforting others," I say as nicely as possible.

"That is all right. I should not be forcing my problems off on you," Lilith says looking up at me.

"No, I didn't mean it like that," I say quickly.

"I understand what you meant," Lilith says with a half smile. "I will tell my father about my recent dreams, maybe he can at least fortify the city better."

"Okay, I am going to the infirmary to talk with Luna and the others about the journey," I say turning down the hallways.

"Wait, that reminds me," Lilith says grabbing me by the arm. "I have some information that may aid you during your journey. You will find many allies, new and old."

"Is that a riddle," I ask slightly puzzled by Lilith's words.

"In a sense, yes," she says smiling. "It will give you something to reflect on during your journey."

"Do you know the answer," I ask glancing down the hall as a guard walks around the corner.

I turn to see if Lilith heard my question, but she's gone. It seems like everyone in this family has the strange ability to vanish without warning. I wonder how they do that. There could be secret passages that are all around the palace. Or maybe they're just faster than I am.

I turn back and begin to walk down the hallway. The guard is looking around the halls as well. I walk past him as he looks in the opposite direction. I walk around the corner and head down the staircase before he turns back around. Maybe it only takes a little practice to navigate these halls in order to elude someone. I walk down the stairs for a moment and then emerge on the floor of the infirmary. I walk to the infirmary door and open it slowly. Before I open the door I hear someone clear their throat behind me. I turn around to see the guard from only a few minutes ago.

"Are you Ivan," he asks.

"Yes," I say slowly. "Why?"

"I have a message from the doctor, Tori," he says. "She says that she, Luna and your friend are at your bed chambers. They are administering to the dragon."

"Thank you," I say, as I close the door.

"You are welcome," he says.

The guard turns and rushes off down the hall. I turn and walk back down the hallway and up the stairs to the floor of my room. I reach my room and open the door. Luna is sitting in the chair by the wall again. Scott is leaning against the far wall watching Tori administering to Arrok. As I step into the room everyone pauses what they're doing to see who has entered.

"Well how's he doing," I ask.

"He is improving significantly," Tori says standing up. "He is asleep, which is good considering how much he protests about not needing help. He still hates taking any herbs or medicine, says they taste too vile."

"I have an idea then," Luna says as she stands up. "Place the herbs in his food. Then he will unknowingly take the medicines."

"All right," Tori says. "That is a good idea."

Tori stands and walks over to the door and talks to a guard as he passes by. I can hear her mumble something and then the guard walks off.

"Well we will have some meat here shortly," Tori says. "Since we are all here, should we discuss the journey to the Dragon's Den?"

"I agree," Luna says. "We are supposed to leave in three days, but if preparations are made we could leave in two."

"But I was hoping to get Arrok to come along with us," I say quickly. "Can he really recover that fast?"

"Dragons can heal at a faster rate than humans," Tori replies. "So in two days he could be ready."

"Did he really say he'd come with us," Scott asks, as he walks over to us.

"Well I asked him earlier," I say quietly.

"And he agreed to come," Scott says in disbelief.

"No. He said he would consider it," I say, regretting that I mentioned it.

"Yes. I have considered," Arrok says yawning. "I am going to accompany you on your journey."

"It is decided then," Luna says looking at Arrok. "When do you think you will able to fly?"

"Two days," he says shortly.

I smile and look at Scott. I can't tell if he is mad about being wrong or that we're going on another journey.

15

THE TWO DAYS BEFORE the journey go by much faster than I had anticipated. I spend them on the training grounds with Luna, trying to master my berserker ability or in my room talking with Arrok. Scott continued practicing medicines and potions with Tori. Arrok made some kind of amazing recovery, no doubt due to the medicine that has been hidden in his food. The wound on my shoulder had also healed, probably because of the remnants of the vampire's touch that were left in me. The wound opening is now the as big around as a pencil and should be completely healed by the time we reach the Dragon's Den.

I stand on the balcony of my room, looking out at the dark three-quarter moon night. The moonlight streams into the cavern city, basking it in a soft blue. I look back into my dark room. Arrok is sitting on his bed mat staring at the floor.

"I wish that doctor would let me fly," he says grumpily.

"She's only trying to make sure you don't hurt yourself," I say, walking back into my room.

"I think that she is trying to drive me insane," he says, raising his head. "I am fine and could have flown yesterday. But no, I cannot fly until she says so."

"Well," I say smiling. "It's dark out and you're not exactly a bright colored dragon. Why don't you go for a quick flight, I'll watch the door."

"You never cease to amaze me Ivan," he says stretching. "I will return shortly."

Arrok opens his wings as far as the room will allow. Fully extended his wings could be about thirty-five to forty feet. Closing his wings he takes one step back then runs full speed out of the room and off the balcony. He soars through the air and I can tell he's enjoying himself. I walk to the door and open it slightly and lean against the wall. In case there are any signs of someone coming. Arrok and I have made a lot of progress over the last few days. He actually wants me to spend time with him now. He asks at least a hundred questions about my life back home and my hobbies.

The sounds of footsteps break my thoughts. They become louder and I peer through the gap in the door. I can see Luna walking this way. I turn and look out to the balcony just in time to see Arrok gliding in. I quickly shut the door and hurry quietly to him.

"Oh, that was great," he says gratefully.

"Quick, act like you're asleep," I say glancing at the door. "Luna's coming this way."

Arrok takes his time until the door knob turns. In an instance he is on the mat pretending to sleep and I'm on the balcony looking over the city again. I turn as the door opens and try to look surprised.

"I heard voices," Luna says quietly. "So I hope it was alright that I did not knock."

"That's all right," I say, walking back into the room. "I guess you couldn't sleep either."

"No, I am too impatient," she says. "I have not even slept tonight."

"I'm just worried about how this trip is going to play out," I say. "There's too much else to do anyway."

"Like keeping guard so Arrok could slip out for a short flight," she says smiling. "Well Arrok, how was it?"

"It was fantastic," he chuckles with his eyes still closed.

"How did you know," I ask with a smile.

"Because I would have done the same thing in your position,"

Luna says looking out past the balcony. "That and he flew right past one of the windows near the hallway when I was on my way here."

"Really," I say looking down at Arrok.

"What? I am only happy to stretch these wings," he says defensively. "That doctor should have let me fly sooner."

"You are not in any trouble," Luna laughs. "That goes for both of you."

Arrok and I look at each other and I can't help but smile. I find it strange that Arrok and I have started to bond as friends. It seems that we both are good at stirring up a little mischief. Maybe a little more than we should, but I bet that we will get into more trouble in the future.

"Well we are going to have dinner before we depart," Luna says. "Scott and Tori will meet us in the dining room."

"Okay," I say looking at Arrok. "Are you going to meet us up there?"

"Yes. I will see you in a moment," he says.

Arrok stands and launches himself out of the room and off the balcony. He performs a few loops then pulls up out of sight.

"You two seem to have become closer," Luna says looking at me. "Are you ready?"

"Yeah, hold on a second," I say.

I walk to the edge of the bed, grab my sword and then attach it to my waist. I walk to the door and open it for Luna. She steps out into the halls. I step into the hallway and gaze back into the room. It will be a while before I set foot here again.

"Is something wrong," Luna says, stopping a few feet from me.

"Everything is fine," I say as I shut the door. "Just thinking about how long it will be before I'm back here."

"We should not be gone for long," Luna says thoughtfully. "Possibly five days at the very most."

"How far is the island from the mainland," I ask as we start to walk down the hall.

"You will see when we when we reach that part of the journey," Luna says.

We turn the corner and begin walking up the stairs. I hope nothing goes wrong on this trip. The last one caused me to have a hole in my shoulder. I'm in no mood for more injuries.

"Here we are," Luna says stepping out of the staircase.

I follow Luna out into the hallway and we turn the corner.

"This place looks different from the other floors," I say. "Why are there so few torches here?"

"This floor is only for the royal family," Luna says as we approach the dinning room. "Since we are vampires, so many torches would be of little use to us. We are gifted with the ability to see in the dark."

"You're able to heal instantly, see in the dark, and walk silently," I say admiringly. "Is there anything that vampires can't do?"

"There are many things that we cannot do," Luna says reaching for the door. "It is not as fun as you make it out to be though."

Luna reaches for the door but I step in front of her blocking her reach for the handle.

"What do you mean by that," I ask.

"There are some things that we cannot control," Luna says looking at the floor. "Like our craving for blood, the abuse of our abilities, and our differences with the humans."

"I'm sorry," I say quietly. "I didn't mean to pry. It's just that you seems so happy being a vampire. I find myself envying you from time to time."

"Are you saying that you want to be turned," Luna asks quickly. "A human cannot be turned unless death is upon them, and even then they must want to be turned."

"I don't want to be turned," I say calmly. "I was born human and I'm going to stay that way."

"Oh. It is just the way you said you envied us," Luna says looking up at me. "I thought you. Never mind. Let us eat before our departure."

I step to the side and open the door for Luna.

"Thank you," she whispers. "Let us keep that conversation to ourselves."

"Okay," I whisper back with a smile.

We walk into the golden lit room were Marcus is sitting at the head of the table. Lilith sits at the first chair to his left. Arrok and Iris lay on the balcony talking quietly."

"Please sit down," Marcus says with a wave of his hand. "Tori and Scott will be here shortly."

Luna walks around the table and sits next to Lilith. I remain standing for a moment. Marcus looks up at me strangely.

"Are you all right Ivan," he asks.

"Yeah, I'm fine," I say slowly looking at Lilith. "I'm going to talk with Arrok until Scott and Tori get here."

I walk across the room and catch Lilith staring at me. She says something to Marcus and gets up from her seat. I reach Arrok and Iris on the balcony. Whatever conversation they were having seems to have ended.

"So how was the flight up here," I ask.

"It was wonderful," Arrok says. "I am looking forward to flying to the Dragon's Den. The journey will allow me to become strong again."

"So that's why you chose to come along with us," I ask.

"That is not the only reason for my accompanying you," he says shortly. "I have other reasons, but I do not feel that they need to be discussed at this time."

"Okay then," I say as I turn to walk back to the table.

I almost walk into Lilith as I turn. She has a worried look about her and her eyes seem distant. She slumps slightly instead of standing straight like she normally does.

"Hey Lilith are you okay," I ask. "You don't look so good."

"I have not slept," Lilith says shortly. "I cannot, knowing what is going to happen."

"You still haven't told the council, have you," I whisper so the others don't here. "You should say something."

"I have told you, the council will not listen," she says sadly.

"Then you should at least tell your own father," I say, in an urging tone. "He deserves to know what is going to happen to his people."

"But how can I tell him," she asks quietly. "I can't bear to think of war, of the lives that will be lost."

"Think of how many lives can be saved if you tell Marcus," I say encouragingly. "You could change the entire outcome of this battle."

"You make my burden sound so light," she says with a half smile. "I should tell him."

"I think it would help you out a lot," I say. "And everyone else."

"Let us be seated," Lilith says motioning to the chairs around the table.

I walk over to the chair facing across from Luna and sit down. As soon as I slide my chair into place the door opens. Scott and Tori walk in and take their seats.

"So what did we miss," Tori says cheerfully.

"We were only waiting on your arrival so we could begin the meal," Marcus says.

As if they had been signaled, a small group of servants walk through the doorway. They carry silver trays laden with food. Two servants walk to Arrok and Iris and place two trays of meats in front of them. Two more walk to the table and place a meal similar to last time in front of us. The first tray has a variety of meats with some seafood this time. The second tray is heaped with fruits and vegetables.

"Let us eat," Marcus says.

Marcus, Luna, and Lilith place rare steaks on their plates. Tori and Scott select the steaks that are cooked through. I wait until everyone has selected a meat before I spear a rare steak and place it on my plate. No seems to notice that I have a vampire's meal on my plate.

We eat our meals, but don't exchange many words. Everyone seems to be focused on the journey. I know that everyone is thinking about the journey, except Lilith. She didn't say anything during the meal. Scott is the last one to clear his plate.

"The meal was great," he says as he pushes his plate away.

"So, how much longer until we leave," I ask eagerly.

"We can leave now," Luna says. "Our provisions are at the outer wall."

"Then I guess we're ready," I say.

I stand and push the chair back under the table. As I look at everyone I catch Lilith's eyes again. She looks at me and then to Marcus.

"So what is the seating arrangement this time," Tori asks.

"I will ride on Iris," Luna says. "Ivan will ride on Arrok, and you and Scott will ride on Lux."

"Wait. Lux is coming with us again," Tori asks excitedly. "He is a wonderful travelling companion. But why is he not here?"

"He is with the provisions at the outer wall," Luna replies. "So let us not keep him waiting then."

We walk to the balcony were Arrok and Iris sit waiting. Luna and Tori mount up on Iris. Scott looks at Arrok suspiciously, like he's going to get bit. I walk up to Arrok and just look at him.

"Are you going to get on or are you going to just stand there staring at me," Arrok asks.

"I am, it's just that we've never tried this before," I say cautiously.

"I assure you that I am just as good a flyer as Iris," he says calmly.

"Okay," I say.

I mount up and sit down slowly on Arrok's back. Arrok shifts slightly under me. He's not quiet used to having a person riding on his back. Scott mounts up too and gets settled.

"Is everyone ready," Luna asks.

No one says anything to her, we all just nod. Arrok shifts a little more under me.

"Then let us go," Luna says high spiritedly.

"Wait," Lilith shouts. "There is something I have to say."

"What is it," Marcus asks walking up beside her.

"It is about the war," she replies grimly.

16

"WHAT DO YOU HAVE to tell about the war," Marcus says concerned. "Please tell us."

"The werewolves will attack here," Lilith says quietly.

"Yes. We are making preparations for their attack," Marcus says gently. "Is that all that your dreams have shown you?"

"No," she says looking at Marcus. "Their numbers are greater than you have predicted. They are gathering their forces. They will attack and these walls will fall."

"What," Marcus exclaims. "Are you sure?"

"Yes," Lilith says shakily.

I look around at the others Scott and Tori have a look of genuine surprise. Luna leaps off the back of Iris and rushes to her sister.

"How long have you known this," Luna says, grasping Lilith by the shoulders.

"For around three days," Lilith says in a trance.

"You should have told someone sooner than this," Luna shouts. "Father could have sent us the Dragon's Den days ago."

"Luna," Marcus says sternly. "Your sister is not the same as you. You take after your mother more than I care for you to. You are a fighter. Lilith is not, she has given many helpful predictions in the past. And as your older sister you should respect her."

I can see that his have words hit Luna hard. She stands a few feet from Lilith, just staring at the floor. Her face shadowed by her hair as she looks down.

"You are right father," she says looking up. "I do respect her, and the gift that she has been blessed with. But we could have been on the journey back by now. If the werewolves do attack it will be in full force."

"This I already know," Marcus says. "If they do attack before your return we will hold them off."

"I am sorry to put more pressure on the situation," Lilith says.

"You are not causing the situation to become any worse," Marcus says as he walks over to Lilith and places his arm around her.

"We should get going," I say looking sat Luna. "Lux is waiting for us."

"Yes we should go," Luna says.

She walks to Iris and climbs onto her back. She looks over at me and nods.

"Let us go then," Iris says.

Iris kicks off and circles above the balcony. I sit and wait for Arrok to take flight. He extends his wings and then folds them close to his body. I look back at Scott to see if he's ready for takeoff.

"What's taking him so long," Scott whispers.

Before I can give him an answer, Arrok launches us into the air. We circle once to level off and then we begin flying towards the mouth of the cave. Iris is flying a few yards ahead of us, but it only takes seconds for Arrok to catch up. As we fly Luna looks over at us.

"Does it feel different to fly with passengers on your back," Luna asks as she as she looks at Arrok.

"It does feel strange, but I am not one to give up on a challenge," Arrok replies.

"So I'm a challenge am I," I retort. "You're quiet a handful too you know. Especially with all the new friends you've been making lately."

"Hopefully we won't encounter any of our, friends, during the journey," Tori says thoughtfully.

"I can agree with that," Arrok laughs.

There's something different about Arrok lately. It's like he's actually trying to get along with people. But it doesn't seem like an act, it's like he really has changed in the last few days. Maybe Tori drugged him during his recovery. What ever the cause is I think I can get used to it.

"This journey is going to be different," Scott says. "I can feel it."

I turn around and look straight into his eyes. He looks at me, somewhat concerned.

"What," he asks suspiciously. "Why are you looking at me like that?"

"You had another dream, didn't you," I say accusingly.

"Yeah, I did," he says quickly. "We're not going to encounter any problems. That goes for werewolves and those two dragons."

"Well I hope your right," I sigh, as I turn back around.

We fly out of the cave and over the fields. The moonlight plays off the small ponds and streams in the fields. A slight breeze moves the wheat making an ocean of moving shadows and pale moonlight. I look ahead and can make the form of Lux sitting on the dark wall top. As we fly closer I can see three haversacks next to him.

Iris circles twice and then lands on the wall. Once she's settled Luna and Tori jump off her back. Arrok dips low and pulls up at the last second as he lands on the wall. I jump off and turn to Arrok.

"You know you're right," I say. "You're not that bad at flying with passengers."

"I told you I was up to the challenge," Arrok says.

"He may be the type of dragon that you like riding with, but I'll stay on Lux," Scott says as he jumps off Arrok. "He does a little too much fancy flying for my liking."

"You have not seen half of what I am capable of," Arrok growls, his teeth glowing in the moonlight.

Scott doesn't say anything, but he does take a few steps back from Arrok. I can't tell if Arrok is really angry with Scott or if he's just toying with him.

"Okay," I say, breaking the silence that Scott and Arrok have created. "Who's sitting where?"

"There is enough room for each of us to carry a haversack," Lux says. "As far as riders, Scott may ride with me. Is there anyone else?"

"I will," Tori says excitedly. "I think you are wonderful to travel with."

For some reason Tori has taken an interest in Lux. I wonder if they would even form a pact. Lux seems to be enjoying being the dragon of choice.

"Thank you for your kind words," Lux replies with a bow. "I am honored."

"Then let us be on our way," Luna says.

I pick up one of the haversacks and heave it onto Arrok's back. It seems that the haversacks are made to fit the backs of the dragons. They have a slight curve so they fit snuggly on the dragon. Scott lifts the second haversack onto Lux's back and climbs on. He helps Tori up and looks at Luna. She's having a little trouble getting the haversack onto Iris's back. I walk over and help her push it up.

"Thank you," Luna murmurs under her breath. "This one has more weight than the others."

"You're welcome," I say quietly. "What's wrong?"

"I should not have lost my temper with Lilith," she whispers. "She has already done so much for me, for us."

"What do you mean," I ask.

"She told me of you," Luna says looking up at me. "Remember? You are going to save my life."

"Oh yeah," I say, recalling what she told me in the hidden cave. "But, what did you mean by; she has done so much for us?"

"Oh, I," she stutters. "I meant, us, everyone in Haven."

"Okay," I say half heartedly. "Are we ready to go then?"

"Yes," Luna says shortly.

"You know you shouldn't be down about what happened," I say over my shoulder. "Cheer up."

"You never seem to see the bad in me," Luna says smiling.

"Everyone has faults," I say. "There's no sense in dwelling on others' shortcomings when we have just as many."

"You are right," Luna says as she continues to smile.

I walk back to Arrok and climb up onto his back. I lean back a little to the extra space Scott's absence has provided.

"Ready," Iris asks.

She looks at Lux who gives her a nod. She then looks at Arrok and he does the same. Without a word Iris launches into the air followed by Lux and then Arrok. We climb high into the air and level off. The moon gives off enough light for me to see. I can tell that Scott and Tori are having the same problem. They're squinting towards the ground, trying to make out anything below.

Luna seems to be in her element now that I've made an attempt to cheer her up. She leans back on Iris and stares up at the moon. She must have seen me looking her way because she looks at me and smiles. Her eyes and hair seem to glow just as much as the moon does. Whatever was troubling her back at Haven must be forgotten, or at least put to the side. I just smile back at her and lie back on Arrok and stare at the moon too.

I wonder if Arrok has any family at the Dragon's Den. He had spoken about how he had lived there when the gray dragons tried to recruit him.

"I can't see anything out here," Scott complains. "Even with the moon being out."

"Oh, it is not that bad," Luna say cheerfully. "I can see perfectly fine. Besides look at how beautiful the moon is."

"You know, I have to agree with you," Tori says, gazing up at the moon and extending her hand. "It is so large that I feel like I could just reach out and touch it."

We all just sit and fly in the soft glow of the moon. No one says anything to break the quiet around us. Then a long and mournful howl cuts into the night. Once it fades another howl rises up from a different location. The howls continue until a high pitched howl, almost like a scream, shatters through the other howls. Then there is only silence again.

"What was that," Scott says, his voice seems unnerved. "Why were they howling like that, and did you hear that last one?"

"Those were scouting parties," Luna says grimly. "No doubt that there are many more out there. I only pray they do not attack until we return."

"They may still be gathering their forces," I say quietly. "It would be nice if they didn't attack at all."

"We can only hope," Tori says. "I am one of the head doctors in Haven. If they attack the other doctors are going have their hands full."

"Do we need to fly any faster then," I ask.

"I would not mind a change of pace," Arrok says. "Or should we keep to our current one?"

"I agree with Arrok," Iris says. "The sooner we reach the island, the sooner we can aid our comrades. We should stop only for us to rest and drink."

The dragons almost double their wing beats as we speed forward. The sudden change in pace due to the werewolves below seems to have broken Luna's cheerful mood. She still stares at the moon, but her face seems filled with sadness once again. I wonder if what Scott said is true. No, there's no way. I don't even know how that could be possible. We're too different, but we are a lot alike at the same time. Maybe Scott's forgotten about what he said that day. The one thing that would conflict is what we are.

I glance back at Luna one more time. She looks over at me and smiles again. I smile back and then look at Scott. He's looking at me with one of those, I told you so, looks. I shrug my shoulders and he only shakes his head and looks away.

I lean back against the haversack and close my eyes. A slight breeze kicks up suddenly. I feel it gently move around me, ruffling my clothes. Then I smell it, a hint of decaying flesh. As we fly on the smell intensifies. The air seems to be getting thicker, making it harder to breathe. I look around at the others, but they're not there.

I look around frantically, but they are nowhere to be seen. I gaze over the side and there are thousands of bodies lying everywhere. Humans, werewolves, dragons, and vampires alike are, all scattered and torn on the crimson ground. As I look on in horror I spot someone standing in the middle on the massacre.

Arrok must have spotted her too because he dives towards her without a single world. I keep my eyes locked on the figure. As we fly closer I can see it's a girl. She's wears a sky blue dress, with not a single drop of blood on it. Arrok lands hard and fast and I jump off.

The girl looks familiar, and then I realize who it is, it's Lilith. I quickly span the distance between us. Jumping over bodies and picking my way around the weapons stuck in the ground.

"What happened here," I ask quickly. "What are you doing here?"

Lilith says nothing she only stares at the crimson ground. Then she looks up at me, as if she just noticed my arrival. Her face is stained with tears.

"Protect her," she says in a ghostly whisper.

Lilith points past me with a shaky hand. I follow the direction that she's pointing and I see someone standing still and alone. My heart skips and my palms begin to sweat as I see Luna. She's standing as if in the same strange trance as Lilith. Suddenly a shadow flashes past her. A red spot blossoms on her side. The pain must have registered because she places her hands over the large gash. She falls to her knees and looks up at me.

I run as fast as I can towards her. It seems like an eternity before I finally reach her. By now her hands and most of her hands are covered in blood.

"Luna," I shout as I reach her. "You're going to be okay."

I grab her before she falls back on the ground. I move her hands and know my words are a lie. She only looks up at me. A tear slides down her cheek and she smiles.

"No," I scream as I jolt awake.

I look around at the others. Everyone is looking at me with the same surprised look from my outburst. I sit up and look at my hands. I can't seem to keep them from shaking and they are cold with sweat.

"Hey," Scott shouts to me. "Are you okay?"

"Yeah," I say shakily. "I just had a nightmare, nothing to worry about."

I can't get the picture of Luna out of my mind. She didn't even move to get away from the thing that attacked her. It's like she didn't know what was about to happen. My hands start to shake again and I clench them into fists. I glance over the side of Arrok at the dark rolling hills and small plants below. Everything is brighter than before; I wonder how long I was asleep?

"Are you are right," Luna asks. "You are shaking."

I realize that my whole body is shuddering. I shift my position and try not to think about the nightmare I've just had.

"I'm fine," I say quickly. "How long was I asleep?"

"You've been asleep for about six hours," Scott says, eyeing me closely. "The sun is about to come up."

I look to the east that is glowing brightly. The sun hasn't broken over the horizon, but the sky is bright orange and the clouds are turning dark shades of purple and pink.

"We will stop shortly," Iris says. "Arrok needs to rest, he has not fully recovered yet."

"I am fine," he pants. "I can keep going."

I notice that his wing beats are slower than when we first left Haven. He is now several yards behind Lux and Iris. I glance up ahead and can see a thin dark blue line on the horizon.

"I can make it to the shores," Arrok says between breathes.

"As you wish," Iris says without looking back.

Arrok puts on an extra burst of speed and catches up with the others. It takes less than an hour to reach the ocean. The smell of salt is in the air and the sounds of the waves crashing on the shores are loud now. Lux and Iris circle before they land, but Arrok flies down and slides across his stomach on the soft sand.

"Are you okay," I ask as I jump off. "Is there anything that you need?"

"Only... a good... rest," Arrok says with a raspy voice.

He lays his head down on the sand and closes his eyes.

"Everyone else should rest too," Iris says. "We leave here as soon as possible."

"We may be a while," Tori says. "Arrok is pretty wiped out. There is no telling how long he will need to rest."

"Then we will make that our only exception," Iris says as she lies down a few feet from Arrok.

Lux lies down on the other side of Arrok and soon he's sleeping as well. Iris stares out at the sea for several minutes before closing her eyes and drifting off to sleep with the others.

"We should keep watch for werewolves in the area," Luna says. "The rest of you should get some sleep too."

"I'll take the first watch," I say. "I slept on the way here."

"I'll watch with him," Scott says.

"We will see if we can get a little sleep then," Tori says.

Luna and Tori retrieve the haversacks off the back of the sleeping dragons and place them on the ground. They both grab a blanket and set them on the sand. They lie down and in a few minutes the group is sleeping.

"You didn't have to take the watch with me," I say quietly as we walk away from the others.

"Well I wanted to talk with you," Scott says concerned. "I want to ask you about the dream you had."

"I was just a bad dream, that's all," I say. "It's nothing to worry about."

"I beg to differ," Scott says quickly. "I've seen you have nightmares before. You normally just jolt awake. This time you screamed and you were shaking really bad."

"I don't want to talk about," I mumble.

"Please. You don't even have to tell me the whole thing," He says pleadingly.

"Fine," I say shortly. "I saw death and destruction."

"Is that all," Scott presses.

I sigh, the image of Luna cover with blood. There was nothing I could do. I clench my first and they begin to shake.

"Ivan," Scott says. "You're shaking again."

"I know," I say through gritted teeth.

"I know you're not telling me everything," he presses again.

"Someone I care about was hurt really bad," I say. "There was nothing I could do about it, nothing at all. Well I'm not going to let it happen. Even if it means me dying, I swore that I wouldn't."

"What are you talking about," Scott asks confused. "What did you swear?"

I inhale slowly; I'm getting tired of having to spell everything out for him.

"I swore to Marcus that I would protect Luna," I sigh. "I'm now her Guardian; I have the responsibility to make sure nothing happens to her."

"But, when did this happen," Scott asks.

"Remember when Marcus wanted to speak with me," I say, trying to keep my anger back. "That's when he asked."

"Does Luna know that you're her, Guardian," Scott asks. "Was it an option, did you even have a choice?"

I snap. I can't take any more stupid questions right now.

"Look, Marcus asked me to do this," I almost yell. "Luna is a great friend and I don't want to see any of my friends dead. Not her, you, or Tori, or anybody else."

Scott seems a little taken back by my temper. He takes a few steps back.

"I'm sorry," he whispers.

We stand in silence for a moment. I know that he's processing our conversation. He does it all the time.

"So Luna was the one in your dream," He asks.

"Yeah," I say shortly.

He stops talking and just stares at the sand. I start walking around in a pattern, breathing slowly to calm myself down. I look back at Scott as he stands alone.

"I didn't know that was why you were troubled," Scott says as he looks up at me.

"I told you I didn't want to talk about it," I say, still trying to slow my breathing.

"I guess you were right too," Scott says with a grin.

I just shake my head and continue the watch. I pace back and forth looking for signs of any enemies that may be approaching. After several hours of being on watch I hear someone stirring. I look up to see Luna sit up.

"Hey Scott," I say calmly. "You can go to sleep now."

"Cool," he yawns. "I didn't have the opportunity to sleep last night. I don't think I will ever sleep while we're flying."

Luna stands and walks up next to me. She looks in the same direction as me, but doesn't say anything. I look over at Scott as he curls up in a blanket. I wait until I hear him snoring lightly before I break the silence.

"You could have kept sleeping," I say quietly.

"I cannot sleep," Luna whispers. "I too have had a nightmare."

"Really," I say, a little surprised. "Was yours as bad as mine?"

A tremor runs through her before she says anything.

"I am sure it was," she says, shaking again. "I am going to die."

"What," I blurt out. "What do you mean?"

"In my dream, I die," she whispers. "I am in the middle of the remnants of a battlefield."

"And we were both there," I say quietly.

"Yes, but how did you," Luna stutters.

"I had the same dream," I say grimly. "Only I saw you become injured.

"Yes. A shadow flashed past me," Luna explains. "It felt so real. The last thing I remember was looking up at you. The look in your eyes, I cannot get it out of my mind. I do not know if I died, or if I somehow managed to live."

"You'll live," I say.

"Did you see it in your dream," she says hopefully.

"No," I say in disappointment. "I woke up before I had the chance to do anything."

"Then how do you know I will live," Luna asks.

Her question catches me off guard.

"Because I swore to you father that I wouldn't let anything harm you," I say, hoping these are the right words. "But before you say anything I have a question for you."

"What is it," Luna asks staring at me.

"What did you mean by the look in my eyes," I ask quickly.

"It was more than just worry or sorrow," Luna says slowly. "You didn't just look at me. You stared into my eyes and told me that everything was going to all right. In that moment of the dream I felt calm when you told me that."

I stare into her eyes as I think about the dream. Luna returns my gaze and then looks away.

"So you are the one that he chose to be my Guardian," Luna says changing the subject.

"Why, am I a bad choice," I ask happy to change the subject to.

"No," Luna says glancing at me. "But I had no idea he would ask you, I am pleased."

"Why do you say that, you still barely know me," I say. "All you really know is that I'm a berserker that is going to save you life."

"I know that there is more to you than that," she says coolly. "And why would you save my life if you barely know me as well?"

"I would know more about you if you told me," I shoot back. "But it seems like you being a vampire, means keeping a lot of secrets."

"It is not that," she says looking at the ground. "My father does not think that humans should know our affairs."

"So that's why he looked strange the first night at Haven," I say. "You mentioned the blood lust thing."

"Precisely," she adds. "There are many things that humans do not know."

"I know plenty about vampires," I say glancing at Luna.

"How could you know about us," Luna asks a concerned look on her face.

"Well, I know about how that they are portrayed in the world I came from," I confess. "Some of it I know isn't true, just from being around you."

"Like what," she asks, becoming interested.

"They say vampire burst into flames if they walk in the sunlight," I explain.

"Sunlight does not cause us to do that," Luna laughs. "As you can see, it only hurts our eyes. Our eyes are more sensitive to light than humans. Right now looking straight ahead for me would be like you looking to the sky near the sun."

"That makes sense," I say. "They also say that vampires have superhuman strength."

"We are stronger," Luna says. "But the longer we go without feeding the weaker we can become."

"Let's see what else," I say thoughtfully. "They say that you feed on the blood of humans too."

"What," Luna says shocked. "They believe we feed on human blood?"

"Well, Yeah," I say slowly. "Why?"

"That is strictly forbidden here or at least among those of us who are civilized," Luna says shocked. "We do not feed on humans."

"Why is that bad," I ask.

"Human blood is different from any other blood," Luna says slowly. "Few have ever tried human blood and been able to resist continuing to feed on it. I have heard that a human's blood is sweeter, it is addicting."

I take a step away from Luna. I'm not sure if I should be around her as much anymore.

"So can you smell blood too," I say. "It smells like…"

"Like copper and salt," Luna says suddenly. "But how can you know?"

"There are some humans that can smell it," I say looking at Luna. "But only if it's spilled."

"I did not know that," Luna says thoughtfully. "You see even now you tell me more about yourself than you know."

"I guess," I admit.

"Tell me, are there any other myths about us," Luna asks.

"Let me think," I say. "They always have pale skin; they can fly, and read minds."

"Hah ha, I am sorry," Luna smiles. "That is amusing to me."

"Please explain to me how that is amusing," I say.

"First of all the pale skin is only we have not fed, we cannot fly, but we have excellent dexterity," she explains. "Last of all, some of us can sense emotions, but we are unable to read anyone's mind."

I look at Luna's hands. They seem to be several shades lighter than a few days ago.

"So, is there anything else besides pale skin as a tip," I ask, somewhat worried.

"Stomach pains," Luna says, her good mood suddenly vanishing. "There are some over things, but they vary depending on the individual."

"Is it dangerous for a human to be around a vampire when the lust takes a hold," I ask, a bead of sweat forming on my brow.

"Yes, it is very dangerous," Luna says looking straight at me. "That is how those few vampires know what human blood tastes like."

I can't stop thinking about how pale her skin is now. One question is burning its way into my mind. She's told me so much already, what's the harm in one more question?

"Luna," I say staring at her. "Have you fed recently?"

She stares back at me. Her eyes seem different, almost like a she's fighting to hold something back.

"No," she says, a dangerous smile playing on her lips. "I have not."

17

"LUNA," I SAY WORRY strong in my voice. "Do I need to get away from you?"

"Do not worry," Luna says a hint of pain in her voice. "I can resist long enough to hunt."

"What do you mean by hunt," I ask quickly. "Please tell me you're going to hunt animals, and not us, right?"

"Yes," she laughs. "I would never harm any of you, intentionally."

Luna walks over to Tori's side and kneels down. I place my hand on the hilt of my sword. I can see her arms move, but I can't see what she's doing. Luna stands back up with Tori's bow and a single arrow.

"Do not worry, I will return shortly," Luna whispers as she walks past me.

"What do I do if the others wake up," I ask, removing my hand from the sword. "Is there anything that I should tell them?"

"If they ask anything tell them that I had to feed," she says over her shoulder. "That is the truth."

"Okay," I say quietly.

Luna begins to walk away, and then she stops and looks at me. Her face seems puzzled.

"How is it that you now feel sympathy for me," she asks. "When only a moment ago you were fearful?"

"I don't like to see my friends in pain," I say. "You should go, before you decide to make me your next meal."

Luna only smiles at me and then looks into my eyes, still puzzled.

"How can you make jokes at a time like this," she asks quietly.

"It's just the way I am," I say with a half smile.

She only laughs and walks off across the sand. Once Luna is out of sight I let out deep sigh and sit down on the sand. How hard was it for her to not feed? She could have easily fed on Tori, Scott, or even me. Although she has been a vampire since the day she was born. She probably has control over it more than others.

I look at Scott and Tori sleeping. They have no idea what dangers were just a few inches away, although for a moment neither did I. Iris and Arrok are sleeping soundly as well, they don't stir at all. Lux growls lowly in his sleep. He flexes his claws and then becomes still again.

The minutes creep by and there is still no sight of Luna's return, or Scott and Tori's awakening. I sit quietly and listen to the sounds of the waves crashing on the beach. The sun slowly reaches its climax and then begins its gradual descent. When it feels like an eternity has passed Scott and Tori wake up. It takes then a few moments to realize that Luna isn't around.

"Where is Luna," Tori asks, breaking the silence.

"She went hunting," I say slowly. "She will be back soon."

"Well here she comes now," Scott says, pointing to the darkening east.

Luna strides forward and into the camp. She has Tori's her bow in her right hand and a bloodstained arrow in the other.

"I had to barrow this from you," Luna says. "I hope you do not mind."

"Not at all," Tori replies.

She examines the arrow and then places it in her quiver. I'm not sure if Tori knows that Luna went to feed or not, but Scott seems puzzled. I don't feel like explaining it to him, so I walk closer to the sea. I watch the setting sun as it turns the dark blue waves into shimmering colors of red and orange. I listen to the others talking behind me.

Then I hear the sound of the sand crunching under someone's feet. I look over my shoulder to see Luna walking towards me.

"Are you all right," she asks smiling. "I am sorry if I worried you earlier."

"That's alright," I say shortly.

She moves in front of me, apparently she's not satisfied by my answer. He skin in darker now, but it's still not as dark as of us humans.

"No it is not," Luna says sternly. "Would you really have used your sword against me?"

"I don't know," I say. "You seemed to have control of yourself, but you still put me on edge."

"I want to know," Luna presses. "Would you have used your sword against me?"

"No," I sigh.

"Then what would you have done if I had turned against the others," Luna asks her eyes searching mine for the answer.

"Do you really want to know," I ask.

"Yes," Luna says taking a step closer to me. "I do."

"I would have asked you to take me instead of them," I say, feeling foolish as the words leave my mouth.

"You would sacrifice yourself for them," Luna asks.

"Scott wants to go home," I say. "He deserves that. Tori is important as a doctor, she needs to be there to help others."

"They should be honored to know that you would do something like that for them," Luna says setting her hand on the side of my arm. "It seems that the decision of making you my Guardian was the right choice."

She smiles again and I notice a speck of red in the corner of her mouth.

"You have a little blood right there," I say rubbing the same spot on my mouth.

She takes a step back and quickly wipes it off.

"We should leave now," she says quickly. "I spotted several werewolves in the area. The dragons have awakened, so we need to hurry."

I look back at the others and see all three dragons are awake. They seem just as ready to leave as Luna.

"How long until we are ready to leave," Tori asks quickly.

"We can leave in minutes," Iris says.

"Load the dragons I have an idea," Tori says rummaging through a haversack and pulling out her medical bag. "Ivan, get some drift wood and pile it right there."

"What are you doing," Luna asks.

"I am going to leave a gift for the werewolves," Tori says pulling out a vial of yellow liquid.

I gather up a handful of the wood and set it in a pile. Tori then pulls the stopper out of the vial and lets a few drops of the substance to fall onto the wood. She then takes a dagger out and a dark gray stone. She runs the blade quickly over the stone and a small shower of sparks fall on the wood. One of the sparks hit the liquid and suddenly bursts into flames.

"We need to go, now," Luna says her voice seems dangerous. "We do not have time for your plan."

"All right," Tori says running and climbing onto Lux's back.

Scott rushes and climbs up onto Lux's too. Luna is already on Iris. I didn't even notice her move. I turn and take one step towards Arrok, when a werewolf appears over one of the sand dunes.

"Ivan, catch," Tori yells as she throws the vial to me. "Drop it in the fire, quick!"

I drop the vial in the fire just as the first werewolf rushes towards me. The berserker takes hold almost immediately. I draw my sword and slash out with it at the same time. The blade cuts into shoulder of the werewolf, causing him to step back and lets out an angry growl. I glance behind him and two more werewolves emerge from over the hill.

"Do not even try to get away," he snarls.

"Fly now," I yell.

Lux and Iris both launch themselves into the air. Arrok doesn't move at all, but he roars at the werewolves. The sound is louder than I anticipated and the werewolves stagger back a few feet. I take the opportunity to run and jump onto Arrok's back. I barely have time to sit before we are in the air.

I look down as the werewolves as they swarm around the fire, looking up at us growling. The leader howls and three more werewolves rush around with the others and begin looking up at us howling and baying for our blood.

"Hey Tori," I say as we circle above the werewolves. "What's the vial in the fire going to do?"

As if on command the vial explodes. The flaming liquid spreads out over several feet. One of the werewolves falls dead and flaming to the ground. Four of the others are hit by the fire as it rains down upon them. I can see that one of them is the leader. He runs and dives into the sea with an audible hiss as the flames are extinguished. The others take no time to follow his example.

After a few seconds they emerge from the water. They crawl slowly onto the sand and moan. Large sections of their fur are gone and many other sections singed. Only one of the werewolves sits on the sand untouched by Tori's fire bomb.

"What was that," Scott asks in amazement.

"Oh, just a little something I found a recipe for in the archives when I was bored one day," she cheerfully. "How did you like it?"

"It was quite the display of genius," Luna smiles. "How hard would it be to make some of that for the up coming war?"

"It is not that difficult," Tori replies. "With enough help I could make plenty."

"Can I make a suggestion to your invention," I ask.

"Certainly," Tori says. "I am always open for suggestions."

"What if you cut a hole in the stopper and stuffed a piece of cloth in it," I explain. "It would act as a kind of fuse. Them you could throw it or attach it to an arrow."

"You could still become a teacher yet," Luna says impressed. "You seem to be full of good ideas."

"I have my moments," I say with a half smile. "Well here's another one, shouldn't we leave while those werewolves are distracted?"

"Yes, we should," Luna says as she glares down at the werewolves. "Let us head south."

The dragons veer to direction that I hope is south. We slowly climb higher into the sky as we fly farther away from the mainland. No says anything even when the mainland is almost a green sliver on the horizon. The sea below is a glittering wonder as the sunlight reflects off the waves.

"Hey Scott," I say breaking the silence. "I thought that you said that we weren't going to have any problems on this trip."

"No ones injured," Scott says. "So I don't think that there's a problem."

"Okay, so where is this island at anyway," I ask looking around in all directions. "I can't see anything."

"You will not see if for another few hours," Luna says staring ahead. "This is the most dangerous part of the journey, if you travel by air."

"What do you mean by air, or do you have ships as well," Scott asks.

"Yes we have a small fleet of merchant ship at Haven," Luna replies. "There is a river that flows out of the mountains and empties into the sea. It is a perfect place to hide and repairs the ships. It is also sheltered form the storms that come from the sea."

"How do you reach this place," I ask, my curiosity suddenly spurred. "Is there a tunnel or is it only accessible by sea?"

"Both, actually," Luna says glancing at me. "The tunnel is concealed inside Haven; we have it as an escape tunnel. In case the city walls where ever to be breached. There are around a hundred ships that are always prepared and ready to be used for evacuation."

As the last words leave Luna's mouth everyone goes quiet. I know that their thinking about the war. That there is that chance that Haven will be overrun by werewolves. A chill runs down my spine causing me to shudder. If that were to happen there would be no way to get everyone out. It would be a massacre.

"There won't be any need to evacuate," I say quietly. "We're going to win."

"I hope your words prove to be true," Luna says grimly. "There will be enough killing, without the slaughter of the innocents."

"As long as I am breathing, there are going to be fewer deaths than there should some be," Tori says, her tone surprises me. "My father saved so many lives, but he was unable to save his own. This is my chance to honor his memory and our family."

I can't help but feel sorry for Tori, her father is dead and I don't know if her mother is even alive. Her expression seems to be rage, she keeps her knees pulled up to her chest and her fists are clenched so tight that her knuckles are white. She stares down at Lux's scales not saying anything at all.

A loud splash causes every one of us too look around. I look over the side of Arrok at the dark blue waters below. A strange and fearsome looking creature rises out of the water. It looks like a giant light green snake with fins along its back. Its head is more like a dragon than a snake though. It opens its mouth to reveal a row of gleaming off white teeth. When it reaches the height of it ascent, it quickly closes its mouth with a loud snap.

"What is that thing," I ask.

"That is a leviathan" Luna says. "They are giant sea serpents that feed on anything that touches the water. They have attacked ships and if they cannot find food and they will turn on each other without hesitation when hunting is scarce."

"So when you said this was the most dangerous part of the journey you meant those things," Scott says.

"No, exhaustion of the dragons makes this the most dangerous part," Luna explains. "Because if we were to fall into the water, well you can see what is waiting for us. Not only being ripped apart by the leviathans, but their venom is just as deadly. I cannot remember what the venom does, what is it Tori?"

The sound of her name breaks her from her trance.

"It slowly causes paralysis to the body," Tori explains. "The venom is for prey that is faster than the leviathan. Of course there is no use for the venom to be used on us or a dragon. If we were to fall into the water right now we would be too slow to avoid the creature. But the leviathan cannot control the release of the venom, so we would become paralyzed anyway."

"Sounds like we should just fly high enough to stay out of their reach," I say as I peer down at the calm waters.

Suddenly the leviathan breaks the water again and snaps at us in another attempt. It falls back into the water and swims close to the surface. The many fins cut through the water as it follows under us. I watch the sea serpent for a few more minutes, but I grow bored. I lean back on the haversack and feel the warm sunlight on my body.

"Look at this, quick," Scott shouts as he hangs over Lux's shoulder.

I sit up and look over Arrok's shoulder. The leviathan is still following under us, but a larger one is now following it. It's easily twice the size of the one under us; its scales are a darker shade of green. I watch as it quickly closes the distance behind the smaller leviathan. Then it dives and disappears into the dark waters.

"I thought something was going to happen," Scott complains.

"No, something is going to happen," Luna says. "That one that just went under is much older than this little one. Just watch, you will understand my words in a moment."

We all watch in silence as the small leviathan swims on, it's oblivious of the danger that it's now in. Then it burst through the surface of the water again, only now it's in the jaws of the larger leviathan. The small leviathan twists in the clutches of its captor. It bites feebly as it tries to fight back and tries to break free. The larger leviathan wraps itself around its victim, much like a snake. It then starts to twist just as the smaller, only it is in control.

The waters churn and begin turning a vibrant red as the leviathan's blood spills into the water. Then another leviathan appears followed by another and another. Soon the water is rolling with fins and blood.

"So they're like sharks, they smell blood and they can't resist," Scott say thoughtfully.

"They're not the only ones, I'm sure," I say looking at Luna.

She looks at me in disbelief at what I have just said.

"I'm sure they can't help it though," I correct, but hold my gaze on her.

"They are only animals. They cannot choose from what is wrong and what is right," Luna says looking down at the red foaming waters.

"I never said that there was anything wrong with their cravings," I say. "It's just a part of what they are, they're nature."

Luna seems to have caught on to the message in my words. She's not backing down now.

"Yes, it is a part of them and will be forever," Luna says quickly.

"I don't think any less of them for that either," I reply. "In fact, it makes me even more interested in them than before."

This seems to have caught her off guard, turning the tables of our argument.

"How can you manage to say that," Luna says shaking her head. "Even knowing what you know of them now."

"I don't know," I shrug. "It must be the human side of me that continues to wonder. About their mysteries and the side of them that others don't see."

"You don't know what you are getting into," Luna snaps. "There are some things that are better left alone. It is for the safety of those you care about and your own safety as well. Why can't you see that?"

"Human I guess," I say with a smirk. "But that can always change."

I smile widely now, I know that it is kind of a sucker punch in this argument. Luna looks at me intensely. Her eyes are searching for something in mine, but what?

"You are right that can change, but at the risk to yourself," she warns.

"I've risked my life before," I say coolly. "What's one more time going to hurt?"

"Because it is foolish to do so," Luna argues.

"And what part of it is foolish," I say. "Learning about them or becoming one by chance? You said so yourself that it is possible, I'm sure that it's happened by accident in the past."

"Yes it has," Luna admits. "But to great risk to both. If some are not strong enough it will not matter. That is why one must request it only before dying. It can also be responsible for their death."

"We all take chances at one point in our life whether they want to or not," I say quickly. "Some just make a habit of it."

"It is a very unwise habit," Luna says glaring at me.

"But I can stop anytime that I want to," I say still smiling at her. "Can you?"

"I am always placing someone I care about in danger," Luna says looking down. "It is all because of what I am too."

"We all place someone we care about in danger," I say quietly. "Not because of what we are, but because of the choices we make."

Luna looks up at me; I think she's relieved at what I am saying. Scott and Tori look from me to Luna they didn't understand the point of our argument. I'm pretty sure they think we're still talking about the leviathans. I glance back at the still churning waters. They are almost out of sight now, merely a red foaming speck in the distance.

"We should be able to see the Dragon's Den on the horizon soon," Luna says eagerly. "It has been four years since I have been to the island. I wonder how you family is Iris."

"I am sure they are perfectly fine," Iris replies. "Do you have any family there, Arrok?"

"Yes I do," he says shortly. "I left two brothers behind. I hope they are well."

"They probably stay out of trouble," I chuckle. "They don't go looking for it."

"I suppose," Arrok sighs. "I have always had a knack for finding it though."

"Now there is a talent I would rather not have," Tori says cheerfully. "We manage to find enough of it with just Ivan here, but now that the two of you are together."

"Ivan does excel in that field," Luna says with a smirk.

"I know humans huh," I half laugh.

"Yes," Luna says. "Not all of them though."

"So when are we going to be able to see this island," Scott asks. "How long have we been flying over the sea anyway? I've lost track of time."

"We have only been flying for a few hours," Tori says thoughtfully.

"Once the island is visible it will only be about two more hours to the island," Luna says. "Look there it is."

We all follow Luna's gaze across the open sea. Barely visible on the horizon is a green smudge. I stay focused on the island as it grows larger with every passing minute. I can now make out a mountain rising out of the dense green forest.

"How many dragons are there on this island," Scott asks nervously.

"There close to two thousand," Luna replies. "Their numbers never reach very high. The old ones pass away and many of the young grow and leave the island. But there are still those that wish to stay and continue living away from our conflict."

"So they're not going to be too happy about us coming here to gather allies," I mumble.

"I would imagine so," Luna says.

Luna's hearing is far better than I would have imagined. We sit quietly again as the island looms closer and closer. The thought of thousands of dragons in one place is something I can't imagine. I've only seen a few hundred dragons in Haven but, this place can't be nearly the size of the mountain stronghold.

"How can there be thousands of dragons on an island that size," I ask, slightly confused.

"That is easy to explain," Luna says. "I do hope you know how islands are formed?"

"Yes," I reply. "Volcanoes under the water slowly ooze lava which eventually breaks through surface of the water. Then it continues until it becomes, well an island."

"All right," Luna says quickly. "There is no need of a lesson, you know."

"Sorry," I mumble. "You where saying?"

"Well that mountain is a dormant volcano," Luna says pointing at the island. "The volcano somehow collapsed in on itself, leaving a cavern inside."

"They live inside the volcano," Scott blurts out.

"They live in the mountain," Luna corrects. "It is no longer a volcano, but there is plenty of heat that still seeps through the floor of the cave."

"Then where exactly in the cave do they live," I ask slowly.

"Do you remember some of the openings in the walls of Haven," Luna asks. "Imagine that, only closer and hundreds more.

"Wow," I murmur.

"What about the temperature in the cave," Scott asks suddenly. "It can't be too hot, otherwise they couldn't stand it."

"Well," Luna says.

"I can answer that," Iris says. "I lived on the island for almost one hundred years."

"Wait you're almost a hundred years old," Scott asks.

"No," Iris says. "I am one hundred and four years old. Why is that old to you?"

"Well… Ah… For a human it is," Scott stutters. "In our world we're lucky to get to be ninety."

"That is very unfortunate," Iris says. "Anyway, back to the island. Water collects at the bottom of the cavern. That allows the cavern to stay warm all the time, not counting the tropical climate."

"If the temperature is like that all the time then why do they stay," Scott asks.

"Because of the eggs," Iris says simply. "Think of the island as a nursery. The warmth of the cavern makes it so the parents do not have to stay with the egg to keep it warm."

"It seems very well thought out," I comment.

"Yes it is," Iris says.

No one says anything else to pursue the issues of the island's structure. We only watch as the island continues to grow closer. As the island grows closer as the waters below begin to change. The water is no longer the dark navy blue like at the mainland. It's now a clear light blue; I can see schools of fish darting one way then the other. The water is so clear it looks like it's only a few feet deep.

"It's amazing," I say in wonder. "This place is unreal."

"It is truly beautiful," Luna says quietly.

The island is now close enough to make out some of its features. The forest isn't like the ones on the mainland. Instead of conifers and oak trees, there's a vast tropical forest before us.

Palm trees are scattered across the beaches of the crescent shaped island. The now dormant volcano rises up from the center of the dense green canopy.

Even though the island is beautiful there is one thing that shadows it with a strange gloom. In the cove of the crescent is tall stone pillar, I'm not sure how I managed to miss this mass of rock earlier. I can see from my vantage point that the surface of the stone has been worn smooth by the elements. At its base are jagged rocks jutting dangerously up towards the sky.

"What is that and how did it get there," I ask, pointing at the stone pillar.

"That is the Monolith," Luna says. "It has been here for as long as anyone can remember. There are not even any records of it in the archives. It is one of the true mysteries of our world."

"I'm still trying to figure out the mystery of how this world is here," I say. "Not to mention its inhabitants."

Luna looks at me; her eyes seem to be deep in thought. Does she think I directed that comment at her kind? It doesn't matter to me. I really meant all inhabitants, not a specified group. But I do find the vampires to be the more intriguing creatures of this world.

"We will be landing soon," Luna says.

We soon close the distance between us and the island. We pass within less than a hundred feet of the Monolith. The waves crash into the jagged base with thunderous booms. The Monolith stands dark and forbidding against the peaceful blue skies and crystal clear waters.

"Are we expected," Tori asks.

"No," Luna says shortly. "Do not worry, when they see who we are they will know that we are no threat to them."

"Until they find out we're here to recruit fighters," I say grimly. "Then they might get a little upset."

"Yes, there maybe some controversy over that matter," Luna says.

"Especially since that is the only reason that we're here," I add.

"It would be nice if there was an ulterior motive to our trip," Scott laughs.

What sounds like a growl escapes from Arrok's mouth. Although it could have been the waves crashing off the Monolith. We are now slowly making our descent towards the white beaches of the island. We make it lower than the canopies of the jungle when a roar echoes across the island. The sudden noise startles the dragons just as they are a few feet from the ground. This makes the landing a little more difficult than it should have been. I'm tossed off Arrok as he hits and I slide across the sand.

"Ivan, are you okay," Scott shouts as he jumps off Lux's back.

"Yeah, I'm fine," I say.

I stand up slowly and brush the sand off of my clothes. I can feel the sand in my hair and on my neck. I quickly run my hands through my hair, but I know that I didn't get it all.

"So what was that all about," I say looking at Luna.

"I am not sure," Luna says looking around. "Usually there are at least a few dragons flying around or fishing. There are no signs of them anywhere."

Another roar sounds again. We all look at the relative direction of the sound. Just as the last echo of the roar fades away, hundreds of dragons fill the sky. They don't look the least bit friendly either.

"This doesn't look good," I say placing my hand on my sword hilt. "How many are there?"

"Around two thousand, like I said before," she says in an irritated tone. "I do not understand. Why are they doing this?"

"They look like they are ready to attack," Tori says notching an arrow on her bowstring.

"Why are we even going to fight," Scott asks drawing his sword. "It's not like we're going to win."

"Because I don't think they're going to surrender," I say.

"Now's not the time for jokes," Scott grumbles.

Luna actually laughs. She draws both of her short swords and takes a fighting stance. If now's not the time to make a lame joke, then it's not the time to be laughing at them. Not that it will matter much longer.

"You know this wasn't the welcome I had imagined," I say drawing my sword.

"I do not think it is the welcome any of us imagined," Luna says.

As the word leave her mouth five dragons drop in an arrow formation, straight towards us.

18

THE DRAGONS DROP FAST, spreading their wings at the last possible moment they so they don't collide with us. They wheel back and land if front of us. The dragon in the front must be the leader. From the bulk of muscles under its scales there's no doubt that it's a male. He dwarfs out all the dragons on the beach. His scales are a dark brown, any darker and he would be the same color as Arrok.

"Well, who might you be," his voice booms.

Luna sheaths her swords and takes a few steps forward. She bows low in front of the massive dragon. I take a few steps forward so I am next to Luna. I stand straight and keep my sword at the ready, but not in a way that it looks like I'm going to attack.

The dragon stares at me and he lets out low growl. He then cocks his head to one side.

"Why do you stand before me, and armed too," he asks. "Do you mean to protect her?"

"Yes," I say shortly.

"Do you think you could really stop me if I wanted to take her life," he says menacingly.

"I'm not sure," I say taking a few steps forward so I'm in front of

Luna. "If you do try, I will probably die. But you will not go unharmed. As long as I breathe nothing will happen to her."

"Why do you feel that way," he asks.

"I have been assigned to," I say. "And I won't fail."

He takes a step forward and I take a fighting position. He chuckles under his breathe and then he returns to his original spot with the others.

"I like this one," he laughs to the others. "You are lucky to have him as your Guardian. Do not worry we will not harm you. These are dangerous time that we live in now, we cannot be too careful."

He lets out a deafening roar that echo many times more that the others. I look around as the swirling mass of dragons instantly begins to thin out. Soon there are only a few curious ones left flying around in the air. I turn my attention to the dragon in front of me.

"We need to speak to your leader," Luna says.

"I am the leader here," the huge dragon says. "I am Thunder."

"But the time I was here last there was someone else," Luna protests.

"Yes. That was my uncle," Thunder says bowing his head. "A few days ago those two gray dragons came here. I remember them from before, when they tried to recruit Arrok here."

"You remember me," Arrok asks suddenly.

"Indeed, a trouble maker like you can never be forgotten," Thunder laughs. "You were always up to something, you never cared much for authority either. Anyway back to our conversation. Those two came here again, only this time they brought two others with them."

"Dragons," Luna asks.

"No. They were humans, or maybe they were like you," Thunder says thoughtfully. "No one here ever saw their faces. They kept black cloaks on and never said a word the entire time they were here."

"So what happened to your uncle," Luna presses. "Surely he had more sense than to join them."

"He did, believe me," Thunder growls. "That is why they killed him."

"No," Luna gasps.

"They killed him while he slept," Thunder roars.

His outburst is more than I can handle. I flinch as his lets out another roar of rage. I bet it would only take me one guess as to how he got his name.

"The next day they were gone, and he was dead," Thunder says in a quieter tone.

"Did anyone join them," I ask, taking a step forward.

"Not a single one," Thunder says satisfied. "Most of them remember what happened to Arrok. Those who did not were quickly informed."

"That is good news," Luna says.

"Yes, I suppose it is the best news in a while," Thunder admits. "Wait, there is other good news."

"What might that be," Luna asks her eyes becoming brighter.

"We have guests," Thunder says looking at his companions. "Go tell the others that they are not a threat to us."

"Of course they are not, they are still alive," One dragon remarks.

Before Thunder can say anything to him the four dragons launch into the air. They fly off towards the dormant volcano. Thunder sighs and examines our rag tag group.

"Well there are some faces here I do not recognize," Thunder admits.

"Oh, let me introduce you to everyone," Luna says. "The red dragon is my pact, Iris. The golden colored dragon is Lux. This is Tori our doctor and her apprentice Scott. I am Luna and this is my Guardian Ivan."

"And I already know Arrok," Thunder interrupts. "I am being rude. Please follow me inside; we should seek shelter from the storm."

I look at the sky at the mention of a storm. Much to my surprise the south is growing dark with black rain filled clouds. I keep my eyes locked on the storm. A flash of lightning causes me to blink.

"Yes thank you," Luna says shortly.

Everyone mounts up onto the dragons and we launch into the air. Thunder leads us over the thick lush jungle. I'm glad we didn't have to make the journey to the mountain on foot. If the floor if the jungle is half as thick as the canopies up here it looks like it would take days to navigate.

We glide into the mouth of the large cavern and not a moment too soon. Arrok and I are the last in the group, just as we pass into the cave a blast of wind rushes past us. The ferocity of the wind brings back the memory of the night of back home. Just before Scott and I were taken through the gateway. That seems like years ago now.

I look out at the darkening skies as the wind roars past the entrance of the cave. There are still a few dragons trying to navigate the winds. As soon as they try to spread their wings the wing rips them open and carries away from the cave. Then they close them and drop back towards the cave.

"Are they going to be alright," I ask.

"Yes," Arrok answers. "It is a little game that the younger ones play. A test of who is the best flyer."

"Did you ever play," I ask.

"I did," Arrok answers shortly.

"What happened," I prod.

"They would not let me join after awhile," Arrok laughs. "I kept winning."

We sit and watch the dragons play their game for a few more minutes. Once all the dragons have landed in the cave it was clear that it was a strenuous game. The last two dragons to enter had been neck and neck the entire time. They collapse on the cave floor exhausted.

"It is also a game of the foolish for those that do not know when to stop," Arrok informs. "You stayed out too long."

The two dragons only look up at him and nod their heads, still gasping for air. Arrok walks off leaving the two on the floor. I walk after Arrok as he heads towards the others. I walk slower, viewing the cave as I go.

The cave isn't nearly the size of the one that houses the city of Haven, but it is very impressive. Stalactites and stalagmites are everywhere; I suppose the ones at Haven were cleared out. More room for builds on the floor and the ones on the ceiling would pose a hazard if they broke. That's my guess at least. The walls of the cave are covered with large holes. It almost looks like a bee hive with the opening evenly spaced. I glance at some of the openings on the floor level. There are dragons in some of them.

I continue along, still gazing at the complexity of this place. It seems that the openings won't hold any more than two adults. A third full grown dragon would make things a little crowded. But if there are only two it seems quite spacious. I walk along behind Arrok watching dragons fly in and out of their apartment like dwellings. We come to a large open area where there are no stalagmites on the floor.

The rest of our group is already there with Thunder. They sit in a nearly complete circle waiting for Arrok and me to arrive. We both sit down and we now have a whole circle. Everyone looks around as if making sure that no one is missing. When everyone stops looking around Thunder is the one who break the silence.

"Now that we are out of the elements we can continue our conversation." Thunder says his voice booms and echoes through the cave. "Where were we?"

"You told us of how the two dragons left," Luna says, picking her words carefully. "None of you ranks joined them."

"Oh, yes," Thunder says grimly. "They said that they were going to make this land the way it was before the humans took it from us. They said that humans should be happy with the world they wanted in the first place."

"Wait a second," I interrupt. "I'm lost here. What do they mean by the world we wanted in the first place?"

"We were all from your world originally," Thunder explains. "When your world was young we all lived in peace, but that soon ended. Humans began settling down and staying in one place. Many settled where the land was fertile and animals for hunting were abundant."

Thunder looks at me to make sure I'm keeping up. I nod at him to continue.

"This upset the dragons," Thunder continues. "We were very territorial at the time. Soon a conflict broke out between our two races. The war lasted for several years. Then everything changed when the human found, what we now call gateways. They would retreat from the battlefield, and of course we were set on driving them away. Then the gateways opened, our numbers slowly dwindle. Then there were none of us left."

"Okay that explains how your kind came here," Scott says. "What about the werewolves and the vampires. How did they come here?"

"I can explain that," Luna says. "By the time the humans finally forced the dragons out it was what you call, the dark ages. This is when the werewolves took advantage of your superstitions. On nights of a full moon they would descend from their hiding places feeding on anyone foolish enough to be out alone, or in small group. You believed in safety in numbers. You then commenced to hunting and weeding out of the werewolves."

"By weeding out do you mean killing or the use of the gateways," I ask.

"Both," Luna says. "Those that would not go to the gateways were killed. But then only your high leaders knew of the gateways and there locations. Years past and many of our kind went into hiding. Few dared to venture among your kind for fear of meeting the same fate as the others."

A heavy shame begins to weigh on my shoulders. I can't believe we could do something so terrible. I know that at some point we find the vampires too.

"Unfortunately some of us became careless," Luna says. "They took up jobs and even started families, all of which looked human of course. They began feeding on humans occasionally, and then one was captured. The humans found that they could heal faster. They took our gift and used it against us. They tortured their captive until they gave up the whereabouts of the others. Then they would finally end their life when they had the information that they wanted."

I can't even look at Luna as she tells the story. I don't want to know that my kind was responsible for so much pain and suffering, but I can't stop listening.

"The humans form a group dedicated to hunting vampires," Luna says her voice unchanging. "They called themselves slayers. They became the only ones left that knew about the gateways besides us, and they used them. Since we look just like humans it took them longer to find us. We don't even know if they managed to remove all of us."

This makes me feel a little bit better, to know that a few of them weren't uprooted from their home.

"When explorers discovered the new world we fled to it," Luna continues. "But it was already too late; it only took them another decade to erase us from their world and their history books. That is our story of how we came here. Of course the gateways still work perfectly well, as you two know."

I stare at the floor; I don't want to even see the faces of those around me. I stand and walk away from the group without a word. I walk back through the cave to the entrance. It seems that just as fast as the storm had arrived it's now gone. The ground is wet and littered with branches and debris. But the sun is now setting and the island is growing darker.

I walk out into the jungle not caring about the coming darkness, or were I'm going. I just have to get away so I can think clearly. I find a narrow path in the jungle; most likely it belongs to one of the animals that live here. It doesn't matter to me were it leads. So long as it leads me somewhere. The minutes become longer and I begin to wonder if I'm travelling in a circle. I know that it would be useless to try and turn back now.

Just as my body tells me to turn back, as the doubt enters my mind, I emerge on the beach. The gentle sounds of the waves lapping at the sand distract me from my thoughts. The moon sends white glowing shimmers off the water. I walk over to a fallen palm tree and sit down on it. The air is warm and humid even at night; I look up at the moon. All the clouds in the sky have been swept away by the winds of the storm.

I hear the sudden crunch of sand, but I make no effort to draw my sword. I don't care right now.

"What happened to you back there," Luna asks. "Are you all right?"

"Yeah, fine." I say shortly. "What are you doing here?"

"Is it not obvious," Luna says. "Everyone was worried about you. Someone had to find you."

"How did you find me," I ask, still not able to look at her.

"I followed you scent," Luna informs me. "Another advantage of being a vampire, we can smell blood. But I cannot smell the individual's blood."

"Oh," I mumble.

"So, what is wrong," Luna asks sitting down on the fallen tree next to me.

"It's your history," I explain. "We caused you so much pain, so much suffering. Now here we are trying to take this world too. Do you know what we do in our world now?"

"I cannot say that I do," Luna says.

"We went to war with each other," I say. "We drove all of you out and now we're trying to drive ourselves out."

"It is not your fault," Luna says. "You were not the one to drive any of us out."

"But my kind did," I say through gritted teeth. "We were still responsible. Now here I am fighting against the ones we got rid of."

"You are not like those before you," Luna says comfortingly. "You are helping us, not forcing us out."

"I don't know," I say. "I still feel somehow responsible for what we did."

"You should not," Luna says.

I don't say anything in response to her words. I only gaze around at the moonlit beach. Then something catches my eye, something glowing softly at the dark edge of the jungle.

"What is that," I say as I stand and walk towards it.

"Oh, that," Luna says getting up and walking beside me. "That is a flower."

"Why is it glowing," I ask.

"It is called a Lunar Luminous," Luna explains. "Most people just call it a moon flower, because it glows like the moon."

"Are they poisonous," I ask kneeling down by the glowing patch.

"No they are not," Luna says.

I pick the flower and examine it. It looks just like a tulip. Except the petal are a little more open like a rose and it glows. The petals are white and glow the same dull light blue as the moon.

"It's amazing," I say.

"They are my favorite," Luna says touching one of the flowers. "My mother named me after them."

I think for a moment and then the realization hits me.

"I would have never thought," I say.

"Neither did my father," Luna laughs. "He says as soon as she said the name he agreed."

"Well then this is for you," I say handing the flower to Luna.

"What for," she says confused.

"My way of saying sorry for all the things that have happened to your kind," I say.

"Thank you," Luna says taking the flower. "But you have done nothing to us. This place is my home, I was born here. There is nothing you can do about that. You seem to have become fond of this place yourself. Do you not miss you home and family?"

"I miss my family," I say. "That's it."

"I never felt the same as everyone else there," I confess. "I didn't want to be like everyone else. You know go to school, get a job, never really do anything great or important."

"And now you are here," Luna smiles "Making enemies, fighting all the time and you seem quiet comfortable about it too."

"That I can't explain, back home I never fought, but here it seems like a way of life," I say. "Here it comes natural to me. Do you think the passing through that gateway has something to do with it?"

"I cannot say," Luna mutters. "It could be, or maybe you understand your true purpose here. You did not feel at home there because you truly were not."

"How can this place be my home when I wasn't ever here before," I ask.

"Maybe not you, but an ancestor," Luna says. "You could have someone in your bloodline that came here and somehow returned."

"But if they returned why don't you," I say. "You, the werewolves and the dragons could take back what you deserve. You would be nearly unstoppable; you would have the element of surprise."

"Why do speak like this," Luna asks horrified. "They are your kind."

"Let's face it my kind isn't all that great," I say coldly. "I often find myself hating them. We thrive on conflict, we trust lies and call them truth and we go about thinking we're good people for it."

"As soon as I think I know you," Luna says sadly. "You show me a new side of you that I never knew existed. I still want to know why."

"I'm sorry," I say. "It's because of what you and Thunder said in the cave. About how you came here, it makes me sick. If you took back that world they deserve their fate. I deserve that fate."

"I did not think that our history would upset you," Luna says. "But not everyone here holds a grudge as you think."

"The werewolves do," I yell my voice echoing across the beach. "You'll never understand what I'm feeling right now. I don't even know if I understand what I'm feeling."

"Then tell me," Luna says quietly and calmly.

"I'm human," I say darkly. "They hate me, because I'm human. Not because of whom I am, but what I am. There's an immense hate directed at humans."

"I am sorry," Luna says quietly.

"It's not your fault," I say. "It's mine. If they want to kill me, they can."

"Do not talk like that," Luna interrupts.

"Let me finish," I say. "If they want to kill me they can, but I'm going to take as many of them down before I do. Like I said war is all we're good at. Not that it's going to help. I heal slowly; my body is weak compared to every creature here."

"You truly dislike being human," Luna says slowly.

"Sometimes I do," I say shortly. "I'm one of the few that's not like all other humans, but being human makes everyone else think I'm just like them."

"You want to be turned," Luna says shaking her head. "As I have said before I am not allowed to under these circumstances."

"I know," I say calmly. "I don't want to change. I just want to prove that we're not all the same. But now that you have spurred my interest, how does one become a vampire. Is it the bite like in our myths?"

"No," Luna says with a smile. "It's the blood. It changes the human's body until there is no more human left in the person. I hear it is quiet painful too. Some have actually died during the process of turning. I have heard someone in the infirmary that was turning. His screams filled the halls for four days and nights. In the morning when everything was silent, we thought he was dead."

"It was Simon, wasn't it," I ask.

"Yes, how did you know," Luna asks.

"I guessed," I say. "Anyway does the turning time the same amount of time for everyone?"

"It is different for the individual," Luna explains. "Just like the cravings to feed. The longer the turning takes the less pain there is, but the shorter the time the more pain."

"So if one was to turn faster," I say.

"It would more likely kill them," Luna says looking at the ground. "If the wounds have caused a large amount of blood loss, the turning will also happen faster. There have only been a handful of people that have turned in a single day or night and lived."

"Wow," I say. "I'll just stay a human, pathetic huh?"

"You give yourself less credit than you think," Luna says.

"Yeah," I say unconvinced.

We walk back to the fallen palm tree and sit down. We watch the waves as they collide with the shore. The moonlight plays across the water and time drags on. Then the sound of wings becomes clear over the waves. The sound grows and then Iris and Arrok land quietly on the sand.

"We were concerned," Iris says. "We came to make sure everything is all right."

"Yes everything is fine," Luna says. "Is Thunder still waiting?"

"Patiently, yes," Arrok says looking at me. "For how much longer I cannot say."

"Let's go then," I say walking across the sand and climbing onto Arrok's back.

Luna climbs up onto Iris and we take off. We fly silently over the jungle that took me hours to navigate. It only takes minutes to reach the cave. As we fly into the cavern, but the dragons don't land. They fly straight back to the now semicircle group that's waiting for our return. We land quickly and assume our original seating arrangements.

"So," Thunder says glancing at me. "Now that everyone has returned, why have you come to our island?"

"We seek your aid," Luna answers. "The werewolves are going to attack Haven with the help of those two dragons."

"So you have come to gather allies for a war that does not concern us," Thunder says his patience now gone. "Is that the only reason you have come to my home? To try and tear us from the peace that we have just as they did?"

"No, it is not," Arrok says.

"And what other reason might that be," Thunder asks. "Well speak up."

"I have come to form a pact," Arrok says looking down at me. "With the boy."

19

THERE'S AN AWKWARD SILENCE after what Arrok has just said. All eyes in the circle fall upon us. They shift from Arrok to me and back.

"Really," Thunder says amused.

"What," I exclaim. "Why would you want to make a pact with me? I haven't done anything for you to want to."

"Quiet the opposite," Arrok says looking down at me. "I have been looking back at the last few weeks. You have saved my life twice and almost lost yours one time by doing so. You were the one that was interested in who I was and who I am. You took my mind away from the pain while I recovered."

"I didn't really know I was doing that," I say still shocked. "I mean I tried to help when I could."

"You did and for that I would like to return the favor," Arrok says. "We both share a common goal."

"And what is the goal," I ask.

"To survive here," Arrok says in a low tone. "You yourself have seen what it is like here. It is a dangerous place with few friends and many enemies."

I look around at the others. Their eyes are still fixed on us. All of them have a shocked and confused expression, except Luna. She sits smiling as she watches the scene unfold. Could she have known about this before me? I look at her a moment longer and she nods.

"This is really unexpected," I say. "Are you sure this is something that you want to do?"

"There is no doubt in my mind," Arrok replies. "All you have to do is give your answer when you are ready."

"Yes," I breathe. "I would be honored."

"Excellent," Thunder laughs. "Let the tests begin."

"Wait, what," I stutter. "There are tests?"

"Certainly," Thunder says. "If there were not we could never tell if you truly trust in your pact."

"But isn't just wanting the pact enough," I ask.

"Somewhat," Thunder says. "Then there is a trust that goes deeper than just wanting the pact. There is the trust in your pact to protect your life, and trusting the other's decisions when they are right."

"Okay," I say. "Let's get started on the tests. I'm ready."

"Well let me make amends," Thunder says suddenly. "I have just realized something. Arrok you said that he has saved your life twice, correct?"

"Yes," Arrok answers.

"Then I believe we can make an exception," Thunder says thoughtfully. "You see the first test would have been the human's willingness to protect his pact. If what you said is true, then we can make minor adjustment."

"You don't have to," I say eagerly. "I will take the test if it is something that I have to do."

"No," Thunder says sternly. "I have seen your determination already. You seem to be very eager to embrace death and yet you never do. You honored your agreement to protect the girl on the beach when you arrived. When you became angered by our history and left, Arrok told me of what you did for him on the beach and what you did in the air shortly there after. You have more than passed the first test."

"Thank you," Arrok and I say at the same time.

We both look at each other for a brief moment. He seems different now that I know his intensions. He no longer seems like he's trying to avoid the company of others. Obviously he wants to form a pact, oddly enough with me.

"The next test is sort of two tests in one," Thunder says. "It will require trust from the human and the determination of the dragon to protect him."

"Okay," I say before anyone else can say anything. "I'm ready."

"There will be one minor complication though," Thunder says suddenly. "It takes place on the Monolith. Any event that involves a creature so much as touching the Monolith tends to draw a crowd."

Great, now we get to have a bunch of dragons watching us. Shouldn't a pact be more private, not a public viewing? A pact is between two not two thousand.

"It will not be a problem," Arrok says. "Let them watch if they want to, they have seen the tests of a pact here hundreds of times before, they know what is going to happen."

"What's the big deal with the Monolith anyway," I ask.

"Well no one knows how or when it was created," Thunder replies. "It does not help that around a hundred years ago a human decided to dive off of it."

"How did that go," I ask, knowing the answer already.

"He successfully made the dive," Thunder says. "Unfortunately he forgot about the leviathans that sometimes come into the cove."

"Back in our world there are thrill seekers like that everywhere," Scott says. "They're all adrenaline and no brains. The more dangerous the situation they can find the faster they'll throw themselves into it."

"Well that's not entirely true," I counter. "Look at you and me, at half of us here. We're about to go fight thousands of werewolves. Where's the thrill seekers now?"

"You're right," Scott says with a smile. "I guess, but you seem a little more eager to fight them than I do."

"I guess," I say with a smirk. "Back to the next test though, when are we going to do this?"

"As you have seen, it is night," Thunder informs. "It would be wise to begin in the morning."

"We will," Arrok says shortly. "Come there are some vacant nests over there."

Thunder launches himself into the air and flies deeper into the cave. I stand and watch him disappear as the cave angles down. I look around at the others as they mount up on the dragons. I climb onto

Arrok's back and we launch into the air just as the others do. Arrok flies towards the wall and lands in the highest opening.

"How do you know that this one doesn't belong to any other dragons," I ask as jump of his back.

"Everyone one of us has a unique smell, just as you do," Arrok explains. "This nest has not been used in years."

"Okay," I say looking around the small cave. "You know I would have never guessed you to have wanted to make a pact with anyone."

"What do you mean," Arrok ask confusion clear in his voice.

"When we found you on the beach," I say picking my words carefully. "You didn't seem to want any help, you seemed angry at the world."

"I was not angry with anyone but myself," Arrok says coldly. "The only thing I was focused on was revenge. When I was attacked again, I wasn't as angry then as confused. Here was a human that did not know me, yet he was risking his life to protect mine. The entire time that you were unconscious I blamed myself."

"The whole losing consciousness thing was my fault actually," I say rubbing my shoulder were the claw had punctured. "I shouldn't have jumped off Iris's back."

The sound of wings causes me to look out at the opening. Iris flies by, just low enough for Luna to jump off into the mouth of the nest. She looks from me to Arrok and then back to me.

"Thunder would like to speak with you," she says.

I walk to Arrok's side and start to climb on his back.

"I am sorry," Luna says. "I meant just Arrok."

"Oh, okay," I say stepping away from Arrok.

Arrok looks suspiciously at Luna and then jumps out of the cave. I look at Luna just as Arrok did. I feel slightly uncomfortable around Luna when we're alone. There's nothing stopping her from attacking me if she decides to get hungry, or thirsty. But I don't think she would resort to that, at least that's what I'm counting on. I look at her again and she smiles.

"What," I say cautiously. "You're looking at me funny."

"I just can't believe you are forming a pact," she says continuing to smile. "You know that you are becoming attached to this world. Do you not miss your home?"

"Probably not as much as I should," I admit. "Like is said earlier, I only miss my family."

"Are you going to stay here," Luna asks.

"I don't know," I say. "I guess we'll find that out when the time comes, if that time comes."

"You know I am surprise that Lilith did not have a dream of this and warn you," Luna says.

A dream of the pact would have been helpful, wait now I remember. The day that I talked to Marcus, when he wanted me to become Luna's Guardian, I met Lilith in the halls. She said that I would gain allies, new and old. She must have meant new allies as the dragons of this island and old allies meaning Arrok. I'm no even going to worry about it this time.

"Yeah that would have been nice," I say. "It doesn't matter though. So can you give any tips on what the next test is going to be?"

"I can," Luna smirks. "But I am not going to. No one gave me any tips when I formed my pact."

"It must have been harder for you to do," I say.

"What do you mean," Luna asks quickly. "Why would it have been harder?"

"You were younger when you had formed your pact," I say correcting myself. "You must not have seen as much battle before."

"It was not until I formed my pact with Iris that I found battle," Luna says. "But in this world it is almost a way of life and with an impending war we need fighters."

"Isn't that why we're here," I ask.

"Yes," Luna says slowly. "But Thunder is not happy about that. He knows that everyone here is knowledgeable of our coming war."

"But it's not their fight," I say.

"Yes," Luna says glumly. "This is going to be difficult."

"Wait I have an idea," I grin. "Arrok was the one that seemed like he would never form a pact with anyone, right?"

"I suppose," Luna says slowly. "What is your point?"

"We use our pact as a means of spurring their want to fight," I explain. "This will probably cause a lot of the ones that are ready to leave anyway, to come with us."

"It sounds a little farfetched," Luna says doubtfully. "But it seems to be one of our only options."

"I know," I laugh. "I hope it works."

I walk to the edge of the cave and sit down at the mouth. I let my legs hang out into open space. I watch as the dragons carry out there daily routines. One dragon sits on the floor of the cavern watching several smaller ones wrestling around. They are easily waist high to me. Luna walks over and sits on the lip of the cave too.

"Are those hatchlings," I ask as they jump on each other.

"Yes," Luna replies. "They are only a few days old."

"Shouldn't their parents be taking care of them," I ask.

"Their parents are out hunting," Luna explains. "You would be surprised by how much they eat while they are growing."

"How big are they when they are born," I ask. "They look pretty big right now."

"They are usually about a quarter of the size they are now," Luna says smiling as she watches them. "They are only a few months old."

"Are they capable of speech," I ask. "Or are they like us and take more time?"

"No they are capable of learning while still inside their eggs," Luna says looking at me strangely.

"What," I ask. "You're looking at me strangely again."

"It seems strange when you said, like us," Luna says. "I know what you meant by what you said, but it makes it sound like we are of the same kind."

"Yeah sorry about that," I say picking my words carefully this time. "I thought it would have been easier than saying vampires and humans. Guess it doesn't really matter now because I just said it anyway."

"I see your point," Luna laughs. "Oh look Arrok is returning and with Iris too, looks like it is time for me to go. You have a big day ahead of you tomorrow."

"All right," I mumble. "See you tomorrow."

Iris flies ahead of Arrok and streaks by the mouth of the cave. I look over at Luna, but she's not there. I look back at Iris and I can see Luna sitting on her dragon's back. She looks as if she is laughing. Arrok flies up and lands in the cave just behind me. I slide back slowly so I don't fall off.

"So how did your conversation with Thunder go," I ask as I dust off my pants.

"It went well," Arrok says. "This is for you; it is from your doctor friend, what is her name again?"

Arrok stretches his claws forward a drops a blanket in my arms.

"Thank you," I say. "Her name is Tori."

"Ah yes, now I remember," Arrok says. "I am still trying to remember all of your companions' names, now that I am going to be an addition to them."

"You'll make it official tomorrow," I say as I roll out the blanket.

"Yes," Arrok mumbles. "We should rest. We have a long day ahead of us."

"Hope it's not too tough," I yawn.

"It is nothing that you cannot handle," Arrok laughs. "Now rest."

"You too," I say as I curl up in the blanket and close my eyes.

It felt like I only closed my eyes for a few minutes and then morning is already here. It's hard to imagine that an entire night just passed. I stretch and sit up; luckily I didn't toss and turn in my sleep. I'm not any closer to the mouth of the opening then when I was when I went to sleep. I look behind me at the empty cave; it seems Arrok is already up. I stand up and walk to the edge. How am I supposed to get down now?

As I stand at the mouth looking down a dragon flies into the cave. I turn as is turns around in the cave. I recognize its golden scales and know its Lux.

"Greetings," he says with a bow. "Arrok is busy at the moment, helping with a hunt I believe. I have been sent to collect you, are you ready?"

"Yeah, let's go," I say climbing slowly onto Lux's back.

As soon as I am on Lux, he leaps out into the spacious cave. We soar quickly to the area of the cave that we held the meeting last night. Everyone is there except Arrok and Thunder. Lux lands and I jump off.

"Iris and I are going to join the hunt with Arrok," Lux says.

"Have fun," Luna says.

Lux and Iris launch into the air and fly off towards the mouth of the cave. I watch them fly away until they are out of sight. After they are gone I look around at the four of us. Luna sits silently, almost like she is meditating. Scott drums his fingers on the floor. Tori has a small fire going with a pot suspended above it with something bubbling inside.

She stirs it a few times large wooden spoon and then produces three large sea shells form her haversack. She then dips the shells into the pot and hands one to each of us, keeping the last one for her.

"What is this," Scott says as he sniffs the shell.

"It is a shrimp stew," Tori says.

"All right," Scott interrupts taking a huge gulp of the stew.

"With red pepper in it too," Tori finishes.

Scott instantly starts fanning his mouth with his hand and sucking in air. Tori bursts into a hysterical laughter as she watches Scott rush for a haversack and frantically search for a flask of water. When he finally finds one he drains half of it in a few drafts. Luna only smiles at the event, she doesn't have a shell of stew though. She only sips from a small silver flask. I'm too engrossed thinking about the test to join Tori or worry about Luna's eating habits. I sip slowly at my soup feeling the light burn of the pepper as flows down my throat; it feels good and seems to calm my tense body. Before I realize it the shell is empty.

"Do you want another serving," Tori asks, holding out her hand for the shell.

"Yes please," I say, my mind is still picturing the Monolith.

"Here you go," Tori says cheerfully, holding the shell out for me.

"Thanks," I say as I take the shell.

I take slightly larger sips of the stew this time. The burn is intensified now. I don't know if from the larger amounts that I'm consuming or if there is more pepper settled at the bottom of the stew. I finish my second shell of stew and set the shell on the floor beside me.

"Do you want a third helping," Tori asks.

"No thanks," I say. "The stew is excellent by the way."

"Thank you my father used to make it every chance he got," Tori says. "It was the only thing he could actually cook."

"As good as it is I would have guessed he was a chef, not a doctor," I compliment.

"You now that is what his friends told him," Tori says looking down at her almost empty shell. "Still wish he was here."

Luna gets up and walk over to Tori's side and sits next to her. She places an arm around Tori's shoulder.

"We all wish our passed loved ones were with us," Luna says softly.

"But as long as we keep then in our hearts and memories, the will always by with us."

"I guess your right," Tori says in a low voice.

Tori sniffs once and then seems to be back to her cheerful self. I can tell some of this is put on, but Luna's words did have some affect. Tori finishes her stew and pours a little water from her flask into the shell. She sloshes it around and pours it out, then wipes it out with a cloth. She tosses the cloth to me and I do the same.

"So are you ready for your first test," Luna asks. "Here come the others."

I look over my shoulder as the four dragons fly over head and land around us. Thunder seems to be in a very good mood today.

"Good morning," he booms. "Are you ready for the next test?"

"As ready as I'm going to get," I say standing and stretching.

"Excellent," Thunder says. "Then we shall begin."

Everyone climbs onto their assigned dragons. Luna rides on Iris, Scott and Tori on Lux, and me on Arrok. Obviously no one rides on Thunder; I honestly think no one would want to. The only way someone would is if they were deaf. We fly out of the cave without a word. The sun seems almost too bright after being in the dim lit cavern.

We fly over the jungle and out over the sparkling cove. We head straight towards the Monolith. It stands just as dark even in the early morning sunlight. The sun is above the horizon so the waters are not shimmering red and gold. We land on the top of the Monolith. As everyone jumps off the dragons fly away. The only dragon that remains is Thunder. I watch Arrok and the others fly to the beach and land. They look like toys since they're so far away.

"This test will determine that you truly trust your pact with your life," Thunder explains.

He lets out a roar that causes everyone on the Monolith to flinch. After the roar fades another roar sounds from the beach. This must be some kind of signal.

"Your friend is ready," Thunder says. "Are you?"

I nod once.

"Good," Thunder says. "This is what you must do. You will leap from here and your pact is going to catch you."

"What," Scott blurts out.

His reaction speaks for the both of us. I stand completely still. It's one thing for me to risk my life to help Arrok, but to risk it just to pass a test. I walk to the edge of the Monolith and glance down. It seems like a thousand foot fall, and then jagged rocks, then whatever might be lurking under the water surface that I can't see. I can feel my heart begin to beat faster with anticipation.

"Do you trust your friend to catch you," Thunder asks again.

I turn and look at each of my friends as they stand behind Thunder. This could be the last time I see their faces. So I'm going to commit them to memory, just in case. Scott looks extremely worried. Tori seems happy to be here as always. Luna stands staring at me just like Thunder, waiting for me answer.

"Yes," I say, more confidently than intended.

"Good," Thunder says. "Then..."

Before he can finish, I out stretch my arms and fall backwards off the Monolith. As I fall I see Luna's expression change to shock and she rushes forward as if to stop me from falling. Why would she do that?

20

THE ONLY THING THAT I feel is the wind roaring past me and tearing at my body as I fall. I can't open my eyes, not that I really want to right now. As I fall I keep picturing Luna's face as I fell from the Monolith. It was almost like she didn't want me to jump. But last night she was so happy about me forming a pact, had she lied?

It feels like I've been falling for too long, the jagged rock at the bottom must be close by now. Arrok hasn't caught me yet, I guess I did the right thing by memorizing their faces. That was the last time that I will ever see them. With every passing second I expect to feel the hard and sudden impact that will end my life. Each second that I don't hit makes my heart beat faster.

Then I hit something hard, my eyes instantly snap open. I'm lying on Arrok's back. I roll about until I am sitting like I normally do when we fly. He pulls up and flies quickly to the top of the Monolith. He lands and I jump off onto the weathered black stone. Everyone seems relieved except Luna, she seems enraged.

"That was awesome," Scott shouts.

Luna looks at him and he falls silent. Then she turns her cold blue eyes on me. What's wrong with her all of the sudden?

"What the hell is wrong with you," she yells.

"What's wrong with you," I say stunned. "We passed the test."

"Let me explain," Thunder roars. "When you said you were willing to trust Arrok with your life, you passed the test. You were brought up here as a sort of bluff. I was about to tell you that when you jumped. Luckily Arrok did catch you."

"I'm sorry I didn't know," I mutter; the apology is directed more at Luna than Thunder.

"There is only one more thing for the both of you to do," Thunder says. "You must now recite the pact; this will take place in the Den."

I climb onto Arrok's back as Lux and Iris fly up and land. Thunder takes flight first, Iris and Lux then follow. Arrok sits for a moment and then flies behind the others.

"Did you know it was a bluff," I ask.

"No, I did not," Arrok says. "I am only glad I was able to reach you in time. Regardless of your actions, I think we did quiet well."

"I'm still sorry," I say.

"I believe you caused more trouble for your friend Luna more than me," Arrok laughs. "She is quiet upset."

"Yeah I know," I say. "I'll try to talk to her later."

"Good luck," Arrok says. "You and I are the center of attention now, you will be lucky to even eat at the banquet."

"Wait, what banquet," I ask my voice louder than I expected.

"The one in honor of our pact," Arrok explains. "I saw the other catching leviathans for the feast."

"How could they have captured one of those things," I ask in amazement.

"Not captured, killed," Arrok corrects. "It is being prepared now, being cooked in one of the giant hot springs I believe."

We reach the cave and fly inside. There are dragons lining the walls as they sit in their caves. They sit silently as we fly to the end of the cavern where we had met last night. We land in front of Thunder and the others. I jump off and stand next Arrok.

"Now for the finally part of your pact," Thunder says. "Please repeat after me."

I swear this pact and will uphold
Until the day of my death behold
Only when I here the dark symphony

Will this pact no longer be

We both recite the pact in unison, our two voices one as they echo through the cave. The last words linger in the air for what feels like an eternity.

"You have now formed a pact," Thunder says. "Let the feast begin."

There is a literal roar of applause from everyone in the cave. The sound is deafening and takes several minutes to die down. Once it is silent in the cave Thunder lets out a roar. This roar isn't quiet as loud as before, but still causes me to wince. All heads turn to the direction behind Thunder. Two of the dragons that had landed with Thunder when we arrived fly over head with a steaming leviathan. This must have been the one Arrok had mentioned earlier.

They fly over us to the center of the cavern and gently set down the meal to be on a long table of stone. Other dragons fly in from the jungle and set down many different types of fruit and several types of edible plants. In an instant there is an enormous feast before us.

"Please those who have a pact will sit at the head of the table," Thunder instructs as he sits down at the end.

Arrok sits to Thunder's left at the first available seat; I sit to the left of Arrok. Iris sit across from Arrok and Luna sits across from me. She still looks angry at me for jumping off the Monolith. Next Scott sits to my left and Tori sits to Luna's left. After that all the others just crowd around. Lux manages to sit next to Scott so our group is together at the stone slab table.

"Let the feast begin," Thunder says.

There are plates with knives and forks set out for us. They look like they are from our haversacks. All the other dragons just tear readily at the fresh meat. I look down the table and can see several dozen other leviathans that have been brought in so everyone may eat. They are uncooked and some blood spills out, but not as much as I thought there should be.

"They drained most of the blood outside," Arrok explains. "Even we dragons do not like to be too messy."

Scott just stares at the leviathan in front of him.

"How are we supposed to get to the meat," he whispers to me.

Arrok must have heard him because he runs a claw along its side.

The smell of cooked meat fills the air with a warm aroma. All the dragons that are eating this one are eating mostly from the top. I cut a portion from the leviathan.

The meat is excellent, but there is a lack of conversation. Scott and I exchange a few words. Luna says nothing the entire time. I make a point to talk to Tori since Luna isn't yielding any words or change in mood.

Once we finished the feast it is nearing nightfall. Many of the dragons wander off to their apartment like caves and retire for the night. I walk to the mouth of the cave, which take a little longer when not flying. I lean against the wall and breathe in the warm air night.

"Hey," a cheerful voice says.

I look over my shoulder to see Tori. I know that Luna wouldn't sound that cheerful right now.

"Hey," I say. "Come to get some fresh air too?"

"Yeah," Tori breathes. "That cave can get kind of hot, especially with those hot springs."

"I know," I laugh. "It makes the jungle air feel almost cool."

"Sure does," Tori says quietly. "I also came out here to congratulate you in person."

"Thank you," I smile. "They weren't much for conversation back there."

"Luna for certain," Tori sighs. "She is really upset with you."

"Yeah I know, I had that same feeling," I say sarcastically. "I didn't know I wasn't supposed to jump. I'll go talk to her tomorrow, give her some time to calm down."

"That would be a good idea," Tori says light heartedly.

"Speaking of good ideas," I say. "You know all about the anatomy of humans and vampires right?"

"Yes," Tori says confused by my sudden change of subject. "Why?"

"If a vampire is wounded they heal right," I hint.

"Yes," Tori replies.

"But what if they can't heal the wound how can they be saved," I ask.

"Well I guess you know that vampires get their strength from blood," Tori asks. "To be honest I have never had to administer a vampire. I have had to watch over some humans the have turned, but not what you are talking about. I suppose that a dose of fresh blood immediately would help. That is the best thing that I can think of. You are worried about the war are you not?"

"How can I not," I say quickly. "Not only am I going to fight, but I'm Luna's Guardian now. I have to protect her."

"Marcus would not have picked you if he did not think you could do it," Tori encourages. "I hope you're right," I sigh. "I really do."

"Of course I am," Tori laughs.

"How can you be so cheerful all the time," I ask. "You're around so much death and pain."

"But I am also helping those who are in pain," Tori smiles. "Helping others makes me happy."

"I see your point," I grin. "Looks like you're right yet again."

"Yep, congratulations again," Tori says, patting me on the shoulder and then walking away.

"Thanks," I say over my shoulder.

I just stare at the dark jungle in front of me. I look slowly up at the moon that is now slightly larger than half now. The moon will probably be almost gone by the time the werewolves attack. I take one more deep breathe and walk back into the hot cavern.

It takes me several minutes to walk around the few dragons that are still lounging around the table. Once I reach the head of the table only Lux, Thunder and Arrok are there. They too seem to have eaten their share of the feast. Thunder breathes slow and deep as if he's about to go sleep. Arrok and Lux whisper to each other, maybe Thunder is actually asleep. I walk as quietly as I can and take a seat near them. Arrok looks up at me as I approach.

"Good you are here," Arrok says. "You need to rest. We leave early tomorrow morning."

"But what about the others," I say. "We came here to gather fighters for the war. We haven't even said anything about that."

"We will tomorrow," Arrok says quietly. "Now we need to retire for the night."

"Okay," I say. "I hope our trip here isn't for nothing."

"As do I," Arrok mumbles.

I climb onto Arrok's back and give a fake yawn. Right now I'm too worried about getting back and protecting Haven. That and thinking about Luna. I might not even sleep tonight. Lux wanders off towards the mouth of the cavern, he seems troubled too. I wonder why Lux hasn't made a pact yet. He seems like a very intelligent dragon. Arrok kicks off silently, leaving Thunder asleep at the head of the table. It doesn't take long for us to reach our cave. For some reason I'm too awake, as Arrok makes a pass by the mouth of the small cave I jump. I land with a soft thud on the stone floor. I look back out at Arrok as he gives me a severe gaze. He glances into the cave and flies off. Where is he going? Maybe he is gong to speak with Thunder about asking for help.

"Impressive," a cold voice says behind me.

I whirl around and grip the hilt of my sword; I fight the urge to draw it. Luna leans against the back wall her face concealed by the shadows. I didn't even notice her when I jumped.

"Hey," I say quietly.

I look at her for a moment, thinking of the right words to say. I'm pretty sure she's still mad me. So I don't want to say anything that would make her shove me out of the cave.

"I'm glad you're here," I say carefully. "I want to say I'm sorry for what happened on the Monolith. I shouldn't have been in such a hurry."

"I am not anger with your reaction," Luna says, her voice not as hard. "I am only glad that Arrok managed to get to you in time. You were not far from crashing into the rocks when he caught you."

"If you're not mad at what I did then why did you react that way," I ask, not too carefully though.

"It's because you are so willing to throw your life away," Luna says her voice cold again. "You are supposed to be a Guardian, you are meant to protect. But it seems like you are in need of more protection than me."

"But I'm here now," I shoot back. "It's not my time to die. But it seems like you are too worried about me to see why I'm a Guardian. I'm not just a Guardian, I'm your Guardian. You're the one that needs protection. Don't you remember the dream?"

"It is strange," Luna says confused. "A human protecting a vampire, this is not a common scenario. Vampires are superior to humans, then why am I being protected by one? I am going to die."

"No," I say placing a hand on her shoulder. "You're in danger, that's why I'm here. I'm here as a shield for you. I'll die protecting you if I have to."

"How can you say this and sound so carefree," Luna asks shaking her head. "You are still so willing to die."

"I'm carefree because I know everyone dies at some point," I say. "And I'm not willing to die; I'm just not willing to let my friends die."

"You consider me a friend," Luna asks. "You do not even belong here. You should be having a different life in your world, living your life there."

"I can't go back now," I say. "I've made a promise to protect you, and until this war is over I'm not leaving. Besides I've lived more here in this short time than eighteen years back home."

"You are too at home here," Luna says moving closer.

"I'm more alive here too," I say calmly. "You've helped me see what I am, who I'm supposed to be."

"Really," Luna asks looking up at me.

"Really," I echo. "So we're leaving tomorrow right?"

"Yes," Luna says, she seems grateful for the change of subject. "Thunder is going to announce that anyone that wants to help us can leave with us. I should go you need rest."

"Okay," I say. "Luna?"

"Yes," she answers as she walks to the mouth of the cave.

"I'm glad I'm here," I say. "I've made new friends and maybe a new life."

"I am sorry to here that," Luna says quietly.

Before I can say anything in return Luna jumps out of the mouth of the cave. I look over the edge just in time to see her land on Iris's back. And she complains about me being reckless, although she can heal if she gets injured. I sigh and lie down on the blanket. I close my eyes and try to fall asleep. I wait for sleep to take me. As I sit with my eyes closed Arrok flies in and lands quietly. He doesn't say anything; he must think that I'm asleep. I wish I were sleeping. It only takes a few more hours before I finally get my wish.

21

DESPITE NOT GETTING HARDLY any sleep I feel very alive and energized. I sit up and wait for Arrok to awake from his slumber. I walk to the mouth of the cave and lean against the wall. It seems that many of the dragons are already awake and roaming about. Until now I hadn't noticed how many of them are old or young.

The older dragons watch over the hatchlings while the parents hunt. This is going to hurt our numbers considerably. Hatchlings are too young, the old ones probably wouldn't make it to the mainland and the parents aren't going to leave their young. So that leaves the young ones that are old enough to decide for themselves. So maybe a fourth of their population is able bodied enough to fight, if they will.

"How long have you been awake," Arrok yawns.

"Not long," I say. "I'm too anxious about how many we'll get to follow us. Will this trip even have been worth making? So far the only good thing that's come of it is my pact with you."

"I have to agree with you on that," Arrok says. "We will have more fighters by the time that we leave. I cannot say how many, but we will have some."

I continue to watch the dragons around me. I feel sorry for those that do come with us. They may be brave, but can they fight? How many will survive to return here? I shake my head to try and silence the unrelenting questions that plague my mind. I look down at the stone slab table that we had eaten at last night. All the remnants of food are gone now. Scott, Tori and Luna are sitting at the head of the table discussing something

"It looks like the others are already up," I say. "You ready?"

"Certainly," Arrok yawns again. "Get on."

I climb hesitantly onto Arrok's back there's something about how he told me to get on that bothers me. Once I'm on, Arrok bolts form the cave. He climbs towards the ceiling of the cave. As soon as it seems like we're about to crash into the stalactites he veers around them. He weaves in between them with ease. I hold my hand out and can almost touch the stone ceiling of the cavern. We start to fly down and he pulls up fast and performs a loop. I tighten my legs as we go upside down and then level off.

"Are you still back there," Arrok asks over his shoulder.

"Yeah, you can't get rid of me that easily," I say.

"Good," Arrok replies.

Arrok flies over the table near the others and begins his descent. He reaches the height that he would land, but instead he flies low to the ground. I know that we are going to meet with the others, but what is he doing. We are almost to the head of the table.

"Jump off," Arrok challenges. "You will have to be prepared for battle maneuvers some how."

I slowly stand up on Arrok's back and balance like I'm on a skateboard. I breathe deep and allow the berserker ability to take hold. I see everything is slow motion as it passes by. We are almost above the others now. I don't give myself to time to back out, I jump. I watch the floor of the cave slowly loom closer. Just as my feet touch the floor I tuck and roll across the floor and stand. Everyone sits watching me. Luna seems less surprised than Tori and Scott.

"You seem to be getting the hang of that," Luna smiles.

"What," Scott says. "When did he do that before?"

"Last night at one of the side caves up there," Luna motions. "He did quiet well."

"Your cave was at the top wasn't it," Scott asks disapprovingly.

"Yeah," I say with a grin as Arrok lands beside me. "I'm going to live up my life while I can."

"I intend on living in general," Scott laughs. "So when is that leader dragon suppose to get here?"

"Thunder, will be here shortly," Luna corrects. "He is going to announce our need for help. I only hope that they will listen."

We sit and watch as the dragons slowly gather in the cavern; they too want to hear what Thunder is going to say. Once almost all of the dragons on the entire island are crowded on the floor of the cave and along the walls Thunder arrives. He lands on a large boulder almost at the center of the cave. The congregation falls silent with anticipation.

"As you all know we live in troubled times," Thunder begins. "Our guests have come here from the fortress city of Haven, they seek out our help. The werewolves have chosen to do what we have not. They have chosen to follow the gray dragons. They have filled the werewolves heads with lies and bring the past forward again. Soon Haven will be attacked by them in full force. There are some of you that have loved ones living there. I ask you now, will you protect them? Will you stand and fight to help your families and our friends."

A murmur echoes through the cave. To my surprise I hear shouts of agreement, mingled with those who disagree as well.

"If Haven were to fall," Thunder yells over the shouting. "Those dragons will find a way to seek revenge against us. We shunned them when we were given the same offer as the werewolves. How long will it be before they cross that little span of sea that separates us from them? Who will go and fight?! You all know me, if I were not your leader I would be the first to go. Our allies are leaving soon. If you wish to follow them meet them at the beach in the cove."

Without another word Thunder takes flight and flies out of the cavern. The inhabitants of the island sit quietly for a moment and then chaos breaks out. It seems that his speech worked in our favor more than excepted.

"What do we do now," Scott yells over the clamor.

"We go to the beach and wait," Luna shouts.

Lux and Iris appear from the arguing mass. They seem to know that we want to get out of the cavern before something happens. Luna tosses me a haversack and I climb onto Arrok's back. Scott grabs a haversack and Tori and him climb up onto Lux. Luna picks up the last and climbs onto Iris. We take off quickly and fly over the dragons as they continue to argue. As we fly out of the Dragon's Den there is a noticeable difference in the noise.

"Finally, I can hear myself think again," Scott says wiggling a finger in his ear.

"I wish we could have avoided a conflict," Luna says. "We are going to have enough of that when we get home."

"You mean when you get home," Scott corrects. "I'm going to find a way out of this place. I don't mean anything against the people here, but there's too much fighting for me."

"I understand," Luna says. "What about you Ivan, do you feel the same way?"

"No," I say shortly. "Well, I'm not sure actually. I suppose, I'll find out after the war, if I live through it."

"You fight well," Luna says. "I have witnessed it, we all have. You will be perfectly fine."

"I am sure that Ivan is also very popular among the werewolves," Tori says. "He killed the son of the alpha male, and that little stunt of ours on the beach. They will be looking for us on the battlefield, I assure you."

There's an edge to Tori voice that sounds strange. It's like she wants to be cheerful about everything. Even when she talks about her father and how she lost him, she still seems to be happy. I guess in times like these it can pay off to be happy, while you're still alive.

We fly over the last stretch of jungle and towards the beach. As we approach Thunder shifts on the empty beach in front of us. He sits and watches as we land on the white sand.

"I am sorry that you have to leave so soon," He says apologetically. "It seems that the others are still arguing. I hate to cause them to be divided after trying so hard to unite them."

"It is all right," Arrok says.

"How long do you think it will be before they're calm," I say. "From out here it sounds like the volcano is active again."

"It may be some time," Thunder replies as he stares at the sand. "Look here come a few of them now."

Everyone instantly turns to see seven dragons flying towards us. As they approach I recognize one of the dragons that were with Thunder when we arrived. The only reason that I noticed is because he's the one leading them. He lands first followed by the others. His scales are almost bone white.

"We will follow you," he says to Arrok and me. "I believe that there are more soon to follow us."

"Thank you Zephyr," Arrok says with a nod.

"We are most grateful," Luna says taking a step forward and bowing slightly. "You do not know how much you are helping us."

Zephyr only nods and gazes over the jungle at the mouth the Dragon's Den. I watch too as three more dragons fly out, followed by five more. The numbers that they come in are small, but at this rate we may get a sizable amount of recruits. The others land and more follow, group after group.

The minutes creep by and more dragons land on the beach around us. I keep count as they land, two hundred and twelve, two hundred and twenty. I can't help but smile at all the dragons that want to help us with our fight. I smile again; I'm even calling it my fight now. I don't know why, but I feel like I have some sort of obligation to help these people. After all, my kind is responsible for putting them here. Another large group of dragons land joining the rest of our small army. The sun is completely up and is beating relentlessly down upon us. There are still now clouds since the storm. It must be about noon right now. I've been counting dragons for hours now. Yet another group lands as I count.

"We are the last," the female leading them says.

That makes eight hundred and seventy-four. Not a bad number I suppose, still smaller than any of us had hoped for though. Over one fourth of the inhabitants here have chosen to fight.

"If there are any of you that wish to stay now is your last chance," Luna says. "You should also know that all of you may not return here to see those that you love."

The only sound on the entire beach is the sound of the wave crashing onto the shore. We all understand too well what waits for us on the mainland. This is our choice, our fight. There I go again with the, we and ours. I let out a long sigh; this is going to by hard.

"Are all of you ready for what lies ahead," Arrok says.

The small army of dragons all roar in front of us. I chill runs down my spine as the roars die down.

"I will take that as a yes," Arrok chuckles.

There are a few laughs from the others. Then silence returns once again.

"Then we shall leave you then," Luna says to Thunder as she climbs onto Iris's back.

I climb onto Arrok's back and lean back on the haversack. Scott and Tori get on Lux and wait quietly. Luna lets out a piercing whistle and Iris takes off with Arrok and Lux close behind her. I look behind me as the dragons on the beach take flight. Once the beach is clear there is only one dragon left. I watch as Thunder slowly turns into nothing more than a speck among the trees of the island. The island soon fades in with the blue of the sea. Only the Monolith is visible against the sky, still dark and forbidding even in the distance.

No one says anything as we fly over the endless blue. All the planning that we've done the last few days is actually taking place now. The only thing that we have left to do is get to Haven before the werewolves do. That's if they're not already trying to claw their way up walls right now. I shake my head to get rid of the image of thousands of werewolves scraping their claws across the stone surface of Haven's walls.

"Are you all right," Tori asks breaking the silence. "You seem as though something is troubling you."

"I'm fine," I reply. "I'm just thinking of how much time that we have left."

"I am sure we do not have much time," Luna says grimly. "That is why we are not going to stop if we can help it."

I glance behind me at our squadron of dragons. Can they make it that far?

"Do not worry," Iris says reassuringly. "The only reason that we stopped on the way here was because of Luna's thirst."

"What," Scott says suddenly. "I thought it was because we needed rest."

I can't help but laugh.

"What's so funny," Scott asks.

"Well she is a vampire," I say sarcastically. "If she didn't feed one of us probably wouldn't be here."

Luna looks at me somewhat shocked; I wink at her and smile. Hopefully she'll go along with the little joke. She looks at me for a moment and then catches on; she smiles and then looks over at Scott.

"It can be very dangerous for those around us," Luna says coolly.

I know all too well that what she said is not just to freak out Scott it's, also the truth. If she couldn't have controlled her cravings that day there is no doubt in my mind that I would have been the first. I was the only one awake, and I don't think I could have been able to kill her if she would've attacked. I know I wouldn't have. Not that I would have had the ability to, but because I couldn't bring myself to hurt her.

"You wouldn't have," Scott says his voice cracks.

"I cannot say," Luna says her voice is serious now. "You will never understand how much we can crave blood when we have not fed. Anyone can be at risk."

I watch as the blood drains form Scott's face. He almost looks as pale as Luna did that day. I felt about the same way that Scott does now. Only I think he's actually afraid of her now.

"Anyway," I say. "She's not going to bite any of us now, so stop worrying."

"Yeah," Scott scoffs. "I think I'd rather take my chances fighting a werewolf before I'd fight a vampire."

"Well you'll get your chance," I say with a smirk. "Besides the vampires are on our side, or we're on their side."

"I do not have any problems with Luna being a vampire," Tori says cheerfully. "In fact I think it would be really weird if she was not."

"What makes you say that," I ask.

"Because the entire time that I have known her she has been a vampire," Tori explains. "Just like I am use to you and Scott being human."

"I see your point," I say.

I stare ahead as the mainland begins to take shape out of the green and brown smudge that it is on the horizon. It's strange how it feels like the trip back is taking less time. Even though the sun as almost at its peak.

"Are we flying faster that before," I think out loud.

"Yes," Iris says. "We do not know if the werewolves are at Haven or not.

"Best not take our time to find out," Arrok says.

"I'll agree to that," I say.

I look over my shoulder at the dragons behind us. None of them seem to be that tired. Although I've seen them play their endurance game before the storm hit in full force. They could probably make the flight to Haven and half way back without stopping. A few of them whisper back and forth, but most of them are silent. Zephyr still remains at the front of all that have chosen to come.

I look back ahead as the mainland continues to take form. I can make out the light brown of the beach and the green hills beyond. Suddenly my stomach growls, I glance over at the others. They don't seem to have heard it. I reach behind me and pull the haversack onto my lap. I open it and rummage through it. I find an apple that's slightly wrinkled. It must have been one of the ones that we brought from Haven. I close the haversack and place it behind me, then take a bite. I'm surprised that it's still very crunchy. I finish the apple faster than hoped for. So I rummage through the haversack again and finish a piece of slated meat.

Scott and Tori have followed my example and are eating some bread that's left over. Luna doesn't eat anything; she only sips from the small silver flask like before. She takes another sip and I notice a little bit of red liquid on her lips. She then rubs her sleeve on her mouth before she puts the flask away.

"Hey we've finally made it back to land again," Scott says through a mouthful of bread.

"It will not be long now," Luna says quietly. "We will be at Haven soon."

I watch the ground for any hint of gray or silver. The air feels still as we fly, I guess it's just the fact that I know what's going to be taking place soon. I continue to watch the ground, just as everyone else does.

"Look there is a large wolf pack," Luna says pointing ahead. "They are going in the direction of Haven too."

I watch as we approach the pack, I can't help but be somewhat impressed by their numbers. They probably outnumber us two to one. There are easily two thousand werewolves all running across the rolling green hills. Their not all just gray or silver either, some are brown or even a rust colored.

"Half of you concealment maneuvers," Zephyr suddenly orders. "Conceal our numbers."

Without a single word or complaint the dragons obey. The ones near the front pull up and back. They then begin flying again above the others.

"That is a good tactic," Luna says. "I suppose from below it would appear that our forces are half of what they are."

"Indeed it would," Zephyr replies.

We continue towards Haven in our new formation. The werewolves still don't seem to have noticed us. Then as the mountains that house Haven begin to take shape and cut up into the skies the werewolves slowly veer away from our path. I watch them until they begin to disappear into the forest in the distance.

"We are almost there," Luna says.

No says anything. The walls of Haven are soon visible as we continue to fly fast. They're still standing. The soldiers that guard the wall tops are still pacing about, and in greater numbers too. It seems that Marcus has doubled the watch in our absence. Luna waves as we approach and several soldiers wave back.

"Land near the training grounds," Luna shouts.

We begin our descent as soon as we pass the wall in the evening sun. As we glide in closer to the ground I can see Simon and a sizable number of soldiers. He seems to be making an example of one of them as they fight one on one without weapons. We land and I jump off and watch as the other dragons land.

"Welcome back," Marcus says as he appears.

He embraces Luna and then turns to the dragons.

"So these are the recruits from the island," Marcus asks.

"Yes," Luna says looking at them. "They are all here by their own will."

"Good," Marcus says looking at me. "You have done well to keep my daughter safe."

"Thank you," I say. "But she's still not safe as long as there's a war to be fought."

"You wish to continue being her Guardian," Marcus asks surprised. "I do not intend on letting her fight. She will be kept safe in the palace until the fighting is over."

"But father," Luna protests. "I have to…"

"No you will not fight," Marcus says sternly. "I am not going to let you risk your life."

"These are just as much my people as they are yours," Luna shoots back.

"I know," Marcus says shaking his head. "But not everyone has to die in order to protect them."

"What about Ivan," Luna asks. "Is he going to fight?"

"That is his decision," Marcus says.

"Yes," I say without hesitation. "I will fight."

22

I CAN TELL THAT I upset Luna the instant the words leave my mouth. I know exactly how she feels, to be left out of the big picture. I've had it done to me many times in the past. I also know that she is an amazing warrior as well. She would help out during the battle more than Marcus thinks. He only sees her as his daughter, not a warrior.

"Are you sure that you wish to fight," Marcus asks again. "This is not your fight or your city."

"Tell me," I say slowly. "Do the people that arrive in this world live in Haven?"

"Yes," Marcus says.

"Then I think it's my fight too," I say. "This is probably going to be where I spend the rest of my life anyway. From what I've gathered the gateways are only one way."

"Then I welcome you into our struggle," Marcus says grimly.

"It's been my struggle since I arrived here," I say with a half smile.

"Are you seriously going to allow him to fight," Luna asks outraged. "Why?"

"Because I can't bear the thought of losing you like I lost your mother," Marcus says sadly. "You and Lilith are all that I have now. If I allowed you to fight and you where killed, it would be my fault. That would crush me."

I had never heard Marcus mention Luna's mother. To be honest I just thought that I still hadn't met her. But now it makes sense of why Marcus is so protective.

"I am not my mother," Luna says coldly.

I can see that Luna's words have done more than just sting Marcus. He looks down at the ground in silence. I can't tell if he's going to snap or remain silent. Instead he only snaps his fingers. I watch as Simon walks up next to him.

"Yes," he asks.

"Simon," Marcus says in a hard tone. "Take Luna to her room. I want you and two guards posted at her door. Do not let her out under any circumstances, is that clear?"

"Yes sir," Simon says with a bow.

I watch as Simon leads Luna towards the second wall that divides us from the city. Iris stirs uncomfortably as Luna is led away.

"I can fly her to the palace," Iris insists.

"No," Marcus says. "You are her pact; thereby you are obligated to protect her. But I am her father, so I too am obligated to protect her."

"Yes, I understand," Iris says looking down.

"I also ask that you stay in a different room for the time being," Marcus says.

"As you wish," Iris says as she flies away.

"Now you must excuse me Ivan, I must speak with our new recruits," Marcus says as he turns and walks away.

I turn and walk towards Arrok. He could easily be mistaken for a statue as he sits in complete silence.

"You are not comfortable with the situation are you," Arrok asks.

"No I'm not," I say irritated. "It's not right that he gave me a choice and not her."

"He is only doing what he thinks is best for his daughter," Arrok says calmly.

"Exactly, what he thinks is best," I argue. "He's not thinking about what others think is best."

"Everything will be worked out," Arrok says. "We should prepare for the coming battle. We do not know how much time that we have."

I breathe deep, trying to clear my mind. I still can't believe Marcus. I've never seen him like that before, although I haven't really seen him that much. I take another deep breath and climb onto Arrok's back. I wonder if I can get to Luna and talk to her. Suddenly my mind is flooded with dozens of farfetched plans to help her escape. It seems strange, thinking of way to rescue someone so they can go to war.

"Are you all right," Arrok says over his shoulder. "You seem distant."

I hadn't even noticed that we had taken off and that we are now half way over the city. I can see the water fountain at the center at the plaza almost directly under us.

"Yeah," I say still not paying full attention to what he's saying. "I was just thinking."

"Let me guess, you are going to try and think of a way to get Luna out and into the battle," Arrok says. "How close was I?"

"Closer than I thought you would get," I laugh. "But we can't just go in now; we have to plan this out. I've fought Simon, and even with my berserker ability I barely beat him."

"So we need to find a way around him," Arrok mumbles.

"Are you really going to help me," I ask, somewhat surprised. "Of course, I am your pact. I may not fully agree with some of the things that you come up with, but there are also some things that you may not agree with that I do."

"I see, so do you have any ideas," I ask.

"You should wait until Simon leaves his post at the door," Arrok explains.

"That sounds like a good plan," I say. "What else do you have?"

"Actually," Arrok says slowly. "That is all that I have thought of."

"Well it's a start," I say. "Wait I have an idea, it'll add on to what you just said."

I tell Arrok of my plan as we fly closer to the palace. He seems to think that it should work. My main objective is to avoid Simon if that's possible. By the time I finish with the finer details of the plan we're at the palace.

"It seems that your friends have already been dropped off," Arrok says as he watches Lux fly by. "Are you going to include them in our little scheme?"

"First of all scheme just sounds like we're up to no good," I say.

"I do not mean to argue, but we are up to no good," Arrok chuckles as we land on the balcony to our room. "Let us call is our plot then."

"Plot doesn't sound that much better," I say with a laugh. "Now you remember what your part is, right?"

"Yes," Arrok says. "I also know what your signal is."

"Great," I say with a smile. "I'll go and see how this goes."

"Good luck," Arrok says.

"Hopefully I won't need any luck," I say as I turn and walk across the room.

I open the door as quietly as I can. As I step into the halls I instantly notice that it is a hive of activity. People with scrolls and books run one way, while others carrying bundles of weapons head the other direction. Many of the people carrying weapons are soldiers, but there are still twice the numbers of guards. This is not going to be easy. I can't go straight to Luna's room in a rush.

Arrok had said that Scott and Tori were here, but the infirmary is in the opposite direction that I want to go. I need to waste some time, but I don't know what to do. I'll just wait in my room for a while, and then I'll go see Luna. I turn around and start back towards my room.

"Hey Ivan," Scott shouts from behind me.

This may be my chance to waste some time, and pick up some useful information.

"What," I say walking slower so he can catch up. "I was wondering where you disappeared to."

"Well when we saw Luna and Marcus arguing we thought it would be a good idea to get out of there," Scott says. "Did you know that Luna's already here?"

"Really," I say, trying to sound surprised.

"Yeah," Scott says amazed. "Simon escorted her here, but they both came on foot. How could they get all the way across the city that fast?"

"Maybe they ran," I say as I open the door to my room and step inside.

"That's still a long way to run," Scott says as he follows me in.

"They are vampires," I say shortly. "Not that it matters how she got here, she's locked in her room."

"I know I already walked by her room," Scott says. "Simon wasn't there though, only three guards."

"What were you doing up there," I ask as I walk to the balcony.

"Marcus asked me if I wanted to fight," Scott says walking onto the balcony with me.

"What did you say," I ask.

"What do you think," Scott says leaning against the rail. "I'm not going to let you go out there and risk your life for people you don't even know. Someone's got to make sure you don't die."

"Thanks," I say punching him in the arm. "But you know that works both ways right?"

"I know," Scott says punches at me.

I step back as he swings into the air.

"I'll make sure that you can go home," I say. "No sense in you staying here."

"Well I'm going to train," Scott says walking back towards the door. "I need all the practice I can get."

"Wait a second," I say rushing up to Scott. "You said that Marcus just asked you if you wanted to fight."

"Yeah so," Scott shrugs.

"Marcus was talking to the dragons when I left him," I say. "He must have flown back here afterwards."

"He must have," Scott says turning to walk away. "Well I'm going to train now."

"All right," I say. "Be careful."

"Come on," Scott says opening the door. "You know me."

"That's the problem," I say under my breath.

Scott walks out and shuts the door noisily. He doesn't even know how much information he's just unknowingly relinquished to me. This means I have to move now, Arrok isn't even in here. That means that he's already waiting for me. I rush across the room and open the door. I look around the halls. There are still a few soldiers walking around with bundles of weapons.

I slip out the door and walk quickly to the stairs. I don't want to waste anymore time. I practically run up the stairs two at a time. I reach the floor that Luna's room is on. I take a few deep breaths and try to slow my rapid heartbeat from the run up the stairs. A soldier cuts around the corner and bumps into me.

"I am sorry," he says.

"That's all right," I say, not even looking at him.

He walks past me and down the stairs. I make sure he's far enough away before I continue. It doesn't take me long to reach Luna's guarded room. The guards stiffen as I approach the door. There are only three like Scott said. There is one on each side of the double doors and one in between them.

"Luna in under isolation," says the one in the middle. "She is not allowed outside her quarters."

"I know," I say blankly.

"Then there is no reason for you to be here," he says.

"I'm here to see her," I say as I stare past him.

I can tell that the other two guards are starting to feel uncomfortable. One of them keeps glancing from me to the speaker. The other continues to shift his stance.

"I won't be long," I say. "If time is what you're worried about."

"You can't see her," the guard says taking a step forward and placing his hand on his sword. "Now leave, we are permitted to use any force necessary."

I chuckle lowly at his threat; this should unnerve the other guards. This completely unnerves the other two guards. They take several steps away from us.

"Then you should know that so am I," I say coldly. "And just to be fair, you should also know that I'm a berserker."

"I don't believe you," he says drawing his sword.

"So you want a demonstration," I say with a smile. "That's fine."

I breathe deep and let the sensation of the berserker take over. I move faster than I thought I could as I hit hand with the back of my fist. He lets go of his sword and I catch it before it hits the floor. As I rise up the blade is only inches from his throat.

"Well," I say. "Am I permitted to see her now?"

"Yes," he stammers. "You can go in and see her."

I lower the sword and flip it in the air and catch it by the back of the blade. I then hand it back to him. He takes it and places shakily back in his sheath. He steps aside and I walk past him. Just as I start to turn the handle he clears his throat.

"You cannot have any weapons when you see her," he says with a smirk.

"That's fine," I say as I take my sword and sheath and hand it to him. "I'll just have to use yours again."

He doesn't say anything as I open the double doors and step into Luna's room. This is the first time that I've seen it. Her room is much like mine, with a few extra pieces of furniture. She has a canopy bed just like all the other bedrooms in the palace. She also has a large mat for Iris and a small two seat couch in one corner. There is also a roll top desk across from the bed. I step into the room and the guard closes the door.

Suddenly from behind the door Luna comes out swinging a vase. I see her coming just a second too late. I step away and the vase smashes into my shoulder. She looks at me for a second and seems relieved to see that I'm not one of the guards.

"That was uncalled for," I wince as I pull a shard of glass from my shoulder.

"I am so sorry," Luna says quickly. "Let me help."

She walks over to me and pulls out two more shards. Luckily there are only six pieces to remove. None of the shards are very big so they didn't do much damage.

"You must really be in a bad mood," I laugh.

"You would be too if your father had you locked away," Luna says. "What do you want anyway?"

"I wanted to make sure you were all right," I say looking at the multiple red spots on my shirt. "But it seems you're doing fine."

"Well that is nice to know," Luna says unconvinced. "How did you manage to get in here? My father said not let anyone except him in here."

"You can do things when you're a berserker," I grin. "Don't worry they're fine. I just showed them that I was capable of taking them on alone."

"So you abused your abilities," Luna says smiling.

"I didn't think of it as abusing," I protest.

"Do not worry," Luna says continuing to smile. "Everyone has to have a little fun."

"Yeah," I say walking towards the balcony. "Speaking of fun, where did you get that vase?"

"Oh that," Luna says. "I had a moon flower in it. I figured it would be enough to knock out one of those guards."

"I think it would," I laugh as I stop in front of the balcony.

"I apologize again for what I did," Luna says stepping up beside me.

"It's all right," I say. "I talked to Scott before I came here."

"Really," Luna replies.

"He's going to fight with us," I say.

"No," Luna snaps. "He is going to fight with you. Is that why you came here, to throw that in my face?"

"No," I say coolly. "This is why."

I take one step onto the balcony and turn around so I'm facing Luna. She glares at me and then I snap my fingers. Arrok flies up from under the balcony and lands quietly in front of us. He looks at me and nods, then to Luna and bows head.

"You are amazing," Luna says hugging me.

"I know," I say putting one arm around her. "Now all you have to do is kick me out of your room. The guards will think that you're still in here, but you'll really be heading towards your secret cave."

"Got it," Luna says letting go. "I will close the drapes too, just in case they decide to look inside."

"All right," I say walking back across the room. "Do you have another vase?"

"One," Luna says walking to the desk and picking up a small blue vase. "Why?"

"I want you to throw it at me when I walk out," I say.

"Are you sure," Luna says. "I have already done enough damage with one of these, but if you say so."

I run and hit the door and then make it sound like I'm scrambling for the door handle.

"All right I'm leaving," I yell as I jerk the door open.

I dash out into the hallway and Luna throws the vase. I know this ones coming so I duck just in time. The vase flies by head and crashes into the wall across from the door. The guards quickly shut the door.

"What happened to you," the one says as he hands my sword back to me.

"Looks like she wasn't happy to see me," I laugh as I take my sword back.

I turn and walk back down the hall as I walk around the corner and I can't help but smile. The plan's working perfectly so far. I attach my sword back to my side. As I move my arm I feel a tinge of pain in my shoulder. There must have been a seventh piece, and it's inside my shoulder. Looks like I'm going to the infirmary after all.

I take the stairs down to the floor of the infirmary. This floor is easily twice as busy any of the other floors that I've seen so far. People are rushing everywhere with bandages, bottle, vials, raw plants and herbs. I walk in between the bustling people and manage to get to the infirmary door. I open the door and quickly step inside.

"Hello Ivan," Tori says in the usual cheerful tone. "What are you doing here?"

"Well," I say hesitantly. "I had a little bit of an accident."

"What did you do," Tori asks.

Her tone sounds like a mother that's just caught her child in the middle of stealing from the cookie jar. She knows that the child's eating the cookies, but she doesn't know how many the child's already eaten.

"I decided to go see Luna," I say.

"Did the guards do something to you," Tori asks quickly.

"No. Luna did," I say.

"I am not even going to ask how you got past them," Tori says shaking her head. "So what did she do to you?"

I turn so she can see my blood speckled shoulder.

"She thought that I was a guard when I walked into the room, so she hit me with a vase," I explain. "We got most of the pieces out, but I think there's a piece buried in pretty deep."

"Let me see," Tori says. "Sit down."

I walk to the nearest bed and sit down. Tori walks to one of the cabinets by the beds. She gets a white clothe and what look like extra long tweezers.

"All right," Tori says sitting down beside me. "You know this is the same shoulder that you took a werewolf claw through. It finally heals and then you get injured again."

I unbutton my shirt so she can inspect the damage. She wipes away the blood and the pressure causes me to wince. She then prods each wound gently. When she touches one and a stabbing feeling emits. I wince again.

"Found it," Tori says to herself as she works. "This is going to hurt."

"Okay," I say gripping the side of the bed.

She takes the tweezers and slides them slowly into the wound. I can feel every movement that she makes. I can even feel them open a little to grab the shard. Once she has it she slowly pulls the small shard of glass out.

"Sorry," Tori says.

"That's okay," I say through gritted teeth. "Do any of them need stitches?"

"No," Tori says looking closely at the shard. "You lucked out this time."

"Well I should get going," I say looking out the past the city.

The sun is almost completely set now. There's not going to be much of the moon left to light the night after sunset.

"Yes, it is getting late," Tori admits. "I still have to stock the rest of the infirmary."

"What ever happened to those explosives that you had on the beach," I ask suddenly.

"I gave the recipe to some of the engineers that Marcus has," Tori says. "He has several hundred working on nothing but it."

"Oh," I say unconcerned. "Does he have anyone helping you?"

"Hardly as many as he has for weapons and armor," Tori snorts. "But I do have help, so I cannot complain."

"That's true," I say as I stand up.

I walk to the door and open it. I take one step into the hallway then stop.

"Do you think what Marcus is doing to Luna is right," I ask.

"He is only trying to protect her," Tori says sadly. "He may not look it, but he does not have much left. Since his wife died."

"How did she die," I ask stepping back into the room.

"No one knows," Tori says in a low voice, like there's someone listening that shouldn't be. She even looks around to see if there is anyone near us.

"She was very adventurous, Marcus thought that when he married her that she would give up her exploring," Tori says. "She knew that it meant a lot to him so she left less and less, because of her two children. Then one day she never returned."

"What did Marcus do," I ask.

"At first he broke down," Tori say shaking her head. "I remember. My father was the one that administered to him. Once he recovered he was different. He sent out hundreds of search parties in all directions. He even left Luna and Lilith with my father in his absence. That is how Luna and I became friends."

"Did they find anything," I ask.

"They found the group that she was travelling with," Tori says. "They were all dead, but her body was nowhere to be found."

"That's terrible," I say shaking my head.

"I know," Tori says. "Luna was only three when in happened too."

"So that's why Marcus acted the way he did," I say thoughtfully.

"Yes," Tori says shortly. "Well I need to get started."

"Yeah, sorry to hold you up," I say.

I open the door again and walk out into the busy halls. I make my way to the stairs and around the few people that are still working. My mind keeps replaying what Tori has just told me. Did I make a big mistake by helping Luna escape? Marcus is going to be furious, and those guards are going to tell him everything.

I emerge on the floor of my room. There's not a single person in the halls. The torches on the walls cast golden light across the polished floor as I walk. I reach my room and open the door quietly. I step into my room and close the door behind me. I'm not that surprised to see a figure stand on the balcony looking out at the city. As I walk towards the figure, I am surprised to see that it's Kain instead of Marcus.

"Hello Ivan," he says without looking away from the city. "How are you this evening?"

"I'm doing all right," I say walking onto the balcony beside him.

"Judging by your shoulder I would say different," Kain chuckles.

"Well besides that," I shrug, that was a bad idea. "So what can I do for you?"

"I have a sort of favor to ask you," Kain says hesitantly. "It is kind of a favor for me and for Violet."

"I can see what I can do," I say willingly. "What do you need?"

"I know you are going to fight in this battle," Kain says. "I want you to kill my father."

"What," I shout.

"Before you object let me explain," Kain says quickly. "My father is the one that is leading the werewolves, and those dragons are the ones leading him. If the werewolves see the alpha male fall, they will break apart indefinitely."

"Cut of off the head of the snake," I say.

"And the body will die," Kain finishes. "Not only that, but you make things safer for Violet and myself. You see I am not going to be able to fight, nor shall she."

"Why," I ask suddenly.

"The werewolves are out for my blood, due to my father," Kain says sadly. "Not only that, but the soldiers here would confuse me with one of the others and try to kill me too."

"Is that all," I ask with a laugh.

"There is one more thing," Kain continues. "This is more of a theory if my father is killed. You see, the werewolves have always been segregated. This is because of my father as well. Once my father is out of the way, I will have the opportunity to become alpha male and unite the packs. Since I am now a friend of Marcus we can finally put this unease at an end."

"Can that much really be accomplished by the death of your father," I ask thoughtfully.

"Yes," Kain says quickly. "He is hungry for power. My brother and I were forced to survive by ourselves while he waged war on other packs for better hunting grounds."

"I'm sorry to hear that," I murmur. "How will I know which one is your father?"

"You will know as soon as you see him," Kain warns. "I am not asking you to personally kill him, but someone needs to end him."

"I will," I say.

"Thank you," Kain says. "I bid you good night."

Kain walks out of the room and leaves me alone. I look around the empty room. Arrok still hasn't returned. I hope there weren't any complications. I walk to my bed and sit down. My shoulder is aching slightly. I lean over and open one of the drawers of a small dresser near the bed. I find clean clothes and grab them.

I head back out into the torch lit halls. I hurry to the stairs and go back down to the infirmary floor. I walk quietly to the bathing room. Just the heat of the room is relaxing. I take a quick bath and put one the fresh clothes. I take my dirty ones and set them in a bin with other dirty clothes. I hurry back to my room and open the door slowly. As I walk in the first thing that I notice is Arrok's sleeping form across from the bed.

I walk as quietly as I can to the bed and crawl under the covers. The soft mattress feels great after sleeping on sand and cave floors. It only takes a few seconds for me to fall asleep.

23

"IVAN," ARROK WHISPERS. "THE sun is almost at its peak."

I moan as I roll over slowly. I roll a little too far and all my body weight is on my shoulder. It causes just enough pain to be uncomfortable and wake me up. I sit up and flex my arm. A sudden burst of soreness emits form my shoulder. I sigh; I guess that I'm going to have to let this one heal naturally.

"When did you get back," I yawn.

"I few minutes after you fell asleep," Arrok says.

"Were there any complications with the plan," I ask.

"None at all," Arrok says pleased. "Only that she wanted to tell Iris about escaping. I told her that it was too risky and that you would not have wanted her to jeopardize your plan. But I told Iris myself, she agrees with us."

"You mean our plan," I correct. "What did she do?"

"She did not say anything," Arrok says. "She should still be at the hidden cave."

"Do you think its safe enough to go see her," I ask.

"I do not see why not," Arrok says.

Arrok walks onto the balcony and stretches out his wings to their full extent. He then launches himself into the air. I get out of the bed and stretch. I grab my shoes and hop on one foot as I put each one on. I yawn and stretch again. Suddenly there's a knock at the door.

"Marcus would like to have a word with you," a guard shouts through the door. "We are here to escort you to him."

Arrok flies by the balcony and we make eye contact. He only nods as the guards rap on the door again.

"Give me a minute," I yell.

I rush to the side of the bed and grab my sword and attach it under my belt. Then without looking back I run onto the balcony and jump over the rail. The air rushes around me as I fall. I look down as Arrok flies under me. I land on his back a little harder than I wanted to. I groan for a moment at the pain and take a deep breath.

"Are you all right," Arrok asks.

"I'll be okay," I say. "Don't head to the cave just yet."

"Why," Arrok asks concerned.

"Those were guards at the door," I explain. "They were going to escort me to Marcus; apparently he wants to see me."

"Do you wish to see what he wants," Arrok asks.

"Sure, why not," I shrug with one arm.

"I only hope that you know what you are doing," Arrok says disapprovingly.

Arrok flies up to the large balcony where the dining hall is. He lands quietly on the smooth marble floor. I jump off and survey the room. Marcus sits at the head of the table just as he usually does. I walk slowly up to the table and lean against a chair.

"I hear that you want to see me," I say.

"Yes," Marcus says slowly. "It seems that Luna has found a way out of her room. She is no where to be seen on in the palace."

"Uh-huh," I yawn.

"My guards say that you were the only one to visit her," Marcus says looking up at me.

I notice that under his eyes are dark from lack of rest. The purple circles stand out against his pale skin, which is lighter than normal. All the war business must be keeping him from feeding. But I'm not supposed to know any of that.

"Yeah," I say indifferently. "I managed to get in, but she wasn't happy to see me."

"How do I know that the vase she threw at you was not just an act," Marcus prods. "That could have been a distraction so she could escape."

"Because," I say undoing the top few buttons on my shirt so Marcus can see my shoulder. "That vase didn't hit me; the first one that she came at me with did though."

"I see," Marcus says staring at my shoulder.

I quickly button my shirt back up. I don't know how long it's been since he's fed. I'm sure he has much more control than Luna, but it doesn't make me feel any more comfortable being around a thirsty vampire.

"So no, I had nothing to do with her escape," I lie. "Why would I help her anyway?"

"I do not know," Marcus says shaking his head. "I suppose since you were her Guardian."

"Until this war is over I'm still going to protect her," I say.

"Then I thank you for your dedication," Marcus says.

There's a knock at the door and Marcus stands up.

"Enter," he says.

The door opens and four guards are standing in the hallway. One of them steps into the room while the others wait outside. He looks at Marcus and bow slightly.

"We went to his room to escort him here," I guard says looking down. "He told us to wait for a moment. We assumed that he was resting and needed a moment to get ready. We waited for several minutes and then entered the room, but he was not there."

The guard looks up at Marcus and then notices me. His expression goes from apologetic to sheer surprise.

"It is all right," Marcus says. "He is here and I have talked with him. You are dismissed."

The guard bows slightly again and then opens the door and walks out of the room.

"It seems you are also quiet resourceful," Marcus says impressed.

"It all depends on the situation," I say with a grin. "If you would excuse me, I have other matters to attend to."

"Certainly," Marcus nods. "I have matters of my own to attend to as well."

I turn and walk back across the room towards the balcony. Arrok seems to be mulling over the conversation. He leans down and I climb onto his back. We take off without a word; only when we are out of sight of Marcus does Arrok speak.

"I cannot believe you," Arrok chuckles.

"What," I ask defensively.

"You lied straight to his face and he did not know the difference," Arrok chuckles again. "I wonder what he will do if he finds out that you had everything to do with his daughter's escape?"

"Probably nothing," I say. "If I make him mad all he has to do is send me into battle like he already is. The only difference is that, right now he doesn't want me dead."

"Let us hope that he does not want you dead at all," Arrok says his tone changing. "Do you want to go and see Luna now?"

"Yeah, if you think it's safe," I say quickly.

"I think that we can go unnoticed for a few minutes," Arrok says looking below us.

He veers sharply to the left and flies straight at the wall of the cave. He veers again once we reach the wall and follow it just as Iris did the day that Luna showed the hidden cave to me. Arrok stops and hovers for a moment and then darts into the crevice. He lands and settles onto the floor in the narrow space. When Iris landed she was able to make her way into the cave and move about. But Arrok is slightly large than her. He barely has enough room to turn around so he can be ready to take flight again.

Once he is situated I jump off and walk slowly into the secret cave. Luna is sitting in one of the chairs braiding her hair into one long ponytail. I walk over to the other chair and sit down.

"So how're you doing," I ask.

"I am managing," Luna says as she finishes the braid. "How is you shoulder?"

"It's healing," I say. "At a human rate, there was one piece that we missed. It was buried under the skin pretty far too."

"I am sorry again," Luna says glancing at my shoulder. "So what are you doing here? I assumed that you would be preparing for battle."

"Not yet," I reply. "I wanted to make sure you were doing okay first."

"I am only waiting for an opportunity to slip into the battle once it starts," Luna says. "Would you hand me that ring?"

I look down at the small table near the chair I'm sitting in. I pick up a thick sapphire ring about as big around as a golf ball. The ring has considerable weight for its size; I examine it for a moment and then toss it to Luna. She places the ring at the end of the braid.

"Arrok has told Iris to come here just before the battle to get me," Luna informs. "I cannot thank you enough. Although I think my father will be trying to question you, if he can."

"I've already talked to him," I say slowly. "He sent guards to my room and I got out before they came in. Then I found him in the dining room. He only wanted to know if I had anything to do with your escape. I told him no and came straight here."

"So you lied to him," Luna says, somewhat shocked.

"Yeah," I admit. "If I didn't, getting you out would have been for nothing. And I would be the one in more trouble than I already am."

"Like going to war is not enough," Luna says. "I'll find you on the battlefield."

"If you do that, then I'm going to have to protect you," I say. "I'm still your Guardian until this is over."

"You do not have to protect me," Luna smiles.

"I know, but you can't be too careful," I say smiling back. "Besides it gives me something to do."

"You should be focused on killing the enemy," Luna says sternly.

"I'll do that too," I say. "I'm going to see if there is anything that I can do to help with the preparations. I guess I'll see you soon."

"I hope that it will not be too soon," Luna murmurs. "Because the next time we see each other, we will be under attack."

"I know," I say sadly.

"I have something here for you," Luna says standing up.

"What," I ask.

"Here," Luna says holding out a bundle of black. "It is lightweight armor, it may help you."

"Thank you," I say taking the armor.

I examine the armor as I unfold it; all of it is jet black. There is a shoulder pad connected to a breast plate and back. It feels like there is metal under the leather.

"It has small overlapping plates of metal to absorb the impact," Luna explains as she puts on a set of armor like mine.

"So it's durable, yet it provides good movement," I say as I put it on.

"Precisely," Luna says sitting back down. "You should go now."

"I'll see you soon," I say as I walk down the tunnel.

I climb onto Arrok's back and he shuffles to the opening of the crevice. He jumps out and opens his wings. It takes a few flaps of his wings before he's away from the wall. I look back over my shoulder and can barely see the crevice to the secret cave.

"Wait," I say suddenly. "Fly out to the wall tops. We might be able to help somehow."

"All right," Arrok says. "But I do not think that there is much left to do."

Arrok flies in a semicircle so we are heading towards the mouth of the cave. Dragons are flying everywhere over the city. Some have people riding on them, other are alone carrying bundles of materials for the battle that will soon take place. I look down at the people in the city streets. There are a lot less than I would've thought. It seems that most of them think staying inside to be in their best interest. Everyone's locking themselves up.

"It is always the quietest before the storm," Arrok mumbles under his breath.

I act as if I didn't hear what he's just said. Why would Luna want to throw herself into the battle? Why do I want to fight or Scott even? He's the one that wants to return home. Me on the other hand, I don't know. I want to see my friends and family, but I feel accepted here. I can actually make a difference, maybe that's why I'm fighting.

"It would seem that Marcus has increased the guards on the walls," Arrok says. "He also has a suitable sized force here too."

I look down at the barren fields. All of the crops look as if they have been harvested. There are still some areas where the grasses and plants are waste or chest high. For every piece that has been harvested it seems that a soldier has taken its place. There are easily forty to fifty thousand soldiers. I hope that the werewolves don't even have a third of the size this force has. Arrok lands softly on the ground, I jump off and walk over to Simon. He must be out of a job now that Luna's escaped. He glares at me as I approach.

"What are you doing here," he asks gruffly. "Do not tell me you are going to fight?"

"Why not," I shoot back. "As I recall I beat you went you challenged me, so save it for the werewolves. Is there anything that I can do to help out?"

"Fine," Simon grumbles. "You can take the wall top guards place in a few minutes. The regiment that I am in control of is going to replace them for the next shift."

"All right," I say. "When do you want me up there?"

"When it is closer to nightfall," Simon orders.

"Sir," one of the guards on the wall yells. "We have sighted the enemy. They are massing at the edge of the forest."

"How many," Simon shouts back.

"It looks like several thousand and growing," the guard yells in a panicked voice. "Their number could be close to forty thousand!"

"This is not good," Simon mutters. "I want this regiment on the walls, now!"

I quickly jump back on Arrok's back. He takes off as soon as I'm on. He flies straight to the top of the wall and lands on an open space. All of the other soldiers are running up steps, climbing ladders, and using all available pulley systems to get up or down. I jump off and look around the wall. It looks like they are truly ready for a war. There are torches places on every battlement. There are cauldrons bubbling over fires, boiling with what looks like oil or water. There are also large piles of rocks in between the cauldrons. Long bows, short bows and thousands of quivers of arrows line every empty space that appears. Where there are no bows there are pikes, spears, swords, and shields.

I now turn my attention to the distant forest fringe. It looks as if a massive fog has settled on the ground and is slowly swirling towards us. There are definitely more than forty thousand. They easily reach fifty thousand. We may out number them slightly, but they are so much stronger.

"How can we win against them," a soldier says in horror.

"Because if we don't, we're dead," I say calmly.

Everyone watches as the mass grows closer and closer. It moves slowly across the open ground with no end in sight.

24

THE WEREWOLVES GROW CLOSER as the day goes on; they're in no hurry at all. They know that we're not going to run, we have no where to run to. The horde stops about one hundred yards away from the wall. There are no less than forty thousand werewolves on the stretch of hills and open grasslands below us. I look over my shoulder at our numbers. We barely have more men, but so much less muscle compared to the werewolves. I watch as Simon as he gives out orders to his group of men on the wall. Below in the fields behind the wall there are others giving orders to their regiments.

"So do you think that we have a chance of winning," I familiar voices asks softly next to me.

I look to my left, and to no surprise I see Luna. She has her short swords at her sides and a long bow with a quiver of arrows on her back. She seems abnormally calm. Her eyes seem to sparkle like true sapphires in the setting sunlight.

"Maybe," I breathe. "I just hope that we can win without losing too many men."

"They will probably wait until it is dark to attack," Luna says staring at the mass.

I watch as the werewolves lounge around on the ground. Even

though they all have chosen to fight they still stay in their original packs. They keep several yards away from each other. Then from the midst of the werewolves the two dragons emerge. They fly low over the horde of werewolves as they make their way towards us. The first thing that I notice that is different about them, they're carrying passengers.

"Look," Luna points. "Those must be the cloaked figures that Thunder had mentioned."

We watch as the dragons land in the space between the werewolves and the wall.

"We would like to talk with the vampire and the human," one says.

"They are the ones that rescued our enemy form our grasp," the other finishes.

Luna and I look at each other at the same time. Before I can say anything Iris is one the wall next to us. Luna climbs on her back and looks down at me.

"You should ride with me, it is too dangerous for Arrok," Luna says.

I walk to Iris's side and start to climb up, when I feel a strong hand on my shoulder. I look behind me to see Simon glaring at me.

"I should have known that you where behind her escape," Simon says in a voice as hard as stone. "You are going back to the palace Luna."

"No, she's not," I say turning around and drawing my sword in a flash. "If you haven't noticed there is a whole army of werewolves at your doorstep. I think that you should worry about them before you try to worry about her."

"Fine," he snorts and walks away.

"I expected him to make a much bigger deal out of it than that," I say to myself as I sheath my sword.

"He will later," Luna says.

I climb onto Iris's back and she dives off the wall. We reach the meeting place in only a few seconds. Iris lands in a hurry and Luna and I jump off. We stand next to Iris not moving any nearer to our enemy.

"You two have caused a great deal of problems for us," the first dragon says.

"Much more than we would have liked," the other continues.

They remind of identical twins that finish each others sentences.

But looking closer they do seem to be alike in every aspect, except one. The second dragon has a pink section on his neck were a wound has been but has now healed, it look like that scales haven't returned to their normal color yet. He is the one that I managed to hit with my sword when we rescued Arrok. That was probably one of the stupider thing that I've, next to jumping off the Monolith.

"We have come to negotiate," the first dragon says.

"A surrender of sorts," the second finishes again.

"Yours that is," the first interjects.

"I am sorry, but you are wasting your time," Luna says. "Besides we are not the ones to talk to if you want surrender."

"Then you and everyone that stands against us will die," a male voice says.

Every muscle in my body tightens as two cloaked figures step out from behind the dragons. The male must be the one on the right. The frame alone betrays them. The figure on the left is shorter and thin. The one on the right is taller and wider. Both of them throw back their hoods at the same time. I was correct.

The girl has blonde hair that looks just like Luna's. Her eyes are like rubies in a fire light, which sparkle dangerously. Her skin is as white as chalk. The man doesn't look any older than me. He has short black hair that is unkempt like mine. He might only be a few inches taller than me, and is more muscular, his eyes are darker than his hair almost black. He is also just as pale is the girl next to him. They both look like evil versions of Luna and I. The girl smiles and I can see the set of fangs, which makes her a vampire. Just by their skin color being the same I can guess that her companion is a vampire too.

"Then that means we can't afford to lose," I say coolly.

"You are arrogant," the male says in an irritated tone. "What makes you think that you can win?"

"What makes you," I shoot back.

"I think that I am going to kill you first," he says menacingly. "Or should I make you and your friend here slaves?"

"Come now Victor," the girl says suddenly.

Her voice is soft like velvet. Her tone is soothing much like Lilith's voice, only slightly more dangerous.

"I told you if we are victorious that we would not do such a thing," she continues. "They deserve to live just as much as we do."

"No, they do not Jenna," he says coldly. "Do you remember who forced us into this place? It was those pathetic humans, just like the ones that stand before us now."

"I am a human," I retort. "But she is not."

"Is this true," Victor asks in surprise.

"It is," Luna says bearing her teeth almost like a wild animal about to attack.

"Then join us," Victor says extending his hand. "We can drive out the humans here. They should be happy with their world, not invading ours."

"It seems like you are doing to us what we did to you," I say.

"Yes," Victor says. "I think it is our right to have some revenge."

"Tell me then," I say suddenly. "Were you alive when the humans drove out your kind?"

"No," he replies bitterly. "I was not."

"I wasn't alive for it either," I say. "So why are you wanting revenge for something didn't happen to you, and I didn't do it to you."

"Because if it had not happened we would be living among you where we belong," Victor fumes. "We should not be here!"

"I think we can agree on that," I say casually.

"Do not try to befriend me," Victor shouts. "We agree on nothing!"

"Victor calm down," Jenna says softly. "Save your hostility for the battle ahead."

The way Jenna acts is almost like she doesn't even belong with him. She's so calm and patient. Victor on the other hand is short tempered and irrational.

"Fine," Victor breathes heavily, and then his eyes dart to Luna. "You still have not given me an answer; do you wish to join us?"

"I am sorry, but my place is protecting my people," Luna replies calmly.

"We are your people," Victor says through gritted teeth. "I was once a member of your city. I was shunned by every single person that I came in contact with. All because I tried human blood, hah! You will never know the true power that their blood will give you. It makes us stronger, faster, and even allows you to sniff out an individual's blood. It is a marvelous thing indeed."

"Then you were right to be cast out," Luna says coldly. "There is no place for your kind here."

"We are the same kind," Victor says trying to keep his temper under control. "The only difference is that I truly understand what this gift is. You waste your existence by drinking blood from foul animals. Now that I think about it, I think that you might be more pathetic than the human next to you."

"Enough," Jenna says sternly, her ruby eyes shining with a suppressed fury. "There is no need to insult a sister of our kind. If she does not wish to join us then that is her choice."

"Her last one," Victor grumbles. "I am leaving."

Victor turns and walks to the gray dragon on the right. He converses with him for a moment and then climbs onto the dragon's back. They take off and circle above us a few times, and then they fly off to the center of the werewolf horde. The second dragon then takes flight and follows in the same direction as the other dragon.

"I must apologize for my husband's behavior," Jenna says smoothly. "He can be a little overbearing sometimes. Now back to our conversation."

Jenna begins to walk towards us, her movement is so graceful. Her body doesn't recoil at all from her footsteps. Even though she moves so evenly it does little to ease my suspicions. I place my hand on my sword and partially draw it.

"There is no need for that," Jenna says only a few feet from me. "I am not anything like Victor. I do feed on human blood, but I do not take their life in the process. I have more control over my abilities than he does, though I do not admit it while in his presence. Even now I have not fed in weeks. Your blood has a unique smell to it."

Jenna steps nearer to me. Her face is only inches from mine as she inhales deeply.

"I knew that some warriors have an, alluring scent but this is different," Jenna says, still close. "You are a berserker."

I take a few steps back and draw my sword. Jenna stays where she is unmoving. She doesn't seem surprised at all by my actions.

"How can you tell that just by smelling me," I ask quickly.

"Just as Victor said earlier, it is a gift given by the blood of humans," Jenna says. "It is a shame that your friend has not tried it yet, maybe one day she will."

"Never," Luna snaps. "I will not become an abomination like you and Victor."

"Ah," Jenna breathes. "You are fearful of what you do not understand. What a pity. No, the true abomination is Victor. You will soon find out what I mean, on the battlefield."

"I will be looking for you," Luna says coldly. "Not him."

"Do not bother," Jenna laughs. "I do not share the lust for war. I am not going to fight."

"If Victor is so evil, then why are you with him," I burst out.

"He was not that way when I met him," Jenna says.

I can hear a heavy sorrow in her voice. She looks down at the ground in silence for a moment then looks back up. I look over at Luna, she is unmoved by Jenna.

"He has lost control of himself after he drank of human blood," Jenna murmurs. "I was once a citizen of you city too. We were married and happy; we both ran a small store together. Then one day he brought home a flask of blood. This was no strange occurrence, yet that one was. It was not the blood of an animal, but a human. I drank unwittingly."

"That's sad," I admit. "Why didn't you just let him leave and you stay?"

"Because my skin had already changed," Jenna says rubbing her hand. "That is how they know. Our skin stays as white as bone."

"You got what you dissevered," Luna retorts.

"That may be true," Jenna says. "What Victor has in store for you and your people is not what you disserve though."

Jenna takes a few more steps forward until she is in between Luna and me. She leans in close enough to touch me.

"They plan on attacking at nightfall," she whispers to me. "Be ready."

Then she turns and walks away, picking her way around the lounging werewolves. She looks back at us and then is lost from sight.

"Do you really believe her," Luna bursts out in anger.

"I don't know," I say sheathing my sword. "She may be on their side, but she doesn't seem to care that much for Victor. I think that she holds him responsible for making her what she is."

"It does not matter," Luna says walking back to Iris. "She is an enemy."

"Maybe," I mumble.

Arrok flies down and lands on the ground next to Iris. I climb onto his back and get ready for him to take flight, but he sits unmoving. Iris takes flight and begins circling over us.

"What're you doing," I ask urgently. "You do see that there in an army of werewolves less than a hundred yards from us, right?"

"Yes," Arrok says. "We should go."

"Yeah that would be a good idea," I say quickly.

Arrok kicks off and flies up to the wall. I can tell by the distant tone in his voice that he's thinking about something.

"So what did you think of Victor," I ask sarcastically. "He seems like a real piece of work."

"Indeed he is," Arrok mumbles. "But Jenna, I think there is some good in her."

"What do you mean," I ask. "She feeds on human just like he does, how can she be good?"

"She does not approve of this war," Arrok says thoughtfully. "I would not have put it past Victor to have sought out the two dragons, just to form a plot of revenge."

"So you could pick up on that much of the conversation from the wall top," I ask.

"Yes," Arrok says. "That and flying above when they did not know.

"So you think that Victor is out for revenge," I murmur. "Do you think we could get Jenna to come over to our side then?"

"Not with Victor still alive," Arrok says as we land on the wall top. "You saw how he reacted to Luna when she said she was fighting with humans."

"Yeah," I say as I jump off Arrok's back. "He's going to make my Guardian job a lot more difficult too."

"You should not worry about him that much," Arrok says gazing out at the werewolf horde. "Yes he is very unstable, but he will be more worried about carrying out his revenge on every human in sight. The chances of him finding you with two armies this size are very slim."

"I hope you're right," I say.

I look up at the sun as it sinks lower in the west. If what Jenna said was true, then we don't have much time left. I look around at the wall top at the other humans and some vampires. I find myself trying to pick out the vampires from the humans. If I'm correct in the handful I've spotted then there aren't many. But there is one that I do recognize the easiest of all. Luna strides towards us with an infuriated look on her face. I glance at her as she stops next to me.

"Is what Jenna said still bothering you," I ask.

"No, and why do you even take the time remember her name," Luna retorts. "Besides I have another problem to deal with now. Simon reported me to my father while we were dealing with the Forsaken."

"So we have a problem," I say grimly. "Like the other vampires and the werewolves weren't enough do deal with. What are the Forsaken anyway?"

"They are vampires that have been cast out of Haven for drinking human blood in," Luna explains coldly.

"Oh," I say shortly. "Does the human blood make them stronger?"

"Yes," Luna sighs. "It also makes them faster, just as the one Forsaken had mentioned."

"Victor," I correct.

"Yes," Luna says with a tone colder than ice.

A group of soldiers moving towards us causes me to look up. I let out a long sigh. In the midst of the soldiers are Simon and Marcus. Simon seems to be in a good mood about his success. Marcus is the exact opposite; his face looks as hard as the stone wall top he's walking on. Luna turns to face her father as the group stops.

"I told you that you were not going to fight," Marcus shouts sternly. "You have disobeyed me yet again."

"I am not going to go through this again," Luna says coldly. "I am going to fight, look out there. They do not care if I fight or not, they are going to attack."

Marcus opens his mouth to speak but Luna cuts him off.

"There is more," she says quickly. "There are two of the Forsaken that are working with the dragons. They are the ones truly leading the attack, not the dragons."

"Well at least one of them for sure," I say.

"You," Marcus shouts as he just notices my presence. "Arrest him! You will not lie to me in my own home."

Three soldiers begin walking towards me. The one in the lead grabs my shoulder. As soon as his hand touches me the berserker ability takes over me. I grab his hand and twist it as hard as I can. He drops to his knees as his arm nears the point of breaking. He lets out a cry of pain and tries to make me release him with his free hand. I twist a little more and I can hear his shoulder let out a loud pop, followed by another cry of pain.

"Why can't you see that there are bigger things to worry about than who fights," I say very irritated now. "Let her fight! She only wants to protect those that can't protect themselves. She understands the situation that she's putting herself in, just like every other soldier on the field. They're protecting the ones they love."

The soldier wiggles slightly under my grasp.

"I don't want to lose my daughter," Marcus says in a hard tone.

"If you do not let me fight than you will lose me anyway," Luna says slowly. "The Forsaken have offered me a place at their side, I told them no. They threaten those that I care about, and they will die for it."

"I'll protect her Marcus," I say as the soldier moans again. "You're daughter will return to you alive. I swear it."

Marcus lets out a long slow sigh. He stands silent for a moment; I know that he's thinking over our conversation.

"Fine," Marcus says. "But if she is killed, then so will your life end. I too swear this."

"Then I'm going to be fine," I smirk.

I let go of the soldiers hand and he falls the ground. He lets out a slow moan of pain as he grips his shoulder. The other two soldiers, that were smart enough to keep their distance, help him to his feet. He walks off towards the long flight of steps. Marcus and his group of soldiers turn and walk away. Marcus has a look of concern and sorrow on his face as he strides down the steps. Simon's expression is of pure disappointment, probably because his plan to have me arrested has failed.

"Thank you," Luna says softly. "You didn't have to do that."

"I'm still your Guardian until this is over," I say.

"I meant nearly breaking that soldier's arm," Luna smiles.

"Oh, sorry," I say.

We turn and watch the last golden sliver of the sun as it disappears behind the horde of werewolves. A slight breeze ruffles our clothes; it pushes the few clouds that are in the sky away from the quarter moon.

It hardly puts off enough light for me to see. All around us the soldiers begin lighting torches and place them on the battlements. The light from them makes it almost impossible to the werewolves below.

I look over at Luna as she stares up at the moon. The glow from the torches mixed with the bit of moonlight causes her eyes to shine. She looks at me and smiles, and then her smile fades.

"What," I ask.

"There is something very important I need to ask you before we go to battle," Luna says, her voice is barely above a whisper. "If you are wounded trying to protect me…"

She falls silent as if searching for the right words.

"What are you trying to ask me," I press.

"If you are wounded to the point of no recovery," she continues. "Do you want me to turn you?"

"As fascinating of a creature that a vampire is I don't think I can live as one," I say. "I don't know why."

My words seem to have hurt Luna. She looks down at the stone.

"All right," Luna mumbles.

"The only reason is because I don't intend on dying," I say trying to cheer her up. "I'll be fine. If I'm dead then I can't fulfill Lilith's dream of saving you."

"You know I had actually forgotten about that," Luna laughs.

"Really," I ask in surprise. "That's the only reason why I told Marcus I was going to stay your Guardian until after the war."

"I truly cannot thank you enough," Luna says.

"You don't have to thank me," I say.

I walk to the edge of the wall top and lean on the battlement. A torch to my left flicks back and forth in the soft breeze. Suddenly the sound of clanking wood emits to the right of me. I look to my right, expecting to see a soldier picking up some spears. Instead there's something hanging on the battlement. I look closer and can see that it's several pieces of gnarled limbs and a deer antler. Attached to it is a thick rope made of vines. It slides back like it's going to fall off the wall, then it catches and the rope goes tight. I lean over the battlement a little and squint into the darkness. My eyes have to adjust because of the light form the torches.

My blood turns cold and my palms begin to sweat. A werewolf is climbing up the rope with lightning speed. Then another hook catches to my left. I back up from the edge as thousands hooks fly up over the edge.

"What is going on," a soldier shouts.

"They are grappling hooks," Luna shouts.

It only takes a second for the soldier to realize what's happening.

"We are under attack," he shrieks in panic.

It only takes another second for chaos to set in. I set my hand on my sword and prepare for the werewolves to swarm over the wall.

25

I DRAW MY SWORD AND rush to the nearest grappling hook and start to hack at it. The rope it so thick that it takes five or six slashes to sever it. I'm rewarded with the sound of a werewolf's surprised howl, followed by a crunching thud. I move to another hook and almost get my arm ripped off by the werewolf climbing up it. It grabs onto the edge of the battlement and begins pulling himself up. I slash out at its arms. My blade cut into both arms and it collapses then slides off the battlement.

I pause for a second to view the chaos all around me. Many of the soldiers are hacking away at the grappling hooks near them. Some are picking up the large rocks and dropping them on the werewolves. Others are taking a slightly riskier tactic, they are armed with pikes. They wait until the werewolves are close enough, them they thrust out madly at them. Some of the werewolves make to the battlements, like the one I killed, before they are cut down.

"Ivan," Luna yells over the pandemonium. "They are coming over the wall, I need help."

I turn quickly to see a group of four werewolves ripping their way through a small squad of soldiers, making their way straight towards Luna. I run as fast as I can towards the fight. Another werewolf comes over the battlement in front of me. I slide under him like a baseball player sliding into home base. As I slide out the other side I thrust up with my sword. The blade glides smoothly into his throat. I scramble to my feet just as the werewolf stumbles off the battlement.

"Ivan," Luna yells again.

"I'm coming," I shout back.

I run to her side and glance at her to make sure that she's not hurt. She catches me inspecting her.

"I am all right," Luna says. "Look out!"

The group of werewolves is upon us now. One of them is wounded, the others are perfectly fine. Two of them dart around us to our opposite side. Another werewolf comes over the battlement. Now there's two in front of us and three behind. I face the three that are not injured. Luna presses her back to mine as she faces the others, then the werewolves charge.

The berserker takes over once again as they fall upon us. The first werewolf comes in low trying to slash out at my legs. I stand my ground and slash down at it. It dodges to the side and quickly recovers, then an arrow pierces it chest followed by another. It falls to the ground dead and I glance in the direction of the arrows. Maria, Simon's sister smiles with satisfaction. I can feel Luna behind me moving rapidly as she repels the werewolves. The second werewolf lunges for my throat. I slash up as hard as I can. My blade encounters some resistance as it cuts through my enemy. It swings one last time in an attempt to kill me. I duck as its claws whistle over my head. The third werewolf takes one step forward and I charge it. I spin as it slashes out at me and the claws miss me. I extend my arm and the blade cuts through its chest. Just as it is about to attack again I stab my sword into its neck and quickly pull the blade out.

I turn to help Luna with the werewolves attacking her. Just as I stand up she spins causing the sapphire ring in her hair to crack into a werewolf's snout. I move forward and finish it before it recovers.

"Here come more," Luna shouts.

"It's too crowded up here," I shout over the clamor of battle. "There's not enough room to fight."

More werewolves are making their way over the battlements. The soldiers that are left on the wall top are dwindling quickly. The soldier below on the ground can't get up the steps fast enough to repel the werewolves that are coming up, or eliminate the ones already on the wall. Suddenly a horn sounds long and low over the screams and ring of steel.

"What is that," I shout.

"The dragons are about to assist with the battle," Luna shouts back to me as she cuts down another werewolf.

I look to see about half of the dragons that we recruited fly out of the cavern. On each of them is a single rider. But they also have what appear to be large quivers filled with short spears. They fly over the fields and split into two groups. The first half flies out past the wall and begins to attack the werewolves that are climbing up. The second group drops lower and begins to carefully pick off the werewolves that are battling our men.

"I have an idea," I shout. "Can you handle yourself for a few minutes?"

Luna cuts down another werewolf and smiles over her shoulder.

"I think I will be all right," she replies.

"Good," I yell back.

I run to a section of the wall that is not yet overrun by werewolves. I let out a shrill whistle. Arrok lands beside me in an instant, he must have been flying above. I sheath my sword then snatch up a razor sharp battle axe and jump onto Arrok's back.

"What are you doing," Arrok asks quickly.

"Just fly along the edge of the wall," I yell as he takes off. "We're going to cut as many of those ropes at possible."

Arrok wastes no time in getting into position. He turns at an angle so that his wings don't hit the wall. I hold the axe out as it scrapes along the wall sending sparks showering from the stone. One by one the ropes are severed as we fly. Many of the ropes are not cut all the way through, but the axe does enough damaged for the weight of the werewolf to make it snap. We cover the small section of the wall that is most under siege. Arrok dodges in and out of the flying spears being thrown by the riders.

Arrok flies up above the fighting. He hovers for a moment as a large group of werewolves begins to tear their way through the soldiers. He dives towards them like bolt of lightning. They notice him just as he strikes. Arrok lashes out with his claws ripping into every werewolf that gets in his way. He passes over them several times, and after each pass the group thins out.

"Jump off and finish them," Arrok shouts. "I will try to eliminate more."

Arrok swoops down and I jump off as he grazes the wall. There aren't many werewolves left in the group, but there are enough to pose a problem for me and the six other soldiers that are near them. As the werewolves charge at us the berserker takes over again. I throw the battle axe at the lead werewolf with all the strength I can gather. The axe flies straight and it slices into the arm of the werewolf. Yet it still charges towards us. One of the soldiers has a bow with half a quiver of arrows. He calmly notches an arrow and fires it. I watch as the arrow buries into the werewolf forehead, it takes one staggering step then falls off the edge of the wall.

The other werewolves are among us before the body hits the ground below. I draw my sword and begin hacking into every werewolf in my reach. My body seems to be moving on its own as I watch. My sword feels just like it's an extension of my arm. It glides through the air and through my enemies with ease. I continue to cut down werewolves one after another. Then the berserker stops. I'm standing in the middle of the gore breathing heavily. My clothes are saturated in blood. There are easily seven werewolves around me. I look over my shoulder at the six soldiers.

"Let's clear this wall top," I shout. "Come on!"

They follow with a dumfounded look on their faces. We slowly make our way through the small groups of werewolves that are left. We destroy any grappling hooks that we come across. We stop to gather more weapons and soldier that can fight. Soon we are at a small group of wounded soldiers. Scott is among them with a five long slash marks across his chest. They extend from his left shoulder down to his waist. Some of the other soldiers have improvised and bandaged his chest as best as they can.

"Scott, are you all right," I ask as I rush to his side.

"I'll be okay," he grins. "It's just a scratch."

"That's a pretty big scratch," I laugh. "Hold on."

I stand up and whistle for Arrok again. It only takes me a few seconds to spot him this time. He dives down and tears a werewolf off the wall, just as it comes over the battlement. He then circles once then lands several feet away from us.

"What happened," Arrok asks. "Are both of you all right?"

"I'm fine," I say. "This isn't my blood, but Scott's been hurt pretty badly. Can you fly him to the infirmary?"

"Certainly," Arrok says.

I kneel down and help Scott up. I have to practically drag him by myself to Arrok and push him onto his back.

"I agree to fight in a war and get wounded before it really gets started," Scott winces.

"You won't be missing much," I laugh.

"From the looks of your clothes you haven't missed a single werewolf," Scott nods at me. "I got a few, and then one of them got me."

"Don't worry about me," I say. "Now you need to get to the infirmary."

"I will return as soon as he is in good hands," Arrok says, and then he takes flight.

"Look there is the last of the werewolves," a soldier shouts.

I look in the direction that he's pointing. There are only a handful of them left. They are packed tightly together slashing out furiously at any soldier that gets too close. Many of the other soldiers are abandoning their swords in favor of pikes and spears. They stab menacingly at the werewolves. Only one of the people in the group of soldiers is killing the werewolves one by one. Luna in their midst carefully firing off arrows from her bow.

I rush over to where she stands. She fires another arrow and it buries into a werewolf's chest. It falls to the ground with out a sound. Soon all of the werewolves in the group are dead. The wall top is clear of any threats, for now.

"That seems to be the last of them," Luna says in a satisfied tone.

A cry of victory rings out from all of the remaining soldiers.

"What is your orders ma'am," asks a soldier with a long gash in his arm.

"Signal for the dragons to start landing," Luna says. "We need to get all of the wounded to the out of here before the next attack."

"Yes," he says as he bows.

He rushes off and converses with another soldier that has a long bow. The soldier notches an arrow and places the tip over one of the few remaining torches. The tip catches fire and he shoots it high in the air. I watch as the arrow lands in a small pond out in the fields. Then more of the dragons that we recruited fly out of the city. They fly in a large arrow formation, until they reach the middle of the field. Then they break off and land at different areas of the wall. Only about two soldiers can be placed on a dragon, sometimes three for the dragons large enough.

"This was only a small victory," Luna says.

"But it was still a victory," I say. "That's going to help morale."

"Yes," Luna agrees.

"Are you okay," I ask looking at a section of her sleeve that's been cut.

"I am perfectly fine," she says looking me over carefully. "Are you?"

"Yeah," I say quickly. "It's not my blood."

"All right," Luna says looking to the skies. "Good, here come the other dragons."

I look up at the dragons as they fly out in all directions over the fields. Some land on the ground, but many land on the wall top around us. As soon as a dragon lands the soldiers that are able help place the wounded on the backs of the dragons. The entire area becomes alive with activity. I assist with the moving of wounded soldiers onto dragons. Weapons are collected and positions refilled with the soldiers that couldn't get to the wall top in time.

Time passes just as the dragons do. Once most of the wounded soldiers are out of the way I stop and look around at the carnage that is left. We lost a lot of soldiers, but the werewolves suffered just as we did. I look down at my clothes for the first time. I knew that there was blood on me, but my shirt is almost completely consumed in crimson. The moonlight causes the blood all over the wall top to shine and appear almost black.

Most of the torches are being replaced since many were lost in the first attack. I walk cautiously to the edge of the wall and peer over the battlements. There are hundreds if not thousands of werewolves lying dead below us. I turn around and lean against the battlements. I slowly slide down it until I'm sitting on the ground. I stare at my bloodstained hands. Someone comes over and sits down quietly beside me. I continue to stare at my hands. Then I feel the person's hand on my arm. I look over at Luna with little surprise.

"Are you sure that you are not hurt," Luna asks concerned. "You seem troubled?"

"I almost lost it," I say staring into her eyes. "I almost lost control of the berserker ability. I was killing werewolves one after the other, but I was only watching not acting. My body was though, yet I wasn't telling it to."

"Maybe it was for the best that you could not control it," Luna says. "If you would have had a single error in your ways you would probably be dead."

"I know," I sigh. "So what do we do now?"

"We retaliate," Luna says coldly. "You remember Tori's little invention that you used on the beach?"

"Yes," I say thinking of the ball of flames erupting from the campfire.

"Well it seems that your idea for a type of fuse will be put to the test as well," Luna says with a devilish grin. "Are you ready to see the werewolves pay dearly for their attack?"

I nod in silence. Luna stands up and takes her bow off her shoulder. She reaches into a pouch on her belt and pulls out a vial. There is a piece of cloth stuffed in the end.

"Get ready to retaliate," Luna shouts.

I stand up to watch the test of this new weapon. Funny how a doctor, one who's purpose is to help those in pain, has developed a weapon for war. What a display of irony. The soldiers follow her example; they pull out vial form pockets, bags, and chests. They attach the vials near the end of their arrows. They then notch the arrows on their bowstrings and pull them back. Luna lights the cloth on a torch and aims the arrow high in the air.

"Fire," she shouts and lets the arrow fly.

At first it looks like a single meteor streaking across the night sky. Then the meteor is joined by thousands of others streaking brilliantly across the night. They rise into the sky and then fall on the werewolves below. Luna's arrow is the first to hit. It strikes a werewolf and buries into it and then it explodes with a muffled pop. The werewolf is enveloped in flames, just as thousands of others. The soft thuds are set off everywhere below. Everyone on the wall top cheers at the new weapon's success as it wreaks havoc on the enemy.

"It seems that you and Tori are quiet the inventors," Luna smiles.

"No. She invented it, I just made a suggestion," I say.

"You are too modest," Luna says. "Fire another volley of arrows, this time without the weapon!"

"What are you doing," I ask.

"Just a little extra damage to what has already been done," Luna says smiling again.

I watch as everyone on the wall top notches arrows again. They aim high just as they did before. They let the arrows through the sky; they are just as black as the night. The howls of anguish are still ringing out from the fires when the second volley hits. More howls of pain and rage sound below us. The fires make it possible for me and the other humans to see the werewolves falling everywhere.

"That should keep them back from the wall now," Luna says satisfied. "They should at least be smart enough to keep out of range of our arrows."

I sit back down on the wall lean back on the battlements. Maybe they will just surrender now, cut their losses and get out while they can. I know that they're not that smart though. Especially if Victor is the one leading them, he's probably screaming out orders for more grappling hooks. They'll find another way to attack or get past our wall. My stomach lurches and I take slow deep breaths.

"Ivan," Luna says looking down at me. "What is wrong with you? You seem ill all of the sudden."

"I'm fine," I say slowly. "But I'm not going to be, none of us are going to be when the wall falls."

"Oh no," Luna gasps. "I forgot all about what Lilith had said. When do you think that they will strike?"

"I don't know, but we need to be ready to evacuate this wall top quickly," I say as I stand up. "We need to get the rest of the wounded to the infirmary or past the second wall."

Luna only looks at me smiling. She seems pleased with me somehow.

"What," I ask quickly.

"You are such an enigma," she says smiling still. "You are able to fight, you are knowledgeable of many things, and you seem to take charge of the situation when the need arises."

"Like I said before, I'm only making a suggestion," I say.

I look out at the small fires that now dot the land before us. The werewolves did move out of the range of the arrows, but there are still some licking wounds where the fires are. It must cause them too much pain to try and move. Then someone steps into the light of one of the fires. Victor is standing very confidently in the orange glow. He no longer has his cloak on since it's dark now. Instead he is in a type of light armor similar to mine and Luna's. It's just as black as his eyes. He raises his hand and begins to smile.

"Is that Victor," Luna says through gritted teeth.

"Yes," I say coldly. "Kill him."

Luna slowly picks up her bow which is leaning on the battlement. She notches an arrow in it and takes careful aim. Victor lets his hand fall, and like a signal Luna fires the arrow. I can't even see the arrow as it flies through the sky. So I keep my eyes locked on Victor. Then he stumbles back a few steps. I watch as he pulls an arrow out of his left forearm.

Instead of yelling out threats to us or moving, he starts to laugh. He laughs likes the lunatic that his is. Then he stops laughing, but the laughter echoes around us. As the echo fades a slight whistling sound begins to grow louder. I look up to see one of the gray dragons flying away. The other is flying towards us with a large boulder in his claws. The whistling grows louder, and then I realize what it is. I look to see a smaller boulder hurling towards us.

"Watch out," I yell.

The berserker takes over and I dive out of the way, taking Luna down with me as the boulder flies just a few feet above us. We land on the wall and a panicked cry rings out. One soldier wasn't fast enough and was knocked off the wall. So that was a signal that Victor had given, that would also explain the malicious laughter.

"Do you mind," Luna says.

I look down at Luna as she is under me.

"Sorry," I say quickly as I scramble up.

I hold out my hand and help her up and then the second boulder hits. The second boulder makes contact with the wall, causing it to shake. A large crack shoots up the side of the wall, but it still holds. The soldiers around that area move away. Many others soldiers instantly begins firing arrows up at the dragons.

"Get everyone off the wall now," I shout. "The wall is going to fall, there's nothing we can do. Retreat to the inner wall!"

Some of the soldiers take my advice and start running down the steps and climbing down ladders. Others continue to defend the wall. The first dragon returns with another boulder and drops it as he dodges arrows and spears. The boulder hits just below the impact of the first. The crack grows larger as the boulder shatters from the collision. The wall is thick, but it won't hold at the rate they are dropping the stones.

The second dragon returns with yet another and lets it fall. The wall shakes again and a section of the wall slides out of place with a low grinding rumble. They are slowly working their way down the wall. They're weakening it from the top to the bottom. Slowly cracking it until the section it loosened enough to fall. The two dragons return and begin dropping the boulders at the top again, but at a different location. We continue to fire arrows and through spear feebly at them. They are too experienced at flying to be taken down by us. The boulders shake the wall again. A large V shaped crack is beginning to form on the side of the wall now. More debris falls from the wall.

"The wall is not going to take much more," Luna shouts to the small group that remains on the wall.

Luna looks around at the few wounded left on the wall. She searches the sky frantically for the other dragons. Then five of them fly down lead by Zephyr. They quickly land.

"Get these wounded back to the doctor as fast as you can," Zephyr orders.

The wall shakes again. Zephyr sways slightly. His head snaps up to the gray dragons as they both fly away for more boulders.

"Can none of you wound them," he demands.

"They are too fast," Luna says. "The wall is not going to hold."

The cracks are almost to the ground below now. The wall is going to fall it takes any more heavy hits.

"Then I shall try," Zephyr growls.

The dragons return and drop their boulders on the wall. The section of the wall lurches forward, then back slightly. It groans under its own weight and a cracking sound begins to emit from under us. The two dragons turn around to fly back, then Zephyr launches into the air and flies straight for them.

Zephyr slams into the first dragon and they lock into a death grip spiral. They slash out viciously with their claws and gnash at each others throats. The second dragon continues to go for more boulders. Just as they are less than a hundred feet from the ground they break apart and swoop up. They lock onto each other again and continue their bloody struggle.

They are not as far from the ground this time when they release each other. The second dragon is retuning with a large boulder. He seems to be struggling with this one. Zephyr spots him and flies toward him as fast as he can. Just as he is about to crash onto the dragon the other rakes his claws along Zephyr's back. The memory of Arrok lying defenseless as he was attacked flashes through my mind. Zephyr roars out in agony as he spirals down to the ground. As soon as he hits the ground he goes silent. I watch expecting him to recover and gather himself back up, but he doesn't.

"He's dead," I whisper.

The dragon that he attacked flies painfully beside his comrade. Then the other dragon lets go of the boulder. It hurtles straight into the middle of the V shaped cracks. First there's a shudder just like the others. Then it continues as the section begins to crack more and then crumble.

"Get off the wall now," Luna shouts.

But for some of the soldiers it's too late. The section of the wall begins to fall apart. I grab onto a ladder and slide down it as fast as I can without falling off. I hit the ground hard and instantly start running away from the wall. Luna is somehow beside me running too. When we are far enough away we stop. As the section of the wall falls it also widened. I don't think that the dragons intended on that, but I'm sure they will use it to their full advantage.

I look around at the few soldiers left that tried to defend the wall. There are only sixteen others besides Luna and myself, so eighteen total. A handful of people are all that remain on the frontline. The last bit of rumbling fades and the dust begins to settle. As the dust clears from the wreckage a large dark gray werewolf stands on the ruined stone. Its chest is covered with the scars of past battles. It lets out a deep howl, which is followed by others. Then werewolves begin pouring through the opening in the wall. There are too many of them for us to fight. We all turn and start running for our lives.

26

I RUN AS HARD AND as fast as I can. The field seems eternal as I try to put some distance between me and the werewolf horde. All of the other soldiers have the same idea as me. They scatter and run for the wall with all their strength. Luna is slightly ahead of the group with no trouble at all, just another advantage of being a vampire.

We enter the chest high grass about half way across the field. I risk a glance behind me to see if the werewolves are close. They're too close for my comfort and that's all the motivation that I need to keep running. Some of the other soldiers are starting to lag behind though. One of them trips and falls to the ground. He screams out as the werewolves fall upon him, and then he falls silent. One by one the soldiers are caught by the werewolves. Most of them just can't keep up with Luna and me. But when Luna starts to slow I know I have to do something.

A werewolf leaps at me from the side as I run. The berserker takes over instantly, but I don't have time to draw my sword. I duck as the werewolf flies over my head. I barely turn my head to see where it lands as one of its claws grazes my forehead and then slides slightly down onto my cheek. The claw misses my left eye by only a fraction.

"Arrok," I shout between ragged breaths.

I can't catch my breath long enough to attempt a whistle. My lungs are burning for the air that they aren't receiving. My heart is beating so hard I fear it will burst out of my chest. I can feel the blood coursing heavily through my veins, just as much as the fear is. Panic slowly pushes the berserker out of me, which causes more panic. I look around quickly as part of my vision blurs red from the blood.

"Arrok," I shout again.

Another soldier is taken down by a werewolf; this one was only a few feet from me. Arrok swoops down and flies low over the filed towards us. A wave of relief surges through my and I put on an extra burst of speed. Arrok gets lower to the ground and is almost to me. I jump as high as I can and he manages to get under me. I land on his back and gasp for air.

"Luna," I rasp. "We... need to help... her."

"Give me a moment," Arrok shouts.

Arrok circles back and flies low to the ground again. I draw my sword and continue to gasp for air as my sides ache. Arrok turns side ways as he flies; his wings are almost scraping the ground. He tucks his wings in closer to his body and gets closer to the ground. A werewolf jumps up towards us but Arrok is focused on getting to Luna. I strike out with my sword and severe the werewolf's arm. It lets out a howl of pain as it falls back to the ground.

"There she is," Arrok shouts. "I am going to flip upside down so the werewolves will not be able to attack us as easily. You grab her when she jumps."

I quickly sheath my sword and tighten my legs around his neck. He flips upside down and I outstretch my arm. I can't see out of my left eye because of the blood that is leaking into it. I only hope that Luna can make it. Luna jumps and grabs onto my arm. I grip her arm just as much she does mine. As Arrok turns she lands on his back behind me.

"Thank... you," she gasps.

I only nod as I breathe heavily too. She leans against my shoulder as we fly over the last stretch of the fields. Arrok dives low and gently lands on the wall. I fall off him more than climb down. I crawl to the edge of the wall and lean against the battlement. Luna manages to jump off and stumbles over to the wall and sits down too.

"Did any of the other... soldiers make it," I ask.

"I do not… know," Luna replies shortly.

A dragon lands with one soldier on its back and then a second lands with two more. They all fall off the dragons' backs like I did. They were definitely with us.

"These are the only other survivors," a soldier says to Luna.

"Get them to… the infirmary," Luna says slowly. "They deserve to rest."

The soldiers barely manage to climb back onto the backs of the dragons. Once they are finally on again, the dragons take flight and fly straight towards the palace.

"So what are we going to do now," I ask as I catch my breath. "Lilith's dream proved to be true."

"It would seem so," Luna replies. "This wall will not fall though. This is where we will stand and fight."

I close my eyes and breathe slowly. That was very cliché; I can't even count the number of movies I've heard sayings like that in. But I suppose that this time it really is a life or death.

I stumble to my feet; it seems my body is still recovering from the run across the field. There are still werewolves coming through the gap in the wall at a steady pace. Almost all of the fields below are covered by packs of werewolves. Most of them are making themselves comfortable on the soft grasses. A few of them wander around the fields.

"So what are we going to do now," I ask. "We can't let them break this wall or the entire city will be massacred."

"Look closely at them," Luna says staring out at them. "They are recovering just as we are. Many of them have been burned by our new weapon; see how they lounge in the streams and ponds?"

"Yeah," I say as I watch. "So is there a way to stop the flow of the water?"

"Unfortunately no, the streams are fed by an under ground spring," Luna sighs. "There is no way to stop it."

"There's a way, we just haven't thought of it yet," I mumble under my breath.

"They have probably wised up to the new fire arrows by now," One of the soldiers says. "We will need something that they will not see as easily or expect."

"Poison them," another soldier says. "Those springs that you just mentioned run all over those fields."

"That's a good idea," I say turning to Luna. "What do you think?"

"Think that you just got promoted," Luna says to the soldier. "Now let us find a proper poison."

"So we're going to see Tori," I ask.

"Indeed we are," Luna says.

She lets out a whistle and Iris lands on the wall next her, I whistle too and in an instant Arrok is next to me as well. I climb onto his back and we take off. Luna and Iris are already in the air. We fly faster than normal towards the palace. I know that we don't know how much time there is before the werewolves attack again or the dragons launch another salvo of boulders in an attempt to bring this wall down too. Although with one dragon wounded they might not be able to.

"We will need to hurry," Luna says. "I am sure that Tori will have her hands full with the wounded, and the infirmary is going to be in chaos."

"Okay," I say shortly.

We cover the grounds over the vast city in a short time. As we fly closer to the palace I can see that there a fair number of soldiers and palace guards on the walls. The air around the infirmary balcony in buzzing with activity, dragons are flying in with wounded soldiers and additional supplies.

"There's not enough room for us to land," I say to Luna as we hover.

"We do not have that land," Luna says.

Iris swoops down as one of the dragons take off from the balcony. Iris turns around so that she's facing us as she hovers near the balcony. Luna stands up on her back and runs between Iris's wings until she reaches Iris's hind legs, then she jumps and lands on floor of the infirmary.

"Are you ready," Arrok asks.

"I guess we'll find out," I say.

Arrok swoops down as Iris moves away from the balcony. He takes her place and turns away form the balcony. I stand and run shakily down his back and then jump. I land hard on the marble floor of infirmary balcony and stumble once before I catch my balance.

"That was not a bad performance," Luna says with a laugh.

"But may I suggest that in the future that you wait until he is a little closer."

"Why, how far was he from the balcony," I ask.

"About ten feet or so," Luna says thoughtfully. "Now we need to find Tori and a suitable poison."

I stand in silence as I gaze at the damage the soldiers received. Some are missing arms and legs. Others are lying on beds covered in the blood that seeps through their bandages. Then there are those that are not wounded badly like me, but they have broken down into frantic sobs. They're not much older than me, probably only nineteen or twenty. The dragons continue to land and nurses rush to pull the wounded soldiers off. I walk over to one of the dragons and help a nurse with a soldier. He has several long gashes running down the back of his leg.

"Thank you," the nurse replies in a tired voice.

"Where do you need him at," I ask.

"On that open bed over there," she says pointing.

She rushes off to help with the unloading of the other soldiers. I throw the soldiers arm over my shoulder and help him stumble to the bed.

"Ah," he winces, and then laughs. "I guess you are not able to kick a werewolf when they get too close."

"You know I did the same thing," I laugh as I help him lay down. "You've got it worse than I did though. What's you're name?"

"William," He says through gritted teeth. "Looks like you got a nice little nick too."

I raised my hand to my face and feel the cut running down my face. I wince as I put too much pressure on the wound.

"Looks that way," I laugh. "So, William how many did you manage to kill before one got you?"

"Not nearly enough," William scoffs.

The nurse comes back with a handful of materials and begins to remove the shredded cloth from around the wound. I stand up and walk away.

"Wait," William shouts. "You did not tell me your name."

"Ivan," I say over my shoulder.

"I shall remember that name," He says slowly. "Good luck."

"Thank you," I say as I walk away.

I walk out of the infirmary and into the hallways. There are wounded soldiers lining both sides of the halls. All of them are bandaged up and each has a blanket to sit on. Many of them are talking to one another. I pick my way around the few soldiers that are closer to the middle of the hall. Luna is talking quietly to one of the nurses. They finish their conversation and Luna walks towards me.

"It would seem that Tori is administering to Scott," Luna says.

"I didn't see them in the infirmary," I say.

"They are in his room," Luna explains. "We should hurry, is will also give you a chance to see your friend."

"Good," I say quickly. "Let's go."

We walk to the staircase that is at the end of hall. We make our way up the staircase to the same floor that my room is on.

"I didn't know that Scott's room was on the same floor as me," I say thoughtfully as we walk. "If I would have known earlier I would have visited him."

"Most of the time you were not in the condition to be up and about," Luna says quietly. "Ah, here we are."

She opens the door slowly and it lets out a slight creak. She stops for a moment and then fully opens it without another sound.

"So how long will I be stuck like this," Scott complains from inside the room.

"Longer than you want if you do not sit still," Tori says sternly.

Luna and I walk into the room and I can't help but feel sorry for Scott. His shirt is off and I can see the extent of his wounds. The gashes run longer than they seemed before. The five long marks dominate his chest. Tori cuts the thread to the last stitch.

"That looks like it hurts," I say lightly.

"It does," Scott grunts. "Can't breathe very deep and one of the cuts is starting to itch."

"The medicine will soon take affect," Tori says. "Then you will be asleep and motionless."

"Did you give him a dose of vampire's touch," I ask.

"Yes," Tori says. "Are you all right though? Your eye was not damaged was it?"

"No I'm fine," I say quickly as look away.

"Here you can at least clean the wound," Tori says handing me a damp cloth. "I do not wish to seem rude, but there must be a fairly important reason for you to track me down. Especially with an army of werewolves and one wall breached."

"How did you know that the wall fell," I ask as I wipe the cloth over the wound on my face.

"The soldiers that were able enough to talk informed us." Tori says as she bandages Scott's wounds. "Are the new weapons not working?"

"No it seems that they are smart enough to keep out of range of the arrows," Luna informs. "We were hoping that you could tell us if there are any poisons that we can dump into the water."

"Why do you want to poison our waters," Tori asks concerned.

"We only want to poison the waters that are being used by the werewolves," Luna says quickly. "They have been badly burned by your invention, so they are using the water to ease their pain."

"There is a poison that I can make with the resources that we have," Tori says. "It causes severe dehydration of the consumer's body."

"How does that work," I ask.

"It is not a very pretty sight," Tori says wrinkling her nose at the thought. "It involves a lot of vomiting."

"Oh," I say dropping the subject.

"How long will it take you to create this," Luna asks.

"Give me until one hour before sunrise," Tori says packing up her supplies into her bag. "I will also need twenty-five soldiers, if you can spare them."

"Certainly," Luna says with a devilish grin. "I look forward to seeing this."

27

THE TIME DRAGS BY slowly as Tori prepares the poison. Every minute feels like an hour. I continue to help in the infirmary since rest doesn't come. The nurses manage to save William's leg, but he will still have some time before he can walk again. I'm surprised when a small group of soldiers approach me as I lay another soldier down on a bed.

"Are you the berserker," one of them asks.

"Yes," I say without looking over my shoulder.

"We were the others that managed to survive on the wall top two of us ran across the field with you," another explains. "Do you think we are going to be able to push them back?"

"I believe that we will," I say turning around and facing the group. "Why do you ask?"

"We are not about to give in," one soldiers shouts.

"I only wish to try my blade against those filthy dogs again," another growls.

"You should be careful then," a man says as he walks by the group.

That voice is very familiar. I turn and see Kain as he begins to bandage a soldier's arm.

"A half-breed," the soldier gasps. "What is a half-breed doing treating our troops?"

"Who better to administer to a wound created by a werewolf, than one that is part werewolf," Kain remarks. "You would be surprised by the workings of a werewolf's mind. They only wish to inflict pain on those that they see as enemies. Unfortunately that is you, and your comrades."

On of the soldiers in the back steps forwards and draws his sword.

"How do we know that you are not with the werewolves that are outside these walls," he asks in quivering rage.

"If wished to kill you then you would be dead right now," Kain says as he continues to work. "If you are not going to use that then put it away, enough damage was already been done as it is."

The soldier seems to be taken back by Kain's commanding attitude. He steps back in rank with the other soldiers and sheaths his sword.

"Are all of you going to fight when we retaliate," I ask.

"Yes all of us that stand before you will also stand at your side during battle," the lead soldier says.

"Why are you saying this to me," I ask somewhat impatiently.

"You saved three of us during the first attack on the outer wall," the lead soldier says. "We owe you."

"It's war," I say. "I was simply doing my job, which was eliminating the enemies that were in front of me. I apologize if I sound rude, but I have to help with the other wounded."

"Yes, all right," the lead soldier says bowing and then walking away.

The group walks out of the infirmary. I turn and help a soldier up form his bed.

"Are you sure that you're up for walking on that leg," I ask as I support most of his weight.

"I should be able to," He grunts as he staggers away from me. "Thank you."

He walks slowly out of the infirmary and down the hall with the others. The halls slowly fill with more soldiers and the infirmary finally begins to empty out. Nurses are now changing out the bloodstained bed sheets for new fresh linens. I walk over to the last soldier that is standing up. One of his arms is heavily bandaged and in a sling. He walks out the door and sits down in the hall.

"Are you not supposed to be fighting the werewolves," Kain says as he walks up to me. "Not helping their victims, that is my job. What has caused you to come here?"

"We needed a change in tactics," I say with a yawn. "Tori's the one that is going to make that happen, and since there has been a cease of attacks I came here. I thought that while I'm here I'd lend a hand."

"You have done well," Kain says. "You have helped us greatly."

"Thanks," I say with another yawn.

"You should rest," Kain urges. "You have been up longer than most of the people here."

"Yeah," I say. "How long is it until sunrise?"

"I would say a few hours at the most," Kain says thoughtfully.

"I think will go rest for a little bit then," I say as I walk out the door into the halls.

I feel very self conscious as I walk among the hundreds of wounded soldiers that line the halls, and probably the halls on many other floors. Here I am walking by them with nothing more than a cut on my face, while they're wounded worse than me. I can feel their eyes on me as I cut the corner and begin walking up the staircase to my floor. As I climb the stairs I can feel my eyelids begin to droop. My footsteps feel heavier than normal now. I emerge on my floor and trudge down the last stretch of hallway to my room. I open the door and kick of my shoes as I stumble wearily to the bed. I change out of my bloodstained clothes and throw the old ones into a basket near the dresser.

Falling onto the bed I hear the deep breathes of Arrok next to me on his mat. I take my sword and set next to the bed along with the armor. I lay my head on the pillow and match my breathing to Arrok's slow rhythm. I really hope that Tori's poison works. I guess that I'll find out in a few hours. I close my eyes and fall asleep.

"Ivan," a voice says shaking my arm. "Ivan wake up, it is almost sunrise, time to test Tori's poison."

I roll over on the bed and sit up. I rub my hand over my face and touch the cut.

"Ah," I wince. "I forgot about that."

I look up to see Luna standing at the edge of the bed. She has my sword in her hand and seems eager to be on our way.

"Tori is at the wall waiting with the poison," Luna says as she tosses my sword at me. "We should not keep her waiting."

"Okay," I say catching my sword.

I stand up and attach my sword back to my waist and slip my shoes on. I look to see if Arrok is awake, but he's not even in the room.

"He took Tori to the wall," Luna informs. "Iris will take us."

Iris is sitting on the balcony waiting for us. I put on the armor as we walk across the room to the balcony. We climb onto Iris's back in silence. She takes off and flies straight and fast towards the wall that separates us from the werewolf horde. Iris flies at a speed that makes me tighten my legs around her neck. The streets below are almost completely empty. Only a few people roam the abandon streets and alleyways.

As we approach the wall the empty streets begin to fill with soldiers. They are all armed and awaiting their orders. Iris circles once and lands on the wall next to Arrok and Tori.

"Sorry we are late," Luna says as we jump off Iris's back.

"Not at all," Tori says cheerfully. "I just arrived with the poison. I suppose that you are ready to see its effect?"

"Yes," Luna says shortly.

"We were fortunate enough to find the source of the stream with the most output of water," Tori explains. "It just happens to be right next to this wall."

"That is excellent news," Luna says with a grin. "Then what are we waiting for?"

"Well you see," Tori says slowly. "Most of the werewolves are watching us, even now."

"So we need a diversion," Luna says quickly. "That should not be a problem."

"Whatever the diversion is I'll help," I say stepping forward. "It will need to be something that makes them look away from the wall, right?"

"That is correct," Luna says. "But I cannot think of a proper diversion."

"Wait look," Tori says pointing to the wall top. "Look at that one werewolf; he is bigger than the others."

"That is the alpha male of the werewolf horde," Arrok says. "If I remember there customs correctly, then if the alpha male is killed the one who did so becomes the new leader. Although it must be someone that is a part of one the werewolf packs. You see he must have defeated all of the other alpha males in the separate pack, which is why they follow him."

"I see," Luna says. "But we cannot challenge him, but I know of two than can."

"No," I say quickly. "Kain and Violet will not fight him."

"Why not they are of werewolf blood," Luna presses.

"Before the werewolves attacked Kain spoke with me," I explain. "If they were to go down there every werewolf in the horde would rip them apart. You see the alpha male wants them dead."

"Why would he," Luna asks.

"I guess because they didn't agree with him," I say. "That's only my guess though."

"Fine, then we will need to find a different course of action," Luna says.

"Whatever the diversion is, we need it to inflict damage on the enemy at the same time," Arrok says. "That way we get something extra out of the plan."

"Okay let's drop some troops on the wall and attack the werewolves," I say thoughtfully. "Then when the poison is in the water, the dragons can pick us up and bring us back here."

"What do we do if the werewolves overwhelm us," Luna says. "You know before the poison is in the water?"

"I didn't think of that," I admit. "What do you mean by us?"

"I am going to fight with you," Luna says.

"Not on the wall top it's too dangerous for you," I protest. "I would prefer not to see if Lilith's dream proves true or not."

"We both know that it will," Luna says glumly looking at the ground. "She said that the wall would fall and look at what happened."

"Fine," I say. "But you're not fight on the wall with me."

"Then what do you propose I do," Luna says annoyed.

"Arrok will land me on the wall top," I explain. "Once he's out of the way you and Iris will attack from the air. Use arrows, spears or whatever you want. But promise me one thing, if those two gray dragons appear you get back here. Don't even try to fight them."

"I am not going to leave you there to be killed by the werewolves," Luna protests.

"You're not," I say looking at her. "If things get to dangerous for me on the wall then Arrok will get me off before the werewolves can do anything."

"It sounds like you have this planned out very well," Arrok says surprised.

"No," I admit. "I just thought it up when Luna said that we needed a diversion. I'm making this up as I go along."

"That is very comforting to know," Luna says concerned. "Do you have anything else that you have just made up that we should be aware of?"

"None that I can think of," I say with a grin. "How long will it take you to get ready?"

"Not long," Luna says as she walks to the one of the pulley platforms that is filled with weapons.

She grabs a long bow and two full quivers of arrows off of it. She puts one quiver at each side of her waist and slings the long bow over her shoulder. She then walks back to us and climbs onto Iris's back.

"Ready," she says with a grin.

"Okay," I say climbing onto Arrok's back.

"Wait," Tori yells. "I have an idea that will help us greatly, here take these."

Tori hands me a small bag and a torch.

"Thanks but it's bright enough for me to see," I say.

"Very funny," Tori scoffs. "That bag has the vials of fire that we used. You can drop them on the werewolves again. That way when they jump into the water they will then be poisoned."

"Good idea," Luna says.

"Thank you," Tori says smiling. "It would seem that I am not the only one that is good at making things up as I go along."

We take off and start flying over the werewolf horde. It seems that most of the werewolves are inside the wall. They crowd around the streams and ponds lapping up water and soothing their burns.

"Look how many of them are in the water right now," I mumble.

"Yes," Luna whispers. "It seems our plan will work."

The sun continues to rise in the morning sky as we fly closer to the ruined wall. Below I can hear the sounds of the werewolves stirring. There are howls of surprise and growls below as we fly closer to them.

"I will cover you from the air," Luna says quietly. "I will try to take out the ones that are giving you trouble."

"Yeah thanks," I say. "Here we go."

We make our descent towards the wall top and a sizable group of werewolves. Arrok swoops down and I jump off over the group. I can feel my heart pumping as I fall down on the werewolves. I miss one's head by only a few inches, as soon as my feet touch the ground the berserker takes over. The werewolves seem surprised by arrival, but then that surprise turns to anger.

My sword flashes out and cuts down the first werewolf. Another gets too close and I hit it in the face with the torch. It howls in pain and falls from the wall. I'm surrounded by werewolves on both sides; if I want to escape then I'll jump. I glance up and see Iris circle above us. Arrok is not anywhere to be seen. I only hope that the two dragons don't decide to make an appearance.

"You have a lot of nerve," a deep savage voice growls. "You must truly wish to die."

I look to see the huge werewolf from that emerged first on the wall when it fell. Now that I'm closer to him I can see even more scars crisscrossing his body. This must be the alpha male of the horde, Kain's father.

"Why are you here," he snarls.

I say nothing as he steps forward. As he comes closer I point my sword at him in silence.

"What is this," he asks. "What kind of trick is this?"

He takes another step closer and then an arrow streaks down and into his arm. He ducks low as if he is about to attack as another arrow flies down. The arrow misses him and buries into one of the werewolves next to him. It falls to the ground without a sound and the arrow protruding from it neck.

"So you have a friend in the air do you," he growls. "Your friend has fewer arrows than there are us, but you already know that."

The werewolves behind me begin to move closer. I spin and cut down another that is within the reach of my blade. Then one lunges at me, I step to the side as an arrow flies past my face and into the werewolf's chest. Another follows right behind him and my body begins to move again. Dodging claws and gnashing teeth as I move.

Werewolves are now making their way up the steps towards me, replenishing the spaces left by their dead companions. Luna continues to keep a constant stream of arrows falling around me, easing my situation. Kain's father only sits and watches as I struggle against the impossible odds. Every time I see a glimpse of his face I know that he's laughing wildly.

"Stop," he laughs. "This is too entertaining."

Even though the fighting has ceased for the moment Luna fires again. This arrow sinks into his shoulder. He lets out a howl of pain. I sheath my sword; I only hope I won't need it again.

"You friend in the air is becoming quiet an annoyance," he snarls. "Watch as she fires her last arrow."

He howls one time and then begins to laugh. I watch as he continues to laugh uncontrollably. Then he looks to the sky, I follow his gaze and my blood turns to ice. The two dragons are flying at Luna and Iris at a breakneck speed. The berserker drains from my body instantly.

"Luna," I shout. "Get away!"

I can't make out her face but I know it's showing confusion. They are almost upon her now. I take a deep breath and let out a long whistle. My heart continues to pump as I search the skies for Arrok.

"What is wrong," he chuckles. "Is the friend that dropped off you not coming back?"

Iris has noticed the two dragons thankfully and is now flying away from them, but not fast enough. I watch as the first dives towards Iris. Then Arrok drops from the sky like a black bolt of lightning. His claws rip through both wings of the attacking dragon. The dragon falls like a stone, and he flaps his ruined wings in a futile attempt to fly. The werewolves on the ground scatter away from his direction.

Kain's father lets out a howl of rage as the dragon crashes into the fields below us. The second dragon hovers for a moment and then abandons the chase. Arrok is now flying quickly towards us.

"If I cannot kill your friend then I will settle for you," he growls. "It will not be a quick death, I assure you that."

"If I die so do you," I say holding the torch in front of him.

"I am not afraid of your little torch," he scoffs.

"Do you remember the arrows that fell on you last night," I say coldly. "As you know they were not normal arrows. Well I have the vials that cause those explosions. All I have to do is light it and we both go up in flames."

"You lie," he snarls with confidence.

I glance up at the sky as I reach into the bag, Arrok will be here shortly. I pull out the vial and hold it near the torch. Every werewolf on the wall stops in their tracks. I can now hear the sound of Arrok's wings as he grows closer.

"It looks like I'm not going to die after all," I say grinning.

"Ivan jump," Arrok shouts.

I touch the cloth fuse of the vial to the flame and throw it down as I jump off the wall. I land on Arrok's back and he flies higher. He stops and hover for a moment, then the explosion sounds with a thud. We watch as several werewolves fall from the wall top. Some of them hit the ground in a howling ball of flames.

"Good timing," I breathe. "A moment longer and they would have attacked anyway."

"Was the one you were talking to the alpha male," Arrok asks.

"Yes," I say coldly. "He is the one that we had to kill in order to break the chain of command in the werewolf horde."

"Well he is not dead," Arrok mutters.

"What," I yell. "The explosion should have taken him down."

"He is running across the fields after us," Arrok informs me. "I do not know what he intends to do, but there are a lot of others following him."

"Great," I sigh. "I hope that the poison is in the water, which should buy us some time."

We fly over the last stretch of fields and the werewolves follow all the way to the wall. Arrok circles above the werewolves and lands on the wall next Luna and Iris. I jump off and rush to the edge of the wall. The werewolves are a massed near the wall; Kain's father is at the front of the group. The deep scars on his body are now mixed with burns and singed fur.

"That was a feeble attempt to end this battle," he roars out. "All that the human did was kill a few werewolves, hardly enough to stop us."

"At least he doesn't suspect that it was a diversion," I whisper to Luna.

"That is good," Luna whispers back. "Are you all right, from here it looked like you had a little trouble."

"I'm fine," I say reassuringly.

"It seems we are at a stalemate then," Kain's father continues to rant. "You are too cowardly to attack us."

"Yet the human and vampire that just attacked you receive no exemption of being cowards," Luna shouts. "It would seem that you have misjudged our bravery."

"Two attacked us," he shouts back. "Not an army!"

"Yet this human almost acted as one," Luna retorts.

"Don't make it sound like I'm the best warrior here," I whisper. "I'm far from it."

"I am just buying us more time," Luna whispers under her breathe.

"What, why," I ask suddenly. "Did you not get all of the poison into the water?"

"The poison is in the water," Luna says with a grin. "We have just added on to the plan a little."

Luna turns to a soldier behind her. He has a long bow in his hand and one of the new fire arrows in the other, only the vial in closer to the tip of the arrow. He notches the arrow and draws the bowstring back. Then every other soldier on the wall that has a bow does the same thing.

"Wait for the signal," Luna says.

"Are you still there or have you hidden from us again," He continues to taunt.

"I am still here," Luna says. "I cannot say the same for you though."

That must have been the signal because every arrow that is in a bow fires. Thousands of arrows rise in the air, but none of them are lit. Many of the werewolves run away so they are out of range. The sound of breaking glass and howls of surprise are all that I hear for a moment. Then there everything is quiet again.

"It that all that you have left," he fumes. "Firing arrows with a strange smelling liquid?"

"No we have normal arrows as well," Luna replies. "Simon fire whenever you are ready."

I hadn't even noticed Simon amongst the ranks of soldiers. He's holding a long bow that is much bigger than a regular longbow. He notches an arrow and pulls back the bowstring and there is a deep creak of the bow. The arrow looks more like a small spear than an arrow. Right behind the large broad head tip is an oil soaked cloth.

"I am ready," He grunts.

A soldier rushes forward with a torch and lights the cloth. Simon takes careful aim and lets the bowstring go. The string propels the arrow with a heavy whoosh. I watch the arrow fly through the air like a comet with the speed of lightning. Kain's father looks up a moment too late. The arrow flies straight through his chest. The cloth slides off the arrow and sticks to his chest and begins to consume his body in flames.

The alpha male's body falls to the ground with a heavy thud. Then the flames slowly start to engulf his body. The other werewolves creep closer to the body to inspect the corpse of their fallen leader. Suddenly the added part of the plan makes sense to me.

"The ground is covered in the liquid," I gasp. "That fire is going to set the whole area up in a firestorm."

"Yes then the werewolves will be forced into the poisoned waters," Luna says.

The flames encase his body and then touch the ground. The liquid sets fire and spreads quickly across the fields and tall grass. Werewolves everywhere are engulfed in ten feet high flames. It looks as if none of them will survive the flames to reach the water. Then one by one they plunge into the water.

"It is working," one of the soldiers says excitedly. "Now we can attack!"

"Not yet," Simon says. "We will wait until the flames die down and the poison takes hold."

"Then we will attack tomorrow before sunrise," Luna says. "That will ensure that the flames will have died and that many of the werewolves will be dead or lost their will to fight."

"What do we do until then," I ask. "It's only been a few hours since sunrise."

"You can go back to the palace," Luna says. "You have been up most of the night and then the battle today must have you fatigued."

"Thank you," I say with a nod. "If anything happens don't hesitate to get me, it doesn't matter."

"I hope that I will not have to," Luna says.

I can feel the heat from the fire below as I walk to Arrok. I climb on to his back and get ready for him to take off.

"You did well," Arrok says. "You are becoming a true warrior."

"I'm only doing what I have to in order to stay alive," I say. "I don't think of myself as a warrior."

"Regardless of what you consider yourself you are," Arrok says as he takes off. "A warrior finds battle and you seem to do that."

"Maybe," I sigh. "It seems like here battle is all that happens."

We fly over the empty streets of Haven. Since the wall fell it doesn't seem as safe anymore. Although since one of the dragons is now dead, the chances of the other wall falling is very slim. The werewolf horde is now crumbling from lack of leadership and their lack of morale is spreading like the poison that they now wallow in. The only problem left is Victor and Jenna. We reach the palace and Arrok lands on the balcony to our room. I jump off and walk into the center of the room. I'm starting to feel the weariness of little sleep and battle weighing down on me.

"Are you going to rest now," Arrok asks as he walks to his mat.

"I will," I say. "I have one thing to do first."

I walk to the door and open it. I stick my head out in the empty hall. Walking out into the hall I shut the door behind me and rush towards the infirmary. Hopefully Kain is still there helping with the wounded. I reach the stairs and take them two at a time. I come out on the infirmary floor and pick my way past the soldiers. Kain is kneeling by a soldier near the door; he looks up and can see that I have something important to tell him.

"What has happened," Kain asks quickly. "Are you well?"

"I'm perfectly fine," I say. "You father his been taken in battle."

I can see the pain in his eyes.

"I only wish he would not have listened to them," Kain sighs. "But after the war I will fight to take his place. Maybe then there will be peace between the werewolves and those who live here."

"Maybe," I mutter.

"Were you the one to finish him," he asks slowly.

"No," I say looking at the floor. "The vampire named Simon did, he shot him through the heart with an arrow."

"A quick death," Kain says satisfied.

"Yes," I say.

"Thank you," he breathes. "Now I must administer to the wounded."

He walks back into the infirmary. I stand for a moment then walk back to the staircase. The walk back to my room seems so much shorter than before. I sneak slowly back into my room and across to my bed. I take my sword and set it next to the bed. Today was a short yet very productive day for me. I lie down on the bed and fall back asleep.

28

I OPEN MY EYES SLOWLY and sit up in the dark quiet room. I slide slowly off the bed and attach my sword to my waist. I look out past the balcony at the night sky beyond the cave. I guess I slept all day. I walk quietly to the door and open it without a creak. Walking out into the halls I feel as though I'm being watched. Like someone is gently laying their hands on my shoulders.

"Ivan," a voice says from the darkness. "You must come with me."

I turn around and almost draw my sword, because of the sudden voice.

"I am sorry," Tori says stepping from the shadows. "Scott is having some difficulties with his recovery."

"Like what," I ask quickly. "Is he all right?"

"Just come with me," Tori says.

I follow her down the halls and around several corners, and then we reach Scott's room. Tori opens the door without knocking. She rushes into his room and I follow close behind her. Scott is sitting up in his bed. He seems to be doing much better than yesterday.

"Hey," He says excitedly. "Ivan, what're you doing here?"

"Tori said you were having some kind of problem recovering," I say with a laugh. "Looks like your doing pretty good to me."

"I know," he says breathing in deeply. "You want to see the wounds."

Scott stands up out of the bed and starts unraveling the bandages.

"Should he be doing that," I ask quickly.

"Just watch," Tori says slowly.

As Scott's bandages get closer to his body they begin turn deeper shade of red. Then I can see his chest. There are no stitches left in the wounds. Actually there are no wounds at all.

"Wow," I say, very surprised. "You're a pretty good doctor Tori. You've managed to heal him in less than a day."

"I did not do this," Tori says concerned. "His body must have somehow accelerated the vampire's touch."

"That's good though right," I ask quickly.

"I do not know," Tori says shaking her head.

"Well I know," Scott says moving his arms around. "And yes, it's very good."

"We do not know the reason for your quick recovery," Tori warns. "It could be hazardous to your health in the future."

"How can some one healing faster be a bad thing," Scott laughs. "I feel better than I ever have before. Like a new person."

"That is what worries me," Tori sighs.

"Don't worry about it," I say calmly. "If something does go wrong we'll fix it then. Besides I have a counterattack to participate in, excuse me."

"I'm going to," Scott shouts.

"No," Tori shouts sternly. "You may have recovered faster than anyone I have ever seen, but I am putting my foot down here. You are staying right where you are."

"I need to be there," Scott protests. "This is my second chance to…"

"No, it is not going to be your second chance to get injured," Tori cuts him off. "You are staying, even if I have to sedate you."

"Okay fine," Scott says defeated. "There's no need for sedation."

"Well I'm going to go now," I say walking towards the door. "Take it easy on him Tori."

"Oh come on," Scott moans. "You're not going to take her side are you?"

"This war's not over yet," I say opening the door and stepping into the hall. "If I get wounded I want to be in her good graces. Have fun."

I close the door and walk down the hall. Even as I get closer to my room I can still hear Scott's shouts of protest. I smile to myself and open the door to my room and step inside. Arrok is awake and waiting. Luna and Iris are on the balcony, I wonder how long they've been waiting for me to get here.

"There has been a slight change in plans," Luna informs. "It would seem the poison worked far better and faster then we had anticipated. We are going to attack now."

"Arrok are you ready," I ask quickly. "I am if you are."

"I am," Arrok says shortly. "Shall we go then?"

"We are going to push them back past the wall," Luna says without emotion. "This is our final effort to win. We are going to use every soldier in this attack. Our estimates are that we out number the werewolves two to one."

I walk over to Arrok as he moves to the center of the room. I climb silently onto his back and wait for whatever else Luna has to say.

"If you see Victor or Jenna on the field of battle you kill them," Luna says coldly. "They are responsible for this war."

"I understand," I say grimly. "I think that Victor is the main problem, if Jenna attacks me first then I'll attack back."

"Do whatever you think is best for your safety," Luna says. "If I see either one of them I am going to kill them."

"You really do harbor a hatred for them don't you," I ask.

"The Forsaken bring disgrace to all vampires," Luna says bitterly. "Why do you think many of the humans here do not agree with us? They think that the first thing that goes wrong and the vampires will start feeding on them. Only a few human truly understand us."

"Am I one of those humans," I ask slowly.

"Almost," Luna says with a grin. "You know more than the average human here, but there are still certain things that you will never understand."

"Luna," I almost whisper. "I've changed my mind. If I'm wounded during this battle I want you to turn me."

My words seem to have caught Luna off guard. Her eyes become wide with disbelief.

"Are you sure that you want me to do that," Luna asks quickly. "What made you change your decision?"

"I'm sure about this," I say slowly. "I need to be around to protect you in the future. In case this battle isn't the one you're hurt in."

"I understand," Luna murmurs.

"But this is only during this battle," I correct quickly. "If I'm not hurt during this battle, then I'm staying human for the rest of my foreseeable life."

"Then let us test your fate," Luna says with a grim smile.

Luna climbs onto Iris's back and looks at me. She seems saddened by what I've said to her. Honestly I'm more worried about her wellbeing than mine right now.

"Okay let's go," I say quietly.

Iris takes off from the balcony and Arrok follows right behind her. We rise into the air and fly straight for the wall. The urgency of the matter weighs down on me. It must be on Arrok too because he's flying almost as fast as when Luna and Iris were in danger.

"How long before we attack," I ask over the flapping of wings.

"As soon as we arrive," Luna says. "All of the soldiers have been positioned on the ground. It is only by chance that the werewolves have not yet attacked us."

"Then lets hurry," I say quickly.

We cover the stretch of city in a short time. As we fly over the wall I can see our army. Luna was right, almost all of the soldiers are on the ground waiting silently. Every soldier is clothed in black armor similar to ours. Arrok and Iris drop from the sky and fly low to the ground in front of the soldiers. Luna jumps off and lands without a sound. I jump off and land with a light crunch on the charred grass. The sound causes one of the soldiers to flinch. He must not have even heard Luna land or the dragons that just flew over him. Luna walks to a soldier that's at the head of the army. Arrok and Iris lands silently behind us as well.

"Are all of you ready," Luna asks in a hushed voice. "We are going to push back the werewolves now. We have superior numbers and morale, but they have more strength. If you see a follow warrior struggling you help him. Do you understand?"

A roar goes up from every soldier on the ground. The air vibrates and the ground trembles as the soldiers let out their battle cries. Then another roar sounds out. Louder than the first and not of humans and vampires, but of every dragon that is in Haven. The dragons fly out over the fields and high above the remnants of the werewolf horde.

"Are you ready," the lead soldier yells.

The others answer with another united roar. Then they charge towards the werewolves. Luna turns and faces Iris for a moment then jumps onto her back takes off into the air. I follow her example and jump onto Arrok's back and he also launches himself out of the charging army and into the air. We grow closer to the enemy with every beat of the dragons' wings, and I can't help but wonder what the others are thinking. Are all of them fighting for the safety of just their home? Are others fighting for glory and fame, or because their fathers and grandfathers fought in the last war?

I look ahead as the dragons dive down and snap at the disoriented werewolves. Some of the werewolves are forming into packs and clawing back at the dragons. The werewolves that are slower are only torn from the ground by the claws of the dragons. Even though we outnumber the werewolves, there are still too many for my liking. It looks as though only about one-third of the werewolf horde was destroyed by the attacks, fire, and poison.

"We are going to drop near the edge of the werewolves," Luna shouts. "We will reach them before the others do on foot."

"Good, more for us then," I shout back with a grim smile.

"Remember what I said about the Forsaken," Luna shouts back. "We kill them if we spot them."

We reach the werewolves several hundred yards ahead of the charging Haven army. Arrok swoops down and swats a jumping werewolf out of the way as if it were noting more than a fly. As soon as I jump off Arrok's back I draw my sword. I hold the blade down and pull my feet up a little. I land on top of an unsuspecting werewolf and drive the blade into its back. It lets out a short yelp of surprise and then falls to the ground.

I spin around to attack the next werewolf and come face to face with Luna. A werewolf charges at her back and I stab past her into the werewolf. The werewolf falls and I move on to the next one. All around us the werewolves are being picked off by the dragons. The others are focused on Luna and me.

"It looks like we're going to have fight our way back through," I shout over the battle.

"It would seem we are too far behind the enemy," Luna yells as she drops another werewolf. "Our forces are still not here."

Our forces, I'm still not used to hearing things of this world as including me. As we fight I can catch glimpses of our soldiers growing closer. They're only about one hundred yards away now. A few have broken away and are less than fifty feet. I strike out at every werewolf I can, not even taking time to see if they fall dead or wounded. I know now that I'm truly fighting for my life. The sound of our soldiers' battle cries grows louder as they approach us. They can't get here soon enough to help.

Then a howl goes up from one of the werewolves. The werewolves turn from the chaos we're creating and charge towards the advancing army of Haven. Then there is a deafening sound as the two groups collide. I can't hear anything over the sound of the battle. Screams of pain and howls of anguish fill the air. Luna and I continue to fight our way out of the mass of werewolves. Although now they are more focused on the opposing army and less on us, but there are still those that wish to end us.

"We're not pushing them back," I shout as I cut down another werewolf. "This isn't working."

"Give it time," Luna shouts back as she hits a werewolf in the face with her sapphire ring. "They have no leader they will soon loose faith in their cause."

Two werewolves rush towards me and I dodge to one side. I slash out and hit one of them as I move. Another werewolf crashes into me and knocks me to the ground. A werewolf appears out of the confusion and lunges towards me. I kick out, catching it in the leg causing it to lose its balance and fall on top of me. Not what I had in mind. It scrambles around trying to get to a position that it can attack me. Suddenly a soldier stabs it in the back with a claymore. The blade goes straight through and I can feel the tip gently prodding into my chest. Then he pulls the sword out and rushes back off into the battle. I quickly get back to my feet and rejoin the fight; yet another werewolf comes before me. I slash out at it, but it dodges my attack and swings its claws at me. Two of the claws make contact with my left forearm. Rage consumes me faster than the pain does. I run my blade through the werewolf before it can retract its arm.

"Push them back," Luna shout to anyone that can hear her. "Push them back past the wall."

A shout goes up from the army and we all start fighting harder than before. The fury of the berserker begins to course through my body. Things slow again and I'm only focused on killing my enemies. My blade flashes before me again and again as it glides through every werewolf in its reach. Then I start walking forward through the disorder. Now most of our soldiers are among the werewolves fighting everywhere. Some are struggling against their enemies; others easily overcome the werewolves and move to help the others of our army.

Then a werewolf begins to flee, followed by another. They rush towards the gap that has been torn in the wall. I continue to walk towards the opening cutting down any enemy that chooses to come near me. I have a strange feeling like I'm being watched by someone. My body continues to move as I try to shake the feeling. I'm in the middle of a battlefield; of course people are looking at me. Now I'm less then a hundred feet from the gap in the wall. Werewolves are now running past me with no intentions of killing me, but only to flee for their lives.

"Ivan," Luna shouts. "What are you doing?"

I stop and look over my shoulder at her, there are hardly any werewolves left inside the wall now. Many of the soldiers are now running past me to pursue the werewolves further. Luna runs up to me as I stand motionless.

"What," I ask as the berserk continues to pulse through me.

Luna seems surprised by my response, like I'm not myself. A werewolf that is lagging behind runs up behind Luna. It rushes towards her with its claws outstretched for the kill. My blade flashes past Luna face and into the chest of the werewolf. Her eyes are wide as I pull the blood covered blade out of another fallen foe. Then the berserker fades from me. The fatigue of battle suddenly overcomes me. My heart starts beating faster and my breathing becomes heavier.

"So it looks like we've done it," I say.

Suddenly Luna's expression turns hard as stone. She's not looking at me, but past me to the rubble of the wall. I turn to see Jenna standing on the pile of ruined stone with her ruby eyes fixed on us. Before I can do anything Luna is rushing towards her with both swords gripped tight in her hands.

"No," I shout as I run after her. "Luna, wait!"

She doesn't respond as she rushes towards Jenna at speeds known only to a vampire. Luna jumps up the sections of broken stone to where Jenna is standing. She swings out her swords focused only on killing Jenna. I reach the bottom of the rubble, just as Luna and Jenna go out of sight down the other side of the wreckage.

I climb as quickly as I can up the sections of shattered wall. I lose my footing and start to slide but grab hold of a groove in the stone and continue until I reach the top. Luna is still continuing her onslaught against Jenna with all her might. I'm surprised that Jenna is not using weapons of any kind, she only jump and ducks away from Luna's attacks. I jump as quickly as I can down the stones until I reach the ground on the other side of the wall.

I run across the grasslands and try to get closer to Luna as she fights. Then Jenna jumps out of the way again and runs into the small groups of soldiers and werewolves that are still fighting. I watch her as she dodges swords and claws, then she's gone from sight. Luna is trembling with frustration as she walks towards me. She is a good distance away as I look around the battlefield. Bodies litter the ground before me. A sudden chill runs down my spine, this is too familiar.

"Luna run," I yell as I start running towards her as fast as I can.

Luna looks at me strangely as I try to get to her. Then a figure cloaked in black flashes in front of her. Luna's expression becomes confused suddenly as she looks down. Her hands move to her stomach as red blossoms across her shirt. As she falls to the ground I see Victor several feet away with a bloody dagger. I push myself harder to reach Luna, yet I keep my gaze on him. He smiles at his success and then licks the blood from the blade. I drop my sword as I reach Luna and kneel down by her.

"Ivan," she says.

"Don't say anything," I say quickly. "You're going to be fine."

Luna shakes her head as I take her blood covered hand in mine and she squeezes lightly.

"I'm not going to let you die," I say.

"There is nothing that you can do," Luna whispers.

"No," I say as my mind races. "I promised you that I'm going to protect you."

She only looks up at me, smiles weakly and then she closes her eyes.

29

I HAVE TO DO SOMETHING; there's got to be some way to save her. A hundred thoughts are running through my head right now. With every second that I do nothing Luna is closer to death. I can't focus on anything with my mind is skipping from one thing to the next like this. I take a deep breath to try and think clearly, even if it's only for a moment. The only thing that I can focus on though is Luna. Why did I let this happen?

More blood leaks onto the ground as I try to think. My mind flashes back to Victor as he moved past Luna. Then he as stood there with her blood dripping from his dagger, he tasted her blood. That's it, blood!

"Hold on Luna," I say quickly.

I pick up my sword and place the palm of my right hand on the blade. I grip the blade run my hand down the sword with one swift stroke. I grit my teeth hard as the blade scrapes across the bone. Blood runs freely out of the gash. I make a fist the best I can to stop the bleeding for a moment.

"Drink this," I whisper to her.

I open my hand and the blood runs into her open mouth. She takes several deep drinks, and then passes out. I rip off the right sleeve of my shirt and wrap it around my hand. I want to find Victor. I want to kill him for what he's done, but I can't leave her alone. I let out a sharp whistle and watch the sky. Arrok flies over my head with Iris right behind him. Both land hastily and rush forward.

"Luna," Iris gasps. "Who has done this?"

"One of the Forsaken," I say as I pick Luna up in my arms. "The one named Victor. We need to get her to the infirmary. This war's as good as over now."

"Get on," Arrok says.

Arrok bows low so I can get onto his back with little difficulty. He takes off slowly this time, with Iris flying nervously beside us. She stares at Luna and rarely glances in the direction that we're flying.

"What did you do to your hand," Iris asks as she continues to stare. "It is heavily bandaged."

"I cut it to the bone," I say. "It probably needs stitches."

We fly over the ruined wall and over the burned and blood soaked fields as fast as Arrok can fly. I wonder what Marcus will have to say about this. He will be anger at Luna for fighting and me for helping her to do it. But I also helped save her, so he shouldn't be as mad at me. It looks like all of Lilith's dreams proved true. The wall fell, the werewolf horde was much larger than we had imagined, and I did save Luna's life, or at least for now.

We fly into the cave and over the city of Haven. People are now coming back out into the streets. Some are cheering at our victory; other are crying for those that they know won't be coming back. I hope that we can get Luna to the infirmary in time to make a difference. The palace is growing closer, but it seems so slow. The wound on Luna's stomach is still bleeding. When she had been injured before the wound healed shortly after. So why is this wound not closing as fast as before?

"Is she still bleeding," Iris asks concerned.

"Yeah," I say. "The wounds aren't healing that well, why is that?"

"She was wounded with a poisoned blade," Iris growls. "It slows the healing of injuries of any vampire it cuts. Since her wounds are more serious her body cannot heal as fast as it should. But when you had her drink of your blood it sped up the healing, but only a little."

"How did you know that I gave her my blood," I ask, trying to hide my surprise.

"The area of your wound is not that of a werewolf," Iris says still staring at Luna. "And in the short time that I have known you, you do not seem the kind of person that would not try anything to save someone you care about."

"Do you think it will make her like them," I ask. "Like the Forsaken?"

"I do not know," Iris says glancing ahead. "Take Luna to her room, I will go to the infirmary and get Tori."

"All right," Arrok says.

We separate from the Iris and fly around to the side of the palace. Arrok veers up and then swoops down to a balcony. He lands gently and without a sound. I slide slowly off Arrok's back and walk softly across Luna's room. I lay her gently on the bed and walk quickly back to the balcony.

"You might want to go to our room," I say quietly. "Iris and Tori will be here soon."

"All right," Arrok says turning to fly away. "Ivan."

"Yeah," I say looking as Luna as she lies motionless.

"Even if she does change you did the right thing," Arrok says in a low voice. "Your job was to protect her."

"Look at her," I say angrily. "She's like this because I didn't protect her."

"That may be true," Arrok says. "But you saved her life, or at the very least helped her live a little longer."

Arrok takes off before I can even say anything in return. I stand alone on the balcony and watch Luna. The only way I can tell that she's still alive is by the rise and fall of her chest as she breathes. I walk quietly across the room to the corner where a chair sits. I pick the chair up and carry it to the edge of the bed. I sit in the chair and wait for Tori to get here.

"Luna," I whisper. "I don't know if you can hear me or not. But I'm sorry if I've ruined your life. If I had never come here you'd be all right."

"No," Luna mumbles.

She shakes her head slightly, but her eyes remain closed remain closed. Her hands wrap around her sides and she doubles over in pain.

"Luna," I say moving closer. "Luna, are you all right?"

I look around frantically trying to think of what to do. Then Iris glides into the room and Tori jumps off quickly. She runs to the edge of the bed and pulls Luna onto her back. She moves Luna's hands and looks at the wound; she then places her hand on Luna's forehead.

"How long has it been since she was wounded," Tori asks.

"Not long," I say quickly. "No more than ten minutes. Can you help her?"

"Yes," Tori says opening her bag and rummaging through it. "You need to leave."

"But I can help," I protest.

"The longer I stand here and argue the less time I have to try and save her," Tori shouts. "Now get out!"

I turn and walk from the room as Tori begins to treat Luna. I close the door behind me and sit on the floor across from the door. I don't care how long I have to wait here. I close my eyes and take a deep breath. The image of Victor smiling at what had done burns in my mind. I will kill him for what he's done, it doesn't matter what happens to Luna. I hope that she lives, but if she dies. I shake my head. There's no need to think like that. Then faint footsteps grow louder until they are near me.

"How's she doing," A voice says.

I open my eyes and I stand up. Scott is leaning against the wall next to me.

"I don't know," I mutter. "Tori's trying her best right now. What are you doing here anyway?"

"Tori was still tormenting me when Iris flew in," Scott explains. "What happened to her exactly? All I heard was Luna's hurt, come with me."

"She was wounded with a poisoned blade," I say sitting back down. "She's not healing like normal."

"So what are you going to do now," Scott asks.

"I'm going to wait right here until I find out how she's doing," I say. "Then I'm going to hunt down the one that did this to her and kill him."

"You know who it was," Scott asks surprised.

"Yes," I say shortly. "He will die slowly."

"Did he get you too," Scott says nodding at my hand. "That cloth is soaked."

I look at my hand and realize that it hurts. The cloth is now soaked with blood and a few drops fall onto the floor.

"No I did this to myself," I say trying to ignore the, now throbbing pain. "I cut it to the bone."

"Why would you do something like that," Scott asks.

"Because if I hadn't Luna would be dead right now," I say.

"Oh, I forgot, she's a vampire," Scott says. "I keep forgetting that. So now you're going to become one of them?"

"What," I ask quickly. "No, she only drank my blood."

"If I were you I would be worried that if she wakes up she'll be after the rest of your blood," Scott laughs.

"How can you laugh at a time like this," I shout. "There's a chance that she'll die and you're out here laughing."

"I wasn't laughing about that," Scott retorts. "I was…"

"Look I don't care," I shout back. "It shouldn't matter to you anyway."

"What is that suppose to mean," Scott asks.

"You're going home after all of this," I say. "You can go back to your family and other friends. You can forget about this place and go back to the life that you had before."

"That sounds like a good idea," Scott says as he walks off. "I don't see why you care so much about a vampire. You're becoming too attached to this place."

"I care because she is a friend just like you," I shout. "But I'm starting to doubt who my friends are now, or what I even care about."

"Yeah me too," Scott says then walks off down the hall.

I sit against the wall and take another deep breath. I've left one war to partake in another. What am I going to do now; the war is pretty much over. Am I too attached to this place? I haven't really even thought about home that much. How long has it even been since I left home? Do I belong there or do I belong here? I shake my head and sigh. There are too many questions and there is only one question that I want answered. Is Luna going to survive?

I look up at the door and stare it its dark color. I hope it will open soon and Luna will come walking out with a smile on her face, or even Tori telling me that Luna is going to be all right. Anything would be better that this eternal waiting.

"My daughter will survive," Marcus's voice says to the left of me. "She is strong."

"I only wish there was more that could have done," I mumble.

"You brought her here," Marcus says calmly. "The Forsaken that did this will be punished."

"I know," I say. "I'm the one that's going to do it, but how did you know that it was one of the Forsaken?"

"Your friend told me just moments ago," Marcus says.

"But I didn't tell him it was one of the Forsaken," I say thoughtfully.

"Well I am the ruler of a city," Marcus explains. "So thereby I must know the habits and techniques that my enemies possess. Only a Forsaken would do something this cowardly."

"Yes he is a coward," I say gritting my teeth.

"Are you all right," Marcus asks. "I know that you are troubled by what has happened to Luna, but were you injured during the battle?"

"Just a few cuts and bruises," I say touching the cut over my left eye.

"Well you hand does not look like a minor injury," Marcus says pointing at my right hand. "How did you acquire that?"

I'm really getting tired of explaining this to every person that comes around. But maybe since it was the only thing that I could think of to save his daughter Marcus will have a different reaction.

"I cut my hand so Luna could drink the blood and start to heal faster," I almost whisper. "It was the only thing that I could think of."

Marcus's reaction is different from Scott's, only his is worse. His hands begin to shake with rage.

"My daughter has drunk the blood of a human," Marcus shouts. "This is unacceptable!"

"It kept her alive long enough to get her here so Tori could help her," I say quickly.

"Do you not know what the Forsaken are," Marcus spits. "Or how they became what they are?"

"Yes I do," I reply.

"So my daughter has betrayed our secrets with you as well," Marcus fumes as he moves quickly forward. "You do not understand the situation that I am now in."

"What would you have done in my position," I shout back. "I wasn't going to let her die!"

This seems to surprise Marcus for a moment and then it only adds to his anger. He rushes forward and slams me into the wall. He pushes with a strength that I couldn't have estimated.

"I did not want her to go into the fight," Marcus says baring his fangs. "You where the one that helped her escape, I know that now. Also because of you my daughter has become one of the Forsaken."

"Will you honestly tell me that you would evict your own daughter from this city," I ask. "The daughter that you raised and cared for all these years?"

"No," Marcus says suddenly. "But I will evict you from this city."

I push Marcus back with more strength than I thought I had. We now stand in the middle of the hallway, evenly matched. I grin at the surprised look on Marcus's face.

"Then that will make two worlds that I don't belong in," I say. "If you're going to do something then just end me."

"You came from that world," Marcus says his tone changing. "Why would you not belong there?"

"Because I felt more alive here," I say as I stop pushing against him. "I've helped you gather allies for a war that wasn't mine. I protected your daughter, tried to save her lived, fought to protect your city. Now this is the payment I receive? Do whatever you want to do, you will anyway."

"So you merely acted as a mercenary on our behalf," Marcus asks.

"No I didn't," I say. "I tried to help the people I've come to care for."

"That is no excuse for what you have done to those that I love," Marcus shouts.

"If you're going to banish me from your city then go right ahead," I say coldly. "But I want you know one thing. You don't need more enemies right now, especially with one ruined wall. Also if you send anyone after me to kill me or track me, they won't be hunting a human anymore."

"What do you mean," Marcus says baring his fangs again.

"I'll just have to find a vampire and have them turn me," I bluff. "Only I will embrace what it truly means to be one."

"You will never understand what it means," Marcus says grimly.

"I have been a vampire all my life. Being turned is the hardest thing you will ever experience, even though I have not felt this I know by those who have. You will die during the turning if you are not strong enough."

"I won't have to if you can just see that I was trying to save your daughter's life," I almost shout. "I thought having her alive would mean more to you than this."

"It does," Marcus says slowly. "I apologize for my outburst. I just cannot imagine having to banish my own daughter. I acted out of fury."

"I'm sorry too," I say. "I've come to know Luna rather well since I've been here. I think that she has enough control to not feed on humans. If she does I'll probably be the first one that she comes after, since she's tasted my blood. And just so you know, I would never betray the rules that vampires live by. But since I'm planning on staying human you don't have anything to worry about."

"I will admit that you do have wits about you," Marcus says with a smile. "In the future use your abilities wisely."

"I only wanted to show you that what I did was in the best intensions of Luna," I say. "I'm not about to go against you and an entire army."

The sound of the door opening causes Marcus and me to both turn. Tori steps out of the room and sighs. Her shirt has blood on it from whatever she's been doing to Luna. She wipes her hands off on her pants and looks up at us.

"Luna is going to be all right," Tori sighs. "I had to stitch the wound so she would not bleed to death. There is good news though, since Ivan gave her of his blood the healing is speeding up, I had to remove three of the first stitches because of the healing."

"This is excellent news," Marcus says smiling. "You have done well, both of you."

Marcus walks past Tori and walks quietly into the room. I look at Tori as she wipes off more blood from her hands.

"Do you think she'll become one of the Forsaken," I ask slowly.

"I cannot tell," Tori says. "Her skin is paler than before, but that could also be form the loss of blood."

"I hope that's the only reason," I say.

"As do I," Tori says looking at the floor.

The door opens and Marcus walks out with a grim look on his face. He doesn't look up as he walks down the hall.

"You can see her if you want," Tori says.

I walk to the door and open it slowly. I step into the room and shut the door. Luna is still lying motionless on the bed. Tori must have changed her into some fresh clothes. Her skin is several shades lighter than it should be too. It's even lighter than the day that she hadn't fed. I walk to the chair and sit down again. I'll wait until she wakes up.

30

IT'S BEEN TWO DAYS since the battle ended and Luna was injured. It's been about that long since I've slept too. I've spent most of that time next to Luna waiting for her to wake up. It wasn't until earlier today that Tori made me leave. She said that if anything happens that she would contact me immediately.

"Do you want another cup of tea," grandma asks breaking me from my trance of thoughts.

"Oh, no thank you," I say. "How much do I owe you for the tea?"

"You do not owe me anything," she says smiling wide. "Remember I said that the next time that come here it would be free."

"Are you sure," I ask.

"Of course I am," she says smiling again sending more wrinkles across her old face. "Now you tell your friend Luna to come by too next time."

"I will," I say standing up.

"See you next time then," grandma says walking away.

I push my chair under the table and walk out the open door. The streets are back to normal. Merchants shout of their deals and discounts. Others see for themselves if the deals are worth it and others carry out their various errands of the day.

I walk along, weaving in between the people as I think. Why hasn't Luna waken up yet? Her wounds are completely healed and her skin has become slightly darker. Did I do everything that I could to help her that day? I clench my hands into fists so hard my knuckles turn white. I will remember Victor's face until the day that I die. I will kill him even if it causes me to die to in the process.

I stop walking and look up at the wall that separates me from the fields beyond. No one seems to like being close to the wall. Everyone avoids the open area between the last group of buildings and the wall that protects them. I turn around to walk back into the city and a small group of kids are blocking the way. There are about ten or so by my count. Three of them hold baskets filled with a variety of flowers. Then a young boy that seems to be the leader steps forward, he appears to be around eleven or twelve.

"Sir," he says in a rather confident voice. "I noticed that you have a sword, by any chance did you fight in the war a few days ago?"

"Yes I did," I reply.

"Good," he says looking back at one of the other kids.

"Look," one little girl suddenly shouts pointing with a short finger. "The dragons are going home!"

I look up at the mass of dragons as they fly out of the cave. I notice near the end of the group one black dragon flying next to a red one. They stop before they fly over the wall and turn back around. They fly towards the palace, but the black dragon stops for a moment then begins its descent towards us. Arrok lands a few feet from me and folds his wings. The kids all take a few steps back at the sight of Arrok's size.

"Don't worry," I say slowly. "He's not going to bite you."

They all look at me and then to Arrok. He nods at them and they shuffle slowly back forward.

"Like I was saying," the boy says picking a flower out of the basket. "We are giving a flower to every soldier that fought in the war. It is our way of showing our thanks for what they did."

He steps forward and holds out the flower. I take and slip it into the loop that holds my sword so it won't get crushed.

"Thank you," I say. "It's people like you that this world needs more of."

All of the kids beam with pride at my words. I walk to Arrok and climb onto his back. He crouches low and launches into the air. We fly high over the city and straight towards the palace.

"What's going on," I ask breaking the silence.

"Luna is starting to stir in her sleep," Arrok says. "Tori believes that she will soon wake."

"That's good," I say. "How long has she been like that?"

"Not long," Arrok says thoughtfully. "Only about an hour, it took me a while to find you. Iris even helped me look for you; she is actually the one that spotted you."

I lean back and think of where I was when they spotted me. Those kids must have gone through a lot flowers already. I wonder if there are other kids doing that too. I set my hand near my sword and touch the flower. I grasp it gently and hold it up so I can see it better. My heart aches as I look at the flower, it's a moon flower. I stare at it as it glows softly in the dim cave.

Arrok flies around to the side of the palace and lands silently on the balcony to Luna's room. I jump off quietly and walk quickly across the room to the edge of the bed. Luna lies still, but she moves her head from side to side occasionally. Her lips move as though she's talking to someone and her eyebrows furrow as if the reply isn't one she wants to hear.

The door opens and I turn to see who it is. Tori walks into the room and shuts the door. I sit down in the chair by the bed and watch Luna. Tori walks up beside me and set her hand on my shoulder. I let out a sigh and slump down in the chair.

"I know that you are worried about her," she says comfortingly. "Marcus is worried too."

"He's worried about her for different reasons," I say. "He's afraid that she's going to become one of the Forsaken. I'm worried that she'll never forgive me, no matter what she becomes."

"You saved her life," Tori says softly. "There is no reason for you to be forgiven, you have done nothing wrong."

"I hope you're right," I sigh.

"You need to get some rest," Tori says. "You have not slept for almost two days now. Let me watch her for a while, if anything happens I will come and get you myself."

"I'm okay," I say defiantly. "I'll wait here."

"Let me rephrase that," Tori says stepping in front of me. "Get some rest."

"Fine," I say. "I need to change the bandage on my hand anyway."

"Is it causing you any trouble," Tori asks. "Are the stitches still holding?"

"Yes," I say waving my hand in front of her.

I stand up and stretch, I guess I am a little more tired than I want to admit. I look down at the bandage on my hand. The wound still tends to bleed when I move my hand too much. I move it slightly and a small tinge of pain emits from it. I look at my good hand; I'm still holding the moon flower. I move closer to the edge of the bed. I take the flower and slip it into Luna's open hand. She slowly closes her fingers around the stem and holds it.

"You'll tell me if anything changes," I say turning around and looking Tori in the eyes.

"I promise," she says smiling. "Now go get some rest, you look awful."

"Thanks," I say. "You look great too."

"I always do," Tori says with a smile.

I walk back across the room and smile for the first time in two days. Arrok sits patiently on the balcony as I climb onto his back and he flies off the balcony.

"You know it is good that you are finally going to get some sleep," Arrok says. "I was starting to worry about you."

"Why are you worried about me," I say. "I'm going to wake up."

"I can understand that you are upset about Luna," Arrok says. "But you need to take account for your health as well."

"I guess," I mumble. "Maybe I was too worried about my health that and not enough about Luna's."

"Why do you blame yourself," Arrok asks.

"Who else am I going to blame," I ask.

"Victor," Arrok says in a low voice.

I grit my teeth at the mention of his name. Arrok flies around to the front side of the palace and lands on the balcony of our room. I jump off and walk to the bed. I sit down on the edge of it and take off my sword. Arrok shuffles over to his mat next to the bed. He lies down on it and stares at me.

"You are not resting," I chuckles.

"I'm going to," I yawn.

I fall back on the bed and close my eyes. Then two days of no sleep and too much worry all come crashing down on me. I only hope that I'm going to wake up to Tori saying that Luna is awake. It only takes a few minutes before I'm dreaming.

Unfortunately my dreams aren't pleasant; it's only one memory playing over and over. Luna is standing on the battlefield and a dark figure flashing past her. I see Victor's twisted smile as he licks the blood from his dagger. Then everything repeats again and again. I can't break the cycle of torment. No matter how fast that I run I can't stop him from hurting her, and no matter how loud I yell she doesn't see him until its too late.

"Ivan," Tori says shaking me awake. "Luna is awake!"

"What," I say jumping up. "How long has she been up?"

"Not long," she replies excitedly. "I had to run down here to tell you."

I get up and run from the room, leaving Arrok and Tori in the room. I run down the hall and turn in the nearest staircase. I take the stairs two at a time until I reach the floor the Luna is on. I slide out into the hall and almost knock over a guard. I run down the halls and finally reach Luna's room. I take a deep breath and open the door slowly. Luna is standing on the balcony leaning on the rail as she looks out at the city. She turns as I shut the door and a look of surprise shows on her face.

"Feeling better," I say with a grin.

"Ivan," she shouts as she runs across the room.

She slams into me and hugs me. I catch my balance before she takes us both down. I put my arms around her.

"Thank you," she says as she looks up at me.

"For what," I ask.

"Several things," she says. "First for saving my life, I do not know how to repay you."

"You're alive," I say. "That's payment enough."

"All right," she says smiling. "Then second for the flower, I awoke holding it. At first I thought that my father placed it there. Then Tori told me that it was you. Where did you find it?"

"A group of kids were giving out flowers to soldiers as thanks," I explain. "They gave me a flower, but I didn't even notice until I was on my way here."

"Well I love it," she says resting her head on my shoulder. "You know there is one more thing I have to thank you for."

"What's that," I ask.

"You have given me a new ability," Luna says quietly. "Remember how Victor said that human blood gives a different strength?"

"Yes," I say slowly.

"I can smell your blood," Luna says taking a deep breath. "I could always smell blood, but now I can smell the individual's blood."

"Really," I say with a smile. "What do I smell like then?"

"I cannot explain it," Luna says confused. "You have a smell that is different, you smell of this world even though you are not of it. It is a somewhat alluring scent, I like it."

The door opens and we quickly let go of reach other. Marcus strides into the room and hugs Luna briefly. He then steps back and looks at her carefully.

"Are you well," He asks.

"I am," Luna says looking at me. "I owe that to Ivan."

"I already know of what he has done," Marcus says glancing at me. "I am, grateful."

The door opens again and Lilith rushes into the room. She collides with Luna the same way as Luna did with me.

"I knew that you would be perfectly fine," Lilith says cheerfully. "My dreams were very clear. Ivan I thank you for saving my sister."

"I didn't do that much," I say looking at eh floor.

"Cheer up," Luna says. "I am here now."

I look up at her and smile. Luna's sapphire eyes seem to have a renewed sparkle to them.

"That reminds me," Lilith says. "How do you feel about returning to your world?"

31

"WHAT DO YOU MEAN," I ask excitedly. "Is that even possible?"

"It is not normally," Lilith says calmly. "But there are exceptions to all things."

"Tell me how," I say. "I should get Scott, he'll be thrilled to know that there's a way back home."

"Shall we discuss this over dinner," Marcus says with a smile. "I believe that this is an event that we need to plan out carefully."

"That is a wonderful idea," Luna says glancing at me. "When do we need to meet at the dining room?"

"Does sunset sound pleasing to everyone," Marcus says still smiling. "We can celebrate Luna's recovery as well."

"Certainly," Lilith says. "It gives us time to think things over."

"Wonderful," Marcus says. "I will send for all of you when it is time. Right now I must give a speech. Our soldiers have done a remarkable job of protecting the city and all those that live therein."

Marcus walks from the room and leaves the door open.

"I need to tell Scott what time we're going to have dinner," I say. "Excuse me."

I walk towards the open door and I can hear Luna and Lilith whispering. I step into the hallway and begin to shut the door.

"Ivan," Luna shouts.

"What," I say stepping back into the room.

"Thank you again for what you have done," she says.

"You're welcome," I say looking into her eyes.

I glance at Lilith as I walk from the room, she's grinning widely. There's something that she knows that I don't as of right now. I shut the door behind me and walk to the staircase. I take my time getting down the stairs as I think about the near future. I'm going to be able to go home. I wonder what my parents will say; can I even tell them what really happened? I step out onto the floor that Scott's and my room is on. I walk to the door that I assume is Scott's. I knock on the door and wait for a reply.

"Enter," a voice says.

I open the door slowly and step into the room. I look up as I shut the door. Kain and Violet are sitting on a small couch together. They both seem surprised to see me, just as I am to see them.

"Sorry," I say stepping back. "I thought that this was Scott's room. I'll just go."

"You do not have to leave," Kain says quickly. "I actually needed to talk to you."

"Really," I say somewhat surprised.

"I want to tell you that I am grateful for your help," he says. "Because of your efforts I can now unit the werewolf packs, maybe under different leadership we can live in peace. It pains me that my father had to be killed in order to achieve this, but it was the price that had to be paid."

"I'm sorry for your loss," I say looking down at the floor.

"You should not be shameful of what happened," Kain says standing up. "Besides you were not the one to finish my father, it is not like you were responsible."

"I know," I say. "So how are you going to restore order to the packs?"

"I will find the strongest werewolf that is trying to become the alpha male and defeat him in a fight," Kain says thoughtfully. "I only hope that they will see things differently now that my father is out of the way."

"Well I hope the best for you," I extending my hand.

"Thank you," Kain says shaking my hand. "We will be leaving tomorrow."

"So will I," I laugh.

"Where are you going to go," Kain asks letting go of my hand. "There are not many other places that you can go here. There is a city in the frozen wastelands to the north, but I do not know of any others."

"I'm going back to my world," I say with a smile. "I've done so much here; I'm really going to miss this place."

"You will miss a world that struggles to desperately to live in peace," Kain asks shaking his head.

"I guess so," I shrug. "I've really found out more about who I am and what is real."

"Then I wish you well in your travels," Kain says with a nod.

"You too," I say as I turn and walk from the room.

I open the door and walk into the hallway; I take a few steps across the hall and stop at the door to my room. I take a deep breath and open the door. Arrok looks up at me from the mat that he's laying on. I shut the door and walk across the room and sit down on the edge of the bed.

"I assume that Luna is well," Arrok says.

"Yes," I reply shortly. "She's fine."

"Then what is troubling you," Arrok asks cocking his head to one side.

"Lilith says she knows of a way to get Scott and me home," I explain. "I really want to see my family, so they know that I'm all right. Yet at the same time I've become attached here too. I've come to care about the people here and I've even made a pact with you. What do you think that I should do?"

"I think that you should do what you think is best," Arrok says. "If that means that you must leave this place then so be it."

"But I made a promise to you," I say quickly. "We made a pact."

"I know," Arrok says in a low voice. "But you would not be breaking that pact."

"Maybe," I mumble.

"There is something else that you are not telling me," Arrok says.

"I can see that there is something still troubling you, other than the decision of going home."

"I don't want to leave the people that I've come to care about," I say slowly.

"Are you talking about Luna," Arrok asks in a hinting tone.

"Well she is one of the people I care about," I say quickly. "If that's what you mean."

"You care for her in a different way," Arrok says a little more serious.

"Yes," I sigh. "Fighting together has made us closer."

"Something that could possibly be more than just liking her," he hints again.

"Whoa," I say suddenly. "You mean something more like love?"

"I never said that," Arrok says.

"I don't think so," I say defensively. "Besides she's a vampire and I'm only a human. I don't think that would work."

"You are right," Arrok agrees. "But you can change."

"No," I say sternly. "I've seen what some of them have become, the Forsaken. I don't want to take that chance and become like them."

"True," Arrok yawns. "Well I am somewhat tired after flying over the city for half the morning looking for you."

"I'll leave you alone then," I say as I get up.

I walk across the room and open the door. I shut the door quietly behind me and walk down the hall towards Scott's room. I walk around the corner and almost walk into Scott.

"Hey," Scott shouts. "What are you doing here?"

"My room's on this floor too," I say.

"I know that," Scott says. "I figured that you would be with Luna now that she's awake."

"I've already been to see her," I say quickly. "I have more good news too. Lilith knows of a way for us to go home."

"What, are you serious," Scott shouts.

"Yes," I say. "Marcus has invited us to dinner tonight so we can talk it over."

"Okay," Scott says. "But what are you going to do?"

"About going home," I ask.

"Yeah," Scott says glumly.

"I don't really know," I say. "I want to see my parents, but I've become attached to this place too."

"I know what you mean," Scott sighs. "I could've gotten used to helping in the infirmary and the constant fighting isn't so bad."

"Are you thinking about staying," I ask hopefully.

"Not a chance," Scott laughs. "But I think I know what you've going to do anyway."

"Why," I ask concerned.

"Remember I had a dream that you where going to stay," Scott says. "You fit in too well here to go back. You have a purpose here."

"Your right," I sigh. "I don't know though."

"Well do you want to go up and talk to Luna some more," Scott says. "I haven't had a chance to talk to her yet."

"Yeah let's go," I say.

We walk to the staircase that's only a few feet from us. Scott walks ahead of me by a few steps as we climb the stairs. We walk out on the floor of the royal family. We walk down the halls to Luna's room. Scott knocks on the door and we both stand still.

"Come in," Luna's shouts.

Scott opens the door and we step inside. Luna gets up from the bed and walks quickly to Scott.

"You look great," Scott says as they briefly embrace.

"So do you for someone who was gashed open by a werewolf," Luna grins. "You recovered faster than I did."

"That's weird isn't it," Scott laughs. "Well it's good to see that you're doing better."

"Thank you," Luna says glancing at me. "You're back soon."

"Just making sure that you didn't get into anymore trouble while I was gone," I say smiling.

"You know I am sure that father will not care if we are early for dinner," Lilith says as she stands up.

"Shall we," Luna motions towards the door.

I walk to the door and open the door for Luna and the others. Scott walks by and gives me a strange look. Luna smiles as she passes by and Lilith grins again as she leaves the room. Her grin isn't directed at anyone though; it's as if she's grinning to herself. I shut the door and walk with everyone down the hall.

"So how do you know that we can get home," Scott asks over his shoulder.

"I have seen the way in my dreams, among other things," Lilith replies with a grin. "It seems that the gateway reverses, but it rarely happens. So you must get there tomorrow morning before it is too late."

We walk down the halls in silence. I guess that we're all thinking about tomorrow now. We reach the two wooden doors that lead to the dining room. I stop for a moment and open the door for everyone again.

"I almost forgot," Luna suddenly says. "We need to invite Tori."

"I'll go and get her," Scott says. "Do you know where she is?"

"She should be in the infirmary," Luna says thoughtfully.

Lilith walks into the dining room and Luna follows her inside. Scott walks off down the hall to the staircase. I walk into the dining room and shut the door behind me. Luna and Lilith are already on the large balcony talking as the sun begins to go down. I was only a few steps behind them when I came in, yet they covered the distance of the room in that short time. I walk to the long table and take the same seat that I have the last few times I've eaten here.

I still don't know what I should do. The more I think about it now the more I want to stay. I know that I've made it sound like I wanted to stay here before, but that's because I thought I wasn't going to have a choice in the matter. I lean forward in the chair and rest my head in my hands. Then I hear the door open.

I look up to see several servants carrying platters walk into the room. Other set down plates and silverware. I get up from the chair and lean against one of the pillars.

"Marcus will be here shortly," one says to me. "He sent us here in advance."

I only nod and watch them as they leave. Then everything is quiet again. I can hear Luna and Lilith talking to each other on the balcony. I strain to hear any hints of what their conversation is, but I can't make out a single word. Time passes by slowly and then the doors open again.

Marcus strides into the room with Scott and Tori right behind him. He walks across the room and stands by his chair. I walk to my chair and stand as he clears his throat to get Luna and Lilith's attention. They walk to the table and stand with the rest of us.

"This meal is to commemorate the recovery of my daughter Luna," he says smiling. "I don't know what I would do without either one of you."

He takes his seat and we all do the same. I sit in the same chair I was in a moment ago. Lilith sits as does Scott and Tori, but Luna stands for a moment. She then walks around the table and sits next to the right of me. I look at her somewhat confused. Everyone else look confused to, except for Lilith. She only grins again and looks at Marcus.

"After you Luna," Marcus says.

Luna selects the first piece of steak from a platter that has a pool of blood settling at the bottom. We all then select what we wish to eat and we talk about what has happened in the last few days. I know it will only be after the meal that we talk about tomorrow. The dinner goes by much faster than I expected or hoped for. Once everyone has finished the servants come back and take our plates away.

"Now to what I have dreamed," Lilith says breaking the silence. "The directions are very simple. You only have to fly southwest until you reach the forest. There will be a small stream that runs into the forest. Be there before sunrise."

"That sounds simple enough," Scott says.

"It is now night," Marcus says. "You should get some rest before you leave. I am sorry to cut this gathering short. It is my fault really; my other obligations conflicted with my schedule."

"That's fine," I say. "I need to make some preparations anyway."

Everyone gets up from their chairs and I walk to the door and open it. I walk out into the hallway and hold it open. Scott and Tori walk out and walk down the hall. Luna walks out and stops, she looks back at Marcus and Lilith as they talk.

"It seems they are going to talk," Luna says looking at the floor. "I will go with you and Scott tomorrow, to wish you farewell."

"Thank you," I say letting the door shut. "I'll see you in a little while then."

Luna looks at me for a moment then walks off to her room. I turn and walk to the staircase. I stroll down the stairs to my floor and hurry to my room. I open the door quickly and quietly. Arrok remains asleep as I move across the room to the small desk near the balcony opening. I find a piece of parchment and quill. I dip the quill in the inkwell and begin to write down my feelings, before the final journey.

32

THE TIME FLIES BY as I scribble on the parchment. When I finish writing I fold the paper up and stuff into my pocket. I get up and walk out on the balcony and take a deep breath of the cool air. This is it, I've made my decision. A knock at the door causes me to turn around. The door slowly opens and Scott walks in.

"Are you ready to go," He asks quietly.

"There is no need to whisper," Arrok says. "I have been awake for some time."

"Luna and Iris will be here soon," Scott says in a normal voice. "Then we'll leave and go home."

"Great," I mumble. "I guess we won't be carrying a bunch of stuff with us this time."

"Doesn't look like it," Scott sighs.

Arrok gets up and shuffles out onto the balcony. He stretches his wings and yawns.

"Here come Luna and Iris," he yawns again. "You can get on so we can leave."

I climb onto Arrok's back and Scott climbs on behind me. Iris swoops down and hovers in front of us. Tori is also with Luna.

"I thought I would come along," Tori says. "You two always manage to find trouble."

"Not this time," Scott laughs.

"Are you ready then," Luna asks.

"Let's go," I say.

Arrok jumps off the balcony and opens his wings. He levels off and flies next to Iris. We fly over the dim torch lit city. For some of us it will be the last time to fly over Haven. I look down at the stone houses and take in every detail. We fly out of the cave and into the cool night air. I look to the east and can see a soft orange glow from behind the mountains. We turn away from it and start our journey towards the location of the gateway.

"This is it," Scott says. "We're going home."

"I know," I sigh. "Are you going to miss this place at all?"

"Yeah," he laughs. "I might come back for a vacation. What are you going to miss?"

"I don't know," I say touching the piece of folded parchment in my pocket.

We fly out over the fields and past the outer wall, which is already under reconstruction. We fly quietly above the grasslands until I can make out the fringe of the forest edge. I look behind us at the now glowing horizon. The sun will be up soon and we haven't fount the stream yet. My heart starts to beat faster. The ground below us starts to become visible as the sun begins to break over the horizon.

"There is the stream," Luna says pointing ahead. "It looks like we can land there."

Arrok and Iris begin to drop until they are flying along the ground. They stop and hover for a moment as they survey the area. Once they think it is safe enough they land. Everyone jumps off and we all meet near the stream.

"It seems that we do not have much time left together," Luna says sadly.

"Yeah," Scott says looking down. "I'm going to miss all of you, except that one werewolf that got me."

Scott rubs his chest where five long gashes once were. The sun is up enough for us to see clearly. I can see Luna's blue eyes and how they are filled with sadness. Then a cold breeze starts to blow, just like at the campsite. We all walk to the small indention at the edge of the forest.

The cold wind continues to blows and a static tingle begins to fill the air.

"There's not much time left now," I say.

Scott walks up to Tori and embraces her and then he hugs Luna too.

"I wish you well," Luna says.

"Thanks," Scott says walking to the center of the indention.

I take a few steps towards Scott then stop. I look back at Luna and pull out the piece of parchment and sigh. I walk to Scott and hand him the parchment.

"What's this," he asks with a confuse look on his face.

"It's a letter to my parents," I say. "It tells about why I'm not with you and most of a fake story. You can read if you want to, it might give you an idea of how to avoid looking too crazy."

"So you're not coming with me," Scott asks slipping the letter into his pocket.

"No," I say as the static feeling grows more intense.

I walk back and stand next to Luna near the edge of the forest. I look down at her and smile. She looks up at me with tears in her eyes, but she's smiling too.

"You mean that you're going to stay here in this place for the rest of your life," Scott asks. "You're going to live in a banished land."

"No," I say quickly. "If I was to go with you, then I would be living in a banished land."

The wind picks up until it feels like a hurricane. Then a bolt of blue lightning strikes in a blinding flash and Scott is gone.

"So what made you decide to stay here," Luna says wiping tears away from her face.

"I have my reasons," I say putting my arm around her. "You're one of them."